SISTER GYPSY MOON

A Gypsy and Petal Mystery

Karen Leabo

BooksForABuck.com

2003

BooksForABuck.com

ISBN: 978-1-60215-161-1

CHAPTER ONE

The house was purple.

Reeling from surprise, I shut off my Cherokee's engine and stepped out into the 90-degree heat. I took a few steps closer to the plum-colored monstrosity, then a few steps back, but it was definitely purple. With yellow trim. Not even the hippie commune where I'd grown up had sported such a ghastly color scheme.

Well, who cares, I thought. For the next three months, the house was all mine.

I glanced up and down the street. My house wasn't the ugliest. A sagging two-story in the middle of the block was painted lime green, and some of the others were so faded and peeling it was hard to tell what color they once might have been. And I did have a huge magnolia tree.

My new home was in an obscure Dallas neighborhood unofficially known as Psychedelic Heights. Ninety years ago it had been quite swanky, but it had fallen on hard times. Hippies had taken it over in the sixties, drug dealers in the eighties. Now the urban pioneers were staging a comeback for the eclectic neighborhood. The house across the street from mine, a stately gray with white trim, was obviously one of the area's success stories.

I stared longingly at the gray house. In its front yard, a woman in a polyester housecoat watered the well-manicured lawn.

Well, hell, I was stuck with purple. Might as well make the best of it. It was only for three months, at which time Darryl, my darling ex-boyfriend, would go on trial for trying to turn me into a human shish-kebab. The good citizens of Tulsa would throw him in what I hoped would be a very nasty prison, and I would not have to hide like a beaten dog.

I crossed my own brown, weedy lawn, noticing that all of the shrubs were dead except one small, apparently drought-resistant rose bush. The sight of its pale pink blooms cheered me. I stepped into the welcome shade of the wide front porch, then tried to get the door open. But the lock was frozen with rust.

"Yoo-hoo!" a voice called from behind me.

I jumped a foot. No one was supposed to know me here. Who would be calling me? I jerked around, then relaxed a couple of degrees. It was the woman from across the street, the one with the nice lawn, scurrying toward me, waving and grinning.

I managed a return the smile, though I was hardly ready for company. I just wanted to be left alone—safe and alone. I gave the stubborn key another twist, but no dice. I peered through the wavy beveled glass window in the door—like I expected someone to let me in—but all was dark.

"Are you having trouble there?" The woman mounted the steps to my porch. She was a mousy thing, with thinning brown hair streaked gray and cut in a conservative, no-frills bob. She wore not a housecoat, as I'd first thought, but a loose polyester dress, support hose, and flat brown shoes. "Are you our new neighbor?"

I nodded and held out my hand. "I'm Gypsy Larabee."

"Gypsy," the woman repeated, smiling uncertainly and ignoring my outstretched hand. "What an unusual name. I'm Merrilee Haglin. Oh, there's Wade, my husband. I'll bet he can help you with that stubborn key."

A fifty-ish man came out the front door of the gray house, dressed in a badly cut three-piece suit. No one wore suits in Dallas in July.

"Yoo-hoo, Wade, over here!" Merrilee called, waving frantically. "Come meet our new neighbor." He waved back and started across the street.

Merrilee returned her attention to me. "You bought Ruby's house?"

"No, not exactly." I struggled with the stubborn lock some more. "The bank foreclosed on it. I've been hired to dispose of the contents and prepare the house for sale." Hired was a bit of a stretch. I was actually being offered free rent and a commission on the proceeds from selling the house and its contents. Which meant, until I'd actually sold a few things, I was dead, flat broke.

Merrilee clapped her hands together gleefully. "That sounds like fun! I bet this house is just chock full of interesting things. Ruby was such an odd character."

"I have no idea what's in here. Yet," I said, bringing home the fact that I really needed to get on with my day—preferably alone.

But there was no escaping from Merrilee, or her husband, who had made it to my porch, breathing hard and perspiring. Wade Haglin wasn't fat, exactly, but he had that jowly, pale look of someone who needed to exercise. His hair was a peculiar dark gold color with the texture of a Brillo pad. I suspected if he hadn't cut it so short, he would look like a Pekinese with a perm. His collar was buttoned so tight that his fleshy neck bulged over it. His beefy hand gripped the crook of a plain wooden cane.

"Hello," I said cordially.

"Wade Haglin, nice to meet you," he said, giving me a critical once-over.

"That's Reverend Haglin," Merrilee clarified. "He's the pastor at the church down the street—Lambs of the Good Shepherd?"

I nodded as if I'd heard of it.

"We like to get to know all of our neighbors, and to let them know that our doors are open for anyone in need of spiritual guidance."

I needed a lot of things—a can of WD-40 topped my current list—but spiritual guidance wasn't one of them. "How nice of you," I said blandly. As a child I was dragged to one weird church after another by my hippie parents, churches with names like, "Disciples of the Sun" and "Holy Temple of the Orange Blossom."

The last time I'd been baptized, at age thirteen, the preacher had held me under the water so long I'd inhaled a half-gallon of scummy pond water and two tadpoles. I was now a confirmed non-church-goer, and I did not want to be saved. Not this afternoon, anyway. I still had to unload the back of my Jeep.

"Well, we're certainly pleased to have you," the Reverend said. "Ruby wasn't the kind of neighbor decent people appreciate."

I sighed, frustration rising in my throat. Just what I needed, bigots for neighbors. I didn't know much about Ruby, but my sister, Petal, who had set up these living arrangements for me, had mentioned Ruby was black. I held my tongue and jiggled the key some more. I was too tired and it was too hot for a debate on racial equality.

Then Merrilee tittered with laughter. "Oh, Wade, that sounded terrible! What must Gypsy think?" She touched my arm. "We aren't prejudiced. We have lots of African-Americans in our congregation. Hispanics, too. No, we had a problem with Ruby because she was a fortune-teller."

"She did the Devil's work," Haglin clarified. "Her so-called business was an evil blight on the neighborhood. Good riddance, wherever she is, that's what I say. Oh, here, let me get that for you." He reached for the key in my hand.

Still reeling from the Haglins' leap from fortune-teller to devil-worshiper, I let Wade try the stubborn key, though I couldn't imagine him having more luck than me. His hands looked soft and weak, even for a minister. But with one determined twist, the lock gave and the door was open.

"Thanks," I said, stepping into the dark, musty interior. "It was very nice meeting both of you."

I thought they'd take the hint, but they followed me right inside. "Need any help with Ruby's things?" Merrilee asked.

Oh. My. God. I didn't just need help, I needed the EPA to check the place out for biohazards. My new employer, Texas Fiduciary Savings, had warned me Ruby's place was "cluttered" and needed a bit of TLC. In my mind, that meant crowded bookshelves and too many junk drawers. "Cluttered" did not mean boxes stacked ten feet high in every corner and rooms so full of dusty, grimy, filthy, spider-infested debris a body could barely get through.

"Dear Lord, protect us," Wade Haglin murmured.

"Are the walls ... brown?" Merrilee asked in a tremulous voice.

"With moss green trim," I confirmed.

I wandered through the downstairs, moving furniture as I went, stepping over tools, broken appliances, stacks of Christmas decorations, and a rusty bicycle, with the Haglins trailing behind. Five main rooms made up the downstairs—a large foyer, a living room with fireplace, a dining room, and an extra room my grandmother would have called a parlor, plus a long, thin kitchen running along the back—circa 1950 appliances. Some walls were brown, some half-covered with peeling, flower-power wallpaper. Smelly shag carpeting in various nauseating hues covered the floors.

"The light fixtures are sort of interesting," Merrilee offered, her busy eyes darting here and there, taking it all in.

"The wood trim is probably salvageable, if you strip it," Wade added. "And this bay window is nice."

They were trying to be optimistic, but it was hard to appreciate a window when the glass was so filthy a Texas summer sun couldn't penetrate it.

A wide, curving staircase led upward to more unimaginable horrors. Overwhelmed, I sank onto one of the steps.

"Will you be all right here?" Merrilee asked, her face wreathed with concern. "We have some emergency supplies at the church for, you know, people in crisis. And I can help you dispose of some of this junk, if you like."

Kind as Merrilee's offer was, I didn't want her help, and I really didn't want anything to do with another homeless shelter—I'd just left one. I wanted, needed to be alone. In solitude, I could appreciate the fact that I was in a safe, quiet place with doors that locked and no squalling babies or smelly diapers nearby. I could sleep here without lying on top of all my earthly belongings to prevent them from being stolen. If and when I bought food, I wouldn't have to share it with a dozen hungry roommates.

Fortunately Wade saved me the awkwardness of turning down Merrilee's help. "We'll be late for our shift at the homeless kitchen," the Reverend reminded her.

She sagged. "Yes, dear."

Finally they left, promising to invite me over for iced tea and cookies once I was settled. Feeling a little guilty, I hoped they didn't follow up. They seemed nice enough, but Bible-thumpers always made me a bit uneasy.

Anyway, I hadn't moved here to make friends. My objective was complete anonymity. I would cheerfully live in a cave, I reminded myself, so long as it had indoor plumbing and no Darryl.

"Well, thanks, Petal," I said aloud. It was all my sister's fault I'd landed in this garbage dump. Desperate to rescue me from the Tulsa women's shelter where I'd been hiding from Darryl, Petal had found this ... situation for me. "No, I haven't seen the house," she'd blithely told me. "But I've met Ruby. She seemed nice enough."

Nice enough for a complete and total slob. Ruby Casserly, former owner of this purple pig sty, was not only hygienically challenged, but she had a nasty habit of never paying taxes and running up credit cards and gambling debts. After years of successfully ducking authorities, she'd finally been caught, and had fled to parts unknown to avoid prosecution. The bank had foreclosed on Ruby's house.

Petal, who was a lawyer, had somehow gotten wind of the situation and had offered my services. No wonder the bank had agreed so quickly to the deal she'd suggested. No one would buy a house that made living under a bridge look good.

My initial plan had been to liquidate Ruby's belongings first, then slap on a little paint and put the house on the market. I'd figured a couple of weeks of concerted effort would take care of it. Now I realized a couple of years wouldn't be enough. And I only had three months.

I decided then and there, staring at red-and-yellow carpet surrounded by hideous lamps, moldering boxes, and things that moved when they shouldn't, that my first priority would be to make one room livable or I would go insane.

I unloaded my meager belongings from the back of my Jeep, then headed for Builder's Corner, where I opened a charge account and bought some spackle, masking tape, brushes, and four gallons of eggshell paint.

It was a start.

Three days later, I was in a slightly better frame of mind. I'd found a bedroom upstairs that was moderately livable, once I'd cleaned the inch of dust off every surface and put clean sheets on the bed. Then I'd started in on the living room. I'd cleared everything out, hauling several loads of trash to the alley. I'd pulled up the carpet, pleased to find hardwoods underneath, though they needed work. Three coats of eggshell paint took care of the ghastly brown walls, and the house's charm started to reveal itself.

If I could just get this one room to shine, some urban pioneer would be inspired by the home's obvious potential and snap it up as soon as I listed it, I thought optimistically.

So, there I was on a ladder slopping white enamel on a window frame when the doorbell rang. Eager for a diversion, I hopped down from the ladder, headed for the foyer, and swung open the door, having forgotten for the moment that I lived in a neighborhood where most folks thought nothing of three dead bolts and a pit-bull.

A pretty Latina girl stood on my front porch. Tall and gangly with just the hint of impending womanhood, she had long, almost-black hair hanging loose and windblown.

She met my welcoming smile with a solemn expression. "My grandmother sent me," she said timidly. "I'm Lupe Silviano?"

I opened the door a little wider, figuring Lupe was no threat. In fact, her granny was probably the nice little lady who'd welcomed me to the neighborhood with a Frito-chili pie. "I'm Gypsy," I said in return.

"Oh, a gypsy!" She sounded pleased.

"Not a gypsy," I clarified. "Just 'Gypsy.' My parents were ... never mind." The girl was far too young to understand why babies born in hippie communes ended up with names like "Sunshine" and "Waterfall," so I dropped it.

I didn't want to be rude, but I had work to do. I was about to ask Lupe to excuse me when her eyes teared up. She grasped both of my hands. "My brother. My brother Jorge. He's only four and he's been gone since last night—"

"Whoa, whoa! Slow down."

She blinked owlishly at me. "Aren't you the crystal-ball lady? The one in the purple house? My grandmama told me you could help. She would have come herself, but she's laid up."

The girl thought I was Ruby.

How in the world was I going to explain to this grief-stricken girl that I wasn't a fortune-teller or crystal-ball reader? I mean, I'd already admitted I was "Gypsy," and didn't gypsies tell fortunes?

As Lupe prattled on hysterically about how her brother had wandered away, I closed my eyes a moment, trying to imagine how frightened she must be—and that little boy! Wherever he was, he had to be terrified. I had no particular affinity for four-year-olds. I'd discovered that at the Wee Luv Daycare Center, the last job I'd been fired from—not my fault. But I wouldn't want to lose one.

"Can I come in?" Lupe asked.

I opened my eyes and shook my head. "Paint fumes," I said. "They're terrible." Needing a break from the fumes myself, I stepped out on the porch and closed the door, though first I checked up and down the street, automatically looking to see if anyone was watching me. I'd become extraordinarily paranoid after coming so close to being incinerated.

"I wish I could help you," I finally said.

"Why can't you?" She studied me a moment. "My grandmama said you were a colored woman."

"I think she has me mixed up with the lady who lived here before ..."

Lupe's gaze dropped. I could tell she was trying not to cry. "You mean you can't look in your crystal ball and tell me where Jorge is?"

"Oh, well ..." I shrugged. "No."

Lupe frowned. "You're not a gypsy? You lied?"

"My name really is Gypsy," I said wistfully.

Eyes downcast, Lupe reached into her jeans pocket and handed me a crumpled ten-dollar bill. "Grandmama says I have to pay you, no matter what information I get."

"Oh, no, I couldn't—" I began, but she tucked the bill into the bib pocket of my overalls.

Lupe turned and bolted from the porch, grabbing her battered bicycle, which she'd left leaning against the steps. She wheeled it around, hopped astride, and took off like a slingshot—right through my little rose bush.

"My roses!" I howled, but I don't think she even noticed. The poor little bush was cleaved in two, some of its blooms hanging forlornly in the heat.

I took the hose and watered it, hoping it would come back. It was the only thing besides the magnolia tree still alive in the whole front yard, and the Purple Palace needed all the "curb appeal" it could get.

I felt bad the rest of the morning, though when I finished the trim in the living room and saw the overall effect, I rallied a bit. Once I refinished the oak floor, the living room would look pretty good. I had one tiny spindle-legged table and an English teapot, left to me by my grandmother. They were the only two items I'd been able to rescue from the fire Darryl had set in my apartment. I would put table and teapot in the middle of the room, and I would come in here whenever the rest of the house got to be too much.

I was poring over the Yellow Pages, trying to figure out where I could rent a floor sander with my pathetic, maxed-out Discover card, when the doorbell rang again. I approached the door a bit more cautiously this time.

I peered through the wavy beveled glass, and for a moment I had to gasp for breath. Standing on my front porch was the most gorgeous god of a man I'd ever seen, the epitome of "Latin lover." His dark, heavy-lidded eyes stared back at me with utter confidence—and how could any man with those looks be anything but confident? He wore a jacket and tie despite the building heat, and he hadn't even broken a sweat.

Normally I would not just throw my door open to a strange man, especially in this unfamiliar neighborhood. But somewhere in the back of my mind I figured, what's the worst that could happen? Rape and ravishment? Even if he killed me, I'd die happy just staring at him as the last of my lifeblood trickled out onto my unfinished oak floor.

I opened the door, only then remembering my own disreputable, paint-spattered state. My long, curly hair was pulled back in a bandanna do-rag, and my baggy, cut-off overalls gave me the approximate shape and size of an automobile air bag. Too late to do anything about it, though.

"Yes?" I croaked, pleased that I could get even that much out. It wasn't often that I got this close to a Hispanic Adonis.

He aimed his piercing black eyes at me. The way he stared made me forget my distinctly unglamorous attire.

"You must be Gypsy." His voice was velvet smooth with a touch of sting to it, like a real expensive tequila. Though his words weren't insulting, his tone was ever-so-slightly insolent.

"That's my name," I admitted cautiously. "And you are ...?"

"Santiago Ramone. Dallas Morning News. May we come in?"

A reporter? And worse, a photographer. A brassy-looking blonde weighted down with a camera bag trudged up my walkway.

My heart started up a panicky staccato. How had a reporter found me? Surely the press wasn't still interested in me. It had been almost a year since the unpleasant incident at Wee Luv involving a toilet and a certain obnoxious pre-schooler's head. Said incident had prompted a wave of embarrassing publicity, ending my short-lived daycare career and almost landing me in jail. Thank God for Petal's legal skills.

Well, whatever the reporter wanted, I wasn't going to cooperate. I'd spent a good deal of time and energy hiding myself from Darryl. I didn't need my picture in the paper.

Quickly I stepped outside onto the porch and closed the door behind me. "No pictures," I said sternly, giving the blonde a quelling look. "What can I do for you?"

Ramone pulled a notebook from the back pocket of his jeans and settled onto my porch railing. Just watching him move, bend at the knees and elbows, made my own knees go weak. With that glowing bronze skin and those full, sensual lips, he was so beautiful, yet somehow dangerous.

"This morning you consulted with a customer, a ..." He read from the notebook. "... Lupe Silviano, is that right?"

"She wasn't exactly a customer," I hedged. I didn't know whether to be relieved or on full alert. Apparently Santiago didn't know anything about

Wee Luv Daycare. But this business with Lupe ... I didn't want it getting around that I'd posed as a psychic to defraud a young girl out of ten dollars.

"But you did talk to her."

"Yeah. She mistook me for someone else." I decided not to mention the ten bucks.

Santiago stared at me, pen poised but still above his notepad. He looked utterly confused. "You don't want any publicity?"

"Absolutely not!"

That really threw him for a loop. He studied me like a bug under a microscope. "You are Sister Gypsy, right?"

I couldn't help it; I laughed. Where had the "Sister" come from? I started to deny the moniker, but just then, Lupe came roaring up the street on her battered bike, hollering like my house was on fire. "Sister Gypsy! Sister Gypsy!"

At that point I closed my mouth. It was going to be a little difficult to argue my identity now.

Lupe got her bike halfway up on the sidewalk then leaped off, letting it clatter to the concrete. She barreled toward me like an out-of-control bullet and grabbed my unsuspecting self in a fierce embrace. "Oh, Sister Gypsy, thank you so much."

"Did you find Jorge?" I asked, tentatively returning the hug.

Santiago rolled his eyes. "As if you didn't know."

"I didn't!" I protested, just as the bimbo-ish photographer started furiously snapping pictures of Lupe's and my hug.

Why didn't I just take out an ad: Darryl, here I am, come get me and bring matches.

CHAPTER TWO

"**Hey**!" I yelled at the blonde. "Stop taking my picture!"

Lupe loosened her clamp on me, but she continued holding my hand while the camera whirred. "All those things you told me—they were a hundred percent right! Jorge wandered into this guy's shed where he stored paint and stuff. The paint fumes made him pass out. Paint fumes! Just like you said."

My attention was on the photographer and the potential damage she was doing to my anonymity. "Did you hear what I said?"

Lupe continued, oblivious. "And as I was leaving, you called out something to me about roses!" It hadn't happened quite like that, but Ramone scribbled furiously.

I grabbed the pen out of his hand. "Call off your camera girl. And I want that film. This is private property, and therefore an invasion of my privacy."

Ramone shot a sideways look at the photographer. She lowered the camera, a mutinous expression on her face, but she didn't offer me the film. He took his pen back from me.

"I went out on my bike," Lupe continued relentlessly, "and I saw Rosewood Street. I found this shed with pink roses growing all over it just like yours, and there was Jorge!"

"Is he all right?" I asked a bit dazedly, only now fully wrapping my mind around what she'd been saying. Had I actually helped her find her brother?

Lupe nodded. "They took him to the hospital, but the doctors think he'll be fine."

I was relieved to hear the little boy was okay, and maybe a bit proud that I had something to do with finding him, even if it was pure coincidence. I gave Lupe's shoulders a squeeze. "I guess it was very lucky you found him."

"Oh, luck had nothing to do with it. It was all your predictions! We took up a collection from the family and a few neighbors. It's not much, but we want you to have it." Lupe pulled an envelope out of her jeans pocket and extended it toward me.

I instinctively backed away. "Oh, I couldn't accept any more money—"

"More money?" Santiago interrupted. "Then you did accept some money initially?"

I turned on him. "I tried to return it."

"You have to take it," Lupe insisted. "Grandmama says it's bad luck if you don't pay a fortune-teller what she's worth." Rather than pressing the envelope on me, she turned and shoved it through the slot on my old cast-iron mailbox.

Ramone made a move to retrieve it, but I swatted his hand away from his target. "Don't you know snooping in someone's mailbox is a federal offense?"

"I have to go now," Lupe said, already hopping down the front steps. "Mama needs me to take care of the other kids so she can stay at the hospital. Bye, Sister Gypsy, and thanks again! Bye, Mr. Ramone!"

When she'd gone, I gave "Mr. Ramone" an appraising look. "You knew she was coming here?" I asked, only now seeing the obvious.

At least Ramone didn't pretend his witnessing Lupe's arrival was a chance occurrence. "Yeah. I was just at her house, covering the story of her finding her brother. When her grandma started taking up a collection for you—well, I just had to meet this metaphysical wonder who pinpointed exactly where to find that little boy." His voice dripped with skepticism.

"First, I'm not a fortune-teller, or psychic, or anything else," I objected. "Lupe mistook me for the woman who used to live here. Apparently the kid took some chance comments of mine out of context and strung them together to make this so-called prediction about her brother's whereabouts."

"But she did find the kid. You aren't going to claim it was your doing?"

"Of course not!"

I guess I was really screwing up the angle for Ramone's story.

We stood there, Ramone and I, staring each other down. He was no doubt thinking of ways to trick me into saying something that would look good in print. I, on the other hand, was busy fantasizing what he would look like without his shirt.

Things could only get more bizarre from there, and they did. A bottle-green Jaguar pulled slowly past my house, then turned around in the neighbor's driveway and pulled slowly back, eventually coming to rest right in front.

The reporter stopped talking to me mid-sentence to stare at the car, which appeared distinctly out-of-place in Psychedelic Heights.

The driver's door opened and a pair of long, shapely legs angled out, the dainty feet housed in a pair of white Farrigamo sandals. Then the total woman emerged, her linen shorts wrinkle free, her frosted blond curls salon-fresh, her lipstick flawless. She stood on the sidewalk for a moment staring at my house, then removed her sunglasses and stared some more, her expression one of frank horror.

Well, okay, I couldn't blame her. The house was purple.

After thoroughly taking in my new digs, she started up the walkway, her upper lip curled in distaste.

I waved. "Hi, Petal."

"Hello, Gypsy," she returned as she gingerly climbed the rickety steps. When she reached the porch, she gave me a brief hug that didn't quite involve touching, then held me at arm's distance to look at me.

"My God, Gyp, what have you done to yourself?" She made a sweeping gesture, encompassing me as well as the entire house.

I cringed. With her dark sunglasses on, Petal hadn't yet noticed the news team, which lurked in the shadows, watching this sisterly reunion with interest. "Petal," I said, gently turning her around to face the journalists, "I'd like you to meet—"

She stiffened and pulled off the shades. "Santiago Ramone!" Obviously Petal knew him, and by the look on her face, she wasn't any too pleased to run into him. She barely acknowledged me as her sister in front of family, much less in full view of the press.

"Petal Ingalls," Ramone said, smiling like a shark.

Petal turned her condemning gaze on me. "Can't you stay out of trouble for ten minutes?" With that she stormed inside my house without invitation, slamming the door so hard I feared for the beveled glass window.

Ramone resumed his frenzied note-taking. He practically chortled. "This is turning out better than I thought it would. Petal Ingalls, visiting a storefront palm-reader."

"Oh, please!" I rushed over to him as the full import of what was happening hit me. I think I actually clutched at his sleeve. "Don't write me up in the paper. You have no idea the damage you could do."

"Then explain it to me. What's Petal Ingalls doing here?"

"She's my sister, okay? Would you forget about Petal? This has nothing to do with her. You can't write me up in the paper because I don't want to draw attention to myself."

Ramone's dark eyes danced. "This just gets better and better. Hiding from the law? Fraud unit, perhaps?"

"Will you please listen!"

The blond photographer actually backed off the porch in the face of my violent angst, but Ramone stood his ground.

"I'm trying to stay one step ahead of a stalker," I said calmly. "He already tried to kill me once. If you put me in the paper, he'll find me. My death will be on your hands."

I might've been overstating the case a little. Darryl was in Oklahoma last I saw him. But he knew I had family in Dallas. He might come looking for me here. And though he had never actually laid a hand on me, he'd burned up almost everything I owned, and he had threatened to cut me up into tiny pieces, then pack me into a garbage can like human Spam.

"C'mon, Ramone, there's no story here. It's a coincidence that I helped Lupe find her brother, nothing more."

Ramone paused in his scribbling and appraised me again, and this time I sensed that he saw something beneath the do-rag and the paint-spattered overall shorts. My legs aren't as long as Petal's, but they're not half bad. "I promised my editor a story about a fortune-teller finding a lost kid," he said, one eyebrow raised. "Have you got an alternative?"

What a slime! Then again, I wondered just what I could bargain with. A night of mindless passion? Nah, that would've been pushing my luck. "How about we compromise?"

Now his curiosity was piqued. "How?"

"I'll admit I helped that girl find her brother by giving her psychic information." What would it really hurt? "But you can't mention my name. Or Petal's. Or the street I live on. And no pictures that show my face."

He shrugged. "Okay. Deal."

We finished up the interview in a matter of five minutes. I gave him some juicy tidbits about how the information just "comes to me in a flash of awareness," and how I sometimes "see into the astral plane." Given where I grew up, I could spout that stuff in my sleep.

Ramone ate it up with a spoon. When he was done, he packed up his notebook and looked at me again. His dark gaze was oddly unsettling, like he was trying to see something behind my eyeballs. He seemed about to say something more personal, but the photographer cleared her throat, and the moment passed.

Ramone thanked me for the interview, then turned to leave, his photographer trailing after him. I started to go back inside but remembered the money Lupe had stuffed into my mailbox. I waited until the reporter's black Blazer had pulled away, then scurried over and retrieved the envelope.

Once back inside, I opened it. It was mostly in ones and fives, but it added up to almost two hundred dollars, all for five minutes' work. I felt really guilty, but not guilty enough to try to return the money. I needed groceries.

While I'd been outside dickering with Ramone, Petal had been inside making herself at home. She'd already located my last clean glass and had filled it with tap water. Now she sat stiffly at the scarred maple kitchen table sipping her water and looking around suspiciously, as if she expected something vile to crawl out of one of the boxes and fly into her hair.

The moment I entered the kitchen, she started in. "Really, Gypsy Moon Larabee, this place is unhealthy."

"You're the one who made all the arrangements! And if we're going to resort to dragging out hideous middle names—"

"You could have backed out once you saw the place. God, I can't believe Ruby lived here. She seemed like a very ... clean person."

"And where would I have gone instead? Your house?"

"Well, no." She seemed abnormally uncomfortable with that idea. "That's the first place Darryl will look if he comes this way."

Thank God she didn't invite me. I couldn't imagine bunking with Petal and dear old Cullen, her husband and my former boyfriend.

She took a dramatic sip of water, then set the glass on the table with a thunk, folded her arms, and refused to meet my gaze.

When I was pretty sure her tirade was finished, I calmly walked to the rust-mottled fridge, pulled out the casserole dish with the Frito-chili pie, and ate the last few bites cold. "Gee, Petal, it's nice to see you too. I'm so glad you dropped by to cheer me up."

"Oh, sister, don't be sarcastic. You know I hate that. What was that horrid reporter doing here, anyway? Don't tell me he got wind of that old toilet-head nonsense?"

The toilet-head nonsense hadn't seemed so trivial a few months ago, when the Wee-Luv Daycare Center had tried to sue me for almost drowning one of the children entrusted to my care. Never mind that Hughey Patterson had gotten his own head stuck in the toilet.

"This had nothing to do with toilets," I assured her as I found another chair and scraped the last few flecks of cheese from the dish. "I helped find a missing boy, that's all." I tried to sound casual, hoping Petal's interest would wane. No such luck.

Petal's jaw dropped.

I sucked on the last few crumbs of cheese, trying not to let Petal annoy me.

"That's astounding!" Petal said. "Where did you find him? How did it happen? You didn't leave yourself open to a lawsuit, did you?"

"I didn't exactly find him myself," I explained carefully. "I, um, offered up some psychic information that led to Jorge's whereabouts."

Petal just stared. Good. Maybe I'd shocked her beyond words. While she processed my revelation in her semi-catatonic state, I re-located the Yellow Pages and resumed my search for a floor sander. With the money Lupe had given me, I could actually pay cash for it.

"Ah, here we go," I said triumphantly. "Builders' Corner rents floor sanders for thirty-five dollars a day."

Petal jumped out of her chair and started pacing. "Explain this to me. You've suddenly turned into a mind-reader or something?"

At that point I had to tell her the whole story, or she would have pestered me with questions for the rest of the day. So I grabbed my backpack and car keys, forcing her to follow me out to the driveway where my Cherokee was parked. I had to make a twenty-minute drive to Builders Corner, and I decided that was as good a time as any to tell my hostage sister all about my temporary change of career.

"So ..." Petal said as I pulled into the do-it-yourself superstore's parking lot, "this was just a case of mistaken identity."

"That is correct."

"Well. Okay. I can handle that. It's just a misunderstanding."

"Right."

"But that awful reporter is going to make you out to be a nut in the paper tomorrow!"

"He promised not to identify me." I firmly believe that life is a series of trade-offs.

Petal huffed out a humorless laugh as we trekked across the parking lot. "You better save a copy of the newspaper for when Mama and Daddy get home. They'll love it."

"They probably will," I agreed. "Didn't Mama used to read Tarot Cards or something?"

"Uh-huh. And Daddy read the bumps on people's heads."

"Then I guess I come by my psychic skills honestly."

"You're like them in a lot of ways," Petal said, and I'm not sure she meant this as a compliment.

Petal and I spent our formative years inhaling second-hand reefer smoke, surrounded by mantra chanting, attending peace demonstrations and "End World Hunger" rallies, eating brown rice and brewer's yeast. I kind of went with the flow. I liked most of the strange people who hung around, and despite my best efforts, I'd ended up leading the same sort of easy-come, easy-go life as my parents.

Petal rebelled in the opposite direction. She'd gone establishment in a big way. About the only thing that remained of the commune in Petal was her penchant for health food.

"It's my name," I said. "How can anyone named Gypsy Moon make something of herself?"

"You think Petal Jade is any better? But I overcame the handicap."

We both laughed, and the mood lightened considerably. Sometimes I really did enjoy Petal, when she loosened up and forgot, for at least a few minutes, that she was an upwardly mobile, ambitious, ball-breaking lawyer.

On the way home I stopped at a grocery store and bought a few groceries with my little hoard of cash—pudding pops, Lean Cuisines, low-fat potato chips, Pepperidge Farm cookies, all the essentials. Petal made me buy herbal tea and a bag of apples.

It wasn't until we were almost home again, with the sander sticking out the back of my Jeep, that I got around to asking Petal why she'd chosen this morning to visit me. She'd certainly made herself scarce when I'd first moved in. Probably she hadn't wanted to get stuck moving any boxes. Unless she was at the gym in a color-coordinated leotard, she didn't like lifting anything heavier than her Coach briefcase. And even then, she didn't want to sweat.

She sighed deeply. "I guess I can't put off telling you much longer." She picked at imaginary dust on her clothes, inspected her perfect nails, cleared her throat.

My hackles immediately rose. Something was terribly amiss for Petal to act like this—fidgety, unsure of herself. "What is it, Pet?"

Without meeting my gaze, she climbed out of the Jeep. I did likewise. I opened the back of the vehicle, and she watched as I tried to wrestle the sanding machine to the ground. It didn't occur to her to help.

"I've left Cullen."

I chose that moment to drop the sander on my foot, for which I was grateful. I had excruciating discomfort to focus on, rather than the reality of what my sister had just told me. I let out a howl of pain and outrage that was probably heard clear to Waxahachie.

"Oh, here, now, it's not all that bad," Petal said quickly, stepping over to comfort me. "Gracious, I didn't know my marriage mattered so much to you."

"The sander," I ground out between clenched teeth, "is on my foot."

"Oh. Oh!" To her credit, Petal tried to lift the thing up to I could slide my poor injured foot out from under. Her efforts were pretty ineffectual, but somehow between us we managed to free my foot, which was bruised but not broken.

"You left Cullen?" I said when I could move my toes again. "That's not allowed. You have to stay and work out your—"

"Now, Gypsy, there are things about my marriage that you know nothing about."

"I know that Cullen is crazy about you." So crazy that he chose Petal over me. I didn't bother to add that part.

Okay, okay, it was old news. I dated Cullen in college. I brought him home one weekend to meet the folks—a risky proposition, given I never knew what, or whom, I might find at the house. Once I'd come home for a visit to find my bedroom had been turned into a chicken coop. But it wasn't my weird parents or their bizarre lifestyle that drove Cullen away. It was Petal, who was a senior in high school. He took one look at her, and I lost him.

Still, the incident had hung between my sister and me for years, clouding every family get-together. We'd been very close as children; as adults, we'd rarely confided anything more intimate than having an ingrown toenail.

"You think Cullen loves me, huh?" Petal folded her arms and stuck her chin out belligerently, adopting a familiar childhood stance. "A fat lot you know."

I resisted the urge to chuckle at Petal's lapse into a kindergartner's syntax only because we were discussing such a serious subject. "Y'all have been married for ten years!" I insisted. "You can't just throw out ten years because ... because..."

"Because he's boffing our interior designer."

"Pardon?"

"You heard me."

"Now, Petal, I'm sure you've misunderstood—"

"It's not a misunderstanding when I walk into our living room and find her bent over the couch with her skirt bunched up around her waist—and she wasn't poring over wallpaper samples. Cullen was??"

I held up a hand to stop her. The mental picture was too disturbing. "Okay, okay."

Suddenly Petal's lower lip trembled. She was usually in complete control of her feelings, so I knew this was serious. Instinctively I put my arms around her. "It's okay, Pet. It'll turn out okay."

I didn't know that at all, but it's the kind of thing people say to comfort one another. The fact of the matter was, I knew in my heart of hearts that Cullen Ingalls was a skunk. He cheated on me to be with my sister, and a cheating man never reforms.

I'd always thought Petal was the lucky one to have snagged him, and I'd always held a grudge about the way she'd worked her cute, blonde, feminine wiles on Cullen that weekend I brought him home. Now suddenly I had a different slant on things. Maybe I was the one who'd lucked out.

I don't know how long we stood there in my driveway behind my open Jeep hugging awkwardly with the floor sander between us, but I gradually became aware that we weren't alone. I opened my eyes and let go of Petal to be greeted by a camera lens staring at me from two feet away. A TV camera, this time.

"Gypsy?" A female reporter with a swoop of dark hair over one eye shoved a microphone in my face. "Is this another satisfied client?"

"Unhh," I managed, ducking behind Petal.

Petal, who was used to being in the public eye, took over. "I'm Petal Ingalls, Gypsy's attorney. She does not wish to be interviewed by the press."

I blinked a couple of times, but no, it wasn't a hallucination. There was Petal, smiling, confident, as if she hadn't just confessed her husband's infidelity.

The reporter signaled her cameraman to turn off the camera. "Did I miss something?" Peering around Petal, she directed her questions at me. "Isn't one of you the fortune-teller who found Jorge Silviano?"

"Yes and no," I said carefully. "I gave Lupe a few ideas, but I'm not a fortune-teller—at least, not a professional," I said, remembering those idiotic quotes I'd given Ramone. I didn't want to come off as a liar.

Of course, the reporter cared not a hoot about my professional status. She wanted me to tell her all about Jorge Silviano—and she wanted me to do it on camera. I declined, she pushed, Petal made threatening legal noises about invasion of privacy. We tried to cut the same deal as I'd given Ramone—a few quotes in return for no filming, but that didn't satisfy her.

"This is television," she said, giving the final word at least eight syllables. "It doesn't work without pictures."

"Sorry," Petal and I said together. Then we retreated into the house as gracefully as we could, considering we were dragging two bags of groceries and a seventy-five-pound sander behind us.

"Of course you'll divorce him," I said a few minutes later as Petal and I shared tea and Pepperidge Farm cookies. Though Petal normally ate nothing containing refined sugar, she gobbled down a couple of the sweet, raisin-studded lumps.

"That's the trouble," she said. "He's already divorcing me. He did exactly what I've always coached my clients to do. He drained our accounts of as much cash as he could, froze the credit cards, and changed the codes on our locks, leaving a couple of suitcases full of my clothes on the front porch."

I couldn't express the horror I felt at the depth of Cullen's betrayal. "Don't you have any cards or accounts in your own name?"

Shamefacedly, she shook her head. "My income is four times what his is, and he's going for spousal maintenance. I outfoxed him though. I resigned."

She dropped this second bombshell almost casually.

"You left the firm? Petal, why?"

"Because I don't want that rat getting half my paycheck!" She stood abruptly and started pacing, her sandals clapping against the rippled, chipped linoleum floor. "I haven't figured it all out yet. I'll have to pay the minimums on those charge accounts if I don't want my credit ruined."

Finally I asked the really tough question. "What are you going to do? How are you going to live?" But deep down, I knew the answer to that.

"I will not move back with Mama and Daddy, even temporarily," she said, her voice barely above a whisper.

Not to mention that they were backpacking through Tibet for the summer, and they'd rented out their house—what used to be the commune, until everyone but them moved out—to some college students.

"Are you wanting to stay here?" I asked, utterly amazed. I just couldn't picture it—Petal, with her designer clothes and her perfect hair and nails, living in this chaotic dump. I narrowed my eyes at her. "You said it was 'unhealthy.'"

"It is. It's awful. But I'll bet it's got extra bedrooms. And I could help you fix it up—"

Again, I held up my hand to stop her. If I let her take charge of my house, pretty soon the place would have that sterile, minimalist look she was so fond of. "You can stay. For as long as you need. But no decorating."

"Not even my own room?"

"Well, okay. You can do your own room."

"Great! Help me get my suitcases out of my car, and then you can show me my room. I'll have a private bath, won't I?"

I couldn't bear to break the news to her about the house's bathroom situation, so I kept silent. Petal could only deal with one tragedy at a time.

CHAPTER THREE

The house had five bedrooms. I was firmly ensconced in the nicest, the big one closest to the upstairs bathroom, and I wasn't going to switch no matter how much Petal whined and tried to make me feel sorry for her. Eventually she reconciled herself to the smallest of the alternatives, because she liked the wallpaper—what was left of it—and the magnolia tree blocked her view of the street, which I'll admit wasn't much to look at. It was also the only other bedroom that wasn't crammed full of Ruby's stuff.

"It's only for a few weeks," she'd said.

I hoped fervently she was right. I could take my sister in small doses only; I hadn't lived under the same roof with her since I went away to college umpteen years ago. When I dropped out my junior year, after Cullen's defection, I didn't even consider moving home and fighting with her for bathroom space.

But here we were again, sharing a bathroom almost as miserable as the one we'd shared at the commune. It featured a claw-footed tub that was large and deep, but that was about the only thing it had going for it. There was no shower; half the tiles were missing, the wallpaper was peeling, the toilet ran, and the pipes shrieked, producing barely enough hot water for one bath, let alone two. I agreed to bathe at night, Petal in the morning.

That night after my lukewarm bath, I went down to the kitchen to fix myself a cup of hot herbal tea, which I hoped would relax me. As exhausted as I was, I was still a ball of tense muscles. Too many things had happened today, and my brain was spinning, trying to process it all.

Neither the bath nor the tea did the job. At one-twenty I was lying naked on the bed with the window open, hoping to catch a breeze—did I mention the house had no air conditioning?—and trying my damnedest to fall asleep.

That's when I heard the noise.

"A cat," I murmured. Had to be. Every night but one since I'd moved in, the next-door-neighbor's cats—she had seventeen—managed to knock over my plastic garbage container in the alley.

The noise came again. It wasn't a cat. It was the unmistakable sound of a crowbar working at one of my downstairs windows; then a muffled tinkling sound. Broken glass.

Bars. I should make the bank buy burglar bars for my personal safety. Not that my newfound resolution would help me tonight. Coming rapidly alert, I reached for the portable phone, which I kept at my bedside, and found empty space instead. The only working phone jack was downstairs, and I'd evidently forgotten to carry the phone upstairs this particular evening.

Figuring there was safety in numbers, I pulled on a long T-shirt, then barged into Petal's room and yanked the sheet off her blissfully sleeping form. Via the streetlight shining through the window, I could see she wore some filmy, sexy nightgown. I don't believe I ever owned one of those.

"Wake up!" I said.

"What?" She was drowsy and pissed all at the same time—a dangerous combination. It meant she would hit if sufficiently provoked.

"I think Darryl's downstairs. I need you to come with me."

Now she was awake. She bolted upright and stared at me. "What are we going to do, beat him up? Are you crazy? Call 9-1-1, then we'll hide in the closet!"

"The phone is downstairs."

That shut her up for all of five seconds. "Are you sure someone's down there?"

"I heard someone prying open a window, then breaking glass."

A loud thunk came from downstairs; Petal froze, her eyes bulging like a frog's. "Oh, my God!" She stood and grabbed my arms. "We are not going down there."

"He'll come up here next! I don't want to stay up here, quivering and waiting for him to find us," I said. I'm not good at waiting. I'm a pro-active kind of girl.

"Then there's only one alternative." She climbed over the bed, went to the open window, and punched out the screen with several good whacks of her dainty fist. The screen made a terrible noise as it hit the porch roof, and I cringed, expecting Darryl to storm up the stairs after us.

"I'm not jumping from a second-story window!" I objected. The mere thought made me queasy.

"We aren't jumping, silly. We'll climb out onto the roof, then work our way over to where that tree branch is, then we'll climb down the tree. Simple."

"For chimpanzees. Petal, I haven't climbed a tree since grammar school."

"It's a snap. I did it all the time in high school, sneaking out of my room."

"I didn't know you ever sneaked out," I remarked, astounded.

"There were a lot of things I never told you."

I was too scared to be stung, but I knew later I would be. In high school, Petal and I told each other everything. "Follow me." Petal slid agilely out the window. I followed, with not quite as much grace. You'd think since she was taller, she'd be the gawky one. No.

We found ourselves clinging to the eaves, scuttling toward the magnolia tree, probably looking like bats adhering to the side of their cave.

"What if Darryl comes out and see us up here?"

"He won't be looking up," Petal reasoned. "He'll be looking for police cars, or nosy neighbors peeking out their windows, or curious dogs that might bite."

Her reasoning made sense.

Once I got the hang of crawling along the roof, it wasn't so hard. We reached the magnolia tree without mishap. Since the tree was at the corner of the house, we also got a clear view of our intruder's beat-up, turquoise truck—and the man himself, who was just then dragging something out the window. He was a tall, slender man with baggy clothes and a hat on backward. Definitely not Darryl, then.

I didn't know whether to be relieved, or more frightened. At least with Darryl, I knew what I was dealing with.

Though it was dark, I was pretty sure the man was black. I tried to memorize everything about him, for the police report.

We were too scared to climb down the tree, knowing he would see us. So we waited, and watched.

"What is that?" I whispered, trying to figure out what he was stealing. Not that I had anything worth much to a kid looking for stuff to pawn for drug money. Although, come to think of it, this guy didn't act like a strung out druggy.

"Boxes," Petal said. "He's taking whole cartons. I'm guessing he'll keep loading up his truck until it's full, or something scares him off."

As he walked almost directly beneath us, I asked, "Do you think he has a gun?" Before Petal could answer, the branch on which I sat abruptly gave way with a loud crack. I grasped frantically for purchase, but everything I touched came loose. I plunged downward, my fall slowed but not broken as I hit about ten more branches on the way down.

"Gypsy!" Petal screamed, forgetting to be quiet. Not that that mattered much at this point. Though I tried not to cry out, my descent was making enough racket to wake the entire neighborhood.

I squinched my eyes closed, bracing myself for contact with the hard ground. Instead I hit a hard burglar. He'd made the mistake of stepping closer to investigate the noise in the tree. I landed squarely on his head, and we both piled onto the ground in a heap of tangled arms and legs.

My T-shirt had blown upward, so that the hem was now over my head, my face covered.

I sat there, the wind knocked out of me, not moving—hoping, I guess, that if I didn't shove the shirt out of my face and look at the burglar, he wouldn't be real.

"Gypsy, are you okay?" Petal called.

"I'm the one she hit," the burglar ground out, struggling to free himself from the tangle of limbs. "Why don't you be asking if I'm okay?"

I finally had the presence of mind to pull my T-shirt down over my bare ass. As soon as I did, I saw the burglar's forearm hurtling toward my face, the tattoo of a bulldog growing larger at an alarming rate. I ducked, but my reflexes at two in the morning aren't up to full speed.

By the time I cleared the stars out of my head, all I could see was the burglar's baggy-jean-clad butt as he ran for his truck. I tried to make out the license plates, but they'd been covered up.

"Gypsy!"

"I'm okay," I finally managed to gasp out. I would be bruised and cut and sore all over, but I didn't think any bones were broken or arteries severed.

The truck took off in a cloud of exhaust.

Petal scuttled down the tree faster than I would have imagined possible. She'd never had much grace as a kid, even after she'd exchanged those knobby knees for feminine curves. I guess all those workouts at the health club had given her more than toned deltoids.

"Are you really okay?" she asked, sounding genuinely concerned. "Do you need a doctor?"

I pushed myself onto my feet with a groan. One knee was sore and my eye throbbed where I'd been socked, but it was nothing a little ice wouldn't cure. "I'll live," I said. "Let's go inside and call the cops."

Since we had no key to use on the front door, we climbed through the broken window the burglar had kindly provided us. "You can call the cops," Petal said haughtily. "I need a bath. On the roof, I think I stepped in pigeon poop." She glided up the stairs. I called 9-1-1, making sure the operator understood that my brother-in-law was a burglary detective. I wasn't of a mind to sit up all night waiting.

My name-dropping worked all too well. A very short time later the cops arrived. Or rather, I should say, cop. When the tall, blond mountain of a man strode into my front hall, my jaw must've dropped to about the level of my navel.

"Hey, Gypsy," he said casually, as if we were acquaintances who'd just run into each other at the grocery store. "Nice decor."

"I wouldn't leave myself open to decorator jokes if I were you."

Detective Sergeant Cullen Ingalls of the Dallas Police Department gave me a hard stare, but he didn't have a smart comeback. Good.

"What're you working for in the middle of the night?" I asked. "And don't the police normally send out a patrol officer on this kind of call?" I wished I'd taken the time to change my clothes. It didn't feel quite kosher, me parading around in my jammies in front of Cullen. Especially when I wasn't wearing panties. Not that Mr. Law-and-Order would look twice at me when he'd had ten years to get spoiled by Petal.

"I'm working overtime," he said. "The Patrol division is short-handed tonight, so I volunteered my services. Anyway, how could I not come running when my dear sister-in-law called for help?" He flashed a surprising grin, and my traitor heart gave a little lurch. He'd gotten me into bed with that grin, once upon a time. No matter what a louse he was, he was still handsome as sin, a Viking conqueror with that white-blond hair and ice blue eyes. After he'd finished making my heart flutter, he looked around, obviously expecting to see Petal. He'd no doubt noticed her car out front.

For everyone's sake, I hoped Petal took a long bath. I figured I could hurry Cullen through the report and get him out of here before she made an appearance.

"So tell me what happened."

We settled into a couple of butt-sprung chairs, and I started from the beginning. I could tell he was trying not to laugh as I related the story of how Petal and I crawled out on the roof and into a tree.

"And tell me again why you didn't just call 9-1-1?" he asked.

"The phone was downstairs, where he was," I said, a trifle impatiently. "Our plan would have worked fine, if the branch I was sitting on hadn't broken."

"You fell out of the tree?" To his credit, Cullen didn't laugh. He studied me anew, and I had to resist the urge to squirm. But it was my bumps and bruises that interested him, not my hot bod. "Are you all right? Looks like you might have a black eye."

"The burglar broke my landing."

Now Cullen did laugh. "Gypsy, I admire your fortitude, but you must know it isn't wise for a civilian to attempt to capture a criminal."

"It was an accident," I reiterated.

"Well, at least you got a good close look at him." He raised his pencil again. "What did the suspect look like?"

"Unfortunately I couldn't see a thing," I admitted. "My T-shirt was wrapped around my head."

At least Cullen appeared briefly intrigued before he resumed his professional mask. "So do we have any description at all?"

I gave him my impression of the burglar's overall height, weight and color, and a description of the truck. "Oh, and he had a tattoo," I added.

Cullen rolled his eyes. "Are you making this up? You couldn't see his face, but you saw a tattoo? On a black man?"

"A tattoo of a bulldog," I said firmly. "On his forearm. It was right in front of my eyes when he hit me."

Cullen's interest sharpened. "Did it look like this?" He made a quick, scribbled drawing of a dog on his pad and showed it to me.

"Exactly! How—"

"The Pit Bulls. They're a gang." I was saved from Cullen's further attempts at interrogation when an old green vase came whizzing toward him. With his usual grace he ducked, and it shattered against the wall behind him. "Nice to see you, too, Petal."

"You!" Petal screamed from the foot of the stairs. She searched around her for another potential missile. I didn't care about the vase; it was a cheap florist's model. But Petal now had her eye on a crystal bowl. I jumped from the chair, though it cost me, ran over to Petal, and took the bowl out of her hands just before she could hurl it at her husband's head.

"You stinking, cheating S.O.B.!" Petal shrieked. She grabbed up a silverplate candlestick, which I also rescued, this time on her back swing. "How dare you show up here!"

Cullen appeared not even ruffled.

"I can't believe you came over here to harass me," Petal said, still maintaining her distance.

"Hey, I didn't even know you would be here," Cullen argued. "I thought you'd be at a hotel. Can I get your statement? 'Cause I have a couple more cases to cover tonight."

"As if I would sit in the same room with you," Petal said. At least she'd stopped throwing things. "Gypsy, you're on your own." With that she flounced away in a cloud of lavender gossamer.

Cullen sighed. Yeah, I had to agree; Petal made a beautiful exit. A moment later he returned his attention to me, all business, as if Petal had never interrupted us. "Can you tell me what was taken?"

"Boxes," I said. "Stuff belonging to the former owner of this house." I stood up and led him into the "parlor," where a section of the room near the stairs was conspicuously bare. "He took maybe five or six cartons before we scared him off."

Cullen scribbled in his notebook, using the gold fountain pen Petal had given him for their tenth anniversary. The skunk.

"And you don't know what was in the boxes?"

"As near as I can remember, all the boxes in that corner were full of papers."

"Papers?"

"Yeah. Old bank statements, letters, coupons, flyers, postcards—like the stuff that always accumulates in your kitchen if you don't go through it now and then."

"I'm not sure I know what that's like."

Oh, yeah. He lived with Petal, who was the queen of neatness freaks. No little indiscriminate piles of paper accumulated anywhere in her domain. Even her desk at work was clear as a mountain lake except for whatever materials she needed for the current task, aligned in perfectly parallel stacks.

"So this burglar took ... basically trash?" Cullen asked, one blond eyebrow quirking up.

"And he was checking the contents of each box. Look," I said, pointing to some of the other cartons that had their lids removed. "He must have looked inside and rejected these." We examined the rejected boxes; they contained a variety of household items, including a toaster, a battery charger, and a clock radio. Things that could be pawned. Why had he turned his nose up?

"What's this?" Cullen asked. He'd found a carton I hadn't yet poked around in. Something shiny peeked through a hole in its newspaper wrapping. Cullen peeled back the paper, revealing a huge crystal ball in an elaborate brass stand.

"Cool," I said, hunkering down to get a closer look.

"This looks like it could be valuable."

"Great! I get a percentage of the proceeds when I sell this stuff." Then I reconsidered. "You know, it seems a little bit odd that Ruby left this behind. She had a side business going as a psychic." I took some other things out of the box—Tarot cards, rune stones, teacups—for reading tea leaves, I guessed. There were books on astrology, numerology, palmistry—everything Ruby needed as a fortuneteller.

"You found a crystal ball?" came Petal's voice. The two of us turned to find her lurking on the stairway landing. "I came back. It occurred to me I should stay and protect Gypsy's legal rights. What if the burglar decides to sue her for assault?"

Cullen rolled his eyes. We both saw right through that one. Petal simply couldn't stand the idea of us talking behind her back.

To his credit, Cullen didn't bait her. Instead he pulled the crystal ball from its nest of newspaper and set it on its felt-lined brass stand. "You mean she actually had the gall to accept money for staring into this thing and pulling some mumbo-jumbo out of the air?"

I thought about the two hundred-plus dollars I'd been given earlier that day—yesterday, actually, since we were already into Thursday morning's wee hours.

"Some people get a lot of comfort from visiting a psychic," I countered, feeling obligated to defend Ruby, who wasn't here to defend herself.

Cullen turned to me, his brows arching in skepticism. "You know from personal experience?"

Petal, for some odd reason, came to my defense. "For your information, Gypsy is psychic. She helped find that missing boy, Julio."

"Jorge," I automatically corrected.

Cullen's eyes bored into me. "You're kidding, right?"

"She's exaggerating," I explained. "The boy's sister misinterpreted some things I said, that's all."

"You're not kidding. I heard about some psychic getting the credit for finding the kid. I couldn't believe the press would give credence to such a wild story."

"But it's true," Petal said. "Gypsy did—"

I quelled her with a look, then returned my gaze to Cullen. His close-minded dismissal of the whole thing bothered me, even though twenty-four hours ago I might've done the same thing.

"Can we get back to the burglary?" I asked as I put the crystal ball away. I hadn't actually touched it before. It felt warmer than I imagined it would. Almost as if the former owner had imbued it with some of her own warmth. Only that was downright silly. It was late and I was tired. That was it. "Will you check for fingerprints? That sort of thing?"

Cullen's mouth turned up at one corner, more sneer than smile. "If you're a psychic, you should be able to figure out who broke into your house."

I was really put out by his rudeness. Whether he believes in psychics or not, I'd done nothing to earn his cavalier attitude about the crime perpetrated on me. The fact that I was offering shelter to the wife he was trying to rip off didn't count.

If I hadn't been so tired, and really aching to boot, I'd have argued with him. I'd been on the debate team all four years in high school. The only one who could occasionally out-maneuver me in verbal sparring was Petal, and that was because she was a lawyer.

As it was, I just wanted Cullen's macho butt out of my house. I pointed toward the door. "Out."

"Look, Gypsy," he said in a slow, reasoning tone, belatedly trying to placate me. "Our resources have been cut to nothing in this year's budget. We can't waste the manpower to have an evidence team trying to solve the burglary of some trash! We aren't going to find this guy. There are dozens of skinny black guys in this city with Pit Bull tattoos on their arms. Put some ice on that eye and invest in a security system."

I knew he was right, but I wasn't about to admit it. I pointed to the door again. With a shrug, he left.

I wasn't too tired, however, to round on my sister. "Petal, how could you have told him I was psychic?"

Petal held her hands out in a gesture of helplessness. "I don't know. It just leaped out of my mouth. He was personally attacking you, and though we've had our differences, family is family. It was my sisterly duty to defend you."

I thought back to an incident in grade school when Lugey Healy had been making fun of our mother—not an uncommon occurrence, given that Mama was wont to show up at school in her ripped bell-bottoms and love beads, in a noisy snit about sexism in the curriculum or racism in the way we chose teams in gym class. I'd learned not to let that stuff bother me, since I pretty much agreed with my mother's position, if not her methods or her wardrobe. But Lugey knew he could bring Petal to tears, and he kept after her until the inevitable happened.

Still, through her tears, Petal was harboring a powerful anger against the unfairness of having parents who embarrassed her. And when Lugey, who probably outweighed her by fifty pounds, leaned over her to get in one last verbal lick, she'd up and punched him in the nose.

I think I knew, even then, that Petal would make a good lawyer. She'd started out defending the down-and-out who couldn't speak for themselves, and she'd won a bunch of money on personal injury suits, criminal defense, and divorce cases—usually on the side of the underdog.

That's why she'd jumped to my defense when Wee Luv had me arrested, then sued me. And that was why she couldn't resist defending my right to be a psychic in front of a man who would never be convinced.

I gave her a hug. "Thanks, Pet," I said.

CHAPTER FOUR

Santiago's story made page one, along with a huge color photo of Lupe's and my embrace. The photo did not show my face, but no one could miss the fact that my house was purple.

"How many purple houses do think there are in Dallas?" I asked Petal, who read over my shoulder as I munched on Cocoa Puffs. She delicately nibbled on a power bar.

"Why? You don't think Darryl will see this, do you?" Petal asked.

Darryl was crazy as a bed bug, but I didn't think he would be reading the Dallas paper on the off chance I'd made the headlines. "Nah. But it gives me the creeps. If he were really smart, he could find me."

"Then you have no worries." She read silently for a minute or two, 'til she came to my quotes. "Gypsy, you sound like a first-rate crackpot."

I laughed. "Yeah. My fifteen minutes of fame—no name, a picture of my rear end that looks like a twenty-five-pound bag of flour, and I sound like I was raised in a hippie commune."

"You were raised in a commune."

"But my butt does not look that big in real life."

Petal chewed determinedly on her power bar.

The floor sander and I got on moderately well. While I bullied the machine into removing a zillion layers of varnish and paint splatters off the living room floor, Petal got bored and started poking around in Ruby Casserly's stuff. I'd already salvaged the obviously good items—some furniture, a couple of lamps, some oil paintings. The rest I was planning to go through after I got the living room set up.

I was working on a particularly stubborn spot on the floor when I heard a loud crash and a shriek from Petal. I switched off the sander, but my arms—my whole body—continued to vibrate. "Petal?" I hollered. "What happened?"

"This house is booby-trapped!" she called back, sounding supremely irritated. "It's a personal-injury lawsuit waiting to happen."

I decided I'd better go see what had set her off. I found her sitting on the bottom step of the staircase, rubbing her head. One of Ruby's green Melmac plates was overturned at her feet, a bunch of apple slices scattered across the floor. A plastic tumbler lay near the piano, its former contents splashed across the floor and forming a skim milk lake.

"What happened?" I asked.

"Something attacked me," she said, pointing to an object lying on the floor several feet away. It was around three feet long and thin, loosely wrapped in newspaper. "I guess I bumped that stack of boxes with my elbow, and that stick, or whatever it is, toppled off and hit me in the head. Am I bleeding?"

I dutifully examined her perfectly coifed blond head. She had a knot, all right, but the skin wasn't broken. "You'll live."

I helped her clean up the mess and lectured her in my best big-sisterly fashion about the dangers of taking food up to her room. She didn't pay me any mind until I mentioned she might attract cockroaches. That produced a delicate shiver and a solemn promise that she would never eat outside the kitchen again.

Only when things had settled down did it occur to us to look at the object that had walloped Petal. I pulled off the newspaper and masking tape while Petal watched, revealing a fine mahogany walking stick with a jewel-encrusted brass head.

"Are those jewels real?" Petal asked breathlessly.

"I don't know." I knew nothing about how to tell real gems from fake. Plus, the brass head was gummed up with a crusty brown substance that dulled the finish. I'd seen some brass cleaner under the sink, so I dug it out and gave the walking stick a once-over. It cleaned up nicely.

Petal had been looking over my shoulder the whole time. "That's kind of pretty, in a gaudy sort of way."

I had to agree. But as I examined it in the sunlight streaming through the kitchen window, even my unpracticed eye could tell that the gemstones were fake—and several were missing. Still, I could get a few bucks for it. I was planning to have a yard sale some weekend soon. I stuck the gaudy cane in an umbrella stand in the front hall.

I started to return to my sanding when Petal reminded me that we needed to shorten that stack of boxes by the stairs before someone got seriously hurt. "I've handled dozens of personal-injury lawsuits," she reminded me. "You wouldn't believe the crazy accidents that happen in people's homes. I could sue you right now."

"And get what out of me?" I grumped. "My one and only asset is the Jeep, and I still owe money on it."

"You could declare bankruptcy!" Petal said brightly.

"Maybe we both can," I countered. "We could get a two-for-one special." Her smile dimmed at the reminder of her own precarious financial state.

Though I only had the sander for twenty-four hours, I decided I could spare a few more minutes to reorganize the offending boxes. Petal helped by pointing and directing, and saying things like, "Oh, be careful. Don't hurt your back." Once we started moving the boxes around, we couldn't resist opening some of them to check out the contents.

Going through Ruby's possessions was kind of like opening one of those mystery grab bags they sell in cheesy mail-order catalogs. Some of the stuff we found was interesting or useful, some was downright weird, and the rest was trash.

After a few minutes of working peacefully on arranging a stack of books in a bookcase, I realized Petal had disappeared. Curious, I searched among stacks of cartons, rolled-up, threadbare rugs, hideous lamps with no shades, and springless chairs. When I found her, she was sitting on the floor in her neatly pressed linen shorts and silk blouse, staring at Ruby's fortune-telling accouterments.

"I think this thing's really old," Petal said, tapping the crystal ball. "Better have it appraised before you sell it."

"Sell it!" I objected. "No way. I'll keep it and use it to divine the future." I flopped down beside her and waved my hands over the mass of utterly clear crystal, doing my best gypsy imitation.

"This is all so impossibly sordid," she said. "Ruby always seemed very normal."

"Hmmm." The wheels in my mind whirled. "It might make a nice sideline."

"What are you talking about?"

"I could put up a sign out front—you know, 'Sister Gypsy Moon, Psychic Readings, five dollars.' It could supplement my income."

Petal laughed. I loved her laugh, so unlike the rest of her—full bodied, robust, uncontrolled. "What income? Anyway, aren't you forgetting something, 'Sister'? You aren't really psychic! You're starting to believe your own press!"

"Do you think some people really are psychic?" I countered.

She thought for a minute. "Well, no. I mean, that would be silly. No one can really see into the future or read minds. Although ..." She closed her eyes. I remained silent, curious as to where her thought processes were leading her. Finally she opened her eyes again. "There were times when Mama read those cards ..."

A chill crept up my spine. Were we remembering the same thing? "When she talked to Grandma?" I said softly.

"Yeah. She used to give us messages from Grandma, and they felt so real." Petal absently fluffed the Tarot cards, which were soft and worn with age and use. "I believed it when we were little."

"Mama was just trying to help us to not miss Grandma so much," I said sensibly.

Petal sat up straighter, suddenly herself again. "Of course. No one can talk to dead people."

"But that's my point," I said. "If no one really has psychic powers, then I'm as qualified as anyone to give readings."

"You're not really thinking about doing this, are you? It would be ... fraudulent."

I shrugged. "It could be a lot of fun." I picked up the palmistry books and studied one of the diagrams inside, comparing it to my own hand.

Petal gave me a suspicious, sideways look. "We are not related. There's no way we share the same DNA."

The cops didn't immediately find our burglar, of course, but we had no further incidents. I returned the sander to Builders' Corner, stained and waxed my living room floor, moved a couple of Ruby's better pieces into the room along with my table and tea pot, and declared it my oasis.

Petal worked on her resume, searched the want-ads for lawyer jobs, painted her toenails, hung weird pictures on her bedroom walls, and worked on the divorce settlement she was planning to demand.

We took turns fixing dinner, which wasn't much of a treat since neither of us was Martha Stewart. Cup o' Noodles with canned fruit salad was my specialty; Petal favored microwaved soy burgers and steamed broccoli.

Petal spread her stuff all over the bathroom, a predictable development. I complained about it, also predictable.

My black eye faded to the point that it looked like purple-and-green eye shadow. I experimented with Petal's make-up, fixing up the other eye so it matched.

"Nice," Petal commented. "You could hang out at the Jefferson Arms and look right at home."

The Jefferson Arms was an apartment house down the street where a bunch of hookers lived.

Finally I couldn't put off the inevitable—I would have to have a yard sale. My stash of cash from Lupe had dwindled to nothing.

For the next couple of days, I unpacked junk, dusted it off, and stuck price tags on it. I hauled empty boxes and newspapers to the dumpsters at the church down the street—not Reverend Wade's church, but the Baptist church a few blocks further. Psychedelic Heights had quite a selection of churches. I guess my diverse neighbors had some pretty awesome spiritual needs.

I threw away an enormous amount of Ruby's old papers, figuring it was best to remove temptation should the burglar have any ideas about a return visit, but I kept the photo albums. It would have bothered me to throw away someone's family snapshots.

I got up at five in the morning on Saturday to start putting out the merchandise for the yard sale. I ran clothesline from the magnolia tree to the porch and hung out tons of clothing, a strange mishmash of Ruby's polyester, some old T-shirts and shorts of mine, and a few cast-off designer dresses Petal had put out because, for the first time since passing the bar, she needed money.

I ran an ad in the paper, so the expected crowd was gathering as the sun rose. It took all my effort and attention just to keep people from walking off with my merchandise during the confusion.

I sold a couple of hundred dollars' worth by 8 a.m. Kitchen appliances moved briskly; a toaster, a blender, a waffle iron. But business flagged by nine. I had few buyers by the time Petal, alert and perfectly groomed as always, made an appearance.

"One of my dresses sold!" she said excitedly after examining the gaps in the clothes. "How much did you get?"

Petal had priced the dress at twenty dollars. Apparently she hadn't done much shopping at yard sales. "I was offered five, I asked for ten, we compromised at seven."

"You sold a Donna Karan dress for seven dollars?" she screeched.

"You told me I could bargain."

"I didn't say to give the stuff away!"

"If you wanted to supervise, you should have gotten up at a decent hour!"

"I've been up since six!"

A potential customer who'd just gotten out of the car by the curb froze at the sound of our strident, sisterly argument. From the corner of my eye I could see her slowly turn and try to slink back to her car unnoticed.

"Good morning!" I called out to her with total cheerfulness, as if the argument had never happened.

Petal joined in. "Can I interest you in some barely worn designer dresses?"

The woman flashed a nervous smile, darted into her car, and drove away.

"Well, great. We scared off the first customer I've had in fifteen minutes."

"Has it been this slow all morning?" Petal asked.

I unzipped my fanny pack to show her the wad of cash I'd taken in. "You missed the rush. Wanta bring me some coffee?" I asked hopefully.

"You can get it yourself," she said with a petulant pout. "I'll stay out here and guard your valuable merchandise."

"Well, my, didn't we wake up on the wrong side of the bed." I flounced inside, needing a break not only for coffee but for the bathroom. I had just poured myself a cup of Folgers and had it perfectly doctored with cream and sugar when I heard Petal yelling for me.

"What?" I asked as I emerged onto the porch, shielding my eyes from the bright morning sun as it peeked above the rooftops across the street. It promised to be a hot one today. I made a mental note to put out some cold Cokes to sell to thirsty shoppers.

Petal looked uncharacteristically flustered. "This lady wants a reading."

Oh, dear.

"You're not Ruby," the stranger on my porch said the moment she saw me. It wasn't an accusation; her tone was one of bewilderment. She was tall and lanky, about fifty, with frizzled bleached blond hair and a face that showed a lot of what I delicately term "character." And she looked like she was about to cry.

"No, I'm not," I said gently. "My name is Gypsy. Here, come sit down." I showed her to a painted metal chair on the porch. "Tell me what you need help with."

Petal stared with her mouth open as I led the woman to a place of relative privacy, but she didn't intervene.

The woman's name was Helen, and she also lived in Psychedelic Heights, about four blocks from me. She told me a long, heart-breaking story about her husband's terminal cancer. He'd died six weeks earlier.

"I know I need to get out of the house and start living again," Helen said on a sigh. "My doctor, my daughter, my friends, they all say if I don't pull myself out of this, I'll waste away and die myself."

"Is that what you want?" I asked. Sister Gypsy, psychic therapist.

"No, I don't want to die," she said. "But I loved Bill so much ..."

Not to trivialize her grief, but this was almost too easy. She felt guilty for wanting to go on with life.

I thought of the crystal ball, and the offhand comments I'd made to Petal about doing psychic readings. Would it hurt to try? I'd listened to my parents do readings before. They usually gave people commonsense advice or validated their decisions. Mostly they just listened.

I closed my eyes for a few moments and took slow, deep breaths, wanting to choose my words just right. "Bill was a loving and generous man," I said. I knew that with certainty just from my brief conversation with his widow.

"Oh, yes," she said, as if I'd uttered something divinely inspired.

"Sounds as if he always put your happiness before your own."

She nodded vigorously. "Always."

"Where he is now, I'm sure he wants only for you to be happy. He doesn't want you moping around, grieving for him and endangering your own health. He wants you to eat your vegetables and drink your milk." I added this last part because the woman looked too thin and a trifle pale.

She'd already admitted that her friends and family worried about her "wasting away."

Her eyes got big and she grasped my hand in a death grip. "I have iron-poor blood," she said, using a term I hadn't heard since those Geritol commercials from my childhood. "Bill was always telling me to eat spinach!"

A little chill wiggled up my spine. All right, so I'd made a lucky guess.

"Are you talking to Bill?" she demanded.

"No," I said quickly. Billing myself as a psychic was bad enough. I wasn't about to become a medium as well. Just the thought of talking to dead people gave me the willies. "These are just feelings I have, impressions." And that was true enough.

"Then you can't ask him where the insurance policy is? We've turned the house upside down and can't find it, but I know he had one. Before he died he said it was in the desk, but I can't find it."

I thought about this logically. The man knew he was dying; he would no doubt have his affairs in order. According to Helen, he'd been completely lucid to the very end. If he said there was an insurance policy, there had to be one.

"Did he tell you what company it was with?"

"He did, but now I can't remember. I was so rattled."

I half-hoped I would get a psychic flash, that the words "Mutual of Omaha" or "State Farm" would pop into my head. But it didn't happen.

"Well, maybe the problem will resolve itself," I said. "The insurance company might locate you. Or the policy will turn up. Are Bill's desk drawers full?" I asked on impulse.

"To the brim," Helen said. "But I've taken everything out."

"Look behind the drawers. Sometimes things get pushed back when the drawers are too full."

She smiled half-heartedly, stood up, and opened her purse. "What do I owe you?"

I waved her away. "Nothing." Mostly what I'd done was listen sympathetically. There was no better therapy. Anyway, I was just practicing.

"Oh, I insist. You've made me feel much better. Ruby charged thirty for a short reading, fifty for a long one."

Good gravy! "Tell you what," I said. "You can pay me when the insurance comes through." I was not about to defraud a widow out of her pension.

Helen agreed, though not happily.

As she headed to her car, she examined several items, then paused at the clothes rack. She spotted Petal's three remaining dresses. Helen was about Petal's general size and shape, though Petal probably wouldn't have appreciated the comparison.

Helen looked at the price tags, then smiled triumphantly and pulled all three dresses from the clothesline. She walked over and handed them to me. "I'll take these. Three times twenty, that's sixty dollars."

"You're ... you're paying the asking price?" I asked, incredulous.

"Hey!" Petal objected.

Helen handed me three twenties, took the dresses, and walked back to her car looking very self-satisfied.

Petal snatched the twenties out of my hand and stuffed them into her pocket. "What were you trying to do, talk the price down? Jeez!"

I didn't have the heart to tell her she'd just pocketed my psychic consultation fee.

I was in the process of fixing macaroni and cheese for lunch when someone wandered in. "Yoo-hoo, Ms. Larabee?"

I instantly recognized the high-pitched nasal voice as that of Merrilee Haglin. Not wanting her—or anyone—to witness the disaster area that was my kitchen, I turned down the burner and hurried into the foyer.

"Your sister said I could come inside," she said, sounding defensive. "I hope you don't mind."

I did, but I pasted on a smile. "What can I do for you?"

Her arms were full of items she'd gathered from the yard sale—a leather-bound copy of Moby Dick, a tattered teddy bear, and the walking stick that had walloped Petal. "I can't find a price on the walking stick. How much do you want for it?"

"Oh, how about thirty bucks?" I said, naming what I thought was an outrageous price, figuring she'd make a counter-offer. That was how the yard-sale game was played.

She nodded eagerly. "Okay. Let's see, the teddy is two and the book eight. That makes forty even." She reached into the pocket of her housecoat/dress, pulled out two twenties, and handed them to me. "I can fix up this teddy bear and give it to one of the kids at the homeless shelter. And Wade will love the walking stick. In fact he had a similar one, but it was stolen from him a few months ago. He has a slight limp, you know." Then she lowered her voice. "War wound. Viet Nam."

I was starting to like Merrilee, at least a little. For one thing, she hadn't tried to dicker the prices down like everyone else. And I liked the fact she was buying a bear for some homeless kid. I even found myself seeing Wade in a new light. He'd fought in Viet Nam, been wounded. Probably he'd seen terrible things. That was enough to make anyone turn to religion.

"Who's the book for?" I asked.

"Oh, me, I guess. I don't read much, but it'll look nice on the shelf."

I walked her outside, where she paused to examine an oak desk. I'd priced it at $300, figuring I might get half that. My heart went pitter-patter. Merrilee had paid full price for all of her purchases without a whimper.

"Are you interested in the desk?" I asked hopefully.

She hesitated. "It's very pretty. But I couldn't spend this much money without Wade's approval. I'll bring him back over later to have a look, if it's still here."

"Any time," I said.

She left with a cheery wave, and I returned to my macaroni and cheese, which had turned into orange concrete in my absence. But I have strong teeth. I served up a hunk for me and one for Petal.

Some of Helen's friends showed up after lunch. Apparently they'd all been clients of Ruby's, and Helen had let them know a new psychic was in the neighborhood. Most lived nearby and, like Helen, just needed a sympathetic ear and someone to validate what they felt, what they wanted to do anyway. So I set up a small table on the porch, put the crystal ball on it, and gave readings to anyone who wanted one. The crystal ball was mostly a prop; I rarely even pretended to look into it.

I didn't have a set fee, since I had no idea what was reasonable for a rookie psychic. I simply asked people to contribute whatever they thought the reading was worth. To my surprise, most people dropped money into the jar, sometimes a lot of money.

Petal gave only a token objection to my activities. She was embarrassed, but she knew none of her friends would be cruising Psychedelic Heights, so she didn't worry so much about being associated with a crackpot. Besides, I think she was intrigued by the fact that I could make money just by listening to people and giving them commonsense advice.

"Aren't you taking this thing a bit too far?" Petal asked during a slow time.

"I'm having fun," I said. "People seem to like it."

"I'm worried you're leaving yourself open for litigation. What if someone follows your advice, and it's the wrong thing?"

Petal was always worried about litigation. "If that were possible, fortune-tellers all over the country would be clogging up the court systems. Besides, I'm not telling people what to do. I tell everybody they have to make their own decisions."

Petal would have argued further, but an angry male voice interrupted. "What on God's green earth is going on here?"

CHAPTER FIVE

I looked up, and there was the Reverend Wade Haglin, in fine form this morning wearing a dark blue polyester suit complete with vest, a narrow, striped tie, and a starched white collar buttoned too tightly around his fleshy throat. He gripped his new cane in one beefy hand flaunting white knuckles.

The man strode right up to me until we were nose to nose. I did not like people invading my personal space, but I wasn't about to back down. Merrilee trailed behind him, her small brown eyes watching intently.

"Can I help you with something?" I asked as civilly as I could manage. "A new vacuum cleaner, perhaps?" I gestured, Vanna-like, toward an old canister vac with a broken electrical cord.

"What exactly do you think you're doing?"

"I think I'm having a yard sale," I said. "What do you think I'm doing?"

"Consorting with the Devil!"

Now things were becoming clear. He did not approve of fortune-tellers; he'd stated that pretty forcefully on his first visit to my house. The sight of me sitting on the front porch with a crystal ball and a jar full of money must have given him quite a turn.

I had a choice, here. I could tell him where to stick his pathetically misinformed assumptions, or I could mollify him. On the one hand, he was a neighbor, and his wife had her eye on a three-hundred-dollar desk. I didn't want to spend the next two-plus months skulking around my own driveway and front porch trying to avoid a confrontation with them. On the other hand, the unfairness of his accusations got my dander up. Here I was, trying to help people with their problems, and he immediately jumped to the conclusion that I was some sort of succubus just because a crystal ball happened to be sitting on my front porch.

Then I lost the chance to make a choice. Petal intervened.

"Excuse me, I'm Petal Ingalls, Gypsy's attorney." She extended one well-manicured hand. The Reverend shook it cautiously. "Has Gypsy broken some kind of law here?" she asked innocently.

"The laws of God!" Haglin intoned, his index finger pointed upward.

"Last I heard, we had freedom of religion in this country. Suppose Gypsy doesn't believe in your God."

"Petal!" Of course I believed in God. I didn't go to church and I didn't kneel by my bed at night to say prayers, but I knew there was some force out there greater than myself. I'd always figured God was basically a pretty nice guy, and that He didn't send people to hell for looking into a crystal ball or having an occasional sexy thought about their sister's husband.

"If this woman doesn't believe in the One God Almighty, then I pray for her doomed soul."

"And do you have to pray in her front yard?" Petal asked. "'Cause I'm sure she wouldn't mind if you prayed for her. As long as it isn't interfering with her yard sale."

"I'm glad you think this is so funny, Ms. Ingalls." Merrilee spoke up for the first time. "And yes, we'll include both of you in our prayers. But the Bible says we must do more than that."

A couple of customers had driven up as the confrontation simmered; they'd gotten out of their cars, sensed the tension, and slipped away, all of their money still firmly in their pockets, darn it.

"Yes, indeed," Haglin agreed. "We must do everything in our power to save this unfortunate sinner from her vile ways." Before I could see it coming, he grabbed both of my hands and clasped them between his in a death grip. "Will you pray with me, Gypsy Larabee?"

I yanked my hands away and backed up a couple of steps. "Are you nuts?"

"Touch her again and you're looking at assault charges," Petal said.

"Well, Wade," Merrilee said with a superior sniff, "this one's going to be difficult." She passed her Bible to her husband.

He opened it, using a red ribbon page marker, squinted as he tried to find his place, then started in with a baritone preaching voice that practically shook the ground. "Yea, though I walk through the valley of darkness—"

"That's it, buster!" Petal said. "I'm calling the cops." She stormed into the house.

"Don't let that woman intimidate you, Wade," Merrilee said.

Haglin snapped the Bible shut and went with improvisation. I guessed he was farsighted and too vain to wear glasses.

"The Lord said to Moses, 'Thou shalt not put false gods before me!'" he thundered. "The prophets of Leviticus warn us, 'Never suffer a witch to live!'"

I decided this had gone far enough. The Haglins had already scared away three customers. "Do you see any false gods here?" I demanded. "I'm not doing anything even slightly blasphemous!"

"You're consorting with Beelzebub!"

"No! I haven't talked to him in weeks, I swear!"

"You're delving into the Black Arts."

"I'm not either! There are no black candles here, no upside-down pentagrams, no saying The Lord's Prayer backward."

Merrilee gasped. "See, she knows all about those things! Look at that weird make-up she's wearing."

"And I don't make blood sacrifices or run around naked outside or anything. You can check my back yard! No animal bones!"

"This power you have does not come from God," Haglin said.

"How do you know? Anyway, I don't have power," I admitted. "I made a few lucky guesses. And the weird make-up is because I have a black eye, okay?"

Petal came outside with the cordless phone. "Call for you, Gyp."

"Now?" I asked.

"It's Helen. She said the insurance policy was right where you said it would be, behind a desk drawer." She shot a self-satisfied smile at the Haglins.

Merrilee narrowed her eyes, and I could have sworn her hair poofed out a little, like it was trying to stand on end. "No powers, huh?"

I couldn't even retort. A chill crept up my spine, from my tailbone all the way to my skull. My God, I thought, maybe I did have psychic powers. And if I did, where did they come from?

Reverend Haglin had pulled a vial out of his jacket, and now he was sprinkling holy water on me. "Oh, Lord, save this poor woman from the evil forces of darkness that have entrapped her soul ..."

Though the good Reverend had scared away all my potential customers, some of the other neighbors had come out of their houses to watch. Some looked just curious, others appeared faintly amused.

"... I am the Lord thy God!" He was building to a crescendo. Beads of sweat trickled down his face. His whole body quivered. "Thou shalt not put false gods before me!"

Merrilee gazed up at him, eyes shining with pride.

He lunged for the crystal ball, intending to do it harm, I believe, but I whisked it away just before he would have grabbed it. "You break it, you buy it," I said. "It's an antique, and it's worth a couple of hundred bucks at least."

"I would pay twice that, nay, ten times that, if I thought destroying that agent of evil spirits would save you from the fires of damnation."

"Listen, Reverend, you pay me two thousand dollars cash, I give you the crystal ball, and I'm out of the fortune-teller business. Scout's honor." I held up three fingers in a Girl Scout pledge. Never mind that my mother hadn't even let me join the Brownies. At the time she'd considered it right-wing sexist brain-washing.

The Reverend narrowed his eyes. "Were that it was so easy, but the devil cannot be banished with a simple cash transaction."

What a cop-out. I knew he wasn't interested in an easy solution. He wouldn't be happy until I was on my knees, admitting I'd consorted with Satan and begging forgiveness. Fat chance.

"Look, I've listened to about all of this I can stomach," I said. "You're trespassing, and I want you gone."

Petal, meanwhile, had someone from the police department on the phone. She paced the front porch, explaining the situation loudly enough for the Haglins to hear. "You'll send someone out right away?"

The threat of law enforcement intervention finally galvanized the Haglins into a retreat. "You haven't heard the last of this," the Reverend said, shaking his walking stick at me. The tiny paste gemstones glittered in the sun, casting pinpoint beams of light onto my sidewalk. Disco lights for the ants. "I'll be back."

It wasn't quite the same as when the Terminator said it, but I didn't doubt the man's resilience.

As soon as the Haglins had cleared the sidewalk and were heading toward their own front yard, I breathed a sigh of relief.

"He's leaving now," Petal said into the phone. "It's okay." She hung up. "Wow, what a nutcase. He's gonna be trouble, Gypsy." She sighed expansively and glared up at my house, as if it were the cause of all our problems. "In my neighborhood, we don't even see our neighbors, much less brawl with them in the front yard."

For half a second, I let myself fantasize about living in a cozy guest bedroom in The Castle, what I secretly called Petal's gaudy home in Highland Park. What I wouldn't have given for central air and a thirty-gallon water heater... But then I shook my head. I liked knowing my neighbors, even if some of them were a tad weird.

"I'll win him over," I said, more to myself than Petal. "When he's calmer, I'll sit down and explain to him what I'm doing. When he understands I'm not really a devil-worshiper, he'll leave me alone."

"Hah!" Petal plopped back down in her lawn chair. "Does the word 'fanatic' mean anything to you? It would be a lot simpler to just give up the fortune-telling business, you know."

She was right. But I wasn't going to do it. I can't explain why it had so quickly become important to me that I be allowed to continue my little side business. All I know is that it gave me extreme satisfaction to help the Helens of the world. And if I could make a few bucks out of it, so much the better.

"Maybe you could tithe to his church," Petal offered.

"What? No way."

"Money talks. Offer to donate ten percent of your fortune-telling proceeds to the Reverend's church, and I'll bet he starts referring customers to you."

"I'm not giving that narrow-minded old fart anything!" I argued.

Petal sighed again. "You never listen to my advice."

A broken-down old truck pulled up to the curb, and I looked forward to the distraction of customers. A young black man in baggy pants and a black mesh jacket over a muscle shirt jumped out of the driver's side; two pals spilled out the passenger door.

My heart did a flip-flop, and I lectured myself sternly not to fall into the stereotype trap. Sure, they were black. Sure, they were dressed like gang members. But I now lived in an ethnically diverse neighborhood where gang clothes were a fashion statement, not necessarily a lifestyle choice.

"Uh-oh," Petal said under her breath. She had control of the fanny pack with the money, and she put a protective hand over it. I couldn't see the phone, and I wondered how far one of us would have to lunge to grab it.

Were gangs into robbing yard sales? I wondered. You'd think they would go to Highland Park, where garage sales racked up some serious money.

The truck's driver sauntered over to me, obviously thinking he was hot shit on a stick. Angry, hot shit, I amended. His glare activated every one of my sweat glands.

"You the lady bought this house?" he asked in a voice that was deadly quiet, commanding attention. The antithesis of Reverend Haglin's booming baritone.

"I'm living here temporarily." My voice quivered just a tad. Show no fear, I ordered myself.

"That's a mistake on your part," he said. "This stuff? All this stuff here? It's mine."

"You tell 'her, Reggie," one of the other men said.

"I believe it now legally belongs to the bank," I countered. "If you'd like to see the paperwork—"

"This stuff belong to my Aunt Ruby," he said. The other men were prowling around the merchandise, knocking things off tables, kicking furniture, flinging dresses off the clothesline.

"Dial 9-1-1," I said to Petal.

"I'm trying!" she said in an un-Petal-like whine. She was hell on wheels in a courtroom with the full force of the law at her fingertips. In a crisis that involved possible bodily harm, she didn't sound so tough. "The damn phone's out of range or something. There, there I got—"

The man grabbed the phone out of Petal's hands and hurled it across the yard. "I said this stuff belongs to me! Ruby's my aunt, and I'm her heir."

The way he used the word "heir," it sounded like he'd just learned it.

"Is she dead?" I asked, wanting to point out the obvious. As long as Ruby still lived, her heir didn't inherit diddly-squat.

The confident sneer faltered for a moment, and confusion clouded his obsidian eyes. "She not dead," he said clearly. "I be taking care of her things while she's gone."

"She owed taxes," I said, wondering how much this overgrown kid could comprehend. He didn't look stupid, but I suspected he wasn't highly educated. His abuse of the English language was my first clue. "The government seized her house, see, then the bank that carried the mortgage—"

"I know what happened!" He took a step closer. I took a step back. "You got no right to sell this stuff to strangers!"

His nostrils flared, and beads of sweat popped out on his chocolate brown forehead. This wasn't simply a power trip for him. He was disturbed.

"If he wants the stuff, give him the stuff," Petal said. "It's not like Ruby's things are worth much." She looked at Reggie. "Especially now that his buddies are busy trashing the place."

"Hey, don't you be dissing my Aunt Ruby," Reggie said, back to using his deadly-quiet voice. His control was again firmly in place. He turned to his homeboys. "You, Lamar, start loading this stuff up."

He was serious? He wanted all this junk?

Reggie pointed to a table stacked with books, mostly paperback romance novels. "Take them books. You got any papers?" he said to me, pointing a finger in my face. "Photo albums, files, records?"

Suddenly this was sounding familiar. Papers—exactly what the burglar had stolen. The young, black burglar with baggy pants, driving a beat-up truck. Duh! How had it taken me so long to realize I was standing face-to-face with my house-breaker? I should have recognized his voice the moment he opened his mouth. Just to be sure, I checked his arm. There was the bulldog tattoo, big as life.

I had lots more of Ruby's papers in the house, but I wasn't about to tell him that. He didn't seem like the kind of person who would let trespassing laws stand in the way of a little friendly home invasion.

"This is everything that's left," I said, which was a big fat lie. The stuff I'd hauled outside for the yard sale had made a sizable dent, so that I could move around inside the house, but I still had dozens of Ruby's boxes to go through, not to mention a file cabinet.

"Then why don' you invite me in," he said, "so I can see for myself."

"Because I don't want to?" I squeaked.

His two goons had finished wrecking my sale, and now they stood on either side of Reggie with menacing looks on their faces. They clenched and unclenched their fists, as if they were just waiting for a word from Reggie to disassemble me and ... Petal. Where was Petal?

I chanced a look behind me. She wasn't there. I could only hope she'd managed to recover the phone, slip inside the house and call the cops.

I was about to warn Reggie that the police would be here any second when a loud crack sounded behind me and a chunk of the sidewalk right by Reggie's feet exploded.

In less than the time it took me to inhale for a scream, Reggie and company had split up like billiard balls at the break and were ducking behind furniture and tree trunks.

Then my scream came out. With reflexes only slightly slower than my visitors', I hit the dirt.

"Shit, that crazy lady's got a gun!" one of Reggie's friends said. Sure enough, Petal was standing at the front door with a pistol clutched in one hand.

"Petal, are you nuts?" I screamed at her. Though Reggie was certainly frightening, I didn't believe he would kill me. Petal, on the other hand, had missed me by inches.

"Next time I won't miss!" she yelled at Reggie, which didn't comfort me a lot. "You got ten seconds to clear off this property."

They only took eight. By the time I got courage enough to unroll myself from the tight ball I was in and look up, all I could see was the truck's tail lights. I did, however, manage to memorize the license plate.

Petal walked out onto the porch as I stood up and brushed dirt off my leg. There was no sign of her gun. "Are you okay?" she asked.

"Yeah." I didn't know whether to kiss her or sock her. She'd gotten rid of Reggie, true, but she'd almost turned me into Swiss cheese in the process. "Let's go call the cops."

"Uh, I'd rather not."

"Excuse me?"

"First, it's not my gun. It's Cullen's. I sort of borrowed it."

"Oh, terrific," I grumbled, sinking onto the front steps. Any strength in my knees regained after Reverend Haglin's visit had vanished with Reggie's.

"Second, the kid might get it into his head to accuse me of attempted murder. I could probably beat the charge, but I'd just as soon not hassle with it."

I almost laughed as I pictured the cops coming to arrest Petal. How would she weather a night in jail, I wondered? "You're right, you don't want to mess with it. Hopefully we scared the guy off for good."

"He's the same one who broke in, isn't he."

"Yup."

Petal sat on the step next to me. "Are you going to tell Cullen?"

I thought for a moment. I'd have felt better knowing the cops were on to Reggie. Then again, even if they arrested him, he wouldn't be incarcerated for long. "Don't worry," I said, putting an arm around her shoulders, "I won't get you in trouble." Family is family. "What exactly were you aiming for, anyway?"

She wouldn't tell me.

We got some big garbage sacks and stuffed in everything Reggie's friends had destroyed. It wasn't too bad. Mostly they'd just thrown stuff around. We were hanging the clothes back on the clothesline when a black-and-white cruised slowly past my house, then stopped, backed up, and parked at the curb. The cop at the wheel rolled down his window.

"We had a report of shots fired in this vicinity," he said. "You ladies see or hear anything?"

"Not us," I said. "Everything's fine here.

By Monday morning I'd stopped jumping at every door that slammed, and cringing every time a car drove past my house. I'd had no further trouble from Reverend Haglin or Reggie. The Salvation Army had come by to pick up the yard-sale leftovers, and things were sort of back to normal, though nothing had been truly normal since I'd moved into that house.

A steady trickle of Ruby's former clients knocked on my front door all day Sunday. I guess my customers were passing along good word of mouth. I did readings and watched the pile of cash in my tip jar grow. I was afraid to count it, afraid to admit I was actually making money. I figured people would stop coming when they realized I wasn't a professional-caliber psychic, and my "practice" could taper off naturally.

Monday morning was quiet. I shined up some brass candlesticks and hung some pretty china plates in the living room. I'd have to sell them eventually, but for now I would enjoy them. My next project was a beat up old mantle clock.

Feeling pretty pleased with myself, I was in the kitchen pouring a third cup of coffee when Petal came storming through the front door, slamming it behind her. She stomped into the kitchen, dropped her briefcase on the floor, headed for the medicine cabinet, poured four aspirin of questionable age into her hand, and swallowed them dry.

"Problem?" I asked. She'd been on a job interview, though she'd referred to it as "breakfast with a colleague," the partner of a small criminal defense firm where Petal hoped to get gainful employment. It wasn't nearly as prestigious as her last post, but it would have to do, she'd told me that morning. She'd acted as if the job were a foregone conclusion.

"I've been blacklisted."

"Can they do that?" They were the partners at her previous employer, Dykens, Jones & Steele, where she'd been a well-paid associate on the rise. I hadn't yet gotten a straight story from Petal about why she'd left the firm. The first version, which involved quitting so she wouldn't have to pay Cullen support payments, made no sense at all, unless she planned on living without an income into perpetuity.

My ambitious sister wasn't the type to leave a job where she was making six figures unless she had somewhere to go. She didn't.

I hadn't pressed, sensing that Petal would tell me in her own time.

"It's those damned ethics charges," she said, slamming the cabinet door for good measure. She opened the rusty fridge, found a bottle of cran-apple juice, and unscrewed the top.

Ethics charges. This was the first I'd heard. I sensed she was going to unburden herself, so I didn't encourage her. If she thought I wasn't interested, she would blurt it all out until she got a reaction.

"What do you think of this clock?" I asked, showing her my latest project. Glue, furniture polish, and copious amounts of WD-40 had turned a filthy eyesore into a half-decent accent piece that kept time, as long as you didn't quibble over losing a few minutes every hour.

"Old Man Dykens might as well have taken a full-page ad out in the Morning News," she fumed between gulps of her drink straight out of the bottle. "It's totally groundless, and the investigation will exonerate me. Meanwhile, no firm will touch me."

All right, I was biting. "Petal, what exactly have you been accused of?"

"Sleeping with a judge to curry favor. Can you believe it?"

Oh, God. "You ... you didn't, did you?"

"Gypsy, of course not." And then she mumbled something I didn't quite pick up.

"What was that?" I asked.

"I said, I only slept with him after the verdict."

I could not believe my ears. My sister, my own sister, had cheated on her husband. "So all that sanctimonious whining about Cullen betraying you was bullshit!" I exploded.

"He did betray me! He didn't know about Judge Colter."

"Am I sensing a double standard here?"

The fire went out of her. "Maybe." She kicked off her shoes and pulled off her jacket, then sat down at the table with me. "I thought this whole thing would blow over. Gypsy, as God is my witness, there was nothing improper going on during the trial Judge Colter presided over. He was attracted to me. I knew that. But we didn't act on it. Not 'til later. I don't know how his wife found out."

"He was married, too?" This just got worse and worse.

"I made a mistake, okay? The whole thing was very brief. Nobody knew about our ... liaison except maybe Ruby, and she wouldn't have said anything."

"Ruby? As in Ruby Casserly?"

"Yeah. I told you, she was a judge's clerk. I just didn't tell you how I knew the judge."

I groaned.

"Donald—Judge Colter—is the one who told me about Ruby's house. You should be grateful I was sleeping with him."

"Oh, Petal." I should have been furious with her. She'd lied to me, claiming the divorce was entirely Cullen's fault. But at that moment, she was my kid sister with a skinned knee who'd been doing something wrong, something she thought she could get away with.

She didn't need a scolding. She needed to know someone was on her side. "What's the worst that can happen?" I asked.

"I could be disbarred." Her voice gave a telltale tremble. "Or have my license suspended for some period of time, like a year or two. But it probably won't come to that. Until it's settled, though, I don't have a paycheck."

I didn't mind too much sharing my roof and my meager earnings with Petal 'til she got back on her feet, but Petal couldn't stand it. She was one of the most self-sufficient people I knew, and had always been more comfortable as the supporter rather than the supportee. "Can you take on your own cases?" I asked her.

"Sure. I guess."

"One of my fortune-teller clients needs a lawyer for a divorce. I have her name and number."

Petal looked less than thrilled, but the alternative was to continue to sponge off me. "Okay. I'll call her." She unbuttoned her blouse with one hand while tipping the Coke can with the other. "I need your help with something else."

"Oh?" I asked, not liking the off-hand, casual way she'd mentioned it. Petal tended to turn small favors into crises.

"I'm supposed to go over to the house today at two o'clock and pick up my stuff. I need your Jeep ... and your moral support. Cullen will be there, no doubt to make sure I don't touch anything that might be construed as community property."

More than likely she'd need me to keep her from scratching Cullen's eyes out. "Okay," I said. I hadn't been out of the house, other than the front yard, in days, and I needed an excuse to see Cullen anyway.

CHAPTER SIX

The home of Cullen and Petal Ingalls was a sight to behold. They'd bought it two years ago. Cullen had been against it, arguing that until they had kids, their two-bedroom Lakewood bungalow was perfectly adequate for their needs. With the hours they both worked, they weren't home much anyway.

But Petal needed a home that befitted her upwardly mobile station, she'd argued. If she wanted to rise to partner status, she needed to act successful. She needed to wear designer clothes, drive a prestige car, and entertain colleagues and clients in an impressive house in the right neighborhood.

The "right neighborhood" was Highland Park, where Dallas' old money had settled in during the 1920s, a few years after Psychedelic Heights was built. No crumbling old mansion for Petal, though. She found a vacant lot where some house had burned down, and she built a new one—The Castle—complete with walk-in closets, an airplane-hangar-sized kitchen she never used, and a three-car garage. It had been more than they could afford at the time, and when they'd moved in they'd done without furniture in most of the rooms. But Petal had insisted they would "grow into it" as their salaries increased.

With her year-end bonus, she'd hired the decorator.

The decorator had the deliciously awful name of Liz Pastelle. The bitch had done a good job, I grudgingly admitted when I entered the house with Petal at precisely two o'clock that afternoon, our arms loaded down with empty packing boxes—something I had loads of. I hadn't visited The Castle in several months, and the vast rooms of Petal and Cullen's yuppie haven had bloomed in my absence.

Everything was casually elegant, stylish yet livable. I could see no signs of Petal's stark minimalist taste. Another thing that definitely was not Petal were the piles of junk stacked discretely here and there. Clutter drove her nuts. I don't know how she stood it in my house, though she retreated as often as she could to her little oasis of a room.

Cullen was there, dressed in jeans and a rumpled T-shirt with a hole in the shoulder. The man, for all his hunkedness, had never been a fashion plate. Without Petal around to keep his clothes neat and clean, he'd fallen into disrepair. It hadn't taken long, either. The rumpled look had suited him well during college, when it contributed to his overall disreputable image. Now it made him look, well, bad. Like he wasn't getting along too well without his wife of ten years.

Idly, I wondered where Liz Pastelle was, and whether she would approve of her new main squeeze looking like a degenerate.

Cullen's lawyer, a toadish man with bulging eyes that missed nothing, hovered in the entryway as we came in. Petal apparently already knew him. She shook his hand firmly enough to cause a wince and took control.

"Per our agreement, Mr. Tuscan, I'll be removing only my clothing and personal items. This is my sister, Gypsy Larabee; she'll be helping me pack. I'll need the mauve tweed luggage stored in the attic, Cullen, if you don't mind." She looked at Tuscan. "The luggage was a gift from my parents when I graduated from law school."

Tuscan started scribbling in a notepad. "That would have been after your marriage, correct?"

Exasperated, she turned to Cullen. "Cullen, you don't want a set of pink luggage! Tell him!"

Cullen shrugged. "It's all community property, babe. Take it now, and we'll settle up later."

The greedy son-of-a-bitch! I couldn't believe this was the Cullen Ingalls I knew. He'd never been interested in money, or he wouldn't have become a cop. Had his years of marriage to Petal changed him that much?

I started to object, but Petal gave me a warning look. She was the one who ought to be going ballistic right about now, yet she'd abruptly taken on a calm serenity that would have fit well on Mother Theresa in a famine. I guessed she was holding it in, and there must have been a pretty good reason.

"I'll need the computer, too, Cullen," she said.

"Oh, no you don't," he immediately objected. "That's a valuable asset. You can't just—"

"Do you want me to sue for spousal maintenance?" she said sweetly.

"Ms. Ingalls," Tuscan cut in, "as you well know, your husband is the one in a position to ask for support. Your income is more than—"

"I have no income, Mr. Tuscan," she said. "I am no longer employed. No wages to garnish, nothing to fight about. If you want to go after my income, then you better let me have the computer so I can take on some work."

Cullen stared in open-mouthed shock. Gone was any trace of cockiness. "You quit your job?"

"I was fired. The shock of seeing my husband in delecto flagrante, and the subsequent divorce, has traumatized me to the point that I'm incapable of performing the rigorous responsibilities of a law firm associate. I don't know that I'll ever be capable again."

"So you're now, er, self-employed?" Tuscan asked, scratching on a legal pad.

"Yes."

"But she only has one client," I added. Ordinarily I wouldn't have contributed to Petal's petty revenge, but by God, Cullen deserved it. He was behaving like a first-class asshole. He was no doubt paying for his odious attorney with money Petal had earned, doing everything he could think of to jack up the legal fees because he knew in the end Petal would have to pay them one way or another. If he impoverished himself in the process, I was sure he didn't care. He knew how to hit Petal where it hurt.

"Let her take the damn computer," Cullen said, trying to pretend Petal hadn't scored with her announcement. "It's four years old anyway. Not worth much."

Satisfied, I grabbed a couple of empty cartons and a roll of tape and started up the stairs, before I let rip all the insults fighting among themselves in my throat to get out.

"All of your things are in the guest bedroom," Cullen called after Petal as she followed me.

At the top of the stairs, Petal headed immediately for the master bedroom. "So, he thinks he can decide which clothes I'll take?" she muttered. But when she tried the knob, it was locked. All of the bedrooms, we soon discovered, were locked except for the one Petal was intended to enter. Inside was what I guessed to be her entire wardrobe. There were enough clothes in here to clothe a small third-world country.

"This is obscene, you know?" I couldn't help saying. "We'll need more boxes."

"No need," she said. "I'm not taking most of this. You know what he did? He went into the attic, found every box of old clothes I'd stored up there, and spread them out in here to make an impression. Then he took a picture. It'll show up in court."

"You're joking."

"I had one of my male divorce clients do exactly the same thing one time," she admitted. "It shows how generous the husband is in allowing the wife to take her wardrobe with her, and it makes the wife look like a greedy money-grubber who uses all her husband's hard-earned salary to adorn herself. He's using my own tricks against me."

"It's a pretty mean trick, Pet," I said. "I'd say your karma is coming back to haunt you."

"Maybe so," she said with much less ire than I could have guessed possible. "Hell, let's just take it all. Maybe I can sell some of it at a resale shop." She started stuffing clothes willy-nilly into boxes, and I did the same.

Cullen brought down the luggage and loaded the computer and printer into my Jeep. While Petal went through her jewelry box, making sure every piece on the inventory was accounted for, I went downstairs to have a chat with my dear brother-in-law.

He was in the kitchen, fixing himself a sandwich. I got a peek into the fridge; it was pretty barren. Petal wasn't here to do the grocery shopping, I guessed. I'd always thought their marriage was a little more egalitarian, but I was beginning to suspect that Petal was the glue that had held this little household together.

Cullen didn't see me at first, and the expression on his face when he turned explained a lot. He was miserable, and this divorce thing was hurting him every bit as much as it did Petal.

The moment he realized I was there, he schooled his face back to the contemptuous, cocky grin he was so good at.

"Done already?"

"Petal's finishing up."

"How's the shiner?"

I touched my eye self-consciously. "Almost gone. Listen, I need to talk to you."

"If it's about the settlement, talk to my—"

"No, it's about my case. The burglary? You still handling that?"

"Yeah. No progress."

"I think I know who did it," I said, settling on one of the leather barstools along the island breakfast bar.

Now I had Cullen's full attention. "Who?"

"His name's Reggie, and he's Ruby Casserly's nephew. He's a member of the Pit Bulls. He drives an ancient, turquoise Ford Ranchero pick-up, license plate 103-KKD. He's about twenty, dark skin, very dark eyes, and he's missing half of his left eye tooth." One of the little details I'd catalogued when he was bullying me.

Reflexively, Cullen found a pen and something to write on. "How'd you find this out?"

I could have told him the truth, but that would have taken all the fun out of this conversation. Also, the fewer people who knew about Reggie's yard-sale visit, the better. I'd told Petal I wouldn't get her in trouble over the gun. "I saw it in my crystal ball."

"Excuse me?"

"It was a psychic vision."

He dropped the pen. "You're about as psychic as that espresso machine. I'm not in the mood for jokes, Gypsy."

"It's no joke. If you don't believe me, check it out. I bet you'll find that such a person exists, and I'll bet he doesn't have an alibi for last Monday night."

Cullen rolled his eyes. "We're shorthanded at the station right now. I don't have time for wild goose chases."

"Do it anyway," I said. "Or do I have to complain to your superior?"

I knew Cullen would rather waste time looking for a ghost than have to explain himself to his higher-ups.

"All right, all right, I'll look him up. Are you being a pain in the ass to get back at me for Petal?"

"No. You're suffering enough. But I did think you were a better man than this." With that zinger I waltzed out of the kitchen. Petal was coming downstairs with the last armload. She signed off on the receipt, and we high-tailed it out of there.

As we crammed the last two boxes into the back seat, I heard a rustling sound behind me and turned just in time to see one of the well-manicured bushes trembling. Was it an animal? Or a human?

Petal saw it to. She had a flowered umbrella in her hand, and she poked it forcefully into the bush, then jumped back. "Come out of there!"

We were rewarded with a sharp "oomph!" A man rolled out from under the bushes. Petal gasped, and we instinctively grabbed for each other as the man rolled into a crouch, then stood to his full six-foot-three.

Darryl.

"Well, well, well, look who we have here," he said, flashing a smile that used to make my stomach swoop. Now it made my skin crawl. "You wouldn't really hurt me with that umbrella, now, would you, sweetheart?" In a lightning-fast move he grabbed the umbrella out of Petal's shock-limp hand.

He was normally pretty-boy handsome, the main reason I couldn't resist going out with him. But he looked a bit disheveled now, with greasy hair and in need of a shave.

"How long have you been hanging out in the bushes?" I couldn't help asking.

"A long damn time. But I knew you'd show up here sooner or later. Gypsy, we have to talk."

"No, we don't," I said firmly, wishing my voice wouldn't tremble so tellingly. "I gave up talking to you the night you tried to barbecue me." I glanced up and down the street, hoping to see a neighbor I could signal to, but the whole block was deserted.

"I wasn't trying to kill you," he insisted. "I've told the police over and over. You were supposed to be at work. I just wanted to burn up your things so you'd have to move in with me."

"What a persuasive guy," Petal commented.

"I wouldn't have moved in with you," I ground out. "We were broken up. It was over."

"You haven't given this thing a fair chance."

There was no talking to him. We'd been over and over the same ground. He wouldn't take no for an answer.

"You're violating a restraining order," Petal reminded him.

"It's not good outside Oklahoma," he said with a grin. "I checked. Gypsy, my car's parked right around the corner. You just come on with me now—"

"In your dreams. Petal, go inside and get Cullen."

"I'm not leaving you out here alone with this maniac!"

"Maniac, huh?" With quicksilver speed, his demeanor went from eerily besotted to terrifying belligerent. A six-inch switchblade came out of nowhere and snicked open. Darryl took a step toward Petal. "You ain't seen a real maniac. Not yet."

That was enough for me. I screamed bloody murder, hollering for Cullen. Petal joined me. Together we created quite an ear-splitting ruckus.

It didn't take Darryl long to figure out he'd lost the upper hand. The knife disappeared, and as the front door opened he took off at a dead run, disappearing around the corner just as Cullen came out.

"What the hell is going on out here?"

Petal and I pointed and gestured and babbled incoherently. By the time Cullen understood my stalker had accosted us in the driveway, no sign of Darryl remained. I'm not sure Cullen even believed us.

"Oh, forget it," Petal said in disgust. "Next time we're in trouble, we'll call a real man to help us." She climbed into the Cherokee's passenger seat and slammed the door. With a shrug to Cullen, I slid behind the wheel, and we took off. For several blocks I checked the rear-view mirror frequently, but I saw no sign of Darryl or his blue Toyota Celica. The last thing I wanted to do was lead him to the Purple Palace.

"What were you grilling Cullen about in the kitchen?" Petal asked when we could relax a bit.

"I sicced him on Reggie. Don't worry, there was no mention of any illegally snatched gun. Why'd you steal Cullen's gun, anyway?"

"You know, hanging out with you is kind of scary. In the span of a few days you've had one burglar, two people assault you in your own front yard, and a third person assault you in my front yard."

Good enough answer, I supposed.

Later that afternoon, after we hauled Petal's stuff inside and crammed it into every available nook and cranny, we set up her computer and printer. She called the woman who wanted a divorce and met with her an hour later in my kitchen. I did a couple of quick readings and sold the clock I'd just fixed up to one of my clients for two hundred dollars. Not bad. I pocketed twenty dollars—my commission—and hid the bank's share in the silverware drawer.

Once again I hoped things were calming down. Once again, my hopes were futile. Cullen phoned just as Petal and I were sitting down to our dinner of tuna salad, saltines, and Kool-Aid.

I answered the phone, and as soon as Petal figured out who it was she flew out of her chair and plastered her ear next to mine.

"I want a straight answer from you, Gypsy," he said. "How did you come by the name of Reggie?"

"Don't tell him," Petal mouthed urgently, shaking her head.

"I told you," I said, smiling evilly. "I saw it in my crystal ball. What difference does it make where I got the information, as long as it's right?"

"It'll make a helluva difference if the case goes to court."

Petal took control of the phone. "A minor offense like B&E wouldn't earn the guy much jail time anyway," she said, "and he'd probably plea-bargain it down before the case got to court."

"Hello, Petal," Cullen said mildly.

"We just want you to scare the kid a little bit and warn him to stay away from Gypsy's house."

"It may not be that easy," Cullen said. "Reggie Crane has already served time for attempted burglary. The crime occurred last spring."

I had a bad feeling about this. "He was trying to break into this house, wasn't he."

Cullen was silent for a moment. "How'd you know that?"

"I'm psychic," I said, earning a snicker from Petal.

"Anyway, I need you to I.D. the guy from a photo line-up before I have evidence strong enough to haul him in. Is there any way you can do that?"

"Sure."

"I thought you didn't get a clear look at him the night of the burglary."

"My memory improved once I calmed down."

Another silence. "Fine. I'll drop by about eight."

"Oh, great, he's coming here," Petal said after we'd hung up. "That means I have to do something with myself."

She looked fine to me in her color-coordinated, designer gym shorts and tank top. Petal always looked well put together, unlike me, whose favorite fashion statement was "unmade bed." "Petal, why on earth would you want to doll up for the jerk?"

"So he'll regret losing me, of course. So he won't assume I'm sitting home with nothing to do. So it will appear I'm moving on with my life while he's clinging to our house and our things, setting up a shrine to our former married existence."

All arguments that made sense, I suppose, if one had a vindictive streak. Or if one were still desperately in love with her husband. "Why'd you cheat on him, Pet?" I asked.

"You don't have any idea what was going on—"

"Then explain it to me. Y'all had a good thing going. Ten years!"

"Yeah, ten years." She stretched out the phrase, making it sound like a jail sentence. "We were in such a rut, Gypsy. We didn't excite each other any more. He didn't appreciate it when I dressed up for him or ordered a special meal catered for just the two of us. And he never did anything special for me. He forgot birthdays and anniversaries. We stopped talking about having kids."

God, I'd had no idea. Publicly they'd presented the image of a perfect marriage.

"Listen to me. I could be reading out of Ladies' Home Journal. 'Can This Marriage Be Saved?'"

She sank back into her chair and played with her tuna salad.

"Can it, Pet?" I asked. "I know you still love each other."

"He doesn't love me."

"You didn't see him in the kitchen today. This divorce is killing him."

She shrugged. "He filed. What can I say?"

"Does he know about the judge?" I asked.

"I don't know. But if not, he'll probably find out. Tuscan will sic an investigator on the case. Then I'm really screwed." Suddenly her eyes filled. "I didn't want it to end up like this."

"Then tell him. Y'all are so busy trying to best each other that you can't even talk anymore."

"Tell him what? That I forgive him for screwing the decorator? That I was kidding when I went to bed with Donald? We can't go back, Gyp."

Maybe she was right. But it was painful for me to watch two people I cared about tearing each other to shreds.

Petal was hiding out when Cullen arrived at a little after eight. Truth was, I didn't want to see him, either. I was more angry with him now, after the hurtful things he was doing to Petal, than I'd been after he dumped me all those years ago. All this divorce business seemed beneath him.

I looked like hell, wearing ratty cut-offs and a T-shirt dotted with bleach stains, when I let him through the front door. Whatever make-up I'd put on earlier had soaked into my skin, and my hair flew in ten different directions.

I was too exhausted to care.

He gave me a once-over anyway. "Are you okay?"

I didn't fall for that fake concern in his voice. "Why wouldn't I be?"

"For one thing, Petal's living with you."

He was sporting for a fight, all right. If he couldn't pick on Petal, he'd settle for the next best thing. I didn't rise to the bait. "Show me the line-up. I'm busy."

With a shrug, he followed me into the kitchen, where the light was better, and pulled a manila folder from his monogrammed briefcase—another gift from Petal. If not for her, he'd probably be carrying stuff around in a shopping bag, I thought uncharitably.

He showed me seven photographs, unlabeled, all of them depicting young black men. I'd hardly glanced at them when I was distracted by the sound of footsteps on the stairs. Oh, Lord, I thought, Petal's going to cause a scene. I wasn't in the mood.

She entered the kitchen wearing a black leather mini-dress and platform sandals, heavy make-up, her blond hair teased to within an inch of its life. She reeked of expensive perfume. "I'm leaving now, Gyp—oh, hi, Cullen. I didn't know you were here."

In a pig's eye, I thought.

"Uhhng," Cullen said, suddenly inarticulate.

"Don't wait up," Petal said airily, giving us a little wave. "I don't have any idea when I'll be home." She made one of her trademark exits.

After a moment of silence, Cullen asked, "What was that?"

"Your wife, last time I checked."

"Where's she going?"

I shrugged. "I never know." I returned my attention to the photographs, giving a few seconds' attention to each while Cullen recovered. I figured he probably had a woody right now that could cut glass. He'd always been turned on by anything even vaguely slutty. Finally I pointed to the second photo from the right. "This one."

Cullen cleared his throat. "You're sure?"

"Oh, yeah."

"It was dark."

"There was a moon."

"Your, um, nightgown was covering your face."

"I pulled it down just in time."

We stared at each other, challenging, him daring me to stay with such a bald-faced lie, me daring him to call me a liar.

"You're sticking with the crystal ball story?"

"How do you know I'm not psychic?" I asked. Then I opened a cabinet and retrieved my tip jar, which I'd tucked away earlier for safekeeping. "Look at all this money that people give me for my psychic insights."

Cullen issued a low whistle as he took the jar, turning it toward the light for a closer look. "How much money have you bamboozled these gullible people out of, anyway?"

"I don't know. I haven't counted it. But it's not bamboozling. I don't even charge a set fee. They just give me whatever money they think the reading is worth."

"Hmm. Fraud Division might be interested in you."

I gasped. "Cullen! You wouldn't!"

"The laws are pretty gray when it comes to fortune-tellers. Most aren't prosecuted 'cause they're small potatoes scam-artists. But if we're talking about this much cash in the span of a few days—"

"It wouldn't be fraud if I really was psychic," I pointed out.

"But you're not."

"I am. I found that little missing boy."

"That was a fluke. You couldn't do it again."

"Try me." Good God, what was I doing? Setting myself up for failure and ridicule, that was what. But he was so damn sure!

"You want me to give you a missing person to find?"

"Yeah. Why not?" He wouldn't. I was counting on that. He wouldn't want to risk "the boys" at work finding out he'd mixed police business with mumbo-jumbo.

He pressed his lips together and thought about it, though. "If you fail? Which you will, miserably."

"I'll take down my fortune-teller shingle and turn away all potential clients." That wasn't such a sacrifice. I'd sort of been planning to do that anyway, eventually, and if I couldn't solve Cullen's case, I would prove to myself once and for all that I didn't have any special talents.

"And you'll tell me how you found out about Reggie?"

Reluctantly, I nodded. He already knew I was keeping something from him. "But if I solve the case, I have my own demands."

"Such as?"

"You give up this ruthless divorce thing and sit down with Petal and a neutral third party to come to a reasonable and fair settlement."

Clearly he hadn't expected that. "Even if I agree, Petal won't."

"You leave Petal to me. Do we have a deal?"

"Sure. It's not like there's a chance in hell you'll win. I'll call you later with the details of the case."

"And meanwhile you'll talk to Reggie, maybe find out what he was looking for in my house?"

"That's the plan."

CHAPTER SEVEN

Petal returned less than ten minutes after Cullen's departure, drinking a large diet Coke from Jack-In-The-Box.

"Oooh, some hot date," I said. "Did you and Jack have a good time?"

"I don't know what possesses me to do things like that," she said, kicking off her shoes and slumping down at the kitchen table. "The man makes me crazy."

"Petal," I said, easing carefully into my question, "if Cullen were willing to sit down with say, an arbitrator to hash out a fair settlement, would you be willing?"

"In a heartbeat. He wouldn't, though. He's too hell-bent on making me suffer."

I filled her in on Cullen's and my bet, which did little to cheer her up. "Gypsy, you can't expect to find another missing person."

"Why not? I found Helen's missing insurance policy."

"Oh, my God, you're serious."

"Well, I had to do something. Cullen was going to sic the Fraud guys on me."

She rolled her eyes. "Yeah, right. They'd never waste their time on you."

I wished she'd told me that earlier, before I'd made my bargain with the devil.

It was the next morning before Cullen gave me my case. I talked to him with the phone wedged between my ear and shoulder while I watered my pathetic rose bush, which still clung to life.

"Reggie's under arrest," he told me.

Relief washed over me. I could quit looking over my shoulder. "Do you think he'll stay there?"

"Maybe, this being a second offense and all. He lives with his mother, and he didn't make much of an attempt to hide his crime. I found boxes with Ruby's papers in the alley behind his house. Are you willing to testify? Before you answer, I have to warn you that you might provoke the other gang members to seek revenge."

Though it was already close to ninety degrees, my blood ran suddenly cold. "I don't want that, Cullen. It was a minor burglary. Not worth that much hassle. Did you ask Reggie what he was looking for?"

"He wouldn't give me even a small clue."

Rats. That meant he still might come back looking for it. "Let me think about it."

"Okay. You want your test case?"

My stomach swooped. He was calling my bluff! I walked inside the house to find a paper and pad, which I located in the kitchen, then schooled my voice to sound cool and confident. "Fire away."

"I talked to Selma Crane last night, Reggie's mother. She's Ruby Casserly's sister."

"Yes, I sensed some familial relationship between Reggie and Ruby."

Cullen ignored my needling. "Seems Selma's worried about Ruby. No one in the family has heard from her since she left town. There was no reason to believe foul play, no signs of struggle or ransom demands. Plus, there's ample evidence she had intentions to flee. She told Selma as much, and she quit her job of seven years, for one thing. But Selma claims Ruby never would have disappeared without telling her own sister where she was going."

And I'd thought it strange all along that Ruby had flown the coop without her fortune-teller paraphernalia. "So that's my case? Ruby Casserly?"

"Yeah. I figure, it's not an official case, so it's not unethical for me to give it to you."

I rolled my eyes. He was more afraid of embarrassment than anything— always had been. "How long do I have to find her?"

"Well, you found Jorge Silviano in, what, a few hours?"

"C'mon, Cullen."

"Two weeks."

"You got it." I sounded a lot more confident than I felt.

As soon as Petal came downstairs to make her herbal tea, I told her about my mission to find Ruby. She was visibly cheered by the news and a lot perkier this morning than she'd been last night.

"Hey, at least Cullen gave you a person who conceivably could be found. I was sure he'd give you some ten-year-old cold case The Amazing Kreskin couldn't solve."

"Do you really think I can find her?" I asked in a glum voice, wishing I'd never thought of making the bet with Cullen.

"Not with your crystal ball. But we've got a whole house full of clues to this woman's life. If anyone can find her, we can."

"Ohhhh," I said, nodding slowly. "We find her, using ordinary, old-fashioned sleuthing methods—"

"Then claim you got the information in a psychic vision. It's perfect!" Petal's cheerful optimism was contagious. Suddenly I couldn't wait to get started.

"Okay, where do we begin?" I would bow to Petal's greater experience. Lawyers did a lot of investigating.

She thought for a moment. "That file cabinet upstairs. She might keep important information in there."

We thundered up the stairs, two kids on a treasure hunt.

The wooden file cabinet was stuffed full of papers, naturally. We found information about the car she drove, which definitely wasn't in the detached garage. That was a great clue, unless the bank had already repossessed it. We found out what banks she patronized, the insurance she carried, the names and addresses of friends and family. It was a gold mine of leads. We scribbled down information on legal pads.

After an hour of sleuthing, I came across a very interesting item. It was the deed to a parcel of land in Seagoville, a sleepy little farming community just southeast of Dallas.

I showed the deed to Petal. "Ruby could be living on that land even now."

Petal nodded, liking the idea. "As a fortune-teller, she would take in mostly cash. Easy enough for her to sock away a nice, untraceable nest egg, which she could use when the heat from the IRS got to be too much."

It sounded like a good theory. "But why didn't Ruby take her crystal ball with her?"

"Maybe she's retiring."

"But the thing is worth money," I persisted. "She could have hocked it. Shoot, she left behind good silverware, a brand-new television. It just doesn't feel right." I stretched to get the kinks out of my back. Most of my injuries from falling out of the tree had healed, but my back was sore from lifting and toting boxes and furniture.

"She might've been in a hurry," Petal theorized. "Maybe the IRS was at the front door and she ran out the back. And if that's the case, we ought to turn that deed over to the police."

Suddenly I giggled. "Listen to yourself, Pet. You're talking about turning a little old lady into the Feds. Didn't you learn anything from our parents growing up?"

"Hey, I'm a lawyer. I'm sworn to uphold the law. If the system's a little bit flawed, well, that's not my problem."

I guessed there wouldn't be any more protest marches in Petal's future.

In truth, it went against my grain to just blithely sic the cops on poor Ruby. Before I gave the police or the IRS any information, I wanted to know her story and judge for myself whether she deserved to be prosecuted.

"Can you find out where this property is? Exactly?" I asked.

"Sure. I have a contact in the Records Building." Petal had contacts everywhere. Sometimes her efficiency amazed me.

An hour later we were in my Jeep heading for Seagoville.

"The property's just off Highway 175 at the Old Mill Road exit," Petal said. "Not far from Aunt Ceecee's old place."

Seagoville is one of the few underdeveloped areas close enough to downtown Dallas for a comfortable commute. Petal and I had a widowed aunt, Cecilia Brown, who once owned a small horse farm there. When we'd been kids, the height of summer ecstasy was to spend a week or two away from the commune with Aunt Ceecee, as we called her, and our cousins Betty and Judy.

The Brown family seemed so deliciously normal to us. They ate meat and white flour. They drove a pick-up truck without a trace of weird-colored body paint. They rode horses and went to the rodeo, blissfully ignorant of the sexist stereotyping there that would have thrown our mother into a first-class tizzy.

Whenever we visited, Petal and I felt normal, too. We'd lie awake on our pallets at night and indulge in the ultimate fantasy, in which we changed our names to something commonplace like Kathy and Suzy, and lived in a normal house with no chanting, incense, or free love.

Of course, Betty and Judy thought our commune life was exotic and highly desirable. I guess every kid thinks their own parents are weirder, nerdier, or more unpleasant than anyone else's.

The Browns had long since moved away from Seagoville, but Petal and I still knew the area pretty well. We found Ruby's land easily enough, tucked at the end of a long, winding, red dirt road. We parked the Jeep on the edge of the road facing back the way we came, ready for a quick getaway.

"What if we find her?" I whispered to Petal as we got out.

"Plead ignorance," she replied. "We'll say we're, um, checking up on Aunt Ceecee's property."

Sounded like a good cover story to me. The last thing I wanted was to tip Ruby off and have her disappear before we could show her to Cullen.

Ruby's thirty-acre tract of land was quite pleasant, really. Lots of pecan and oak trees dotted the flat terrain, and from the road it looked like there might be a creek passing through.

No sign of a house or trailer, though. Rats.

"We're not really dressed for hiking," I pointed out. We both wore shorts and sandals, and Petal's sandals had two-inch heels. The mesquite brush on Ruby's property was pretty thick in places.

"We came all this way," Petal said, climbing out of the Jeep. "Let's at least have a look around."

Gamely, she plunged through the trees and I followed. We'd never been Girl Scouts or Camp Fire Girls, but as kids we'd spent a few weeks camped illegally on someone's hunting lease, so we weren't completely ignorant of the woods.

We were right about the creek. It was only a trickle during the semi-drought we were in, but it made a pleasing gurgle.

"I wonder what she planned to do with this acreage," Petal said.

Ruby hadn't started a new life here, that was for sure. I felt keenly disappointed, but I guess I should have known finding Ruby wouldn't be this easy.

We turned and started back toward the car. "I think you should talk to Ruby's sister," Petal said. "She might open up to you, tell you things she would never mention to a cop."

"You don't think she'll be just a tad angry with me for having her son arrested?"

"Maybe, but you won't know 'til you—oof!" Petal tripped on something and went flying, landing face first in the dirt.

"Are you okay?" I asked, crouching down to peer at her.

She raised up slowly and nodded. "I think so. Oh, ow, look at my elbow."

An inch-long scratch on her elbow oozed blood.

I took her arm and helped her up. Her knees were scraped, too. Took me back to when she'd learned how to roller-skate.

She looked down at herself. "Damn. I'm such a klutz. Now my knees are going to look—" She stopped abruptly, her face turning white as Ivory soap. She was no longer examining her knees, but staring at the ground, at the root she'd tripped on. Only it wasn't a root.

"Is that ..." I asked in a shaky voice, unable to actually voice my suspicions.

"It's animal bones," Petal said without much confidence.

Surely ..." But we both knew it wasn't. A bony hand, still with bits of flesh clinging to it, protruded from a mound of freshly dug earth. It was almost as if the corpse concealed in the shallow grave had reached out and grabbed Petal's ankle to trip her.

I shivered. "Guess we better go call the cops."

"Let's call Cullen first. He'll tell us the best way to proceed."

"We're not in the Dallas city limits," I reminded her.

"I don't care who we call," she said, sounding slightly desperate. "Let's just get out of here. This place is giving me the creeps."

"Yeah, like the guy with the hockey mask is going to jump out any second and—"

"Cut it out!" She grabbed my hand, and we ran for the Jeep. It was only as we reached the dirt road that we realized we weren't alone. A black Chevy

Blazer was parked about ten feet behind us. The vehicle looked vaguely familiar to me, but I couldn't quite place it.

Please don't let it be Darryl. No one could hear us scream out here in boonie-land. I wondered if Petal had brought her gun.

Petal squeezed my hand until I was sure all the blood was gone from it. "Oh, my God, now what do we do?"

"Just act cool," I said. "We didn't do anything wrong. The person in that car probably has a perfectly legitimate reason for being here."

We slowed down to a brisk walk, trying to act normally. As we drew closer to the two cars, we could see that the Blazer was empty. "Where do you suppose the driver went?" Petal asked.

"He's probably just taking a pee out here in the woods," I replied. I didn't know and I didn't care. I just wanted out of there, back to civilization, freeways and gas stations and fast-food joints. I flung open the door of my Jeep, too late realizing I'd found the Blazer's driver. He was sitting behind the wheel of my car.

I let out a scream that could have awakened the corpse we'd just left behind, and Petal joined me.

"Jesus, give it a rest." The interloper was none other than Santiago Ramone, intrepid reporter.

"Christ, you almost gave me a heart attack! What are you doing in my car?" I demanded. "What are you doing out here in the middle of nowhere?"

"Duh," Petal said. "He followed us."

Santiago gave me a lazy smile, making no move to vacate my driver's seat. "Guilty as charged."

"Why?" I wanted to know.

"You make good copy. What are you ladies doing out here in the woods, anyway? Meeting your coven?"

"For God's sake," Petal said, sounding disgusted, "Gypsy's not a witch. Psychics and witches aren't the same thing. Where do you people get such crazy ideas? Don't you ever do research?"

"My aunt owns property out here," I said promptly. "We were just checking up on things."

"And is that why you came running out of the woods like a banshee was after you?"

Well, he had us there.

"A snake," Petal said, the lie sounding perfectly natural. She was a much better liar than me. "We saw a copperhead."

"Ah." Ramone nodded. Finally, he climbed out of my car, but he stood in the way so I couldn't get in. He looked across the roof at Petal. "Why aren't you at work?"

"I'm taking a sabbatical." She thrust her chin out, daring him to contradict her.

"This wouldn't have anything to do with those ethics charges, now, would it?"

Petal looked truly panicked for a moment, and I wanted to sock Ramone right in his kidneys. But she quickly schooled her features. "I have no comment," she said, climbing into the Jeep.

"Why are you doing this?" I demanded. "Why are you following us?"

"Two stories for the price of one." His mouth quirked up on one side in a crooked smile, producing, of all things, a dimple. Who would have imagined. "I figured if I followed you, at least one of you would do something interesting."

"Yeah, well, you were wrong. We're not doing anything."

"That's not what Sergeant Ingalls says."

Cullen's audacity squeezed the breath right out of me. How dare he sic a reporter on me? I tried not to show Ramone the rage shivering inside me, demanding an outlet. Later. "So, he thought it would be funny to document my failure in the psychic quest for Ruby Casserly?"

"That wasn't exactly how he put it. He figures you're getting your information somehow, but not out of some crystal ball."

Ah. Now it was becoming clearer. Cullen wanted to prove I was cheating. Well, okay, so I was cheating, but I wasn't about to let Mr. Macho Reporter here know that. But what to tell him?

Petal quickly solved the problem. "For your information, Mr. Ramone, my sister is genuinely psychic. She had a vision, right at the breakfast table. And a voice in her ear told her to drive—drive, and she would find Ruby."

Oh, no, I thought. Please, Petal, don't tell him. But it was too late. She was like a runaway train once she launched on a crusade against the evil oppressors—cops and reporters, in this case.

"And you know what?" she continued. "We found something, something very significant."

The cocky smirk abruptly fled Ramone's face. For a split second he believed Petal. Then he thought better of it. "You did not. You're just making that up, hoping I'll print some nonsense to make me look like an idiot."

"You mean like your last story?" Petal said sweetly.

Ramone appeared momentarily embarrassed. Maybe those crazy quotes I gave him had made him look foolish. Though he'd done his best to present me as a scam artist, he hadn't been able to offer a reasonable explanation as to how I knew where to look for little Jorge.

"Print whatever you want," I said. "Just don't forget about my stalker."

"I'm not sure I believe there is a stalker," he said, clearly not intimidated.

I crossed my arms into an ex and wiggled my fingers in a classic spell-casting posture. "If you print anything that leads Darryl to me, I will put a curse on you so powerful your nuts will dry up."

He swallowed, and I fancied he turned a little green. Some people were just too easily suggestible. "I'm just trying to do my job," he said.

"What's your job title, Chief Scum-sucking Bottom Feeder?" I pushed my way past him, got in the Jeep, fired it up and raised a rooster tail of red dust in my wake. In the rearview mirror I could see Ramone standing forlornly on the side of the road, watching me leave. If he had any idea what was in those woods—how near he was to a good story—he wouldn't be so glum.

"The guy's got cajones," Petal said, the estimate sounding not too condemning. "You should have told him about the body. That would have shut him up."

"I was tempted. But I don't think it would be prudent of us to notify the press before the police. Our motives might become suspect."

"Good point. Anyway, publicity isn't all it's cracked up to be."

As soon as we were sure Ramone hadn't followed us, we whipped into a Burger King parking lot and called Cullen on Petal's cell phone. "Thanks for siccing the reporter on me, jerk," I said without preamble.

"What? Shit. He wasn't supposed to confront you. Where are you?"

"Seagoville. Why Santiago Ramone, of all people?"

"Cheap surveillance. I know you're up to something, and it has nothing to do with your supposed woo-woo powers."

"I am not up to anything. I'm looking for Ruby."

"You're supposed to be looking for her in your crystal ball," he pointed out. "Not Seagoville."

"You have no idea how psychics work," I said. "We follow hunches. We ... we hear voices."

"So do schizophrenics."

Petal tapped me on the arm. "Tell him about the body."

"Is that Petal?"

"Look, I'm trying to tell you something. I had a psychic vision."

"Yeah, right."

I tried to remember exactly what Petal had told Ramone, so our stories would match. "Over breakfast. A voice told me to drive—drive to Seagoville and I'd find Ruby. And I did."

"Gypsy!" Petal hissed.

"You mean—" Cullen was having trouble getting his words out. He now sounded very much awake, in full alert mode. "You found Ruby Casserly? Just like that, overnight? When her sister has been looking for her for months? Where is she? Is she there with you now?"

I decided I better level with him. After all, murder is a serious business, and the dead person buried on Ruby's land was now Petal's and my responsibility. "Okay, here's the deal," I said soberly. "We found a body."

Silence while Cullen processed. Then, "As in dead?"

"Uh-huh."

"As in human?"

"Can't say for sure—I'm no forensics expert. But it has an opposable thumb."

Suddenly he was all business. "Where are you now?"

I gave him directions. He told us to sit tight, that he'd come look at the remains, and if they were human, we'd go together to the Seagoville police.

"It'll take him at least thirty minutes," I said after hanging up. I glanced at the Burger King. "You want some french fries?"

"Ugh, how can you even think of eating? My appetite's ruined for a year."

Unfortunately it takes a lot to ruin my appetite. I got the fries and, what the hell, a Whopper, too. Three minutes later Petal was snitching the fries; a year can be very short to Petal.

Forty-five minutes later, Cullen gingerly flicked dirt and leaves off the skeletal remains with a stick. It took him ten seconds to agree with me; they were human. He called in the local cops, who were a little miffed that it took a Dallas cop to find a body in their jurisdiction.

I was hoping Petal and I would be able to slink off once the proper authorities had taken control of the crime scene. No such luck. As one might expect, the Seagoville Police wanted to know what we were doing tromping around in the woods so far from home.

I could bend the truth a bit for Ramone and Cullen, but when it came to going on record with the police, I was unwilling to embellish the truth. Seeing that Cullen was busy talking murder with one of the crime-scene guys, I took the detective aside and explained about Ruby, and the house and the deed and how I wanted to help my brother-in-law find this missing woman. I even emphasized how driving out to Seagoville was all Petal's idea, to prevent any overzealous reporters from concluding I'd found the body psychically.

"So you found the body totally by accident?" the cop asked.

"Yes, of course! My sister tripped over it." I left out any mention of purported psychic abilities.

He dutifully took notes, though I couldn't tell whether he believed me or not.

A reporter showed up—not, thankfully, Santiago Ramone. He was from the Seagoville Examiner, and he was predictably interested in the manner of Petal's and my gruesome discovery. I gave him a brief statement, then Petal and I slid out of there.

"We should have reported the body anonymously," Petal grumbled as we finally drove away, hours later. "Now both of our names will be in the paper. What if Darryl sees it?

I pointed out that it was only the Seagoville paper, and anyway, Darryl didn't read.

"And you dated this guy?"

"He rode a Harley."

Enough said.

CHAPTER EIGHT

My reputation as a psychic got a significant boost the next day without my lifting a finger. Cullen called just after lunch.

"Tell Petal she can come home whenever she wants," he said, sounding a bit glum.

"What?"

"You won the damn bet."

It took me a few moments for the significance of his words to sink in. "Ruby?" My legs wouldn't hold me up any longer, so I leaned against the kitchen wall and slid to the floor.

"As if you didn't know, Madam Fortune-Teller."

Suddenly this psychic detective stuff wasn't a lark anymore. I'd found two missing people within a week. I'd done it through misunderstandings and pure, dumb luck, but never the less, I'd done it.

"Cullen, God help me, I didn't know it was her. I was just razzing you yesterday when I said I'd found her. I assumed the body had no connection to me, that some murderer buried his victim on Ruby's land because it was out in the middle of—"

"Ruby's land? You mean—"

"Yeah. I found the deed here in the house. I thought she might be hiding out there, so I went to have a look. Damn it, Cullen, you don't really think I'm psychic, do you?"

He laughed, a little nervously. "No. But you're awful damn lucky."

Or maybe not so lucky. "This isn't even officially your case," I said. "Why were you tracking down the body's I.D.?"

"Curiosity, mostly. Call it a hunch."

"Oh, sure. It's all right for you to have hunches, but I'm not allowed to be psychic."

"Hunches are entirely different from visions and voices. All cops have hunches, gut instinct."

He was splitting hairs, but now wasn't the time to debate the various manifestations of paranormal powers of perception. I had other problems.

What were the chances, I wondered, that someone would kill a woman, then bury her on her own piece of property? I asked Cullen the question aloud.

"It means whoever killed her, knew her. Knew her pretty well."

"Reggie?" I barely breathed the name.

"He's someone I would question, if it were my case," Cullen answered diplomatically.

"Cullen, the Seagoville police won't hassle me, will they? I mean, don't they always suspect the person who finds the body?"

"That's only on TV. You and Petal don't have any connection to Ruby. You probably never even heard her name 'til after she was already dead and her house was repossessed."

Sure, that was true for me. Petal was a different story. "Just out of curiosity," I said, trying to sound casual, "suppose one of us had known Ruby. Before she died." I had to tread very carefully here. As far as I knew, Cullen was still ignorant of Petal's affair with Judge Colter.

"Then you might have trouble."

My stomach sank. I didn't know how competent the Seagoville police were, but even the most casual inquiries into Ruby's life would turn up her work history with the judge. If the judge was a spiteful sort—as ex-lovers were wont to be—he might make a point of mentioning Petal's previous acquaintance with Ruby.

"I still won the bet," I said.

"Technically. But you didn't prove you were psychic. You just proved you know how to make a lucky guess."

"Doesn't matter. You said if I found her—"

"Yeah, okay. Truth is, I was going to give up the divorce, anyway. It wasn't as much fun as I thought it would be." He paused, and when he asked his next question, he sounded like a lovesick teenager. "Do you think she'll come home?"

"You hurt her bad, Cullen. Really, the decorator? Tacky."

"Not as tacky as boffing a judge. A married judge."

Oh. So he knew.

"Jesus, Gypsy, I'm a detective. Finding out about her affair was child's play. But we've both had our fun now. Tit for tat. I want to put it behind us."

Men. It wouldn't be that easy. Whatever problems had driven Petal and Cullen to adultery were still there.

I felt very uncomfortable having Cullen speak so frankly to me. It suggested an intimacy that seemed ... I don't know. Improper, I guess, given that a teensy part of me—a very bad part—had always wanted to steal Cullen back from Petal. What if I subconsciously gave him bad advice that drove the wedge between them even deeper?

"You'll have to talk to Petal about this," I said, a trifle tartly. "She's not here, but I'll tell her to call you."

"Thanks. And you'll tell her she can come home, right?"

"I'll tell her." But I didn't think she'd jump at the chance. Maybe she'd have been willing to proceed with a cordial divorce, but forgive and forget? The man had been married to Petal for ten years, but apparently he still didn't know her.

Dinner that night was my responsibility, and I was forced to go to the grocery store. It was either that, or we'd be eating peanut-butter and saltines again. I threw on a T-shirt dress, pulled my hair back with an elastic band, and headed for the Fiesta Store, shopping list in hand.

Fiesta caters to the predominantly Hispanic population in and around Psychedelic Heights, which makes it a shopping oddity for a white-bread girl like me. I knew it was different from the Safeways and Krogers of my youth the first time I pulled into the parking lot and saw the market stalls and push carts crowding around the main entrance. You could buy corn on the cob, ice cream, fake designer watches and cheap electronics—all before you even entered the store.

Once inside, I was surrounded by unfamiliar, yet not unpleasant odors while Mexican music blared from the speakers. Two whole aisles were devoted to Mexican products. I'm talking thirty-five different kinds of tortillas, rice, hot sauces, mysterious-looking cans of unidentifiable vegetables, soft drinks with exotic-sounding names and peculiar colors. I liked the store, though, especially for its amazing array of fresh produce, an old-fashioned butcher counter, and authentic Mexican baked goods. I'd gotten used to the music, which was kind of peppy.

I'd decided to try something more ambitious for dinner tonight, spaghetti with Ragu sauce. I bought some lettuce and vegetables for a salad, and a long loaf of bread and a jar of garlic butter.

I was contemplating the bakery case when another shopping cart crashed into mine with such force that everyone in the store must have heard it.

I was about to treat the perpetrator to a few choice words, but the reprimand died on my lips. Santiago Ramone. Again. This time he wasn't smiling.

"You held out on me," he said, waving a copy of the Seagoville Examiner in my face.

I grabbed the paper from his grasp and scanned the front page story, which detailed the finding of an unidentified body. My name wasn't mentioned, for which I was supremely grateful, but Petal and I were identified as "two Dallas women out for a walk in the country."

I guess Ramone had figured it out.

"I didn't hide anything," I argued. "I told you I'd found something. You chose not to believe it."

"You intended for me not to believe it."

"Whatever. Excuse me, please?" I maneuvered my cart around his, no longer interested in the baked goods. I just wanted to take my spaghetti and get out of there.

He followed me doggedly. "Who was buried in that grave?" he asked.

"How would I know?" I pretended interest in the pickle section, finally selecting a jar of gherkins and moving on.

"You were looking for Ruby Casserly. Did you find her?"

"It's an ongoing police investigation," I hedged. "I'm not allowed to talk about it." Which was true. Though Cullen hadn't mentioned it specifically, I knew that when he talked about a case, any case, the information was confidential.

"C'mon, Gypsy. You owe me, after that load of crap you gave me on that first story."

"Load of—you begged me for a juicy quote. You knew it was crap before you printed it." I grabbed a jar of molasses, then moved on to breakfast cereals. I blindly picked out a couple of boxes. Being stalked by reporters blunted my powers of discretion.

"The body is Ruby, isn't it? C'mon, just confirm or deny. Just ... blink twice if the answer's yes."

I tried to hold my eyes open. "I'm not confirming anything. Go away."

"Not til you explain what you were doing out in the woods. And don't tell me you just accidentally stumbled on a body."

"That's exactly what happened." I turned and faced him, deliberately adopting an otherworldly expression and a spooky voice. "This voice in my ear told me to—"

"Oh, no you don't. I'm not letting you sucker me into that again."

"It's more interesting than the truth," I pointed out. "Read my lips. We found the grave by accident. Why do you think we were so freaked when we came running out of the woods?"

"Still, do you think it could be Ruby?"

"Why don't you call Cullen Ingalls? Maybe the M.E. has identified the body by now."

"I tried that. Ingalls isn't taking my calls, and the M.E.'s office won't release any information. They were acting kind of hush-hush about it." Ramone's dark eyes practically danced in their sockets. Clearly he loved the drama and mystery inherent in the discovery of a dead body.

"Which automatically got your attention."

"Right. Damn, it is Ruby. I just know it is. Which means either you're incredibly lucky ... or you're involved in something."

That was the second time in an hour somebody had called me lucky, but I wasn't feeling at all fortunate. It was only a matter of hours before Ramone confirmed the identity of the mysterious body. After that, I was in for another battering from the press.

I headed for the frozen dessert aisle, Ramone in hot pursuit. "What's your angle?" he asked. "Why no cooperation? Do you have something to hide?"

"I haven't got an angle. I don't want publicity. Or have you forgotten about—"

"Yeah, yeah, the stalker. Who is he, anyway?"

I grabbed two boxes of pudding pops, my favorite comfort food. I suspected I'd need them in the days to come. "A guy I dated a few times. He won't take no for an answer."

"Did he hurt you?" Ramone's interest seemed more than morbid curiosity.

"He tried, but I ducked and ran."

"Good for you."

"Not really. It made him mad." Mad enough that he'd made a lot of revolting threats and tried to burn down my whole apartment complex. He hadn't succeeded, but he'd managed to destroy almost everything I owned. That's when I'd high-tailed it to the women's shelter.

"Why are you looking for missing people if you're not psychic?" Ramone asked.

I wasn't about to explain the bet I'd had with Cullen. "Please stop asking me questions."

"How about something off the record?" he asked. Alerted by his change in tone, I slowed my cart down so that I was no longer sprinting through the store. "Like what?"

"You want to have dinner?" His heavy-lidded eyes were making promises I was sure he never intended to keep. Still, my knees went weak. Dinner, drinks, music, air conditioning.

The temptation was powerful, but I forced myself to be realistic. This wasn't about sex. This was about a newspaper article.

"No, thanks," I said, sounding more regretful than I meant to. "There's something about a grilling that ruins my appetite."

"How about if I grill a couple of tuna steaks instead?"

Without my consent, my mouth watered. I hadn't had a decent sit-down dinner in weeks.

"I'll drop the subject of Ruby and psychics and everything else," he continued. "We can talk about whatever you want."

"Then what's the point?" I heaved a case of diet Coke into my cart, then moved on to the dairy section. Two percent for me, skim for Petal.

Ramone shook his head, smiling. "Guess you're not psychic after all, or you'd know what the point is."

My heart started a series of athletic palpitations. He couldn't be saying what I thought he was saying. But when I returned his steady gaze, my suspicions were confirmed. Something besides professional interest lurked in those black-glass eyes.

I resisted the urge to smooth my hair or wipe my damp palms on my dress. This was a joke, right? Hispanic Adonises weren't interested in pale gringas like me. Not that I'm a gargoyle or anything. Petal claims my looks are well above average when I fix my hair, put on decent clothes, and wear make-up.

The problem is, I seldom do those things, and certainly Ramone hadn't ever laid eyes on the dolled-up version of Gypsy. Though I'd reveled in a healthy fantasy or two about me and Ramone and a can of Redi-Whip, I felt distinctly unprepared for the reality of going on a date with him.

Ramone scribbled in his reporter's notebook, then tore out the page and handed it to me. "My address. Come Friday at around seven. I'll have the tuna marinated, the grill fired up, and the wine chilling."

He turned and walked away, no doubt assuming I wouldn't have anything better to do. I didn't, thank God. As he sauntered toward the check-out lines, I made a leisurely study of his tight, jean-clad ass.

I moved through the check-out line in a daze, paying my purchases with a bunch of ones from the psychic tip jar. I had a date with Santiago Ramone.

Not that I would go. This had to be a ploy, I told myself. He would ply me with food and wine, maybe a kiss or two, then coax me into spilling my guts about Ruby. By tonight he would know she was the unfortunate murder victim. Did he really expect me to believe we would talk about lima beans or Mount McKinley if that was my wish?

When I arrived home, I had a new problem. Reverend Haglin and his wife were marching in front of my house with hand-painted picket signs. Wade's sign read, "Say No to Satan." Merrilee's read "Down with Witches ..." The other side said, "... Way Down."

I pulled into the driveway and got out, not sure whether to be enraged by the vicious personal attack, or amused at their pathetic effort. Two people made for a pretty sad picket line.

"I thought you wanted to save me, not send me to hell," I called out to Merrilee.

She looked at Wade, presumably for guidance. Wade lowered his sign and walked up to meet me on the sidewalk. "You've made it quite clear you don't want to be saved. Now I'm trying to save the community."

"Yeah, I'm dragging the Heights down to hell in a hand basket, all right," I countered. "I helped one lady find a lost life insurance policy. I counseled another one to leave her abusive husband."

Merrilee gasped. "Exactly! There are ways other than divorce to deal with a marriage in crisis, but you convinced that poor woman to choose Satan's way."

I didn't consider it Satan's way for a woman to save her own life by removing herself from a man who routinely beat her black and blue, but I already knew this couple didn't listen to reason. "I'm calling the cops," I said. Right after I put away the frozen food. The threat of legal intervention had gotten rid of the Haglins last time.

"Fine, call them," Wade said. "Call the FBI, call the National Guard, call the press. Especially the press."

"We've got a permit to demonstrate," Merrilee added. "It's our constitutional right."

And I have a right to the pursuit of happiness, which at the moment meant living in anonymous poverty, and the Haglins were interfering.

"What'll it take to get you to stop picketing?" I asked.

Wade's response was prompt. "Hand over the crystal ball."

I opened the back of my Jeep and grabbed up all of the plastic bags. I was getting ready to make an exit, and having to return for a second load of groceries would spoil it.

With my arms loaded, I slammed the hatch with my elbow and turned to face the Reverend. I smiled. "In your dreams."

The exit was married somewhat by my ability to find my front door key without setting everything down and scrounging through my backpack. Petal would have done it better.

"Gypsy!" The moment I walked through the door, Petal skittered down the stairs, still in her heels and fuchsia silk suit. Normally her clothes came flying off the minute she hit the door, in deference to the heat that built up in the house during the day. So she must have been rattled. "Thank God you're okay. When I got home from my lunch, they were out there picketing and you'd disappeared. I was afraid that awful preacher and his mousy wife had done away with you."

"They're tempted, I'm sure," I said dryly. "Is there anything we can do to get rid of them?"

"Short of target practice?"

"Petal."

She relieved me of some of the groceries, and we moved into the kitchen to restock the cabinets. "I checked. So long as they're peaceful, and they allow egress and ingress to the house, and they stay out of the yard and don't physically molest your, er, clients, there's nothing we can do."

That's what I'd been afraid of.

"Maybe if we just ignore them, they'll get bored and give up," I said.

"We can hope. Gypsy, what is this? Molasses? Garbanzo beans?" Petal looked at me curiously.

"I got distracted at the grocery store."

She pulled the two boxes of cereal from one of the plastic bags and stared at first one, then the other. Fruit Loops and shredded wheat. "Oh, here's a good choice. Pure sugar, or pure cardboard. You couldn't have chosen something in between?"

"Well, you'd be flustered too if you had Santiago Ramone stalking you down the cereal aisle."

Petal froze in the middle of opening the jar of gherkins. "Ramone? What'd he want?"

"A date."

She looked me up and down. "You're joking."

I glared. "Are you saying he couldn't possibly be attracted to a frump like—"

"Oh, Gypsy, I said nothing of the kind. I just mean, I think he might have an ulterior motive."

I gathered up all the plastic bags and stuck them in the pantry for recycling. "Yeah, me too. That's why I'm not going."

"What? You have to go."

"Why? He's a jerk."

"But he's a good-looking jerk, presumably single, straight, and has gainful employment! You don't run across jerks like that every day."

"Please. I'm not looking for a husband."

"Did I say anything about marriage? I presume you have other needs."

"Please!"

"I wouldn't turn down the opportunity."

"That's the difference between us. You're a slut. I'm not."

Petal pushed up the sleeves on her silk jacket. "Okay, if you want to play rough, let me just remind you that you've slept with my husband? And on the first date."

"He told you that?" I decided then and there I was going to kill the big-mouth liar. "It was on the third date, and it was before you ever met him, and he has no business confiding our sex life to you."

"He's my husband. We've been married ten years. Maybe we ran out of things to talk about." Suddenly all the fight went out of Petal. She sagged into a chair at the kitchen table. "Ten years. And we're just throwing it away. Oh, Gypsy, I'd give anything if I could turn back the clock and undo what I did, what he did. If I only had another chance—"

"Um, Petal ..."

"What?"

"You do. I forgot to tell you. Cullen called a while ago. He's canceling the divorce, and he wants you to come home."

"Oh, he does, does he?" Petal's turn-around from morose to militant was so quick, it made my head spin. "He thinks he can just snap his fingers and I'll go straight home and act as if nothing happened?"

I cringed. "That's what he's hoping."

"He's out of his ever-loving mind. 'Cause you know what? He's the one at fault here. If he wants to drop his suit, fine. I'll file one of my own. I'll kick him out of the house."

I threw up my hands. "Petal, you just said you wanted another chance. I mean, I agree you shouldn't just pretend it never happened. Y'all need some counseling."

"I have a good case. I could take Cullen to the—"

"He knows about the judge."

That took the wind out of her sales. "He does?"

"You've both been very, very naughty. Go home, Petal. Don't throw your marriage away. Cullen might be a jerk sometimes, but as you so recently reminded me, you don't run across jerks like that every day."

Petal firmed her jaw. "Maybe I'll go home. But not today. He's going to have to grovel a bit first."

It was a compromise of sorts, so I left it at that. We had other problems, namely Ruby Casserly. I brought Petal up to date while she took a lukewarm bubble bath.

"How did she die?" Petal wanted to know.

"I don't know." I busied myself by sprinkling some Comet into the rusty sink. It didn't help. "I forgot to ask."

"Are they sure she was murdered?"

"Petal, people who die of natural causes aren't found in shallow, unmarked graves."

"Good point."

"Um, just exactly how well did you know Ruby, anyway?"

Petal shrugged. "Not that well. We were nodding acquaintances. She seemed a perfectly nice woman. But we never exchanged more than a few sentences. I had no idea she was moonlighting as a fortune-teller, for example, or that she had tax problems until Donald told me."

"Or that she had a nephew in the Pit Bulls." I paused, not wanting to alarm Petal with my question. Then again, she was the lawyer, not me. She was probably already exploring mentally the angles that had me nervous. "Petal, did you and Judge Colter end things on a, shall we say, cordial note?"

"Yes, very cordial. The whole thing was short, sweet, and a big mistake. Thank God we both came to that realization at the same time. Why?"

"Well, picture this. The cops are talking to the judge, you know, investigating the crime, talking to people who knew Ruby."

She nodded, though her eyes were closed. She didn't seem all that concerned. "I'm following."

"The judge says, 'Well, isn't that a coincidence. My ex-lover just happened to stumble across my clerk's dead body."

Petal's eyes popped open and a tiny furrow of worry marred her otherwise flawless forehead. "When you put it that way, it sounds awful. God, I'd hate to be called in as a witness or something. As if I need to be involved in any more scandal!"

She flipped the drain lever and stood up, wrapping a large pink bath sheet around her. The towel wasn't mine. I could only assume Petal had snitched it from Cullen. "Well, I don't know what I'm worried about," she said, dismissing my concerns with a bubbly wave of her hand. "Donald doesn't know I found the body."

"He will."

Our eyes met. "Santiago Ramone," we said together.

CHAPTER NINE

The story about Ruby Casserly broke in Friday's Morning News, with Ramone's by-line. By some miracle, Petal's name wasn't even mentioned, but mine was—prominently. Fortunately there was no mention of where I lived, so if Darryl did happen to see the paper, he still wouldn't be able to find me.

Sitting at the kitchen table with our cereal—shredded wheat for Petal, Fruit Loops for me—we took turns poring over the article.

"What is this?" Petal complained. "I'm the one who tripped over the body, and I didn't even get a mention."

"You're complaining?"

"I'm referred to as, 'her sister.' Ramone could have at least called me 'her prominent local attorney sister.'"

"Count your blessings, ding-dong," I said, flipping a Fruit Loop at her. "Ramone kept your name out of it. Now the Judge won't know about your involvement. You're off the hook." More importantly, the police wouldn't know about her connection to Ruby. I breathed a huge sigh of relief.

Petal interrupted me mid-sigh. "Uh-oh. Take a look at this." She passed the newspaper back to me, pointing one perfectly manicured fingernail at a blurb both of us had missed the first time around. "See related story, page C-1."

I rifled madly through the rest of the paper 'til I found section C, the "Today" segment. There was a picture of my house and the Haglins picketing out front.

"Oh, my God! I'm going to kill him!" Ramone's name could go on my list of potential victims, right under Cullen's. The headline read, "Answers from a Crystal Ball?" The article, which I read aloud to Petal, detailed how one local psychic—yours truly—had located two missing persons in one week, and how a local minister was squaring off against all psychics and fortune-tellers, starting with me.

"At best, they bilk gullible people out of millions of dollars annually," the Reverend Haglin was quoted as saying. "At worst, they consort with powers best left alone and drag innocent people with them to eternal damnation."

"What a nut," Petal murmured.

As for the part about me, Santiago stuck to the truth. He explained that I'd learned Ruby Casserly, the former owner of my house, was missing, and that I'd subsequently found her buried in the woods. Even unadorned, the truth sounded a little bit spooky. He also added, "Protective of her privacy, Ms. Larabee declined to be interviewed for this story."

The story went on to interview other local psychics, many of whom claimed to have found missing persons and long-lost objects. The more eccentric of them claimed to have predicted assassinations and shuttle explosions.

"Please tell me I don't sound half as kooky as these folks," I begged Petal. She made no reply.

It could have been worse, I thought, trying to comfort myself.

That was before the huddled masses started lining up at my door. These were not the well-mannered people—Ruby's former clients—I was used to. These people had recognized the purple house from the newspaper, and they were certifiable. They wanted love potions. They wanted me to put curses on their enemies. One woman wanted me to help her win a school board election by using telekinesis to mentally tamper with the votes. One old man wanted me to pray over his glass eye so that his sight would be restored. And one homely teenage girl thought I could help her to marry Leo DiCaprio.

The picket line grew, too. Now it was the Haglins and four others. Sometimes they chanted. Sometimes they sang hymns. They looked hot and bedraggled by noon, so just to show I could turn the other cheek, I brought out a pitcher of ice water and some paper cups. Though I could almost see their mouths watering, not a one of them accepted my offer.

TV crews showed up. Petal made a restrained statement on my behalf, the gist of which was that I'd only been trying to help people and I did not believe I had any special powers that everyone didn't have.

The last straw was when my parents called—all the way from Tibet.

"This is so cool," my mother said. "We heard all about it from your Grandma Larabee. Gypsy, do you really live in a purple house?" She giggled. "And since when did you start using a crystal ball?"

"Recently. By accident."

"And some religious nut is really picketing your house?"

"As we speak."

"Wow."

My mother isn't like other people's mother. She once got herself arrested for walking around topless at a rock concert. The more outrageous my behavior, the more she approves. Sometimes I think she named me Gypsy because people named Gypsy are bound to turn up in the newspapers.

At three o'clock I put a sign on the front porch: No Readings Until Further Notice. The Haglin demonstrators cheered, believing they'd pressured me into it. But it wasn't just them. If all I'd had to face were a few picketers, I never would have admitted defeat. But I was fighting a more personal demon. Did I want to be a fortune-teller or not? Lord knew I needed some way to make a living, and I enjoyed helping people. I was cheaper than a therapist. But I didn't enjoy wading through crazy people all day.

Was I really helping people? More importantly, was I really psychic? Could I find missing persons, and if I could, did I want to? The publicity I was suddenly embroiled in made me more than uncomfortable, and not just because of Darryl. I simply didn't like people thinking I was "weird." I'd had enough of that during my childhood.

At five o'clock I stole some of Petal's frou-frou bubble bath and soaked in the tub. Afterward, I rifled through my closet, wondering if I had anything the least bit stylish. Most of the items hanging there were my friends' cast-offs, given to me after Darryl burned up all my clothes. Not that I'd ever been much of a clotheshorse.

Petal came home from playing tennis—apparently she still had country club privileges—and found me holding outfits up in front of the mirror, a half-dozen of her hot rollers in my hair.

"Oh, my God," she said. "You're going out with Santiago Ramone."

I neither confirmed nor denied, since I still wasn't sure what I would do. "I just thought it would be nice to wear something besides cut-offs and T-shirts, for a change."

"You lie like a rug, Gypsy Moon. That look in your eye says you're planning on getting laid tonight."

"No way! Even if I have dinner with the man, do you think I'd let him touch me? After what he did?"

"It depends on how long it's been since you had sex."

I didn't tell Petal that I'd started counting in years, rather than months. Darryl and I had never done the deed. I'd realized after only a couple of dates that he was a few sheets short of a ream.

I held up the two outfits side by side. "What do you think? Sleeveless white top and skinny black pants, or bright green mini-dress?"

She gave the two outfits a critical once-over. "Are those my only choices?"

"These are the best my closet has to offer." I'd already scoped out Petal's wardrobe, but our tastes in clothes had diverged over the years. She tended toward pastels, tailored suits, silk, linen—stuff that had to be dry-cleaned and/or ironed. I didn't own an iron, and anyway, I liked stretchy knits and denim.

"Go with the black and white," she said decisively. "The green says you're trying too hard. And forget the rollers. Put your hair up. I have some combs you can use."

"So you think I should go?"

"Would it matter either way? You'll do what you want to do, like always."

I guessed she was right. I couldn't resist the temptation, if only for the opportunity to tell Ramone what a slug he was for putting my life in danger.

"What if he's a serial killer or a rapist?" Petal asked. "What if he puts some of that date rape drug in your wine?"

"With his looks, I hardly think he has to resort to rape," I replied sensibly.

"Well, take my cell phone with you, just in case you have to call 9-1-1 in a hurry."

"Don't be an alarmist. I hate cell phones." I didn't particularly like computers, fax machines, answering machines, pagers, or e-mails, either. I was technologically challenged.

"Take it, or I won't be able to sleep."

"I'll be home by ten."

She tucked the phone into my backpack on my way out the door. "Give the bastard hell. And open the car window on the way there. You'll asphyxiate him with that perfume."

I arrived at Ramone's apartment at seven-fifteen, late on purpose. Didn't want him thinking me too eager. He lived in one of those luxury high-rise buildings in the fashionably quirky Oak Lawn, with marble floors, antiques in the lobby, and a real live doorman.

The doorman, a doddering old man with a pleasant smile, had my name on an approved-for-entry list. He let me in, giving me directions on how to find Ramone's apartment. Apparently Ramone protected his own privacy even while he took it away from others. As the elevator carried me up to the seventh floor, I had an attack of nerves. What if he wasn't home? What if he was playing a cruel joke on me, like the time Hank Belton asked me to the prom, then stood me up? Okay, maybe I had some teensy insecurities when it came to men.

Once on the proper floor, the apartment was easy enough to find. I rapped smartly on the door, wishing I'd worn the mini-dress. It was retro sixties empire waist, and I didn't have to suck in my stomach when I wore it.

I'd rehearsed several clever opening lines, but my memory slipped out through my ears along with the rest of my brains when Ramone opened the door. God, he was gorgeous! He even had Cullen beat, and Cullen had been my measuring stick for a very long time.

He wore faded jeans that hugged his thigh muscles, and a pure white, starched dress shirt open at the throat. Nothing else. No jewelry, no belt, and no shoes. I couldn't resist a glance at his toes. They were long and well shaped, making me glad I painted my toenails. I make it a rule never to date a guy with thicker hair, longer eyelashes, or prettier feet than me. Ramone didn't seem at all surprised to see me. He offered me a "I knew you'd come" smile, but at least he had the good grace not to say the words aloud.

I handed him the bottle of dessert wine I'd brought. Every southern girl, even one raised in a hippie commune, knows that you don't show up at someone's door empty-handed.

"Thanks," he said after briefly studying the label. "Come in."

I entered his lair, which I quickly realized was the ultimate millennium bachelor pad. No unsightly stacks of Sports Illustrated or ashtrays filled with cigar butts, but thoroughly male nonetheless. The carpeting was clean and plush, the furniture tasteful wood, the colors strong and dark.

He showed me into the living room, where he'd set out brie cheese and crackers. One wall was devoted to electronic entertainment devices of every description—TV, VCR, CD, DVD. A veritable alphabet soup of boy toys. I could tell which chair was his favorite?-a recliner, comfortably worn. A table next to it held four remote controls.

"What did you think of the story?" Ramone asked without preamble as soon as I'd sat down.

"It made me want to go live in a communist country where the government censors the press."

"That bad?"

"It was a fine story, Ramone. I just wish my name hadn't been quite so prominent—or my house so ... so identifiable. Do you have any idea what kind of crap I've had to put up with today? I mean, I thought we had a deal."

"That was for the first article. This was an entirely different story." He flashed a look of genuine concern. "My editor insisted we use your name. And I had no control over the picture. Your stalker didn't find you, did he? I didn't tell where you live."

"No stalkers, but every crazy in the city now expects me to solve their problems with my crystal ball."

"I interviewed some other fortune-tellers," he said. "They all seemed really happy to get publicity."

"Yeah, but I bet they don't have Reverend Haglin and his sycophants parked at their curbs. Not to mention TV news crews. You can probably catch Petal's act at ten."

"No, thanks. I've seen Petal Ingalls in action before. That woman scares me. Is she really your sister?"

"Yeah," I admitted. "Don't tell anyone."

"Does she embarrass you that much?"

"Oh, gosh no. I embarrass her. She's trying to find a job, and she doesn't want potential employers to know she has—" I all but slapped my hand over my mouth. What was wrong with me? Ramone was a reporter. I shouldn't go blabbing anything about Petal's employment woes to him.

It was too late. If he'd had antenna in his head, they would have been popping out. "I thought Petal Ingalls was on sabbatical."

"She and her employer parted ways recently," I said, trying to make it sound like it was no big deal.

"Why's she hanging out with you? Are she and Cullen separated?"

"Temporarily. They're getting back together." I made a desperate, pathetic attempt to change the subject. "Mmm, something smells good."

Amazingly, my ploy worked. I guess he wasn't all that interested in Petal. "I put the tuna on just before you got here," he said. "I figured if you didn't show, I'd share it with Clarissa."

My hackles rose. Who was Clarissa? I wondered, though I didn't dare exhibit any curiosity. He'd mentioned her just to rattle my cage. Well, so what if he had a girlfriend or a voluptuous neighbor who popped over every now and then for leftovers and sex?

Just as my imagination was going into overdrive, Ramone nodded toward the floor near my feet. "Clarissa."

A cat. Clarissa was a fat black Persian with orange eyes, clearly an overindulged pet. Ramone was full of surprises. Most macho men I'd encountered wouldn't pet a cat, much less own one. Much less name it Clarissa.

"You like cats?" he asked.

I suspected that to say no would deeply offend one or both of them. So I reached down and gingerly petted Her Highness. She arched up to press against my hand. "Yeah, I like cats." I didn't care for the seventeen that lived next door to me, but that was because they yowled at three in the morning and wouldn't stay out of my garbage. Clarissa seemed well-mannered. I had to admit she was kind of cute, with her bulging eyes and smushed-in face.

"Well, I'm sorry the story caused you problems," Ramone said. "I was just doing my job. If it's any consolation, the story's played out now. I'll still be following the Ruby Casserly investigation, but your part is over."

I hoped so. I just wanted things to get back to normal.

Conversation drifted to other topics, and I found Ramone to be stimulating—mentally, that is. I wasn't sure whether he had designs on my body or not. He was a model of propriety. No off-color jokes, no staring at my cleavage, no touching, other than brushing against me when he held my chair.

The dinner was yummy, too—grilled a tuna steak, salad, crusty french bread, and an excellent Chablis. The food on the table could have fed four or five people, and I had to forcibly resist the urge to ask for a doggie bag.

Pleasantly satiated, I followed Ramone out to his tiny balcony, where the charcoal grill was down to embers. The temperature had dropped to a manageable eighty-eight degrees, according to a lighted bank thermometer in the distance. We sat on two reclining lawn chairs, and I felt inexplicably happy, certainly happier than I would have believed possible a few hours ago. The sunset had turned the sky shades of orange and fuchsia; city lights were popping on one by one, and a breeze rustled in nearby trees.

I found myself liking Santiago Ramone. He was arrogant but not insufferable, proud but not conceited, self-assured but with a hint of vulnerability. He'd been trying to impress me tonight, and for some reason my opinion was important to him.

"So what's it feel like to be psychic?" he asked abruptly.

My pleasant frame of mind evaporated. I didn't want to be reminded about my new calling. At least Ramone had waited 'til after dinner to pick my brain.

"I thought you didn't believe in my mumbo-jumbo."

"As a reporter, I have to show healthy skepticism. But I'm not a hundred percent convinced either way."

I looked at him suspiciously. "You didn't hide a tape recorder out here somewhere, did you?"

"Gypsy, I'm wounded. I told you tonight is off the record. I'm just curious how the psychic thing works."

"Off the record? Really?"

"Really."

For some reason, I believed him. "I'm not psychic. I tried to tell you that the first day you came over, but you wouldn't believe me."

"Then how do you explain—"

"Coincidence, misunderstanding, and pure dumb luck. A little commonsense deduction, maybe."

"Intuition?" he probed.

"Maybe," I conceded, remembering Cullen and his gut instinct. "Everybody has intuition. Not everybody listens to it. I'll bet you have hunches sometimes when you're working on a story. Right?"

He shrugged. "I guess. But nobody pays me to read their palm or predict their future with a crystal ball."

"Hang out a shingle. You'll be amazed."

"Can you read minds?" He ran one finger playfully up my bare arm. It was the first time he'd consciously touched me all night, and every nerve ending in my body snapped to attention.

"When we were kids, Petal and I read each other's minds all the time."

"Can you read my mind?" he persisted.

I wasn't sure I wanted to play this game. I decided to take the humorous approach. "You're thinking about tonight's Ranger game, and wondering if you can catch the last couple of innings after I leave."

"Hah! And you call yourself a psychic. You're not even close."

"You think it's so easy, you try it."

"Okay." He leaned closer and put one hand over each of my ears, then scrunched his eyes shut and assumed an expression of fierce concentration. "You're thinking ... you're thinking that you wish I'd shut up and just kiss you."

Damn, but the man was dead on.

He opened his eyes. "Am I right?"

"Mmmm," I managed, which he took as assent. He pulled me closer and touched his mouth to mine.

The man could definitely kiss. With those full, sensual lips, it would have been a shame if he couldn't. But he did everything right. Even with the arms of the lounge chairs between us, he managed to hold me just right, firmly but not in a death grip. The kiss was powerful, commanding, but gentle. It was moist but not drippy.

I hadn't been kissed like that in years. Past high school, most men consider kissing a necessary preliminary to be gotten through in order to reach the good stuff. "First base, yeah, okay, check. Let's move on to feeling up the boobs." Ramone turned kissing into an art. I was completely convinced he would be happy to simply kiss me all evening.

He did touch my breasts, though, gently, through my shirt. With every caress, the heat pooling in my loins moved up a degree or two. I was starting to sweat.

"Think anyone around here ever watches these apartments with binoculars?" I whispered in his ear as he nibbled my shoulder.

"Would you prefer to go inside?"

"Yes." Inside, in the aid conditioning, where I wouldn't drip sweat on him.

With one smooth move he stood, scooped me out of the lounge chair, and lifted me into his arms. I felt very dainty and feminine, and I couldn't squelch a delighted giggle. I wasn't normally a giggler, except sometimes when Petal and I got started.

I thought he would take me to the bedroom, but he set me down gently on the couch. I didn't know whether to be disappointed or relieved, and I was both, I guess. I knew I had no business sleeping with Santiago Ramone, especially not on a first date. But, damn, what were a few more regrets?

Still, his ardor didn't cool just because we were in air conditioning. His hands were all over me. He pulled Petal's combs out of my hair, which came tumbling down in a mass of hairsprayed tangles. Neither was I a model of propriety; I had roving hands of my own. I became consumed with feeling his butt. It was hard as a denim-covered bowling ball, but sexy as hell.

I sucked on his neck, almost giving him a hickey. But I wanted to experience him with all my senses. If I could have inhaled all of him, I would have.

A ringing phone brought us both to a standstill. "Let it ring," I said, knowing with the full force of my "intuition" that if we stopped for the phone, we'd come to our senses.

"I will," he said, nuzzling my collarbone. "It's your phone."

"Mine?" The cell phone. Probably someone trying to reach Petal, in which case, letting it ring made sense. But what if it wasn't? What if Petal was trying to reach me? What if Reggie had come back to the house? Or Darryl? What if one of Reverend Haglin's followers had firebombed the house?

Sometimes my imagination didn't serve me well. I couldn't ignore the phone.

"I better get it," I said. Ramone reluctantly released me. I found my backpack, dug through it, and extracted the cell phone. It took me a moment to figure out how to answer it.

"Gypsy, thank God!" She sounded close to tears.

"Petal? What? What is it?"

"You have to come bail me out of jail!"

CHAPTER TEN

I nearly dropped the phone as all thoughts of passion fled. "You're kidding, right?"

"Would I kid about something like this?" She lowered her voice to a hiss. "Oh, God, you're not within earshot of Ramone, are you?"

"Yes." I worded my next question carefully, so as not to clue Ramone in on the nature of the call. "What seems to be the problem?"

"They think I murdered Ruby Casserly. For God's sake, I barely knew the woman!"

Oh, no. At worst, I thought Petal's affair with the judge might come to light. I hadn't imagined for one minute anyone would believe dainty, feminine Petal could kill, never mind her barracuda image.

"You have to get me out of here, Gyp. They threw me in a holding cell with a bunch of junkies and prostitutes. This one drunk woman threw up on my shoes!"

"Hey, who you callin' drunk?" came a voice from the background.

I shivered, imagining the worst. Poor Petal. She was strong in some ways, but she could not stand dirt or other people's body odor. When she was little she used to scream whenever we had to ride on a public bus, which was often our only way of getting somewhere.

"How would you, um, suggest I deal with the problem?" I asked.

"The magistrate tried to set my bond at a hundred, but I talked him down to twenty-five."

"Twenty-five ... as in, thousand? Where are we going to come up with that much—"

"Chill. You'll only need to come up with around three thousand dollars for the bail bondsman, and they'll want some collateral. You can give them the registration for the Jag."

"Okay. Where, exactly—"

"Look in the yellow pages under surety bonds."

"No, I mean, you. Where exactly are you?"

"Lew Sterritt."

"Can't Cullen fix this?" He could probably get things straightened out faster than I could.

"He's not home. Probably out screwing Liz Pastelle. Hurry, Gyp. I don't know how much more of this I can take."

"I'm on my way."

"What's the problem?" Ramone asked when I'd disconnected. He'd listened intently to my side of the conversation, blatantly curious. Now he tried not to act disappointed that I was leaving, but I could see his jaw working.

"Oh, just a family sort of thing," I hedged. "No big deal, but it requires my personal touch."

"You know, you're a rotten liar."

"I'm not lying! Why would I lie?" I wasn't fooling Ramone. He knew nothing short of a national emergency on the order of an earthquake or a Cuban invasion would be sufficient to drag me away from him just now.

"So you're leaving? Just when things were getting interesting?"

The moment called for something coy, but I didn't have a coy bone in my body. "We'll pick it up later," I said, grabbing my backpack. "It was a wonderful dinner, Ramone. Thank you."

Grudgingly, he walked me to the elevator. "I have a first name, you know."

I guess once you've gotten to second base with a guy, it's okay to use his first name. I'd resisted using it because it was such a sensual name, and to utter it seemed very intimate. But it was a valid request.

I mustered a smile. "Santiago. I'll call you." The elevator arrived, and I stepped on. "Or, you can call me." The doors shut between us.

Benny the Bail Bondsman wasn't a pleasant person. He was sweaty and rather unclean looking, and he hadn't shaved in a few days. His office wasn't any better groomed. The one-room store-front, squatting on the edge of downtown, hadn't seen a vacuum cleaner or dust cloth in any recent decade. Benny sold handguns on the side, which did not endear him to me.

"What's her name?" he asked in a bored voice when I told him my sister was in jail.

"Petal Ingalls."

He looked surprised. "The lawyer? Get outta here. What'd she do, kick some D.A. in the balls?"

"No, she killed someone. I mean, no, she didn't kill anybody!" God, what was I saying? "They've charged her with murder. Her bail is twenty-five thousand dollars."

Benny laughed, showing a mouth full of green teeth. "You're shittin' me."

I figured it was pointless to argue that I would not walk into this disgusting establishment for a joke. I needed Benny on my side.

"Okay," he said, getting down to business. "I charge twelve percent. That'd be three thousand dollars. You got that much cash?"

"How about a Visa?" It was Petal's, and I had no idea whether it would go through or not.

"That'll work. What have you got for collateral?"

I pulled the title and registration for Gypsy's Jaguar from my backpack. "This is Ms. Ingalls' car. It's a '98 Jaguar, bottle-green, loaded. She paid over forty thousand for it."

"You're a bail bondsman's dream." He snatched the title away from me and wrote down some numbers on a form. We had to fill out a lot of forms, providing every kind of personal information imaginable. He asked me everything except my bra size, and I suspected by the way his gaze kept straying to my bust, he wanted to ask me that, too.

Thirty minutes later, I was wandering through the maze of the Lew Sterritt Justice Center, Dallas's state-of-the-art criminal processing building. By my side was Benny's wife, Lucille, who was authorized to post the bond. Like Benny, Lucille, with her beehive of black-and-blond cotton-candy hair, was personality-challenged. Maybe dealing with the dregs of society day in and day out had deadened them to social niceties.

At least Lucille knew where to go. She toddled along in her rubber thongs through various hallways until she found the right office.

She and the clerk seemed to know each other. They had a good laugh over Petal's dilemma, which I thought exceedingly rude. But apparently not too many people in the Dallas legal system had a fondness for my sister.

I'd seen Petal in action a few times, when I came to the courthouse to watch her try a case. In court, she seemed like a different person, like an actress playing a part. She was poised, serious, and determined. She never backed down from an argument, and she usually didn't lose, either. Judges threw her steely-eyed glares when she showed them she knew the law better than they did, but they acquiesced when they had to.

I wondered how many people she worked with knew she had a sense of humor.

In the early days of her career she'd been given every hopeless case, every dog on the docket, the ones nobody thought were win-able. And when she started winning those, the partners at her firm gradually switched her over to the high-profile, big-money cases.

I think she enjoyed the underdog cases most of all.

More papers had to be signed, after which Lucille hot-footed it out of there with an unfriendly reminder that I was responsible for making sure Petal showed at her various court hearings. A few minutes later, a stern-looking guard escorted Petal through a locked door and into the waiting area.

For a moment I just stared. I'd never seen her looking so cowed, so utterly humbled. Her grass-green shorts were stained with God knew what. Her T-shirt, which earlier today had looked so cool and stylish with its little sprigged flowers, was torn at the neck, showing her bra strap. Her hair was flat, and her shoes were missing.

When she looked up, I saw she had a bruise starting to form on her cheekbone.

"Oh ... oh, Petal, what have they done to you?"

I enfolded her in my arms, and she cried on my shoulder like a baby.

"Aw, ain't that touchin'," the guard said.

"Just shut up," I told him. "If you had any part in hurting her, we're gonna sue your ass."

"Shh," Petal said, pulling herself together. "Let's just get out of here, please."

We did. Petal led the way. I'd gotten so turned around I didn't have any idea where my car was parked.

Only after I had Petal firmly buckled in to the passenger seat and all of the doors locked did I ask her what had happened.

"The guards didn't do this to me," she said, touching the bruise on her face. "Another prisoner did."

"It's the guards' responsibility to keep you safe," I reminded her. "Your ... your constitutional rights were violated."

"Drop it, okay?"

I thought Petal was acting pretty weird. She was always first in line to threaten a lawsuit against someone who slighted her.

"Do you have any money?" she asked.

"A little. Why?"

She was rifling through my backpack. "Stop at that 7-11."

I did as she asked. Sensing she'd reached the end of her rope, I was afraid to cross her. She jumped out of the Jeep before I'd come to a complete stop and ran inside the convenience store. I'm not sure she even realized she was barefoot.

Moments later she emerged with a tiny plastic bag and climbed back into the Jeep. The bag contained cigarettes—Eve Menthol Lights—which she tore open. She stuck one in her mouth and pushed in the car's cigarette lighter.

Petal hadn't smoked since law school. I decided it wouldn't be wise to comment on the resurrection of her habit.

Once we were home, I ran Petal a hot bubble bath and ordered her in it. She smelled like a homeless shelter. She told me to burn her clothes. Then she climbed into the tub, slid down beneath the bubbles, and chain-smoked while she told me about her ordeal.

The cops had come for her just after I left for Ramone's. She hadn't thought it was a big deal at first; she'd just assumed she'd been nailed as a witness. When they asked her if she wanted counsel with her, she'd haughtily informed them she was an attorney and she could protect her own damn rights.

Things had slid downhill from there. A detective named Clay Norton— the devil incarnate, from Petal's description—had grilled her for two hours. He apparently knew all about her affair with Donald, the ethics charges she was facing, the impending break-up of her marriage.

"I don't know how they found out about all that," Petal said.

I had my suspicions, but I didn't want to go hurling accusations until I had more evidence.

"He asked me how many times Donald and I ... you know. When and where it all happened. He wanted details, Gyp, and I think those perverted detectives—there was a video camera, so I know others were listening— were just treating themselves to a prurient thrill."

"So did you tell them?"

"I spilled it. I've seen what happens when people lie to protect themselves, thinking no one will ever find out. They always find out, and it always looks bad. So I told the God's honest truth."

I was still confused. "How did this all lead to—"

"A few times we did it in his office," she said matter-of-factly. "Ruby was his clerk. She knew when I came to visit, and how often. Donald's phone calls went through her, too. She was the only one, besides me and Donald, who knew about the affair."

Now the light was beginning to dawn. "And they think you killed Ruby so she wouldn't blab to the ethics committee."

"That's the gist of it."

"That's ludicrous!" I exploded. "Completely circumstantial!" I'd learned a thing or two from watching Perry Mason reruns.

"Unfortunately, you can make a case with circumstantial evidence, especially when the body's decomposed, destroying all the physical evidence. Since they don't know exactly when Ruby died, an alibi won't help me."

"But you didn't know about Ruby's land."

"Norton thinks I did. How else would I have 'discovered' the body?"

"Did you tell him about the deed?"

"Gypsy, of course. I told him everything I could think of, every infinitesimal detail—even about the bet you made with Cullen. He was unimpressed."

I thought for a moment. "The timing's all wrong. Ruby died long before any ethics charges were filed."

Petal shook her head. "Donald's wife made her accusations ages ago. I didn't mention it because I never believed it would come to anything."

"How did she find out?" I asked.

Again, Petal shook her head. "I don't know. We were really careful."

"Maybe Ruby ratted on you."

"It's possible."

But I had my own suspicions. Someone else had known about the affair.

When Petal finally got out of the tub, her fingers and toes were wrinkled as raisins, and there were seventeen cigarette butts floating in the water. She'd smoked the first three in the car on the way home.

"Petal, that's disgusting. Are you done smoking now?"

"Yes." She pulled on one of her filmy peignoirs, a virginal white one. "I'm better, now. Thank you, Gypsy, for taking care of things. I'm going to bed."

She seemed more normal, now, much to my relief. I threw out the cigarette butts, rinsed out the bathtub, then went downstairs to make myself some tea. I thought about my truncated evening with Ramone ... Santiago ... and felt only a twinge of regret. It probably wouldn't have been that smart to sleep with him.

It was nearly midnight when someone knocked frantically on my front door, pulling me out of my chamomile-induced stupor. My heart fluttered as I briefly entertained the idea that Ramone had come over to check on me. I was disappointed to find Cullen standing on the front porch.

"I just got Petal's message. Is she okay? Is she here?"

I slipped out the front door. "Shh! She's asleep. You're a little late with your concern," I said peevishly.

The night had cooled off to the low eighties and a light breeze blew through the branches of the magnolia tree. An altogether spectacular night for lovers. What a waste.

"I tried calling, but no one answered. I tried calling her cell phone, too, but the calls weren't going through."

That was my doing. I'd used up all the batteries, first by keeping it on all the time, then by using it to call several bail bondsmen from the car.

I shrugged and sat on the porch railing. "We managed without you. Where were you, anyway?"

"I was out."

"With the decorator slut?"

"Her name's Liz, and I took her out to dinner so I could end our relationship civilly."

I had a news flash for Cullen—there was no way to end an affair and make it civil. "You've learned a little bit over the years," I commented dryly. "I seem to recall you ending our relationship by bringing over a six-pack to my dorm room."

He cringed at the reminder. "Let's not rehash old news," he said. "Tell me what happened with Petal. All I got was that she'd been arrested and needed to make bail, but when I called the jail they said she'd come and gone already. Was it all those parking tickets?"

"Not quite. Sit down."

He sat in one of the painted metal chairs, and I told him everything, as closely as I could recall it. With every word, he sank lower and lower into the chair.

"Jesus Christ," he finally said. "This is all my fault."

"You told the judge's wife about his affair with Petal," I concluded. It was the only explanation that made sense.

He nodded. "I thought it would be better if Petal didn't know I knew. She'd have been pissed to find out I was having her followed."

"So what do we do next?" I asked.

"We hire the best goddam lawyer in the city."

"Second best," I corrected him. "Petal's the best."

"She can't represent herself. That would be totally stupid."

I agreed.

"She didn't do it, Cullen," I said, just to make sure we were on the same wavelength.

"Of course she didn't do it! I'm putting my money on Reggie Crane. And I'll prove the bastard did it, too."

"You're a Burglary detective," I said. "You don't even work in Homicide."

"I'll investigate on my own time. I've got some vacation coming."

"I'll help," I said. "Whatever you need. Surveillance? How about undercover work? I did a little acting in college—"

"How about you look in your crystal ball?" he asked, only half joking.

I guessed now wasn't the time for me to remind him I wasn't psychic. "I'll do what I can."

He left, promising to come back in the morning and talk to Petal. I went inside and started for the kitchen, intending to rinse my teacup. But Ruby's crystal ball gleamed invitingly at me from its brass stand in the living room.

On a whim, I picked it up, held it between by hands, and stared into it. What was I supposed to see? Forgetting the teacup, I took the crystal ball with me to my bedroom and set it on the nightstand. Maybe I would get some inspiration from it.

"I've decided to represent myself," Petal announced at breakfast the next morning. She was completely herself again, with hair and nails salon perfect and not a single wrinkle in her gold linen trousers and white silk blouse.

She'd carefully applied her make-up so that the bruise on her cheek wasn't even visible.

I strenuously objected to her plan, but she overruled me. "Why should I pay some schmuck two hundred dollars an hour when I can do the best job for free? I mean, who could be a better advocate, me, or some guy who may or may not believe I'm innocent? Lawyers are used to assuming their clients are guilty."

"We'll find one who believes you're innocent," I said.

"I don't want some idealistic, snot-nosed kid fresh out of law school representing me, thanks. I can handle it." She stirred her tea with jerky motions.

"You're emotionally involved in the case," I tried again. "You're not at your best. You can't be thinking straight."

"I work harder when there's a lot at stake. And I always think straight. Always."

"You got into a brawl with a drunk woman last night," I reminded her.

"She started it."

"She attacked you?"

"In a manner of speaking." Petal sipped her tea, peering at me over the rim of the cup. "She made fun of my name."

"You introduced yourself to her?" Seemed like that was just borrowing trouble.

"She was a former client. I defended her on a pro bono case—solicitation. She was guilty as hell, and I got her off with a suspended sentence. But was she grateful? No. Did she learn anything? No. She was back in jail, and she was making fun of my name."

"The point is, haven't you ever heard that saying, 'An attorney who represents himself has—'"

"—has a fool for a client. I'm doing it anyway. There's not another lawyer in this town I trust to do as good a job as I can do."

I was glad Petal didn't suffer any shortage of self-esteem. "What's the first step?" I asked.

"My preliminary trial is Monday at nine. That's when they formally charge me, I plead not guilty, they set a trial date. Then I file a motion for discovery. That's where I find out exactly what evidence they have against me. Once we know what the evidence is, we can start ripping it apart. Anything I can't rip apart, I move to suppress. I'll also move for a change of venue. There's not a judge in this city who doesn't know me or know of me, and most of them can't stand me."

She sounded level-headed enough. Maybe this would work after all. "Why don't they like you, Petal?" I asked with a touch of naiveté. "You're a good lawyer, aren't you?"

"Too good. Because of me, criminals are out on the street."

"Does that ever bother you?"

She poured herself the second half of her cup of coffee and sat down. "Yeah, it bothers me," she confessed. "But someone has to defend them. Everybody has a right to a fair trial. Whether they're guilty or innocent, I make sure they don't go to jail unless the prosecutor presents enough evidence, fairly gathered. I make sure the jury is aware of mitigating circumstances so they can make an informed decision."

When she put it that way, it didn't sound so bad.

"Still, sometimes I can't sleep nights."

The doorbell called a halt to our tête-à-tête. Cullen, probably. "Be nice," I cautioned Petal over my shoulder as I went to the door. "He wants to help. Let him."

"Mornin'," Cullen said as he stepped into my entry hall.

"Where were you last night?" Petal demanded, sounding like a fishwife. "I needed you. If you want me to move back home, you'll have to do a better imitation of a husband."

Cullen didn't fight back. He just stood there, looking at his shoes.

"Who wants breakfast at Edna's?" I asked brightly.

Edna's Cafe was my new favorite restaurant, a throwback to the 1950s and, even better, a mere three blocks from my house. I figured I could think better with my stomach full of pancakes. Edna's decor hadn't changed since the '50s, and neither had the menu. The waitresses popped gum and stuck pencils in their teased hair, and they called everybody "hon'." In the three weeks since I'd moved to Psychedelic Heights, I had become a regular. They greeted me by name.

Cullen, Petal and I found a booth in the minuscule non-smoking section, ordered enough food for a high school football team, and plotted our strategy.

Tension between Petal and Cullen was tight enough to strum, but with a common goal to work toward, they managed to be civil to one another.

Petal planned to keep busy pursuing legal avenues. She would petition for copies of police reports involving Reggie and Ruby, and she would get a copy of Ruby's autopsy report. Cullen would focus on Reggie, talking to his friends, family, and fellow gang members.

My job, for the time being, was to keep searching through Ruby's things. Maybe I'd get lucky and come up with a threatening letter, or some evidence that she'd been blackmailing someone. We didn't know Ruby's romantic history, and it was feasible there was a jealous lover involved, never mind she'd been in her fifties. We also hoped I might stumble across whatever it was that Reggie wanted so badly.

"My job sounds really boring," I complained. "Can't I do something more pro-active?"

Cullen scratched his chin and thought for a moment. "I know. You can talk to your neighbors and find out if any of them saw or heard anything suspicious around the time of Ruby's disappearance. They might know if she had a boyfriend, too."

"What about Wade and Merrilee Haglin?" I asked. "I can't talk to them."

"Of course you can. Tell them you're assisting the police with an investigation, and they'll fall all over themselves to tell you what they know. People love to dish dirt about their neighbors. And you already told me they didn't like Ruby. C'mon, Gypsy, you can do it."

"I'd rather tackle the Pit Bulls," I grumbled.

CHAPTER ELEVEN

It wasn't easy to procrastinate where the Haglins were concerned. When Petal and I got home from breakfast, they were marching in front of my house again, along with about ten followers. The picket line didn't look quite as pathetic as it had a few days ago.

The crowd parted to let my car into the driveway, then shook their signs at me and shouted their slogans, which I'd long since tuned out.

"Are you going to talk to them now?" Petal asked.

"Can't think of a better time." I was sure Cullen was wrong, that the Reverend Wade would refuse to even listen to my request for information. Once refused, I could move on to something more constructive.

As I approached the picketers warily, I noticed how scraggly they were. The men weren't shaved, the women hadn't combed their hair, and their clothes looked threadbare and none-too-clean. What kind of minister was Wade Haglin, anyway? Didn't he preach the "cleanliness is next to Godliness" shtick?

Then it hit me. These folks weren't members of his congregation. They'd been recruited from the homeless shelter. The Haglins were paying people, or otherwise bribing them, to picket my house!

"Good morning, Reverend, Merrilee," I called cheerfully.

The chanting died down. They all stared at me suspiciously, perhaps waiting for me to produce a pointy black hat. It didn't help matters that one of my next-door-neighbor's cats, a black one, wandered up and wrapped itself around my ankles while I tried to carry on a conversation.

"Her familiar," someone whispered.

I nudged the cat away with my toe. "Reverend Haglin, Mrs. Haglin, might I have a word with you in private?"

"Don't bother trying to negotiate with us or cajole us," Wade said, shaking his head rapidly so that his jaws actually flapped. "We aren't leaving 'til you hand over the crystal ball."

"I understand. But this has nothing to do with me or fortune-telling. I need your help with a police investigation. You'd like to help catch a murderer, wouldn't you?"

"A murderer! Oh, my stars!" Merrilee clutched at the front of her dress, but her nose twitched with curiosity.

"Who was killed?" Wade asked, ushering Merrilee and me a few feet away where the other protesters couldn't overhear. Apparently they hadn't read the paper yesterday. Wade leaned heavily on his jewel-headed cane, making me wonder if his bad leg hurt from all the marching.

"Ruby Casserly."

I paused to let it sink in, wondering if they felt any guilt that the object of their disdain had faced her final judgment day. Wade made the sign of the cross.

"I knew that woman would come to a bad end," Merrilee huffed.

"Now, Merrilee, we must forgive sister Ruby her sins. She will need all of our prayers where she's going."

In sync, the two of them closed their eyes and bowed their heads in silent prayer for their fallen sister. In the interest of gaining their cooperation, I bowed my head also and tried to look pious.

A moment later they both raised their heads and opened their eyes, perfectly mimicking one another.

"The loss of one lamb, even a misguided one, is very sad," the Reverend said, sounding suspiciously insincere. "But I fail to see how we—"

"My brother-in-law is a police detective," I explained. "I offered to help out by canvassing the neighborhood, to see if anyone had any ideas."

"But she left this neighborhood months ago," Merrilee pointed out. "I'm sure whatever she got tangled up with had nothing to do with us."

"In the interest of serving justice, we'll do what we can," the Reverend said. "But don't think that means we'll soften our stand where you're concerned."

I could hardly believe my luck. They were going to talk! "Yes, yes, of course. Whatever," I said. "Did you ever happen to notice who came and went at Ruby's house?"

"Goodness," Merrilee said, "she had all kinds of weird people coming and going at all hours. Any one of them could have killed her."

"Where was she killed?" the Reverend asked. "And how?"

"I don't know. Her body was found buried out in the country."

"Oh, that's so disgusting," Merrilee said. "How could anyone do that? I mean, Ruby was an evil woman, but she was a human being, deserving of a proper grave."

"Maybe not on consecrated ground," Waded added thoughtfully.

"I'm sure she'll get a proper burial now," I said, trying not to let my impatience show. "I just need to know if you noticed anyone hanging around her house about the time she disappeared. Any strange cars?"

"There were always strange cars," Wade replied.

"Any that showed up on a regular basis?"

"There was that nephew of hers," Merrilee suddenly remembered. "He came around a lot. They were supposedly very close, but I never liked the looks of that kid. He tried to break into her house last spring, and I called the cops on him." She looked at Wade. "Was that before or after Ruby flew the coop?"

Wade couldn't remember. "Now that you mention it, though, there was a noisy fracas sometime last spring, not long before we found out Ruby was gone. Remember, Merrilee?"

"Oh, yes, quite well. The nephew came over late one night. I always know it's him because of the terrible noise his truck makes. It doesn't have a muffler."

Now we were getting somewhere! "Yes, and what happened?" I asked, hardly able to contain my excitement. Five minutes into my investigation, and already I was gathering useful evidence.

Merrilee proved to be a font of information. "They were yelling and screaming about something. Doors were slamming, curse words flying. The nephew came outside and was yelling something about Ruby breaking a promise."

"Something like that," Wade added.

"The young man was hopped up on drugs or booze, or both. Really, it was just awful."

"It sounds awful," I agreed. "What happened next?"

"I heard the truck start up, and that was the end."

"Did you call the police to make a complaint?" I asked, keeping my fingers crossed.

"I had just picked up the phone to call 9-1-1 when the noise died down," she said. "So I didn't bother."

Damn. A police report detailing a noisy fight between Ruby and Reggie would have been helpful.

The Haglins couldn't provide any more details, no specifics as to this supposed "promise" Reggie and Ruby had argued about. I thanked them and turned to go into the house when Wade called out, "Excuse me! I just have one more question."

I turned. "And that would be ..."

"Why don't you look in your crystal ball and see who murdered Ruby Casserly?"

I smiled sweetly. "I already did that. As a matter of fact, I know exactly who killed her. But the silly police won't accept psychic visions as evidence, can you imagine?"

I briefly enjoyed the twin looks of outrage on their faces before turning and hurrying to my porch, out of the sun. I had my handle on the knob when I noticed a police cruiser heading up my street. Yes! I sat down in one of the metal chairs to watch how the good Reverend and his missus dealt with the law.

To my dismay, the cruiser pulled into my driveway. A stout female officer emerged and headed in my direction.

I smiled a greeting. "Are you going to do something about those idiots in the street?" I asked when she got close enough.

She turned to look at the demonstrators, then back at me. "I don't know anything about any picketers," she said. "I'm just supposed to collect a ..." She consulted a notebook. "... a Gypsy Larabee and bring her downtown."

My stomach sank. "That would be me."

Petal poked her head out the door. "What's going on?"

"I think I'm being arrested," I said forlornly.

The officer shook her head. "No, ma'am, they just want to talk to you."

"Oh." I looked to Petal. "What do I do?"

"You go, of course. I'm counting on you to straighten out that bozo, Norton."

This wasn't how I wanted to spend the rest of the morning, but I picked up my backpack and followed the cop. At least she let me ride in the front seat.

I'm afraid I didn't do a very good job of straightening anybody out. Detective Lieutenant Clay Norton would have made a perfect Marine drill sergeant. Given my automatic dislike for authority figures, particularly smug, superior-acting ones, I did not make a favorable impression. As Norton led me into a sterile interrogation room, I made oinking noises under my breath.

I am my parents' daughter.

He stopped and turned sharply. "Did you say something?"

"Who, me?"

He narrowed his piggy eyes suspiciously at me. "Sit down." He didn't offer me coffee. He didn't treat me with even an ounce of civility, and I returned the favor.

He asked some routine questions for the record, then launched right into the meat of the matter. "Please describe the events of Tuesday, August second of this year."

I told him every goddam detail, down to my choice of breakfast cereal and the fact there wasn't enough mustard on my Whopper. He listened to every word, too, staring intensely—at my mouth, I think. When I finished, he leaned back and scratched the top of his head, running furrows through his graying crewcut.

"According to the report from the Seagoville Police, driving out to that parcel of property was all your sister's idea."

I swallowed, hard. How could I have known the ramifications of my little white lie? "At the time I was trying to deflect attention away from me." And I told him about Lupe and Jorge and Ramone. I even started to explain about Darryl and why I was publicity-shy, but he starting tuning out the explanation, so I shut up.

He asked me how and when I'd come to live in Ruby's house.

"I was desperate for a place to live," I answered in all honesty, remembering Petal's advice about not hiding anything. "I was flat broke, unemployed, and hiding out. Petal told me about this house that was being foreclosed on, and—"

"How did she know about it?" Norton interrupted.

"You know perfectly well she heard about it through Judge Donald Colter, Ruby's former boss. Anyway, I didn't care about the details, I just wanted a roof over my head."

"And how many days did you live there before your sister announced she was moving in with you?"

Alarms went off in my head. "You ... you think she moved in so she could go through Ruby's things and dispose of any incriminating evidence?" I asked incredulously.

"Just answer the question."

I sighed impatiently. "I moved in on July 22. Petal came about three days later, I think."

"Has your sister shown any interest in Ruby Casserly's possessions?" Norton asked. "Has she been looking through drawers or boxes?"

I know Petal thought the truth would set her free, but I couldn't help myself. I had to lie. "She isn't remotely interested in Ruby's things," I answered tartly.

"But didn't she help you search through a file cabinet the day you found the body?"

Oh, hell. Tripped up already. "She was helping me in my effort to locate Ms. Casserly." I explained about my bet with Cullen, hoping Petal's and my stories matched. "She didn't know where that land was, you know. She had to call the County Records office to find the location."

Norton didn't care about that.

We went on like this for more than two hours. By then my butt was aching from sitting on a damned uncomfortable metal chair, and I was thirsty from having eaten all that salty bacon at Edna's. Norton's questions became more impatient, my answers more clipped. His questions were getting redundant. I was repeating myself.

Finally he let me go, and I felt fortunate he hadn't arrested me as an accessory. Though he hadn't said it, he thought I was in cahoots with Petal, that if I hadn't helped kill Ruby, surely I was helping my sister hide the crime.

I had to find my own way home. I took the DART train, then walked the seven blocks home from the train station in blistering heat.

Petal was on the phone when I came inside, panting and wilted. "I'm filing the motion for discovery Monday," she said into the receiver. "Couldn't you just let me have a peek at it?" She paused, then smiled. "Great, thanks, Ike. I'll be right over."

"Who's Ike?" I asked when she hung up.

"Dallas County Medical Examiner's office. Works there part-time on weekends. He's a peach. He's going to let me have a look at the preliminary autopsy report. Do you want to come with me? On the way, you can tell me all about your meeting with the lovely and cordial Clay Norton."

"You're going to the morgue?" My skin crawled at the thought.

"Yeah. Oh, come on, we won't be in the part where the dead bodies are. It's just this office. They'll show me the report, I'll read it over real fast, and we'll leave."

I would have refused, but I sensed she wanted company. Petal had always been a resilient, self-sufficient sort, but the events of the last twenty-four hours had shaken her to the core. Outwardly she was poised and quite normal-looking, but anyone who knew her well—and I knew her better than anyone—could see the subtle signs of stress. She'd broken a fingernail, for one thing, and hadn't bothered to repair it. And she'd forgotten to put on earrings.

"I'll go with you now to the morgue, if you'll help me talk to the rest of the neighbors when we get back," I offered.

The M.E.'s office was in its own building, tucked away in a corner of Dallas County Medical Center, Dallas's largest hospital and the facility of choice for those without medical insurance. Petal parked her Jaguar in the visitor lot. She knew a shortcut to the morgue, which unfortunately took us right through the Emergency Room.

Even on a weekday morning, the waiting room was full of mothers with feverish children, young men bleeding from various scary-looking injuries, an old woman with her arm packed in ice, and one unfortunate-looking gentleman who appeared to have the granddaddy of all belly aches.

I instinctively recoiled at the concentrated suffering; Petal cruised by like she never saw it. Maybe she'd walked this path enough times that she'd become immune.

We walked through one corridor after another, and then outside again until we reached the unassuming, one-story, yellow brick building.

"Every autopsy in the whole county is done here," Petal told me, playing tour guide. "Sometimes six or eight a day."

"Gross." That was a lot of dead people. "They're not all murdered, are they?"

"No, most of them are just people who die of natural causes, or in car accidents. Then there's the suicides, the accidental drug overdoses, anybody who dies in an emergency room or within twenty-four hours of entering a hospital. Anybody who dies at home and who isn't under a doctor's care."

"That doesn't leave out many people."

"The M.E. stays busy, all right."

We walked up to a counter where a young Hispanic man presided. He smiled toothily the moment he spotted Petal. "Ms. Ingalls. Been expecting you." He lowered his voice and nodded toward me. "Who's your client?"

Like I couldn't hear him?

"Oh, that's not a client," Petal said. "She's just my sister, along for the ride."

"Yeah, the morgue's a nice place to visit, long as you're alive," he said. "Who is your client?"

"You mean, word hasn't gotten around?"

"Rumor has it the accused is someone important, but it hasn't made the news yet."

Thank heaven for small favors, I thought. That would all change when Petal was formally indicted. Although, I never knew what to expect with the media. They might relegate Petal's alleged crime to a page-2 article in the Metropolitan Section and a sound bite on the evening news. Or, they might really turn it into a circus. Their reaction depended on how bored they were, and how slow a news day it was.

The biggest question mark was the reaction of my own personal reporter, Ramone. He was going to freak when he figured out what I'd ditched him for last night. I suppose I could've been nice and given him the scoop, since at least I knew he had the capacity to write a fair story. Instead I'd forced him to read the news off the police blotter like every other news hound out there.

He wasn't going to be pleased.

"Can you get it for me?"

"Got it right here," the man named Ike whispered, then reached under the counter and pulled out a thin manila folder without a label. "You won't tell anyone, right?"

"It's our secret," Petal said in a husky voice that suggested more than would ever be delivered. Ike must have known that, but he looked like he was about to melt anyway.

Petal took the folder and headed for one of the two beat-up plastic chairs lining the wall of the dingy office.

We'd just sat down and opened the folder when a man in a white coat whisked through, then skidded to a stop. "Petal?"

Petal jumped and snapped the folder closed. "Oh, hi, Dr. Melrose."

The doctor was a tall, morbidly thin man, probably in his fifties, with military-short, white hair and thick glasses. He approached, a steaming cup of coffee in hand, and leaned down to speak softly to Petal. "Dear God, is it true? Did they really arrest you?"

"I'm afraid so."

Apparently Petal was more popular here than at the police station. She had at least two allies in the morgue.

Dr. Melrose swung his lean frame into the chair on the other side of Petal from me. "Damn. The D.A.'s office didn't waste any time, either. The body was found, what, four days ago?"

Petal nodded.

"I'll bet the D.A. is salivating at the thought of pinning something on Petal Ingalls. Jesus, Petal, what are you involved in?"

"Nothing! The charge is ludicrous. I barely knew the woman. That's why I'm here. The sooner I can find something to clear me, the sooner I can get the charges dropped."

And file a lawsuit for false arrest, I mentally added. Pity the poor district attorney when that happened.

"You got a copy of the autopsy?" Dr. Melrose tapped his foot and frowned.

Petal looked uneasy. She'd promised Ike, but she obviously didn't want to lie. "Yes," she finally admitted. "I'm planning to file a motion for discovery, but—"

"It's all right with me. I don't see any need for formality between us. I know you'll do the appropriate paperwork. What do you think?"

"I haven't really looked at it yet."

As Petal and Dr. Melrose chatted, the door opened and a gurney came through bearing a form covered head to toe with a sheet. Without meaning to, I clutched Petal's arm.

"Is that ..."

"Incoming!" the orderly pushing the gurney announced.

"I thought you said there wouldn't be any bodies!" I hissed.

Petal seemed unconcerned. "Oh, just close your eyes. It'll be gone in a minute."

I couldn't close my eyes or look away. The corpse's hand had slid from beneath the sheet, hanging limply. What looked like a class ring encircled the ring finger, and a smear of dark red spread across the back of the hand.

Good God. I'd gone my whole life without ever seeing a dead body. Now I'd seen two in the span of five days.

I averted my gaze, but then I found myself staring at a series of graphic color photos in Petal's hand, part of the autopsy report. I snapped my eyes closed and took a deep breath.

"Do you want to take a look at her yourself?" Dr. Melrose was saying. "I was getting ready to pull her out again. The D.A.'s office has requested some additional toxicity tests. The indentation in the skull is an unusual shape, and I don't believe the photos do it justice."

"Sure, I'd like to get your personal observations," Petal said. "Sometimes a dry report doesn't convey everything."

Petal stood, and the two of them started toward a door on the far side of the counter, apparently forgetting my existence. They walked past the body, which was still lying there on its gurney while the orderly and Ike did some sort of paperwork.

I could follow Petal and Dr. Death, or I could stay there with the mysterious body. When the body made a noise like it was breathing, my heart tried to leap up my throat.

I must have made some sound of distress, because Ike and the orderly turned to stare. Then they both burst into hysterical laughter. "Better check that one again," Ike said to the orderly. "Some doctor must've jumped the gun."

I decided to take my chances with Petal and Dr. Death. Yes, they were going to have a look at Ruby. But I was sure I could find a place to wait while they attended to their grisly task.

I was wrong. When I caught up with them, they were entering a large room with a sloped concrete floor with drains. Not a comforting sight. Several long, stainless steel tables lined the room—mercifully empty.

"Uh-uh," I said, balking at the entrance. "No more dead people."

"Don't be so squeamish," Petal said. "You have very keen powers of observation. You might see something everyone else has missed." She seemed awfully glib when compared to that semi-hysterical woman who'd run headlong out of the woods in Seagoville. But this was different, I guess. There was control here, protocol, and safety. Apparently this wasn't the first time she'd been near an autopsy. I guess her work required that sort of attention to detail.

"It's not so bad, really," Dr. Melrose said in a soothing voice. "As old as these remains are, there's no blood, nothing more gruesome than some old bones. More like ... an archeological find than a body."

It offended me that anyone would think of Ruby as nothing but a pile of old bones. But I had to remind myself that this man saw dozens of bodies every week. He was bound to be deadened to the emotional assault I was feeling.

"Have we met?" Dr. Melrose asked.

"I'm so sorry," Petal said. "Where are my manners? Dr. Melrose, this is my sister, Gypsy Larabee."

He shook my hands and I tried real hard not to grimace. Surely he wore gloves.

We murmured pleasantries, and before I knew it I was following them into the brightly lit room where the smell of disinfectant was enough to knock over a 300-pound linebacker. An assistant wheeled a cart in from another door, on which was an impossibly small bag. The assistant and Dr. Melrose gently lifted it and deposited it onto the stainless steel table, and the orderly departed.

The doc found surgical masks for all three of us. Then he donned a pair of plastic gloves and opened the zipper.

The smell of death was incredible. Sickly sweet and muskily pungent all at the same time, it immediately overpowered the Pine-Sol smell. The mask filtered it some, but not enough. My eyes watered, and I thought I was going to gag.

Dr. Melrose went about his grisly work, collecting tissue samples from various desiccated organs and depositing them in test tubes. All the while he kept up a steady monologue about the body's condition.

"I'm reasonably certain she died immediately after the blow to her head," he said. "It knocked a good-sized hole in her skull. Probably impacted the cerebellum, rendering her instantly unconscious if not dead. A relatively pleasant way to die."

"Any speculation as to the murder weapon?" Petal asked.

"The old 'blunt instrument.' In other words, not a clue. The hole in her skull was round, about the size of a golf-ball." The two of them bent close to inspect poor Ruby's head. I hung back.

"What's that shiny thing?" Petal asked.

"What?" Dr. Melrose sounded suddenly alert. "What shiny thing?"

"It looks like a sliver of glass or something. Stuck in her hair."

Dr. Melrose produced a magnifying glass and examined the corpse's head with painstaking thoroughness. "Well, I'll be damned. How'd I miss that the first time?" With a pair of tweezers, he extracted the minuscule piece of glass, or whatever it was, from its hiding place and put it in a small plastic bottle.

"So maybe she was hit with a bottle?" Petal hypothesized.

Melrose shook his head. "Unlikely. I've seen those types of wounds before, and there would be a lot more glass. I'll turn it over to the lab and let you know."

"Okay, thanks. Do you think a woman could have delivered the fatal blow?" Petal asked.

He sighed. "Absolutely. With a heavy enough club, even a child can kill."

"There goes that defense." Petal sighed, too.

I just took deep breaths. I was having hot and cold flashes, and a thin sheen of sweat had broken out on my forehead. "Can we leave now?" I said.

"I still have to read the report," Petal reminded me.

"Take it with you," Melrose said. "But if you tell anyone I gave it to you early, you'll never get another favor."

Petal yanked off her mask and smiled. "It'll be our secret."

I didn't wait for the flirtation to play itself out. I bolted for the door. I needed to find a restroom, and fast. Unfortunately, I didn't know where one was. In the middle of the hallway leading to the outer office, I heaved my cookies.

I didn't eat breakfast from Edna's again for weeks.

CHAPTER TWELVE

Petal's indictment was Monday morning. Since I had no clothes appropriate for courtwear, I borrowed something from Petal, a pale green suit that made my skin look a pasty avocado. Plus it was too snug and too short, and the matching size sixes pinched my size-seven feet something fierce.

"This thing won't last long, I promise," Petal assured me. She wore somber gray. She'd toned down her frosted hair with a light brown rinse, and her artfully applied make-up made it look as if she wore no make-up at all. She looked pale and a little tired, which was exactly the desired effect.

The courtroom in the Crowley Courts Building downtown was already a zoo when we arrived. Reporters trolled among the observers like sharks in a school of salmon, searching for someone with a personal knowledge or connection with the crime or its participants. A knot of reporters surrounded a lone, middle-aged black woman in a black rayon Sunday dress.

"Probably Ruby's sister, Selma," I whispered. The poor woman looked like she hadn't slept in days, which she probably hadn't, and her shoes didn't match. Her light brown wig rode slightly askew.

The reporters were sticking microphones in her face, and the bright television lights caused her to squint and hold up a hand to shield her face.

I wanted to grab those media hyenas by their collars and pull them off of her. Petal, sensing my intention, squeezed my arm. "Don't," she said. "You'll just bring them to us, and I can't take it right now."

As one, the reporters turned and stared at us. Maybe Petal's hair threw them off for a moment, but they didn't immediately engulf us. In fact, Petal managed to make her way unmolested into the courtroom and to the defendant's table at the front.

I found a seat in the back and tried to be inconspicuous.

Cullen was there, more rumpled than ever and looking like he hadn't slept much. I actually found him appealing in his more vulnerable moments. He seemed to need a woman in his life to function at his best. Fortunately, those vulnerable moments were few and far between.

"All rise." A skinny woman bailiff introduced the judge, The Honorable James Esterbrook, an austere but attractive young man with full lips and razor-sharp cheekbones. He didn't look friendly. He hardly even glanced at Petal, which made me wonder if he might be gay.

That would be bad. While a gay man might admire Petal's fashion sense or her hairstyle, she wouldn't be able to work her charms on one. There went the sympathy vote.

A warm body squeezed onto the bench next to me in a space that wasn't large enough for a child. I was about to express my irritation at the lout's rudeness, but the reprimand died on my lips.

Ramone.

"Hiya, Gypsy," he whispered without looking at me. I didn't look at him, either. But I could smell him, and feel his warmth radiating next to me. The senses combined to transport me back in time to his apartment, dinner, wine, roaming hands .... My abdomen tingled while an invisible fist squeezed my gut.

"I was going to call you, swear to God," I whispered back. "Soon as things settled down."

"The TV stations scooped us," he said in reply.

"That's not my fault. I didn't give them any information."

"You didn't give me any, either."

"Is that why you asked me to dinner?" My voice rose a little, despite my best efforts to contain it. "So you could pump me for publishable tidbits?"

"You know damn well that's not why—"

"No, I don't know," I said, every insecurity about my appeal as a sex goddess bubbling to the surface. "You make it sound like I owe you special access to private information about my sister, just because you fed me some really excellent tuna."

I felt rather than saw him relax. The tension flowed out of him like water out of a rain gutter. I had to wonder at the fact that I could sense his mood so easily. Had I formed a bond with him so quickly? Or were my sporadic psychic abilities kicking in?

"You really liked the tuna?" he asked.

I leaned over and whispered in his ear, "For me, tuna is an aphrodisiac."

He laid his reporter's notebook in his lap and left it there for the next few minutes.

Just as Petal had promised, the proceeding went quickly. She spoke deliberately, respectfully to both the prosecutor and the judge, but with just a hint of tremble in her voice.

Nice touch, I thought. All those hours we used to hide up in the attic of the commune, trying on various theatrical costumes and pretending to be everyone from Theda Barra to Clint Eastwood, had really paid off.

I'd scarcely gotten comfortable in my seat when the judge banged his gavel, declaring the thing was over. Petal had pleaded not guilty, her bail had been reiterated, she'd entered her own name as council of record—which elicited quite a few gasps around the room.

"She's really representing herself?" Ramone asked me as the courtroom got noisy again. "Isn't that kind of risky?"

"She doesn't believe—" I halted. "Are we on or off the record?"

He flashed that devastating smile of his. "On. I'm working today. If you won't talk for the record, I'll find someone who will."

"Okay, I'm on." Petal wouldn't approve, of course, but I intended to choose my words carefully. "Petal believes the charges will be dropped when another, more believable suspect is found."

"Does she have a lead on another suspect?" he asked, raising one skeptical eyebrow.

"Yes. With the help of her husband, who is a police detective and her staunchest supporter, she's conducting her own investigation."

Ramone scribbled furiously. "So who do you think did it?"

"It wouldn't be appropriate to discuss the case at this time," I said, falling back on Petal's standard duck.

Ramone made his eyes go all soft and sad. "For me? You're sure? You know the paper can't print anything about a suspect until he or she's arrested. It would just be background information, so I'd know where to keep looking."

Those eyes. They almost worked. But then I thought about how Cullen and Petal would both ream me if I started flapping my lips.

"I'm sure," I said, standing and grabbing my purse. Petal had refused to let me bring my backpack. She said it would ruin my courtroom-chic. But I'd found the biggest purse in my closet and stuffed it full of pennies, to use as a battering ram in case the press or bystanders got too pushy.

As it turned out, a couple of police officers were there to escort Petal out of the courthouse and into her car. She motioned for me to hurry up.

"Gotta run, Ramone."

"Hey, what happened to my first name?"

"I'll reserve it for when I'm off the record." I actually winked at him— me, Gypsy Larabee, who doesn't have a flirtatious bone in her body, winked at a man. He probably thought I had a tic.

A couple of other reporters wandered over and attempted to get me out in the hallway, where the cameras and microphones could snag me. They weren't even sure who I was, but they'd seen me walk in with the accused.

I demurred. Darryl didn't read much, but he did watch television.

Cullen grabbed my arm as we were hustled out of the courtroom. "The Dixie Duck, thirty minutes," he whispered urgently in my ear.

I didn't say anything to Petal until we were in my Jeep. The parking meter had run out, and I had a ticket on my windshield. It hardly registered on my irritation scale. After dealing with so many crises lately, I'd become numb to everyday annoyances. I reached out my open window, snatched the ticket from under the wiper blade, and stuffed it into the ashtray.

"Well, that was a heap of fun," I said as I started the engine. "Oh, Cullen wants us to meet him at the Dixie Duck in thirty ... no, now it's twenty minutes."

"Good. We need to tell him everything we found out over the weekend."

So Petal thought meeting Cullen was a good thing. That was a switch. "Have you given any more thought to moving back home?"

She gave a disgusted sigh. "My mind's a little distracted right now, okay?"

"I just thought maybe it would look better if you and Cullen appeared to be reconciled. I mean, if this whole business about you and the judge comes out, and Cullen seems to be squarely on your side, it'll make the affair seem like not such a big deal."

"It wasn't an affair, it was a very brief liaison. And it wasn't a big deal." Petal's voice rose in volume and tone with each word.

"All right! Excuse me for trying to help you to not spend the rest of your life in prison. I mean, can you imagine how sallow you'll look in those orange prison uniforms?"

My attempt to lighten the mood fell flatter than a penny on a railroad track. Petal pulled a coral lipstick out of her purse and applied it to her lips, then put on some blush.

"I hate looking like a refugee from a prison camp," she said as she spritzed on perfume. "And, no, this is not for Cullen's benefit, so you can just stop giving me those speculative looks."

The thought hadn't even occurred to me, but now it did.

The Dixie Duck isn't much more than a little shack on the west edge of downtown, not far from the Trinity River. It serves the best fried chicken in town, but it's such a dump that tourists steer clear of it. Which leaves plenty of tables for locals like us.

Unfortunately, the smell of fried chicken did nothing for me at ten-thirty in the morning, especially since my stomach was still unsettled from my humiliation at the morgue.

Cullen sat in a back booth chowing down on today's lunch special, livers and gizzards with a side of cole slaw. With a napkin over my face, I quickly told him what I'd learned from the Haglins about Ruby's noisy fight with Reggie around the time of her disappearance. Petal gave him a rundown of what she'd learned at the morgue from Dr. Melrose—and then couldn't resist telling Cullen about my barfing up scrambled eggs right in the hallway. He chuckled over it.

"Great, funny, ha-ha. Can we leave now, please?" I pleaded, fearing a repeat of Saturday's gastric performance.

Petal and I both slid off our stools.

"Wait," Cullen said. "I have to warn you all about a couple of other things. The first is that Reggie made bail."

My heart sank. Something else to worry about—being strangled in my sleep.

Petal looked at me, clearly uneasy. "Jeez, Gypsy, maybe we should think about staying in a hotel or something. That guy scares me."

I squared my shoulders and stuck out my chin. "Nobody runs me out of my own house. Cullen, how much does a security system cost?"

"I don't think you'll be staying at your house tonight anyway, Gypsy," Cullen said between licking grease off his fingers. Charming. "There's a search party heading your way."

"A what?" I asked.

Petal looked slightly panicked. "He means a bunch of cops with a warrant and a battering ram."

"There's nothing for you to worry about," Cullen said, then added uneasily, "is there?"

Petal socked him in the arm. "Of course not. Cullen!"

"What I mean is, I know you wouldn't want them pawing through any of your notes—"

"They're all in my briefcase," she said. "The cops won't find anything in the house. It's just that they make such a mess! Gypsy's worked so hard trying to get that house in order, and now they're going to trash it!"

"Define 'trash,'" I said as a series of nightmarish scenes flashed through my mind, combining every movie I'd seen about police abuse.

"Is the order for the whole house, or just my room?" Petal asked.

"The whole house is of critical interest, both because you live there and because Ruby might have been killed there."

A chill ran up my spine. "Why do they think that?"

"Think about it, Gypsy. Ruby's body clearly was moved after her death. At least, that's what the M.E. thinks. Where's the most logical place for the murderer to do the deed? The most private place?"

"No," I said, shaking my head vehemently. I'd given up on the napkin over my face. "I'd know if somebody was murdered in my house."

"Unless the murderer cleaned up afterward," Petal said.

Cullen took a sip of his Coke. "You'll know soon enough. The evidence team has tests they can do to detect even the smallest particle of blood."

"What else are they looking for, besides blood?" Petal asked Cullen. They went on talking, like the thought of my house with blood all over it didn't disturb them in the least. If it was true, I wouldn't be able to stay there another night. Not that I believe in ghosts ...

"Anything," Cullen said. "Murder weapons, incriminating notes, blood-stained clothes."

"Like I'd be stupid enough to keep that stuff around."

Cullen and I both looked at her sharply.

"If I were a murderer," she added hastily, "which I'm not. Would you guys cut it out? It gives me the creeps that you think, even for a split second, that I could bludgeon some poor woman to death."

I shook my head. "Sorry, Pet. Look, Cullen, the cops won't find anything like that," I said in a huff. "We've examined everything in the house. I'm sure they'll take a quick look around, realize there's nothing interesting, and leave."

Petal and Cullen both looked at me, pity in their eyes. "You really have no idea, do you?" Cullen said. "I'll make up a spare bedroom."

Petal gave him a look that could peel paint.

He held up his hand in defense. "Okay, okay, two spare bedrooms. Just temporary, Pet, if that's the way you want it."

Petal closed her eyes and scrunched her face all up, obviously struggling for control. "I can't think about us 'til I'm off the hook for this murder thing. There's only so much a person can handle at one time!"

Her emotional outburst concerned me. She was normally such a controlled person. Even the angry tirades and breaking of glass directed toward Cullen had been carefully calculated for maximum effect. This was real.

I put my arm around her. "You're completely right. First we make the murder charge go away. We'll all put a hundred percent of our energies into that."

We left right after that, and I was unbelievably grateful to be breathing car exhaust instead of grease and burning bird flesh. "What did Cullen mean about the spare rooms?"

"You'll see," she said with a grimace.

I expected the worst when I arrived home, and I got it. First there were Haglin and his troops, over a dozen strong today. The timbre of the picket signs had changed too. In addition to the "kill the witch" sentiments were numerous slogans impolitely condemning me for harboring a murderer.

Then there were the TV crews. They had the temerity to trespass right in my front yard.

Then there was the yellow crime-scene tape encircling the Purple Palace, making it look like a gaily wrapped birthday package. A fireplug of a man with a military-short haircut stood guard on my porch. Behind him, I could see that my front door had been splintered, the beveled glass panes shattered into thousands of shards.

I climbed out of the car, shoved a reporter out of my way with a well-aimed purse, and stomped up to the guard. "You did not have to break down my front door!" I screamed. "I would have let you in! Do you know how much those beveled panes cost? The city is going to have to pay for that!"

"No, they won't," Petal said. She'd come up behind me. "Search warrants give cops the right to run over the damn house with a bulldozer if they want, and they don't have to reimburse you for a dime of it."

Texas Fiduciary Savings wouldn't be pleased about this.

I tried to walk around the guard, but he grabbed my arm. "No one goes in."

"I live here! How long are you going to make me stand out here?"

"It'll take all day, and maybe tomorrow, too, to go through everything. You'll have to make arrangements to stay elsewhere."

I was dumbfounded. Were they ripping up Ruby's sofa cushions, peeling back what was left of the wallpaper? "I need to get inside," I said weakly.

"She needs her medication," Petal added.

Oh, great. The mini-cams were rolling. Now everyone watching the news would think I was on anti-psychotic drugs.

Conscious of the cameras, the guard turned and yelled into the house. "Hey, Ray. The resident is here."

An impossibly young-looking man with a yellow crime-scene investigator's jacket appeared at the doorway. "Oh. Hello."

"Yeah, hi," Petal said. "Look, I know you have a job to do, and we're going to have to stay the night someplace else, but can we at least get some clean underwear and our toothbrushes?"

Resignedly he nodded and motioned for us to come inside. I used my key to open the useless front door, and walked with as much dignity as I could into what had once been my safe haven.

Three steps in, I screamed. My living room. My beautiful renovated living room, my oasis of sanity. It looked like an army had marched through it. A dirty army. Black fingerprint powder was all over everything, including my freshly painted walls. My grandmother's china teapot lay in a million pieces on the floor. Ruby's hand-hooked rugs had dirty footprints all over them.

I walked to the teapot and stared down at it, tears pushing at the back of my eyes, then looked up at the yellow-jacket man. "Was this really necessary?"

"Er, that was an accident," he said. "We'll pay for the breakage."

"You heard him, Pet. You're a witness."

She took my arm. "Come on. Let's just get our stuff and leave them to their pillaging."

Yellow Jacket escorted us upstairs. The rest of the house, at least the parts I could see, looked pretty much like we'd left them. I figured the brutes hadn't gotten around to those rooms yet. I could hear someone banging around in the kitchen, though. It sounded like they were turning drawers upside down and dumping silverware onto the floor. Thank goodness I'd moved my various stashes of cash from the kitchen to my sock drawer.

In a daze, I haphazardly gathered some comfortable clothes, a sleep shirt, a few toiletries, one particular pair of socks bulging with quarters and one-dollar bills, and dumped them into one of Petal's mauve suitcases. I was acutely aware of every noise I heard, and I felt thoroughly violated and still very close to tears.

Yellow Jacket watched every move I made—making sure I didn't try to dispose of evidence, I guess. He personally inspected the suitcase and all its contents. Then, apparently satisfied I wasn't smuggling a murder weapon or bloodstained clothes, he made me sit at the top of the staircase while he watched Petal do her packing.

She finished quickly, then came up behind me and nudged me in the back with her knee, jolting me out of my brood. "Try not to think about it," she said. "It's just stuff. We're alive, we have our health, and some of us have our freedom." Her pointed comment made me realize I was being foolish. Things could be replaced, and, heck, most of the stuff here wasn't even mine. Walls and rugs could be cleaned. The important thing to focus on was proving Petal didn't kill Ruby.

I talked Yellow Jacket into letting me water my drooping rose bush, more to irritate him than anything. At this point, dead plants were the least of my worries.

As I turned off the hose, I heard a screech from Petal, who had been sitting on the porch waiting for me to finish. Now she leaned over the porch railing. "Stop it! Stop it!" she cried. "I have a key. What are you doing, you imbeciles? Do you know how much that car cost?"

Yellow Jacket and I ran over to see what was going on. Two cops, a man and a woman, stood in the driveway by Petal's Jag and looked up at her sheepishly. They'd just finished punching out the door lock on the passenger side.

Petal turned and spoke to me. "What are the odds my insurance covers this?"

CHAPTER THIRTEEN

Cullen wasn't home when we got to The Castle, but Petal was able to gain entry with the numeric keypad. He'd apparently given her the new code.

She'd wanted to stay in a hotel, but I nixed that idea. except for the few dollars rolled up in my socks, I was broke again. I'd dutifully put 80 percent of the yard-sale proceeds in the bank to turn over to Texas Fiduciary Savings, and the rest of my meager cash reserves had gone for groceries and a car payment. I had no income at all due to the suspension of my psychic readings, and I didn't know when or if I'd be in business again.

Petal wasn't in much better shape. She had no job, no savings, and her credit cards also were charged to the limit—a condition that had nothing to do with Cullen, as she'd first told me. Accepting a free roof over our heads sounded like a plan to me.

"He better not even think this means I'm moving back," Petal grumbled as we lugged our suitcases upstairs.

"Anybody ever tell you you're stubborn?" I shot back. "If you don't stake a fresh claim to the man, some other woman is going to snatch him out from under your nose."

"Like who? You?"

I hadn't specifically been thinking of me. The idea of taking over my sister's discarded husband was distasteful in the extreme. But the fact that Petal thought it was such an impossibility really pissed me off.

"Why not me? Once upon a time, Cullen and I were pretty hot."

We'd reached the top of the stairs. She turned abruptly and slapped me. A split second later, her face reflecting the horror at what she'd done, she fled down the hall and disappeared into the guest bedroom, sobbing.

I just stood there, in shock, the left side of my face stinging. I'd been trying to needle her, not enrage her. It wasn't the first time she'd ever hit me. When we were kids, her physical assaults were a fairly regular occurrence. Though I was older by a couple of years, she'd always been tougher and meaner. But she hadn't actually struck me in anger since junior high.

I guess I'd underestimated the psychological toll the murder charge was having on her. Granted, my comment had been a tad mean, but let's face it, she'd overreacted.

I wasn't sure which one of us should apologize first. Since she was the one under duress, I decided it would have to be me. And if she didn't immediately apologize back, I'd have to do something really mean, like substitute depilatory for her hair mousse. Rubbing my face, I walked determinedly down the hall and tapped on the guest bedroom door.

"Petal?" I said.

"Go away. Go steal my husband. Get it over with."

"Would you stop feeling sorry for yourself and listen a minute? You know Cullen is crazy in love with you. He's never even looked my way once since he met you." Okay, that was an exaggeration. The chemistry between me and my brother-in-law reared its ugly head every once in a while, but neither Cullen nor I would dream of acting on it.

Silence.

"I'm sorry I teased you. I shouldn't have done it, knowing how upset you are."

I heard some rustling around. Then the door opened a crack. Petal peeked out at me with one red-rimmed eye. "I'm sorry I hit you," she said, sounding completely insincere. But it was the gesture that counted. She wanted to make peace.

"Can I make you some tea?" I asked.

"No. I need to lie down for a while."

"Okay. Where should I put my stuff?"

"The office, across the hall. The sofa pulls out to a bed." She retreated, closing the door firmly.

I found the office. The sofa was already pulled out and made up with sheets. Cullen's domesticity surprised me, but I guess he was trying to earn a few brownie points.

I changed into shorts and wandered downstairs, at loose ends for the first time in weeks. I checked the locks, ever mindful that Darryl could find me here, but then there was nothing for me to do, no boxes to unpack, nothing to clean or paint or repair. I thought I might go grocery shopping, but I found the kitchen to be fully stocked. Cullen's doing again. Starving, I made myself a grilled cheese sandwich and some tomato soup, one of Petal's and my favorite childhood meals.

Calmer by half, I cleaned up and put the dishes away, then headed for the den, where a large-screen TV lured me in. An hour later, Cullen found me channel surfing between a gravelly-voiced oil painter on educational TV and a Gomer Pyle re-run.

Cullen was dressed casually in jeans and a T-shirt, so he couldn't have been on duty. "Hi," he said, taking in the way I'd sprawled on the sofa, making myself perfectly at home. "Where's Petal?"

"Upstairs. Napping."

He frowned. "You're kidding."

It was almost amusing—the idea of hyper, workaholic Petal, never in bed before midnight, now napping like a little old lady.

"She's at the brink, Cullen." I switched off the TV. "She's falling apart."

He sat next to me on the sofa. "You think we ought to find another lawyer to handle her case?"

I shook my head. "She'd never let it happen. We just need to be gentle with her. And for God's sake, don't bug her about reconciling with you."

He shrugged. "I'm beginning to think that isn't going to happen. Maybe there's been too much water under the bridge." He paused and looked away, suddenly finding a loose thread on the sofa intensely fascinating. "Maybe she just doesn't love me anymore."

I felt this tremendous urge to put my arm around him and comfort him. He looked so lost, so sad. Thank God I'm not that stupid. How many extra-marital affairs start when a woman comforts a man having trouble in his marriage?

"She loves you, Cullen. And she'll come back to you. Just give her more time." I wanted to change the subject. "Where've you been?"

"Talking to your neighbors. I passed their statements on to Norton. He's planning to question Reggie."

"That's great!"

"He agrees the district attorney was premature in filing a murder charge. Apparently the D.A. has a real hard-on for Petal. I knew Petal played hard ball, but I had no idea ..."

"She's not the Mother Theresa of defense attorneys, that's for sure. What have you heard about my house? Have those barbarians turned up anything useful?"

"Rumor is, your house is clean as a whistle so far."

"Told you Ruby wasn't killed there."

"'Cause you'd 'feel it'? You and your sensitive psychic vibes?"

"I found Ruby, didn't I?"

Cullen gave me an appraising look. "You and Petal. That's the most damning aspect of this case. Murderers, particularly first-timers, often lead authorities to a body, even after they've taken great pains to conceal it."

"Really?"

"It's a guilt thing. Sometimes they make an anonymous call. And sometimes, they 'discover' it themselves."

"Hoo, boy. Petal was just along for the ride, you know."

"That's not exactly the story you the Seagoville police. You said it was all Petal's idea."

Damn. My efforts to deflect attention from me had probably put a nail in Petal's coffin. "I was trying to avoid another ridiculous newspaper story. I explained that to Norton."

"Is that why you went over to Santiago Ramone's apartment?"

I felt like a Toyota sideswiped by a DART bus. "How did you know about that?"

"Just answer the question." He tossed me a wicked smile, taking some of the sting out of his interrogation.

"My meeting with Ramone has nothing to do with newspaper stories."

"Is he good in bed?"

"Jealous?" I was careful not to directly answer the question.

Any amusement Cullen might have been feeling evaporated in a heartbeat. "Don't talk to him. You could jeopardize—"

"I haven't told him anything!" Well, almost.

"And you won't. Stay away from him, Petal. I mean it. I never should have dealt with him in the first place. The guy's trouble."

"The guy grills a mean tuna steak."

Cullen actually leered at me. "Back in college, all it took was a Whopper and fries."

What on earth had prompted this uncalled-for attack? On the heels of Petal's slap, it was too much for me. I dumped my cup of tea over his head. "Oops. Spilled."

He grabbed my wrist, wrestled the mug out of my grip and set it on the floor before I could do him further violence.

Then he didn't let go. We sat there, both of us breathing hard from temper and adrenaline and God knows what else.

I came to my senses first and stood up, breaking contact. A number of emotions skittered through my psyche—temptation, regret, pity, anger. Anger won out; it seemed safest. "You and Petal must be the stupidest people on earth. You deserve each other. But I want no part of you two tearing each other to pieces. Leave me out of it." I stomped out of the den.

I left the house, got in my car, and drove aimlessly for a long, long time. When I was in danger of running out of gas, I stopped at the Highland Park Village shopping center. I felt protected among the crowd, and I window shopped for all the things I would never be able to afford, even if I wanted them, which I didn't.

When my feet started to hurt, I bought a movie ticket. With a giant bucket of popcorn for dinner, I sat through two showings of a truly terrible Nicholas Cage action movie. When I was sure it was late enough, I went back to the Castle of Matrimonial Discord. All was dark and quiet.

If I'd thought sleep was elusive the night before, I found it impossible now. I lay on the lumpy sofa bed, hating Petal for taking the comfy guest room, hating Cullen for taking out his sexual frustrations on me, and hating myself for still being tempted to sleep with him. What kind of a person was I?

Then again, I hadn't given in. I suppose that meant I had a backbone somewhere.

I fell asleep sometime around five, then got up at seven. My plan was to shower, dress, and leave the house again before I killed someone myself. I thought maybe I'd go to a bookstore and browse, see if I could find any good books on managing a career as a psychic reader-and-advisor.

The house was still quiet when I emerged from my temporary bedroom, comfortably dressed in cut-offs, T-shirt, and a Texas Rangers cap. I wore my glasses instead of contacts, hoping no one would recognize me.

I was about to sneak down the stairs when I heard giggling—distinctly feminine giggling—coming from the master bedroom.

Those sneaks! was my first thought. They'd been laughing and having great sex while I was stewing with insomnia in my lumpy bed, feeling sad and guilty and plotting how I would get them back together. Wondering if I'd had any part in the friction between them. Hoping that maybe I did, then feeling guilty all over again.

My second thought was one of relief. I was tired of walking through a minefield every time I opened my mouth. The three of us needed to work together as a team to clear Petal, and we couldn't do it if we were busy sniping at each other, slapping each other, and pouring tea over one another's heads.

Optimistic, I continued to my car. The early morning cool, such as it was, felt good against my bare legs, and I tried to enjoy it. Another hour and the sun would be beating down on Dallas, bringing on another record temperature. As a rule I like warm weather, but this summer was wearing me down.

I bought gas, then found a used bookstore on nearby Preston Road, but it was closed until ten. So I located a Starbucks instead, bought a tall iced Cafe Mocha, and settled in to read the newspaper.

I used to like the newspaper. I used to really enjoy sneaking outside of Wee Luv during nap time, sipping coffee, and reading about other people's foibles and conflicts. Now I dreaded it, especially knowing what would be on the front page, but I felt a strange compulsion to torture myself.

Santiago's latest story met all of my expectations. My own quote sounded awful, overly defensive and smart-ass—just the way a murderer's sister should sound. I wondered what Cullen would have to say about it. Whatever it was, I probably deserved it.

There was a picture of me, too, alongside ones of Petal, Selma, and a very youthful-looking portrait of Ruby. At least my hair looked pretty good, I thought, searching hard for something to be pleased about.

"It's not a bad likeness, but you're a lot sexier in person."

I jumped and sloshed some of my mocha onto my leg. Darryl sat at the next table, his face hidden behind a comic book. But I couldn't mistake that creepy voice.

My first instinct was to scream, but fortunately I stifled it. We were in a public place. He couldn't hurt me here, and maybe I could talk some sense into him.

"Fancy meeting you here, Darryl," I said resignedly.

He lowered the comic book. "Seems fate just keeps throwing us together. That must mean something."

"Fate had nothing to do with this. You followed me from Petal's house." It amazed me that I hadn't noticed. I guess Petal's crisis had nudged my problems with Darryl to a back burner.

"But I'm guided by fate. We were meant to be together, darlin'."

"No, we weren't. And the sooner you realize that, the easier it will be on both of us. Do you want me to go to court and get another restraining order?"

"There's no law against sitting at the next table having a friendly chat."

"It's called stalking, and there is a law."

"Not in Texas." He flashed a Charles Manson grin.

"Of course Texas has a stalking law." At least, I thought so. "Well, we do have laws against burning down people's houses," I pointed out.

"Gypsy, don't worry. I won't do that again. I've learned my lesson." He flashed sincere, puppy-dog eyes at me. "I don't want to hurt you."

"Should I be comforted? I'm not."

The puppy eyes turned hard as crystal. "I don't want to hurt you." The slight change of emphasis made my skin prickle. I thought about that knife he'd been carrying, and the threats he'd made right in front of Petal. Back in Oklahoma, he hadn't bothered to hide his arson from anyone. He'd waited in his car for the police to arrest him.

He was the type who didn't care if he got caught. He could knife me right here in Starbucks, witnesses be damned.

The cold latte sat like a lump of frozen lead in my stomach. How was I going to get out of this? If I walked out to my car, he could grab me in the parking lot. I didn't see a pay phone where I could call the police—as if the police would even care. They wouldn't care until he'd sent me to the hospital, or worse.

My salvation came in a most unexpected form. I spied a broad set of shoulders in a pristine white T-shirt coming through the door. The man they belonged to didn't spare me a glance, but went to the counter to order.

I jumped out of my chair and practically skipped over to him, resisting the urge to just throw myself in his arms. "Santiago, finally, you're here!"

Both men looked startled, but Ramone slowly smiled. "Miss me, baby?" He slid an arm around my waist.

Darryl threw down the comic book, staring at me with uncomprehending eyes. I guess it had never occurred to him that I might have replaced him. He got up slowly and walked deliberately toward us, though Ramone paid him no mind. He was too busy staring me, pleased but puzzled by my behavior.

I gave Darryl a hard look and bunched up my fists, ready to defend myself if need be. But all he did was reach around me, uncomfortably close, to grab a piece of chocolate candy from the counter. "You'll pay for that, won't you, baby?"

By the time Ramone noticed what was going on, Darryl was halfway out the door. "Who the hell was that?"

I pulled out of his light embrace. "My stalker."

"Aw, hell, Gypsy, I'm sorry. I shielded you as long as I could, but once you were on TV ..." He shrugged.

"It's not your fault. Darryl's been watching my sister's house. He knew I'd show up there eventually."

"Can't Cullen protect you?" Ramone turned to the girl at the counter. "Regular coffee and a biscotti."

"Cullen's been busy. And I suppose it's just coincidence you turned up here, Ramone?"

"So we're back to last names."

"You expect me to get chummy after the cheap shots you took at my sister? Anyway, I'm not supposed to talk to you at all, using first or last names. Orders from on high."

He frowned. "If that's the way you want it. Can you just listen, then?"

"No," I said, afraid I would weaken. He was so damn gorgeous, and I was feeling alienated and unloved by everyone else I knew.

"Then I guess I can't tell you what I found out from Ruby's sister."

I swallowed the bait whole. "Is there more than what's in the paper?" Selma Crane's quotes had been predictable, about how kind Ruby had been, how she'd never hurt anyone, blah blah blah.

He paid for his coffee and cookie, and we sat down at a table. "Some things don't translate well to print," Ramone answered. "Body language, for instance. Evasiveness. An inability to look a reporter in the eye."

I leaned forward, tingling all over. "Selma's lying? About what?"

"What's it worth to you?"

I resisted the urge to leap across the table and grab Ramone by the collar. "Name your price," I said. I figured I could always say no.

He hadn't expected me to be so cooperative, and he wasn't prepared with a demand. He scratched his head and considered his options. I could only imagine the thoughts going on behind his unfocused eyes, but the lazy half-smile didn't instill me with a sense of safety and well-being.

"Okay, I know," he finally said. "My grandma's eighty-fifth birthday party is next month. You can be the entertainment."

That wasn't at all what I'd expected. "You want me to ... what, jump out of a cake or something?"

He slapped his forehead. "No! This is my Nana we're talking about. You do your psychic thing. Read fortunes for all her old-lady friends, my mom, my aunts, my sisters. They'll love it."

"Deal," I said promptly. Sounded easy enough, and maybe even a little bit fun. I'd never thought about Ramone having a family, but I don't suppose he just popped out of a clamshell fully grown. "Now tell me what Selma said. And this better be good."

"Okay, here's the deal. She's protecting her son. She knows something she's not telling the cops."

The hair on the back of my neck stood up. "How do you know?"

"Every time I brought up his name, she clumsily changed the subject."

"How did you know to bring up his name?" I asked.

"Reggie's been arrested twice now for breaking into his aunt's house. There has to be a connection."

"That's what I've thought all along!" I said. "Cullen's finally convinced Detective Norton to question Reggie, but it's taken them long enough to connect the dots."

Ramone shrugged. "Once the police have a suspect, it's hard to get them to change their minds."

"Because then they have to admit they've made a mistake."

"Right. So they're going to need some nudging." He paused, then said, "Talk to Selma. She hates cops, and reporters aren't her favorite people. She might open up to you. Especially if she believes you're psychic, like Ruby. She believes in that stuff."

"I don't think she'll give me the time of day," I said. "I'm the one who I.D.'d her son in a line-up."

"You can at least try."

Cullen would kill me for interfering. He was already going to kill me for talking to Ramone, if he found out, and I could just imagine what he'd have to say about me telling fortunes at Grandma Nana's birthday party.

"Where does Selma live?" I asked.

"The projects over on Carrington, near the river."

"No way." Not even for Petal would I show my pasty face in territory dominated by the Pit Bulls.

"Okay, how about this? Ruby's laid out at the funeral home tomorrow for visitation. You can go and extend your regrets to Selma."

This suggestion had possibilities. "Wait a minute. They're not actually going to view Ruby, are they? I mean, not to be disrespectful, but it would take one talented undertaker to make Ruby's remains suitable for viewing."

"Don't be gross. The casket won't be open."

"Oh. Okay. Maybe I'll go. Just one question for you, though."

"Shoot."

"Why're you trying to get me to do this? Will a photographer stake out the funeral?"

"Did it ever occur to you that I might just want to help? As a ... friend?"

No, I'm ashamed to say, I hadn't thought of that. In my world recently, kind gestures were highly suspect. "If that's the truth, then, thank you."

"And I might want an exclusive after your sister is cleared."

I knew there had to be an angle. Still, he hadn't made the exclusive a part of the deal. He was just hopeful. "I might just give it to you," I said, hiding behind my newspaper.

It was a small price to pay, and not an altogether unpleasant prospect. He hadn't said an exclusive what.

"Oh, and one more thing," I added. "Can you walk me to my car?"

CHAPTER FOURTEEN

"**You** mean I have to spend another night here?" I blurted out a few hours later when Cullen informed me the police weren't done with my house yet.

"Sorry you find my hospitality so repugnant."

Yes, that was the word. Spending time with the lovebirds made me want to puke. Cullen and Petal couldn't keep their hands off each other. They made goo-goo eyes at each other. They actually were smiling. I would not be smiling if I were accused of murder, no matter how thoroughly my husband had ravished me.

"I appreciate your kindness," I said through gritted teeth. "I'd simply like to return to my own domicile and resume my life."

"Oh, you two stop grousing at each other," Petal said, suddenly Miss Congeniality. We were all in the kitchen, and she was munching on celery sticks filled with peanut butter. "We all have to work together. Gypsy, one more day here won't kill you."

"The sofa bed might," I chimed back.

"You can have the guest room tonight," she said, giving Cullen a sultry look. She seemed more cheerful, more relaxed, than she'd been in weeks. I was forced to conclude that it wasn't the murder charge stressing her out as much as the loss of her husband. Now that the marriage crisis was apparently surmounted and conquered, she saw the murder thing as just one more tactical problem to be solved.

I turned my attention to Cullen. "I'm going to Ruby's wake tomorrow," I announced.

I expected a noisy objection, but he just nodded. "Me, too. It's always interesting to see who shows up, and how broken up they appear to be."

Rats. How could I talk to Selma with Cullen shadowing me? Well, I'd worry about that when the time came.

At ten the following morning, Cullen called from work—he was working some very erratic hours—and informed me the cops were done with my house. Ruby's visitation was from six to eight that night. Cullen said he would meet me at six at the Dally Brothers Funeral Home.

I tried to talk Petal into coming home with me, but she claimed she wasn't up to dodging the reporters who surely were staking out my house. The press couldn't bother her here, because the municipality of Highland Park had some rather stringent rules about loitering. Murder charge or no murder charge, no mobile news units could camp out in front of the Castle.

Apparently Petal wasn't up to taking a shower or getting dressed, either. When I left her shortly before noon, she was sitting in her bathrobe at the kitchen table nursing a cup of tea and greedily reading all about herself in the paper.

I'd already read today's story, which had been relegated to the Metropolitan section. It was mostly a rehash.

During the twenty-minute drive home, I steeled myself for what I would find. But for a change, reality didn't live up to my worst nightmare.

For starters, the driveway, yard, and street in front of my house were almost deserted. No cop cars, no reporters with mini-cams, no Reverend Haglin and his picket line. The yellow crime-scene tape was gone. Everything looked pretty normal, except for the plywood nailed across my door, where the beveled glass had once been.

The only exception was a van parked at the curb with a logo on the side: "Dusty's Dusters." It was a cleaning service. Did I dare hope ...?

Sure enough, the inside of the house was crawling with a team of men and women in matching khaki pants and aqua shirts with the "Dusty" logo on the pocket. They were so busy vacuuming, sweeping and dusting that they didn't even notice my entrance.

At random I picked one of the workers, a large woman with a crop of silver hair that stuck straight out from her head, and tapped her on the shoulder. "Excuse me. Who's paying for this?"

She shrugged. "Ask Dusty." She pointed to a scrawny, banty rooster of a guy in the dining room, vacuuming the nasty red shag rug. Tearing out that carpet was next on my list.

I tapped Dusty on the shoulder, and he jumped a foot in the air before switching off the vacuum.

"Who're you?" he asked suspiciously.

"I live here. Who's paying for this?"

He smiled and winked. "A present from your sister and brother-in-law. You know, I might suggest that you use our service once a week. That way things won't get so ... out of hand."

"Yeah, I'm not much of a housekeeper," I said blandly. I walked upstairs and went back to bed, waking up just in time to take a cool shower and dig something out of Petal's closet worthy of a funeral.

The Dally Brothers Funeral Home was not too far from the housing projects where Selma and Reggie lived. Though the surrounding neighborhood was no more blighted than my own, it was scarier because it wasn't familiar. Plus, I hadn't seen a white person in ten minutes, which made me feel conspicuous.

The funeral home's parking lot was full to overflowing, forcing me to park on the street almost two blocks away. I walked briskly down the cracked, weedy sidewalk, my purse-o-pennies clutched tightly in my hand, ready for action. But my fears were unfounded. I only passed one person, a young woman who nodded pleasantly at me.

Bigoted paranoid, I lectured myself.

A tall black man in a somber suit greeted me and directed me to the Greenleaf Room, which housed Ruby's remains. It was very nearly full, of people and plants. The aptly named space reminded me of the rain forest exhibit at the zoo, minus the chattering parrots. As I eased into the room and searched for an inconspicuous place to sit, I spotted Selma Crane, wearing the same dress she'd worn to court, with the addition of a straw hat festooned with purple flowers. She sat on the front row, and next to her was an aged woman I guessed was her and Ruby's mother. They held hands.

There was no sign of Reggie, the disrespectful little shit.

Cullen was there, as promised, along with Clay Norton. I would have had to climb over too many people to sit next to them?-not that I even wanted to—so I found a chair close to the door and parked myself.

I nearly choked when I recognized the Haglins, sitting close to the front. Those hypocrites! Maybe they were trying to assuage their guilt over speaking so ill of Ruby, treating her so shabbily. Or maybe they were just trying to get a little more publicity. They didn't see me, and I prayed they wouldn't. I wasn't in the mood.

Ruby's plain, dark wood casket rested at the front of the room. It seemed oversized to me, and I caught myself thinking that her poor bones would rattle around in such a large receptacle. Did they pack her up with some kind of padding? I wondered morbidly.

The service was short, but intense. A black preacher stood up in front of the group and pitched a little fire and brimstone. Some of the women started wailing; a baby cried, an older child fussed. A man who identified himself as Ruby's cousin read a brief poem.

Then it was over, and the mourners started milling around, offering condolences to the family. I waved to Cullen and walked out the door, but I didn't leave. I hid out in the ladies' room for a few minutes, hoping he and Norton would scram so I could carry out my plan away from their prying eyes.

It worked. The crowd was thinning when I returned to the Greenleaf Room. The cops were gone, and Ruby sat alone in her chair, pensive.

I slipped into the chair next to hers. "Excuse me, Mrs. Crane?"

She slid her glasses up her nose and peered at me. "Yes?"

"I'm Gypsy Larabee. I wanted to extend my condolences."

"Why, thank you, child. And how did you know Ruby?" she asked, but before I could answer, the light of recognition came into her eye. "Oh, landsakes. You're the one found her."

"Yes, ma'am."

She lowered her voice. "You're the sister of that lawyer gal done been arrested." She tipped her head back to study me more thoroughly. "I saw you on T.V. You got the second sight, just like Ruby."

I nodded. Selma didn't seem too affronted by my presence, but neither was she welcoming.

"I'd like to speak with you privately, if I may," I said.

"What about?"

"About Ruby. I ... I never met her when she was alive, but since I'm living in her house and everything, I sort of feel like I know her."

Selma's eyes grew round, and she grabbed my hand. "You come with me," she said, abruptly standing and dragging me with her.

She led me out of the Greenleaf Room and into a dim alcove, away from everyone's view. I would have been a little bit afraid, except Selma was such a fragile-looking woman, I didn't believe she could hurt me.

"Ruby always said she'd come back as a shade," Selma said, sounding both afraid and excited as we sat on a dusty window seat next to a fake window illuminated by fluorescent tubes. "You've got the second sight. Can you talk to folks in the spirit world?"

"I, um ..."

"It makes sense for Ruby to haint that old house. She lived there a long time, and she was mighty proud of it."

"Her presence in the house is very strong," I said, which wasn't a lie. Her personality came through every time I opened a closet or box. The scent of Cashmere Bouquet was in every dresser drawer.

"Then she can tell you! She can tell you what happened."

"It's, um, not really that clear for me," I hedged. "I'm still learning how to use the, um, second sight. I'm sure I'm nowhere near as good as Ruby was. But one thing is very, very clear. My sister did not kill Ruby."

Selma bit her lip and looked down. "No. I never believed that, either." When she looked up, her eyes were teary. "But it couldn't be my baby, neither."

"Reggie?" I barely breathed the name.

"That police officer came to the door just before the funeral, looking for my baby. Reggie done seen him coming and high-tailed it up to the attic, and Lord forgive me, I lied to that policeman and said I hadn't seen Reggie all day."

"What else could you do?" I said soothingly. "A mother has to protect her son. But ... Reggie should come forward and talk to the police. If he cooperates ..."

Selma shook her head, causing the flowers on her hat to wiggle violently. "The police, they wouldn't treat him fair. A young black man, got a gang tattoo on his arm. They'd be lethal injecting him before he could spit."

She was exaggerating, but I couldn't blame her for her caution. A black gang members did make an easy target for the police when they were looking for a murderer.

"These days it's hard to find someone guilty of murder without hard evidence," I said with only a tad more certainty than I felt. "If he's innocent, they won't convict him."

That was a very big "if" hanging between us.

"He is innocent," Selma insisted. "He's done some bad things, used drugs, had a few brushes with the law, but there's no way my baby could kill. Deep down he's sweet. A sweet boy."

Reggie hadn't seemed too terribly sweet when he was tearing up my yard sale, but I let the observation remain unspoken. Instead I asked, "Do you know what Reggie was looking for when he broke into Ruby's house?"

"Now, he ain't been convicted—"

"I saw him with my own eyes, Mrs. Crane," I said gently. "I identified him in a photo line-up." I figured I better get that out in the open.

She narrowed her eyes at me. "What are you really here for?" she asked, suspicion dripping from every word. "I think you'd like to see Ruby's murder pinned on my Reggie."

"I'm only after the truth," I said diplomatically. "If Reggie didn't kill Ruby, and my sister didn't, then let's work together to find out who did."

Selma brief fire of anger sputtered. "I'd like nothing better. If I tell you some things, do you promise not to tell the police?"

I swallowed hard and nodded, hoping I could keep the promise. Selma seemed like a nice woman. Clearly she loved her son, and she'd tried to raise him right. I found myself liking her, and almost found myself hoping Reggie was innocent.

"There was something going on with Reggie and Ruby," Selma said in a hushed voice. She kept a nervous lookout for eavesdroppers. "Ruby and Reggie, they've always been close. Then, for a few weeks last spring, they was acting funny. Sort of secret-like. Ruby would come over, and the two of them would go off together in another room and whisper and even giggle sometimes.

"Also, Ruby was acting funny in other ways. She'd quit her job, for one thing. And she was talking about moving away. See, she had some money problems."

So I'd heard.

"But then she and Reggie had a falling-out."

"How so?" I asked breathlessly.

"They had a big fight. Reggie was hyped up or strung out on something, God knows what. He went over to her house and raised Cain. From the way Ruby told it, he was throwin' things, cursing, acting right crazy."

That would be the blow-up the Haglins had told me about.

"After he left," Selma continued, "Ruby called to complain about it, only she never said what they was fighting about."

My heart sank into my shoes. If Selma was telling the truth, Ruby had been alive and well when Reggie left her house.

"As soon as that boy got home, I gave him what-for. 'Your Aunt Ruby been nothin' but kind to you,' I says to him. 'She bought you clothes, she took you out for ice cream, and since she got no chilin' of her own, she named you in her will!' I says, 'You got no business disrespecting your Aunt Ruby.' Then I made him go over right then and apologize."

"And did he?" I asked as hope blossomed again. He'd gone back. And he was the beneficiary of her will, though by hiding her body he wouldn't have been in a position to cash in.

"He drove off, and he didn't come back 'til morning. He told me he and Ruby made up, and he slept on her couch. He did that sometimes. I didn't think much more about it."

"Until she turned up missing."

Selma shook her head. "You got to believe me, Ms. Larabee. My baby is no killer. But if the police find out he had a big fight with her—"

"They already know," I said. "One of Ruby's neighbors told them all about it. That's why they want to question him."

Selma's face crumpled. "It looks so bad," she said. "It just looks so bad."

I had to agree. "Talk to Reggie," I pleaded. "Convince him to talk to the police. If he didn't do it, maybe he can help find the real murderer. But if he runs, that just makes him look guilty."

"You're right. You're right." She took my hand. "Couldn't you try to talk to Ruby?"

"I'll try," I said. What could it hurt?

By the time I left Dally Brothers, it was dark, deserted, and a whole lot creepier. On my way to the Jeep, I passed a wino and three gangish-looking teenagers with their girlfriends, all of whom looked straight through me when I gave a polite nod.

I was unbearably relieved when I reached the relative safety of my car. I climbed behind the wheel, slammed the door, locked it, and took a deep breath.

Fraidy cat, I scolded myself.

As I stuck the key in the ignition and twisted, a pair of warm hands fitted themselves around my neck.

I was too scared to scream. Nothing came out. "Ramone?" I squeaked hopefully.

"Wrong," a thoroughly unfamiliar voice said. Certainly not Darryl. Young, black, but not Reggie, either. Jeez, for someone who tried to mind her own business, I had a lot of people gunning for me.

From the corner of my eye I could see my assailant's dark-skinned forearm, complete with a bulldog tattoo.

CHAPTER FIFTEEN

I don't think I'd ever really tasted fear until that moment. I broke out in an instant sweat, but my skin felt cold. I couldn't seem to breathe. My vision blurred, and the guy hadn't even squeezed my throat. Yet.

"What can I do for you?" I asked, trying not to sound like I was about to pee in my pants. "I don't have any money, except for some pen—"

"I don't want money." He shook me and tightened his grip around my neck. "What's money without freedom?"

I said nothing, figuring he'd get around to making a point sooner or later. Since there was no weapon being pointed at me, I hoped that meant my friend didn't have a knife or gun.

"Reggie ain't no killer. Leastways he wouldn't kill his own fuckin' flesh and blood."

"Yes, I agree with you."

"Bullshit. You sicced the cops on Reggie. You told 'em he killed his aunt so's you could save that fuckin' skinny-bitch, white-bread sister of yours. And the cops believe you, 'cause you're a witch or somethin'."

"Trust me, the cops do not take my word on anything, and they couldn't care less whether I'm a witch—which I'm not."

"You I.D.'d Reggie in a line-up."

"For a burglary. That was entirely different." But it was evidence that the cops did in fact listen to me, sometimes.

"You found the old lady's body, and now you trying to pin the murder on my bro."

"I'm trying to help my sister," I said. "That's all."

"Then you better come up with another murderer. 'Cause if Reggie goes down, so do you, know what I'm saying?"

Unfortunately I did. "I'd love to find another suspect. Who do you suggest?"

Abruptly he hit me with something hard on the side of my head. I thought about Ruby and wondered if this was how she'd felt when someone struck her. Then I blacked out.

When I woke up, I was alone. The rear left door of my Jeep was open, though, testament to my new friend's hasty flight. I was so damn scared, I didn't bother to get out and shut it, or worry about whether I was fit to drive or not. I turned on the ignition, put the car in gear, and roared away from the curb like a dozen demons from hell were chasing me. The door slammed on its own.

I hit eighty-five on the freeway. I would have welcomed a speeding ticket just for the treat of seeing a cop. But no one stopped me.

I pulled up in front of my house, shaking like it was ten degrees outside, but I couldn't make myself get out of the car and go in my house alone. Whoever my assailant was, he knew where I lived. Reggie knew where I lived. And if, for some reason, they were under the misapprehension that I had enough clout to get Reggie convicted of murder, they might decide to silence me—permanently.

The Pit Bulls had been involved in murders before. I wasn't being paranoid, not this time. I backed out of the driveway and drove back to the Castle. The lovebirds would just have to put up with me for one more night. Tomorrow, I would figure out some way to keep myself safe in my own home.

I was much calmer the next morning—so calm, in fact, that I decided not to tell Cullen about the previous night's assault. I couldn't identify the man because I hadn't seen anything but his arm, and as Cullen had pointed out before, there were dozens and dozens of Pit Bull members in Dallas. Besides, Cullen's involvement might make things worse. In his white-knight mode, he tended to act first and think about consequences second.

Petal wanted to know why I hadn't gone home, of course. I told her I'd left my contact lens paraphernalia at their house.

"Cullen thinks there might be a breakthrough today," Petal said as she washed out the tea kettle while I loaded the dishwasher.

"Really?"

"Apparently Reggie Crane fled from the police when they went to question him. And he wasn't at his aunt's funeral."

"That's not exactly an admission of guilt," I pointed out. "Gang members have plenty of reasons to avoid cops."

"Hey, whose side are you on, anyway?"

"Just playing devil's advocate." As much as I wanted my sister's name cleared, the idea of Reggie being arrested for Ruby's murder scared the ever-lovin' spit out of me. His gang buddy, I was pretty sure, wouldn't take the news well.

What I really wished for was that mythical third suspect. But no one came to mind as particularly likely.

Determined not to let my fear conquer me, I said good-bye to Petal right after breakfast and drove back toward Psychedelic Heights. But I didn't go home. My first stop was the city animal shelter. It didn't make much sense for me to invest in burglar bars or a security system for a house I didn't own. Anyway, those things take forever to install, and I had no way to pay for them.

A dog, on the other hand, was immediate and cheap.

"I want a scary dog," I announced to the attendant. "A pit bull would be nice." And ironic.

"We got all kinds," she said with a shrug. She led me back to the cages.

I'm not crazy about animals. I hadn't grown up with any pets, unless you counted the chickens Mama and Daddy raised, since Petal was allergic to just about anything with fur. But even I couldn't help but feel bad for all those poor dogs in their concrete-and-chain-link runs. Doomed, all doomed. Except for the one I picked.

It was a burdensome responsibility.

I was trying to decide between a chow mix and something that might have been part Doberman pinscher. Both barked ferociously at me when I stopped in front of their cages. I could only hope whichever one I picked wouldn't bite me once it figured out where the food came from.

"Nice dog," I said to the chow. He stopped barking, came to the gate to sniff my knees, then growled.

One of the Animal Control workers opened the cage next to the chow's and put a leash around the neck of the occupant, a huge, shaggy, mangy, nondescript mutt with elephant feet. It was missing an ear, and its face had more scars than Al Capone. It panted and jumped from foot to foot, eager for a walk.

"C'mon, girl," he said glumly.

I had to ask. "Where are you taking her?"

"Um, well, it's her time, if you know what I mean. I got a truck full of new dogs outside—"

"No!"

"I really have to, ma'am. She's been here almost a week, longer than most."

"I'll take her," I said, grabbing her leash. "This is the one I want."

The man appeared skeptical. "Didn't I hear you say you wanted a watch dog?"

"I want this one," I said stubbornly.

Seeing that I was now in control of the leash, the mutt jumped up against me, then down, then spun around in a circle and barked.

"Oh, she's a fierce one, all right."

I persisted, and fifteen minutes later and ten bucks lighter, I was the proud owner of an I-don't-know-what. Ugliest dog alive.

I stuck her in the back of my Jeep, but within two blocks she'd crawled up front to ride next to me. She'd have gotten behind the wheel if I'd let her.

I decided to call her Bernice, after a not-so-well-groomed woman who'd lived at the commune for a couple of years. "Let's get a few things straight, Bernice," I said. "There will be no fleas. No barking, except at burglars and murderers. No chewing. You'll eat the cheapest food I can find, and no complaining about it. Most important, you will not puddle on my newly refinished living room floor. Understand?"

She panted, giving me a king-sized whiff of doggy breath, clueless as to how close to death she'd come.

My house was much friendlier looking in the summer sunshine. Bernice trotted inside, sniffed out every room, then became very interested in the ill-fitting dining-room carpeting. She sniffed and sniffed, then started pawing at it.

"It's probably the only thing in the house that smells worse than you, all right?" I said. "Why don't you come to the back porch and get some food?" I'd stopped at the Fiesta Store on the way home and bought something called Good Boy Dog Food. My mother would have had a fit, wondering why there wasn't any Good Girl Dog Food. I also bought Milkbones, a bowl, a brush, a rawhide chew toy, a ball, a collar and leash, dog shampoo, and flea repellent drops. The guy at the checkout gave me the name of a vet and informed me it would cost over a hundred dollars just for vaccinations and other preventive care. I didn't even know if Bernice was spayed.

So much for cheap. The security system would've been less.

"Bernice!" I yelled, rattling kibbles in her bowl. "Leave that carpet alone and come eat!"

She ignored me and continued her frenzied attack on the carpet. Maybe, I thought, if I left her to her own devices, she would pull it all up for me and save me the trouble.

She managed to get a corner of the rug up and started tugging on it.

"Hey, come on now," I said, "that's really destructive behavior." I wondered how much obedience school would cost, jacking up Bernice's price tag.

Ignoring me, she pulled all the harder until she revealed a second rug underneath the first. It was marred by a huge reddish brown stain.

Pleased with her progress, Bernice pawed at the stain a couple of times, barked to be sure I'd seen it, then lay down on the ruined carpet and guarded her find.

I went over and patted her on the head. "Good girl," I said. "Smart dog." I rewarded her with a Milk bone. It seemed I'd unwittingly adopted a detective dog. She'd found the murder scene.

I went for the phone, intending to call the police, but stopped after two of the required three digits. How quickly we forget! I'd only just gotten my house back from the Crime Scene Neanderthals. If I told them about this, they'd descend on my house with chain saws, and this time there might be nothing left when they finished.

What would be gained by the police learning the location of the murder? Would it help or hurt Petal? Since Reggie and Ruby's argument had occurred here, at the house, pinpointing the murder scene here might make Reggie look even more guilty.

That was something I hesitated to do just now, given that I liked my own life, such as it was, too much. A better situation would be to clear Petal without directly implicating Reggie.

Vowing not to make any snap decisions, I found a hammer and replaced the "clean" rug over the stained one, pounding the tacks back into place. Bernice didn't bother it again, and for a while seemed content to gnaw on a rawhide.

I needed someone to talk to. Cullen and Petal were out of the question. Insane as it was, I called Ramone.

He seemed surprised to hear from me.

"I thought I'd save you the trouble of stalking me yet again," I said. We agreed to meet at Lee Park, not far from Ramone's apartment building, in two hours' time. In the meanwhile, I took Bernice out in the back yard, hosed her down, dowsed her with doggie shampoo, then let her dry in the sun while I brushed her out. She handled it all without complaint, even sitting still while I cut out some of the more stubborn mats from her coat.

When I was finished, she still wouldn't have won any prizes at a dog show. But she smelled better. I took my own shower, threw on shorts and a halter top, and loaded her into the car. Bernice didn't appear to have a mean bone in her body, but she was big, and I wasn't going anywhere without her.

Robert E. Lee Park is a smallish green space in the heart of trendy Oak Lawn. In the sixties and seventies, it was a notorious hippie gathering place. I could remember going there with my parents when I was five or six and lying on a blanket with my coloring book, largely ignored, while the folks and their friends dropped acid and made a big to-do over cute, blond Petal.

The park still looked much the same, but it was a politically correct place to hang out, now—multi-ethnic, families, singles, gay and straight couples.

And dogs. Lots of dogs.

I thought Bernice would enjoy the dogs, but she acted aloof when any of them brushed close. In fact, she hardly ever took her eyes off me. There were no outward signs of affection, but clearly I had become her significant other.

While waiting for Ramone, I let her off the leash and threw her ball, since she didn't seem inclined to stray. She fetched the ball over and over, dropping it proudly in my lap each time. And when I got tired of throwing the ball, she started bringing me sticks.

One minute I was watching two squirrels chase each other in a live oak tree, the next Ramone was sitting beside me in the grass, like he'd been there all along.

"Jeez, you scared me to death," I said by way of greeting.

Before he could respond, Bernice returned, dropped another slimy stick in my lap, and plopped down beside us, panting and watching Ramone carefully.

"Good God, what is that?" he asked.

"My new body guard."

"Do you think you could have found an uglier dog?"

"You're shallow and superficial. She's very smart, and utterly devoted to me." And she really liked sticks.

In answer to that, Bernice picked up the stick she'd just brought me, took it over to Ramone, and dropped it in front of him.

"Traitor," I muttered.

Ramone gave the dog a token pat. "Did you go to the visitation?"

"Yes."

"Talk to Selma?"

"Yes. And you were right. She's protecting Reggie. But she talked to me in confidence. I promised I wouldn't snitch."

"Not even to clear your own sister?"

"Really, Selma only corroborated stuff we already know. Reggie had an argument with his aunt. And some of the things she told me are illuminating, but not helpful to Petal. For instance, Ruby was definitely still alive after the argument."

Santiago's face fell. "Damn."

"But ... this is off the record, right?"

"If it has to be."

I took a deep breath, knowing I was starting down a slippery slope. A promise was a promise. Then again, I'd only promised Selma I wouldn't tell the cops. I hadn't said anything about reporters. A technicality, but I jumped on it.

"Reggie went back to Ruby's house later. His mother sent him to apologize. She claims he was sorry for fighting with Ruby. He didn't come home 'til the next morning. Said he made up with his aunt, then slept on her sofa."

Ramone's eyes narrowed. "I'll bet. Did his mama check for dirt under his fingernails? Does he own a shovel?"

"I couldn't exactly ask that. I'm trying to stay on her good side."

Ramone sighed. "We need something more, something that will really turn the tide."

"Like a murder weapon," I said.

"You can forget that. It's at the bottom of White Rock Lake by now."

"There's something else," I confessed. And I told him about Bernice finding the bloodstain.

Ramone studied the dog with renewed interest. "You did that all by yourself, mutt?"

I beamed and stroked her behind her missing ear. It was the first time, I realized, that I'd actually pet her. She looked at me suspiciously but tolerated the touching.

"You know," Ramone said, "they train police dogs for years to be able to sniff out dead bodies and drugs and stuff. Maybe Bernice is retired from a K-9 unit."

"I think she's just street savvy," I said.

"You should probably tell the police about the blood," he said after a pause. "If not, they'll just assume you're hiding evidence to protect your sister."

I hadn't thought of that. "I'll call Norton as soon as I get home."

"Any chance you'd let my photographer get a quick shot of the stain before—"

"No." That would not endear me to the police.

An awkward silence ensued. "What about us?" Ramone finally asked.

"There's an 'us'?" I was genuinely surprised. Most guys I'd known, including Cullen, had resisted any phrase that smacked of couple-hood for as long as possible.

"There's unfinished business."

"Well, we certainly can't finish it here in the park," I quipped.

His eyes, I swear, smoldered. "You, uh, need any help fixing your broken front door?"

My breath caught in my throat. If I said yes, he was coming over. The door would be an excuse. We'd be in bed. My loins roiled at the thought.

I opened my mouth to answer, but Ramone's beeper cut me off. It played "Twinkle, Twinkle, Little Star." He yanked it off his belt, squeezed a button on it, and cursed colorfully under his breath.

"Something important?"

"Work," he said enigmatically. Then he winked. "You're making a habit of getting off easy."

"Hey, it's not my beeper," I huffed.

He flashed a smile that was special, somehow, just for me, and my heart glowed like a giddy teenager's. Really, I had to stop letting him get to me like that. He was talking "us." If I were remotely ready to be part of an "us," it wouldn't be with someone who unsettled me to where I couldn't think.

Heck, I'd just acquired a dog. One new relationship at a time.

When I returned home, there still was no sign of a picket line. I hoped that meant my zealot neighbors had given up their quest to reform me or get rid of me. Peaceful co-existence. It could work.

Inside, I found a near-hysterically happy phone message from Petal. "Reggie turned up at the police station, willing to cooperate," she said breathlessly. "We're just waiting for word of an arrest. I've got the champagne and caviar chilling."

Personally, I thought Petal was premature in her optimism. Questioning a suspect was a long way from an arrest, and she ought to know that better than me. But maybe she had some inside information she hadn't told me.

I tried to call her back, but there was no answer. Moments later I knew why when my doorbell started a frenzied ringing. Bernice gleefully barked at the intrusion. I saw Petal's Jag through the living room window, so I knew it was okay to open the door.

Petal and Cullen stood on the front porch, Petal with a bottle of champagne, Cullen with a large pizza. The silly smiles on their faces faded the moment they saw the dancing, panting beast by my side.

"Oh, my God," Petal said, "what is that?"

Poor Bernice. Everyone called her a "what" and a "that." "This is Bernice, my watchdog."

Cullen burst out laughing. "I'm sure. A burglar would laugh himself into a stupor."

Bernice flattened her one ear and glared at him in response, but when he fearlessly stuck his hand out to pet her, she immediately started fawning on him.

"Needs work," Petal said, just before she sneezed.

"Uh-oh." I put the dog out in the back yard.

When I returned, Petal was unboxing the pizza in the kitchen and Cullen was uncorking the champagne. "Is it time to celebrate?"

"It is!" Petal replied. "The police got a search warrant and searched Reggie's truck."

"They used Luminol," Cullen said with great significance. When I gave him a blank look, he explained that Luminol was a chemical that could detect even the slightest presence of hemoglobin.

"You spray it on," he said, "then use a black light. Any traces of blood turn up a fluorescent blue. Even if you wash the blood away, say, with a hose, the Luminol will detect the tiniest amount that's left."

"And?" I prodded.

Petal couldn't contain herself. "Reggie's truck glowed like a neon light. At some point in time, that truck was absolutely awash in blood! It's almost certain the D.A.'s office will bring a murder charge—second-degree, given that he was under the influence and in the heat of an argument—and that means they'll have to drop the charge against me!"

I forced a smile. This was the news we'd all been working toward, right? But I felt a little queasy at the thought of Reggie's truck bed full of blood, especially given Bernice's gruesome discovery. Ruby had doubtless bled a great deal on her own rug. Had there been enough blood left to soak the bed of Reggie's pick-up?

I decided it was time to let Cullen and Petal in on my newest secret. But there was no reason I couldn't have a little fun first. This was, after all, a party.

"That's terrific news, Pet—" I cut myself off, then clutched the edge of the table as if I were dizzy. I unfocused my eyes, hoping to give them a faraway look.

"Gypsy?" Petal said. "Something wrong?"

"Blood. It's all this talk about blood. I feel something ..."

"Feel something?" Cullen repeated suspiciously. "As in, mumbo-jumbo?"

"Psychic vibrations," I corrected him.

"Gypsy!" Petal stood abruptly, letting the paper-towel in her lap fall to the floor. "You're not really having a ... a vision, are you?"

Without replying, I headed for the dining room, doing my best zombie imitation.

Cullen and Petal followed. "Gypsy," Petal said, using her scolding voice, "what are you doing?"

"I see blood!" I said melodramatically.

"Where?" Cullen asked, his gaze searching the room as if some of the red stuff might start seeping through the walls.

"Wait, I'm hearing a voice. Ruby? Ruby, is that you?"

Petal grabbed onto the sleeve of Cullen's shirt. "Stop it, you're scaring me! Cullen, make her stop."

Cullen just folded his arms and smirked. "You're even less convincing than that excuse for a dog."

Excuse for a dog? I'd show him! Ignoring his snide comment, I grabbed the corner of carpeting, and with one dramatic gesture I yanked it up, revealing the hideous bloodstain.

In unison, Petal and Cullen dropped their jaws and gasped. It was almost worth the twin looks of horror on their faces to have my house bombarded once again by the evidence squad. They both looked like they wanted to join

Reverend Haglin's picket line—or maybe skip the formalities altogether and burn me at the stake.

I folded my arms and offered them a self-satisfied smile. "That, ladies and gentlemen, is how it's done."

CHAPTER SIXTEEN

Cullen struggled to act non-freaked-out. "You found this earlier," he said.

Petal sighed with relief. "Well, duh."

I burst out laughing. "But I had you going for a minute, didn't I? Actually, Bernice found the blood. She sniffed it out and ripped up the carpet the moment I brought her in the house. Smart, huh?"

"I don't consider a dog that rips up carpet particularly intelligent," Petal said with a haughty sniff. But Cullen was examining the stained carpet. "Looks like someone tried to clean the stain. And when that proved impossible, they nailed down this old scrap. I can't believe the crime scene people didn't catch this!"

"They sure didn't skimp anywhere else," I groused, remembering Grandma's tea pot.

Cullen looked thoughtful. "Hard for me to picture some drugged-up kid going to this much trouble," he murmured.

"Of course he did!" Petal thumped Cullen on the arm. "He would know where his aunt kept the hammer and carpet nails. It's not something I would do. So this should help me. Right?"

"Selma," I said. "Reggie's mother helped him cover up the crime." But even as I mentioned the possibility, it didn't sit right with me. She'd been too earnest in pleading that her son wasn't a killer. If she'd had any part in her own sister's death, I felt certain she would have admitted it and taken all the blame rather than letting her son go to jail.

"So, what are we waiting for?" Petal said. "Let's call Norton." She fetched the cordless phone and handed it to me.

Two hours later, I was pleading with the same annoying pip-squeak in a yellow jacket not to take a chain saw to my wood floors. The blood had seeped all the way through the bottom rug, staining what used to be very nice hardwoods. The price I hoped to get for this house had already dropped, considering a murder had been committed here. Holes in the floor wouldn't inch the price any higher.

"You already wrecked my beveled glass," I reminded him. "And my tea pot. These narrow-planked oak floors are irreplaceable. Take the carpeting, take the padding, but leave??"

My doorbell rang. I went to answer it, but one of the other evidence techs beat me to it. It was Ramone, complete with his bimbette photographer, looking much as he had the day we met. In other words, breathtaking.

"All right, who notified the media?" Yellow Jacket demanded.

I pretended I suddenly had pressing business elsewhere.

"We've had a stake-out on the house," I heard Ramone explain. I would have to figure out how to thank him later for not implicating me. Through two doorways and into the dining room, he took in the situation with one glance. "If we promise not to interfere, can we take pictures of you chain-sawing Ms. Larabee's floor?"

"Ramone!" I objected from the parlor, where I was eavesdropping.

Yellow Jacket suddenly had second thoughts about the chain saw and how heartless it would look on the front page of the Morning News. "Just take a few splinters," he told one of his minions. "If we need larger samples of the blood, we can use what's in the padding."

Now I really needed to thank Ramone. Power of the press, and all that. He and the camera-girl got what they needed quickly enough, then bolted, muttering something about deadlines.

I was lucky the evidence team stayed only two hours instead of two days, this time. They left behind huge gouges in my floor, but they ripped out all of the dining room carpet and took it with them, saving me the trouble. I covered the stained floor with a throw rug, not wanting any more visual reminders of Ruby's murder. As it stood, I wasn't sure I could sleep here tonight.

Just before Yellow Jacket made his final departure, he addressed me. "I notice your picket line is gone," he said. "What happened to 'em?"

I shrugged. "Don't know, don't care. I'm just glad to be rid of them."

Petal, who'd been filing and polishing her nails in the kitchen during most of the rug-ripping ordeal, spoke up. "I might've had something to do with Haglin's disappearance," she said smugly.

I turned. "You got rid of him?" Too late I realized how that sounded. The entire evidence crew froze and stared at Petal. "I mean ..."

"I merely talked to him, pointing out that, should the charges against me be dropped, his blatant reference to me as a murderer could legally be construed as libel. Criminal libel, given its malicious intent. Punishable by fines, possible jail terms ..." She let her voice trail off with delicious possibilities.

I grinned at Petal. "You know, Pet, sometimes I'm really glad you're my sister." It didn't happen all that often, but when Petal did you a favor, she usually did it up right.

Our celebratory pizza, long delayed, was cold by now, not to mention short by three slices. The evidence guys had ripped us off.

"Let's go out," I said, "my treat." I pulled the last of my stash from my backpack, which amounted to about twenty-two bucks. And a purse full of pennies.

"Gypsy," Petal said, concerned, "is that all you have?"

"Now that Haglin's gone, I can do some more psychic readings," I said blithely.

Petal just groaned.

I opened the back door and called for Bernice. She'd collected a generous pile of sticks on the back porch. I dragged her into the house. "Don't let anyone in," I cautioned her before we took off. As if she could understand me. But, you know, she seemed to.

We ate at Tillman's Corner, an old neighborhood bar whose menu had been yuppified to include trendy sandwiches and salads. Cullen kicked in a couple of bucks so we could afford it. Our food had just arrived, and we'd toasted to Petal's impending freedom, when Cullen's beeper went off. It played something by Bach.

I hate beepers. They never should have been invented. Cell phones, either. People ought to be able to enjoy a meal at a restaurant unmolested by technology. But I had a particularly bad feeling about this particular beep. It was from Detective Norton.

Cullen called him back on his cell phone. Petal and I, our food growing cold, listened with trepidation at the one-sided conversation, which mostly consisted of, "Uh-huh. Uh-huh."

Finally Cullen said something interesting. "Would deer blood produce the same results?" Pause. "Can't you get a sample, do DNA testing—" Another pause. "Uh-huh. I see. You don't believe him, do you?"

Whatever answer he'd gotten to that question, Cullen looked relieved. "It ought to be easy enough to blow holes in his story. I lay odds he won't find anyone to corroborate it, except maybe his mother."

He hung up after that, and Petal and I besieged him with questions.

"It's nothing to panic about," Cullen said. "Norton just wanted to give me a heads-up. Reggie claims he went deer hunting with a buddy last winter. They chucked a dead deer in the back of the truck, and it bled all over everything."

"And this is reasonable?" Petal asked.

"Improbable, but possible. Luminol only recognizes blood, not necessarily human blood. And there's not enough blood left in the truck to take a sample so we could find out for sure."

Petal looked crestfallen. "The police won't just take Reggie's word for it, though, right?"

"That's right. Norton thinks it's a crock. So unless Reggie can find someone to corroborate the story, it won't hold much sway with the D.A.'s office."

"Well, that's something," I said. I took a bite of my cold burger, trying to act normal.

"There's something else," Cullen said. "Reggie has volunteered for a polygraph test. Eagerly."

"Oh, dear." Petal took a sip of her iced tea.

"Lie-detector tests aren't admissible in court, right?" I asked.

"No, but if he passes, that'll be enough for Norton to keep an open mind. It might mean a delay in charging Reggie with the crime."

"And a delay in dropping the charges against me," Petal said miserably.

Our celebration had taken on a distinctly funereal tone.

I decided Petal and Cullen deserved some privacy, so I talked myself into spending the night at my own home. It didn't seem so bad, especially with Bernice there, but I made her sleep in my room with me, instructing her to lie on a rug near the door.

In the morning I awoke to find her not only on the bed, but right next to me, her furry brown head sharing my pillow. When I opened my eyes, I found her staring at me with so much disdain that I felt almost guilty for making her get down.

I let her outside, fed her, then headed for the bathtub, wondering what else I could do to ensnare Ruby's murderer. Actively setting out to prove Reggie's guilt sounded like a distinctly unhealthy proposition for me, especially after I got a couple of breather phone calls that marred the enjoyment of my breakfast Pop Tarts. Probably just wrong numbers, but they unnerved me nonetheless.

So I decided to concentrate on proving Petal's innocence. To do that, I would need to get a more accurate picture of the supposed motive— silencing a witness who could nail her during the ethics investigation—then blast holes in it.

The person to talk to, I concluded, was Judge Colter himself. Through his clerk, I made an appointment to speak to him at five-fifteen that afternoon.

I spent the day in blissful non-communication, weeding out a flowerbed. Bernice kept me company, content to snooze on the porch and wake up every so often to chase a squirrel. Sweaty, filthy, but pleased with my progress, I went inside just in time to bathe and dress appropriately to visit the judge. Petal had taken most of her things with her when she'd left the day before, so I was forced to pull something from my own closet. I found a navy skirt and a light blue T-shirt, flat blue sandals, and no hose. It was just too damn hot for stockings. I doubted if I could even tug a pair up my sweaty legs.

By some miracle I found a parking place near the Courts Building and was actually five minutes early for my appointment. Judge Colter's clerk, a young man—Ruby's replacement—showed me into his chambers.

Judge Colter was a nice enough looking man with pale brown, receding hair and wire-rimmed glasses, but nothing to write home about. I found it nearly inconceivable that Petal had cheated on Cullen with this guy. Brad Pitt, maybe, but Donald Colter?

He glanced up when I entered, held up one finger in a "just a sec" gesture, and returned to his paperwork. Finally, having made me wait an uncomfortable amount of time, he tapped the paper edges onto the top of his desk to neaten them, then laid them aside.

"Sorry," he said, sounding not very. "Have a seat, Ms. Larabee. What can I help you with?"

I sat in one of the low, leather-bound chairs before his desk. His chambers were just this side of shabby, but dignified looking. Without preamble, I launched into a monologue that wasn't very well thought out. "My sister's been accused of murder, the police department has torn up my house, a religious nut has been harassing me, the Pit Bulls have sworn out a death threat against me, my ex-boyfriend wants to turn me into Spam, and I'm having a bad hair day."

His brow wrinkled in pseudo concern. "I'm sorry to hear that." He paused, and an awkward silence hung between us for a few moments while I struggled to collect my thoughts. "Do I have a role in all this?"

Now that I was in the judge's chambers, I wasn't quite sure what I was really after. The mission to come here had seemed clear in my mind when I'd started out, but now I found myself tongue-tied. "I want to help my sister," I finally said.

"I'd like to help her too." Judge Colter took his glasses off and began cleaning them with a handkerchief. "I assure you, if I knew anything that would clear Petal, I'd announce it to the world. But the police have questioned me extensively. I've wracked my brains trying to think of any small thing Ruby might have said that would lead me to another suspect, but I can't think of anything. Ruby was a quiet, efficient clerk who led a quiet, ordered life, so far as I knew."

I thought about her house, and decided "ordered" was the last word I would use to describe Ruby. "Did you know about her fortune-telling business?" I asked.

"Not until recently. It was quite a surprise. She seemed much more sensible than that."

I pushed the personal affront aside. Unless he never watched the news or read the paper—and I couldn't believe that about a county judge—he knew

I'd dabbled in fortune-telling, too. "What about her nephew?" I asked. "Did she ever talk about having any problems with him?"

Judge Colter shrugged, and his answer was a bit more clipped than the last one. "Again, I didn't even know she had a nephew. She didn't keep any pictures on her desk, she took no personal phone calls that I knew of."

He expected me to believe Ruby had revealed nothing of her private life to her boss, despite the fact she'd worked for him for several years?

"Ms. Larabee, the police have been over and over this. I assure you they're running a competent investigation. Why don't you let them handle it?"

"Because I can't just sit home and do nothing," I said. "My sister has been falsely accused of first-degree murder. Anyone who knows her knows she could never—" I stopped as it occurred to me what I really wanted to know from Judge Colter. "Do you believe she did it?"

He thought for a moment, then chose his words carefully. "She had a very strong motive. Her entire career was on the line because of this false accusation—"

"It wasn't false," I said. "My sister told me the whole story."

Colter studied me anew, perhaps gauging how dangerous I could be to him. "I wasn't suggesting the affair never happened," he said, his face twisting bitterly. "God knows, once it's been in the paper I could hardly do that. But there was never any suggestion between us that I would grant her judicial favors. That is the false accusation I'm referring to."

"Yes, of course," I said, wanting to prolong the interview since he was being so chatty. "Please go on. So she had a strong motive."

"Petal knew I would never admit the affair, ethical or not. The whole thing would have blown over ... except for Ruby." He shook his head. "I really thought I could trust her. She'd always been the soul of discretion, not a gossipy bone in her. But, I guess the temptation to tell my wife about Petal was just too much."

I didn't dare mention that Ruby wasn't the one who spilled the beans to the vengeful Mrs. Colter. Dear, jealous Cullen had done us all that favor, and poor Ruby had gotten the blame.

"Ruby was the only one who knew about our little impropriety," Colter continued. "Petal saw her as a wild card, an unknown quantity. And an easy target for an ambitious, calculating woman desperate to save her career."

"You sound like a prosecutor making his summation before a jury."

"I'm just trying to illustrate why Petal makes such a good suspect," he said. "But do I believe, on a personal level, that she did it? Do I believe my ex-lover is capable of murder?" He pursed his lips and thought long and hard before he answered. I didn't realize I was holding my breath until he finally answered. "I can't say for sure. She's ambitious to a fault, she can be ruthless, and she has a powerful temper. I don't want to believe it, but I think it's possible."

"Is that what you told the police?"

"I would never lie to the police. I'm sure, though, they don't care a whit for my personal opinion."

Yeah, right. And pigs fart perfume.

I no longer cared whether I pissed him off. He sure as hell didn't do Petal any favors, the bastard. "If my sister had a strong motive for murder, it seems to me you did, too. It must be unethical for a judge to diddle a lawyer in his court."

He didn't rise to the bait, but only smiled. "Double standard. The powers-that-be have a motive of their own for getting rid of Petal Ingalls. She's not exactly popular. I, on the other hand, am extremely well liked. Nobody gives a fig about my sleeping habits. It's politics, my dear." He looked at his watch pointedly. "Now, if you'll excuse me, my wife is expecting me home for dinner."

I left in a huff, disliking Judge Colter far more than I had when I'd entered his chambers. But I'd gotten what I wanted—another suspect to focus on. Colter might be trying to make it look like he had no motive, but he did. Several, in fact. He could have killed Ruby to save his reputation, which was clearly important to him, given his bitterness toward the unfavorable press. He could have done it to protect his lover. And he could have committed murder out of sheer vengeance against the woman whom he believed had ratted to his wife about his sordid little affair.

Plus, he'd known Ruby far more intimately than Petal had. He might know a lot more about her personal life than he let on—including the location of a certain parcel of land in Seagoville.

I wondered if I had a chance in hell of convincing Norton to take a closer look at Colter. If the judge really was as popular as he claimed, going after him would be a political hot potato.

As I rode the elevator down to the first floor, I zoned out, staring at the lighted floor numbers blinking on and off, and thinking of ways to trap the judge. I almost didn't recognize my own sister when she got on.

We both did a double-take.

"Gypsy! What are you doing here?"

Er, I didn't really want to admit I'd been muddying the waters. No telling how Petal would take it. "Paying that parking ticket," I lied through my teeth. "You?"

"Filing that divorce case you referred to me. Life goes on. Oh, Detective Norton's been trying to get hold of you, but he won't tell me why. He called me at home."

We stepped out into the lobby, where people concerned with their own problems, their own personal dramas, ignored us. Apparently my fears of being an unwilling celebrity the rest of my life were overblown. Fame is a fleeting thing.

Petal handed me her phone, and we found a quiet corner where I could call Norton back. I didn't have the number, but Petal showed me how to check her answering machine remotely. More techy stuff I didn't really want to learn.

It took several phone calls to track him down, but I finally located Clay Norton.

"Ms. Larabee," he said with exaggerated politeness. "Can you meet me at the jail?"

This sounded ominous. "You're not going to arrest me, are you?"

He laughed at my expense. "Nothing like that. Reggie Crane's been asking to see you."

"Me? Why?"

"Don't know. But I want to find out."

"I can be there in five minutes," I said, since I was practically across the street from Lew Sterritt. I asked Petal to go with me, but she shuddered at the thought of going anywhere near the jail.

"Just fill me in as soon as you're done," she said. "I'll wait here in the coffee shop. Hey, maybe he wants to confess."

"To me? I'm sure." What he really wanted to do, I guessed, was to issue more threats. But the summons was intriguing enough that I could hardly ignore it. I caught a trolley bus and made it to the jail with a minute to spare.

Norton met me at the entrance and escorted me through a bewildering array of elevators and hallways, slightly familiar since my visit to bail out Petal. The visiting room, however, was new territory. It looked kind of like a line of bank teller windows, with chairs. Norton had me sit in one of the chairs, then used an intercom to summon a guard, I think. Five minutes later, Reggie Crane sat down in the chair across from me. Though a pane of thick glass separated us, the sight of his strong, arrogant face unnerved me.

Pretty quickly, though, I realized this was a very different young man than the one who'd threatened me and torn up my yard sale. This Reggie looked downright cowed. There was no insolent staring. In fact, he didn't make eye contact, at least not at first.

"You came," he said simply. His voice floated to me through a vent in the glass, like the ones in movie theater ticket booths.

"Curiosity overcame me. What can I do for you?"

He didn't answer me right away. Instead he said, "You talked to my mama."

"Yeah."

"She said you got the second sight, that you can talk to Aunt Ruby."

I said nothing, neither confirming nor denying.

"I seen a ghost once," he said, lowering his voice. "I don't mess with the spirits. I don't want to make 'em mad, neither."

"Spirits only want the truth," I said, and I'm ashamed now to admit that I deliberately inserted an otherworldly tremor into my voice. If Reggie was superstitious, I wasn't above using this small peccadillo for my own devices. Maybe his friends were superstitious, too. Maybe, if they feared I'd put a curse on them, they'd leave me alone.

"That's why I called for you. I want to tell you something."

Why me? I wondered.

"Can they hear what we're saying?" he asked, whispering so that I could hardly understand him.

"The spirits?" That I didn't know.

"The guards," he clarified.

"Oh. I don't think so." Norton had told me the visiting rooms had cameras, for security purposes, but that conversations held there were private. Not that I trusted the police.

"Okay," Reggie said, "here's the deal. I was looking for something in Aunt Ruby's house. And I never found it, so unless you threw it out, it's still there."

"What?"

Again, Reggie looked from side to side and whispered. "A lottery ticket. Worth four million dollars."

"Four million!"

"Shhh!"

I grew faint at the thought of that much money. In my house. At the moment, guarded only by a piece of plywood and a dog about as fierce as a parakeet. Unless I'd thrown out the ticket. Oh, but surely I wouldn't have. I'd gone through all of the papers before tossing them. I recalled finding some discarded scratch-off tickets, but even those I'd double-checked to make sure no winners had escaped Ruby's detection.

No wonder Reggie had been so determined to get into the house.

"She was afraid to cash it in," Reggie said. "She owed the government some money. Taxes and fines and stuff. And she owed other people money, too, Visa and Sears and some banks and a casino in Shreveport. She was afraid that if she cashed it, all them creditors would swoop down on her and take it away."

"And she told you about it?" I asked, hardly containing my disbelief. Oh, yeah, if I had a four-million-dollar lottery ticket hidden in my cookie jar, I'd want a member of the Pit Bulls to know about it.

"She didn't just tell me about it. She thought I should be the one to claim it, since I didn't have no debts or taxes or nothing."

"So what went wrong?"

"She changed her mind, that's what," Reggie said, becoming agitated. "She decided she didn't trust me. She was afraid I'd never give her the money once I had it."

Gee, I can't imagine why she was worried about that.

"I never did nothin' to hurt Aunt Ruby, know what I'm sayin'? In fact, me and the homeboys kinda watched over her house. We caught some punk spray painting her garage once and we beat the shit out of him."

How reassuring that must have been for her, I thought.

"Her not trusting me was like a knife to the heart, know what I'm sayin'?"

I nodded. Betrayal was betrayal, and I was familiar with the pain. "Is that what you fought about?"

He dropped his head. "Yeah. I ain't never fought with Aunt Ruby before. But I was hopped up, know what I'm sayin'? I said some things I didn't mean, some things ..." To my amazement, his eyes teared up. "... some things I wish I could take back."

"Have you told the police any of this?" I asked.

"What's the point? If I admit I was within twenty miles of her house, fightin' with her and shit, they'll think I killed her."

"But you didn't."

"I didn't lay a hand on her. She was alive as a body can be when I left her house."

"Your mother said you went back later," I said.

His eyes got a little shifty. "I told Mama I was going there, but I never saw Aunt Ruby again."

"Then how did the blood get in your truck?"

He rolled his eyes. "A deer. It was a deer. Ask my mama if last winter we didn't eat venison for a month."

I decided not to pursue that avenue. Doubtless the police had asked him thousands of questions having to do with his supposed hunting trip with his non-existent friend.

"So why are you telling me this?" I asked.

"'Cause you're my last hope. The police won't lift a finger to clear me. It's too easy to put a black gang member away and move on to the next case."

"They kept investigating after they arrested my sister," I pointed out.

Reggie laughed without mirth. "Only when you and her old man lit a fire under them. You turned 'em on to me."

I was surprised he knew so much about the investigation.

He read my mind. "Yeah, I make it my business to find out about these things," he said. "I can read the papers. I ain't just some stupid, illiterate gangbanger, know what I'm sayin'?"

"You sure acted like one when you tore up my yard sale," I reminded him. If he expected me to do him any favors, he was going to have to acknowledge how tacky he'd been that day.

"Yeah, okay, me and the brothers got a little out of hand. Four million dollars can make you act crazy."

I'd give him that. "Um, Reggie, did you tell any of the 'brothers' about the lottery ticket?"

"No! I just told you I ain't stupid. I didn't tell nobody."

"What about when you were high? Do you ever say or do things you don't remember when you drink, or use drugs?"

His answer was a bit less emphatic. "I wouldn'ta told nobody about that lottery ticket, high or not. I ain't no junkie, you know. I've shot up a few times, but I'm not addicted, know what I'm sayin'? And I don't get crazy like some people."

But I could see the wheels turning. He was thinking back, trying to remember.

The suspect pool just widened to include all of the Pit Bulls. Any one of them might have gone to Ruby's house to intimidate her into giving them the ticket, and, unlike Reggie, they might not have stopped short of violence.

"So you want me to ... what?" I asked.

"Find the truth. Talk to the spirits or anybody you have to, but find out who really killed my Aunt Ruby, and I hope they rot in hell!"

This last was delivered with so much vehemence, I didn't, at that moment, doubt that Reggie was on the level.

"And find that lottery ticket. Use the money to hire me a good lawyer. That turkey of a public defender they gave me don't know his balls from his butt."

The guard returned just then, signaling that our time was up. Norton reappeared, too. I said good-bye to Reggie, telling him I'd do what I could, and left with Norton.

"So, what'd he tell you?" Norton demanded the moment we were alone in the hallway. He was nearly slobbering with curiosity.

"Nothing incriminating," I said, lying through my teeth. If the matter of this lottery ticket came to light, it would provide a sterling motive for murder. Which was why I kept quiet.

"I know you'll find this hard to believe," I said, "but I'm halfway inclined to believe he's innocent."

Norton rolled his eyes. "Great," he muttered, "just great. We don't have enough to charge him," he said to me. "If we have to let him go, the charges to your sister stick."

"I know that," I said, then added carefully, "Maybe one of Reggie's buddies killed Ruby."

"If you can find a Pit Bull with blood all over his vehicle, we'll look into it," he said dryly. "I don't get it. Do you want your sister cleared or not?"

"Of course I want her cleared. But I don't want the wrong person to go to jail."

"Maybe Reggie'll flunk the lie detector test," Norton said, almost to himself.

Somehow, I kinda doubted that would happen. Reggie would never have volunteered to take the test if he thought he was going to flunk.

I left the jail, anxious to return home and find that four-million-dollar scrap of paper. Maybe it wouldn't clear either Petal or Reggie, but it could buy a heckuva good legal representation for either suspect.

CHAPTER SEVENTEEN

When I got back to the Purple Palace, I turned my house upside down. I made a bigger mess than the evidence guys. But, Jeez, four million dollars! I wondered who would legally own the money. The bank, I suppose, or any number of creditors including the U.S. government, but I at least should get my twenty percent of it. That was the deal.

I tried to tell myself I would dutifully share the loot with Selma and Reggie, but I had this sneaking suspicion I was as greedy as the next person and would try to keep as much as possible. Petal's legal defense could get expensive. Even if she remained counsel of record, she would have to hire other lawyers to assist.

I toyed with the idea of not telling the bank.

Then again, before I could face any of these moral dilemmas, I had to find the lottery ticket. And it was nowhere.

Driven by blatant greed, I searched for hours, tidying and throwing things out as I went. The cleaning needed to be done, I argued to myself, trying to justify all the time I was spending on this potentially fruitless search.

I moved to the parlor, followed by Bernice, who'd been watching my progress suspiciously. In this room, a large portion of Ruby's things still awaited me in boxes. After stacking those up in dangerously high towers to get them out of the way, I focused on the bookcase, where I'd put aside some of Ruby's books. She'd obviously been a voracious and eclectic reader, collecting everything from dry history tomes to Harlequin Romances. I'd kept those that didn't sell in the yard sale, figuring I'd trade them in at Half-Price Books one of these days.

I shuddered to think of all the ones I'd already sold. The lottery ticket could have been tucked away in any of those.

I started to reach for a paperback entitled Lady Luck—an apt place to hide a lottery ticket. But I paused when I saw the crystal ball, which I'd displayed on the bookshelf. I'd helped Helen find her husband's life insurance policy. Why couldn't I help myself find a lottery ticket?

I took the crystal ball down, set it on a coffee table, and sat cross-legged on the floor before it. I closed my eyes, took some deep breaths to relax, then opened my eyes and stared into the huge crystal orb. Bernice lay down beside me with her head on her paws, looking worried for my sanity.

"Ruby, if you're here, talk to me," I said aloud, feeling very foolish. But I'd promised both Selma and Reggie I would try.

Nothing.

How was this supposed to work? I wondered. Would a psychic person actually see something inside the glass, or did the ball simply help you to clear your mind so that psychic impressions could enter and be recognized? Would I hear Ruby's voice, or just suddenly know the truth?

The argument was ridiculous, I thought. I wasn't psychic, and the crystal ball held no power. Yet it did feel relaxing, just staring into the glass and letting my mind empty itself. The ceaseless mental chatter slowed to a standstill.

Still no visions, no voices. Darn.

Growing bored, I noticed how the crystal ball inverted and distorted reflections from the room. I picked out bits of color in the reflection, then tried to guess what caused them. The wiggling, bright green came from a tree outside the window blowing in the breeze; that was easy. Something gold and snaky—the chandelier. A bit of bright pink ... that one was harder. I finally had to look up, wondering what I possessed that was bright, hot pink. My eyes went to the bookshelf, where a set of three photo albums were wedged between A History of South Africa and Dr. Ruth's Good Sex. One of them was pink.

On a whim, I went to the shelf, pulled out the pink album, and flipped through it. These were Ruby's photos, the ones I couldn't bear to throw away. Now I knew what to do with them. I'd give them to Selma.

The photos were ones from recent years, judging from clothes and cars. Birthday parties. Ruby and some friends in their Easter dresses and hats, posing before a church. Even an office party of some sort, because there was Judge Colter with his arm around Ruby, and Ruby looking embarrassed.

I turned the page, and my heart beat faster. Before me were several pictures of Reggie. In some he was wearing his gang colors, in others he wasn't. But the picture that both excited and repelled me was one taken in front of Ruby's house. It showed Reggie and an unidentified friend standing in the bed of Reggie's old truck. Both young men sported triumphant grins as they held up their trophy between them—a bloody, dead deer.

The photo was dated in Ruby's careful script, which I'd come to recognize. The date was from last winter.

"I'll be damned," I murmured. The crystal ball hadn't found the lottery ticket for me, but it had certainly led me to a piece of evidence that would go a long way toward getting Reggie out of jail. Petal was going to be furious that I was working so damn hard to clear Reggie, but I could hardly keep the photo a secret.

I decided to give the snapshot to Clay Norton.

I looked at my watch. It was almost six o'clock, and Norton probably would not be at the station. Most detectives, not counting Cullen, worked regular hours. I'd call him in the morning, and tonight I'd break the news to Petal about the photo.

I was just replacing the album on the shelf when the doorbell rang. I jumped. Bernice didn't. She raised her head, looked around, then waited for me to take care of it.

I grabbed her by the collar and dragged her to the front door. "C'mon, you big lump of fur, act like a guard dog."

Reaching the front hall, wishing I had a peephole in the plywood nailed over my door. I opened the door a crack, ready to slam it and slide the dead bolt if someone I didn't like was standing there.

It was Reverend Haglin, sans Merrilee, looking a little forlorn.

I started to slam the door, but he grabbed the knob and held it open. "Wait, Ms. Larabee. Please. You have every reason to be angry, but I just want to talk."

Relenting, I opened the door. Bernice ran out to greet him, sniffing up and down his legs with admirable thoroughness. I stifled a laugh and let her do her worst.

"Good gracious," Haglin said, "what is that?"

"A very good watch dog," I said succinctly. I did not ask Haglin inside. I did not assume even the slightest hint of civility. "What do you want?"

He tapped his walking stick nervously on the wood porch. I noticed it was a new one, a dark, twisted piece of ebony wood, or something similar, with a smooth ivory head. Looked like real ivory, too, and I wondered if he ever gave a thought to the poor elephant who'd donated to the cause of the Reverend's pride.

"I guess you noticed I called off the picket line," Haglin began.

"Yes, I noticed." I wasn't about to thank him, but apparently he wasn't here seeking gratitude.

"I've had a change of heart."

I waited for him to continue. What new game was he playing?

"After my service Wednesday, one of my parishioners came up to me and spoke on your behalf. She's the daughter of a woman who recently lost her husband."

"Helen?" I asked.

"Yes, that's right, Helen Aimes." He seemed determined to get the whole story out, the words rushing out, so I shut up and let him finish. I was intrigued despite myself, because I'd been sure it was Petal's threat of a libel suit that had shut down the picket line. Maybe it was, and this was just a cover story to save face.

"Her daughter, Margaret, said that after her father died, her mother was inconsolable, that she wouldn't eat, couldn't sleep, would hardly leave the house. But after one visit with you, she was a changed woman—smiling again, showing optimism, regaining an appetite. Plus, she found a crucial missing document. Claims you told her where to look."

I couldn't help it—I glowed. To think that a few simple words to that grieving woman had helped so much!

"I don't claim to know what you do—"

"I could show you," I offered.

He took a couple of steps back. "No, no," he said hastily. "That wouldn't do at all. But it's occurred to me that Satan could not possibly be enlisted to help a grieving widow rediscover her spirit. Ergo, perhaps you're not in league with the dark forces as I once believed."

"I tried to tell you that."

"I'm still not certain that it's circumspect for mere humans to delve into these mysterious matters. The Bible is quite clear—"

"You're not going to start preaching again, are you?"

"Er, no. My new policy is one of tolerance."

"And my sister's warning had nothing to do with your dramatic change of heart?" I couldn't resist asking.

He blushed like a teenager. "Ms. Ingalls's phone call reminded Merrilee and myself that there is a provision of law that presumes a suspect is innocent until proven guilty, and that privilege of freedom to speak one's mind contains with it certain responsibilities not to malign those who are presumed innocent."

A long-winded way to say he'd been warned not to continue his vicious slander against Petal.

"But I assure you," he continued, "her warning would not have prevented my dedicated little band from moving ahead with our protest—if we had still believed it was the right thing to do. It's simply that we no longer feel the protest serves God's best interests."

And the negative publicity was getting too sticky, I wanted to add, but since he was extending the olive branch here, shriveled though it was, I decided not to further antagonize him. The idea of peacefully co-existing with my neighbors was more than appealing.

"Your apology is accepted," I said.

Bernice licked his hand, and he grudgingly patted her head.

"I am a different sort of fortune-teller than Ruby was," I continued, taking the opportunity to be sure he understood he was doing the right thing. "I understand she used to put hexes on people and extorted money to ensure good luck. I don't do any of that. I try to encourage my clients to make positive choices, and payment is strictly voluntary."

"Sounds a little like a church," Haglin said with an uneasy laugh. It was amazing how quickly the man had become almost likable. Well, tolerable, anyway. Humility suited him.

"I see you have a new walking stick," I commented.

"Hmm?" He looked down at his cane. "Oh, this. This is an older one from my collection."

"Are you tired of the one with the jeweled head already?"

"Oh, no! Lately it's my favorite. But I noticed it has a few stones missing, and Merrilee insisted it be repaired. She said it didn't look respectable for a man of my, er, stature to be carrying around a cane with missing stones."

"No, I wouldn't think so," I murmured.

"Of course, they aren't real gemstones," he whispered, as if he were telling me something I didn't know. "Just colored glass. But I like the way they catch the light."

My head was spinning. Oh, my God. Oh, my God! I'd been beating the bushes for a good murder suspect, and here was one under my nose! He'd despised Ruby. He'd thought she was a devil worshiper. Lots and lots of murders had been committed in the name of religion.

I fervently hoped this newest revelation didn't shine out of my face. Obviously something was, because Haglin asked, "Ms. Larabee, are you all right? You've grown pale as a communion host."

"Oh, it's, um, just the heat," I said feebly.

"You need to lie down." He took my hand, concern etched in every line. "Here, let me help you find a chair."

"No! No, no, I'll be fine." I pulled Bernice back inside and shut the door in Haglin's face. Rude, I know, but I wasn't about to let a cold-blooded killer into my house. He'd killed one fortune-teller. Why not another? Who knew how many others he'd done away with in the name of his religious zealotry? He could have made a similar speech to Ruby, gaining her trust, then pushed his way inside and bashed her over the head.

I sprinted for the phone, but it wasn't in its cradle. No telling where I'd left it. A ten-minute search, increasingly frantic, yielded no results. I made a mental note to call the phone company tomorrow and have some more outlets put in. It was dangerous to have only one phone, particularly when I kept losing it.

I finally found it in the kitchen under a pile of newspapers. When I pushed the power button, it beeped and gave me a "battery low" signal. Praying it had enough juice for one short phone call, I dialed Petal and Cullen. Petal answered, sounding annoyed, as if I'd interrupted something.

Well, hell, if news that I'd found Ruby's murderer wasn't enough to get her out of bed, nothing was.

"Petal, I—" The phone gave out.

Great. I could find a pay phone, but I decided to just drive to Highland Park and state my case to Cullen in person. I grabbed the photo album, my backpack, my keys, and Bernice, and headed out the door.

Haglin was in the front yard trimming his hedges, having changed into bermuda shorts and a madras shirt. This was the first time I'd ever seen him in anything but a suit, and the result was so comical I almost forgot for a moment that the man was a murderer. I'd never thought about murderers having knobby knees.

Merrilee was there also, supervising, I guess, wearing a pink housecoat/dress.

She waved at me shyly, then said something to her husband, who also looked up, though with a puzzled expression. I guess he thought it was strange someone who'd been near to fainting fifteen minutes ago was now literally running to her car.

I waved back distractedly, feeling very vulnerable with nothing but Bernice to protect me. Bernice, whose instincts were so keen that she licked the hand of a murderer.

I didn't breathe a sigh of relief 'til I was five blocks away. But even then, my runaway imagination thought up ways Wade Haglin could do me in—putting a bomb under my car, for instance. Or sending me oatmeal cookies—flavored with arsenic.

When I arrived at The Castle, I lurched into the driveway and jumped out almost before the Jeep had come to a complete stop. Not content with punching the doorbell once, I pressed the button five times, each time causing Westminster Chimes to start over.

I heard the clackety-clack of heels on marble flooring, a pause while someone checked the peephole—I felt a pang of envy—then the door jerked open.

"Gypsy!" Petal practically screamed, truly annoyed with me. "What is your problem? First you call and hang up on me, then you—" She cut herself off when I burst out laughing. "Stop it! What is so damn funny?"

She had to ask? She was wearing a black peignoir set with a matching pair of feathered mules. The shorty-pajama-style nightgown, clearly visible underneath the sheer robe, had peek-a-boo cutouts over the boobs. Yet her hair, with the blond frosting back in place, was perfectly styled, her make-up flawless—except maybe for the lipstick, which was slightly smudged. "You look like a Playboy centerfold from the 1950s!"

She looked away, embarrassed. "For God's sake, Gypsy, grow up."

"It's not even seven o'clock, and you're in your jammies!" My laughter took on a slightly hysterical note. I guess it was a release of the pent-up fear from facing Haglin, because I couldn't stop.

"What are you doing here?" Petal demanded. "And you are not bringing that horse into my house." She folded her arms and tapped one mule impatiently on the floor. The little feather poof on the slipper wiggled, causing me to laugh all the harder.

"Please," I said, "go put some clothes on."

She turned and stomped away, as well as she could stomp in those improbable shoes. It was one of her most graceless exits.

I was just starting to get my mirth under control when Cullen appeared. Wearing a ratty bathrobe over plaid boxer shorts and a dingy white T-shirt, his short hair mussed, he was Petal's antithesis in every way. But any urge I had to laugh was instantly stifled by the angry scowl on his face.

"What are you up to?" he asked suspiciously. "And didn't I hear Petal tell you not to bring the mutt inside? You know she's allergic."

He was dressing me down like I was the annoying kid sister, and I didn't like it a bit. Couldn't they figure out that I wouldn't burst in on them unannounced if it weren't important?

"Fine," I said. "I'll put Bernice in the garage. But if you want to know who murdered Ruby Casserly, you'll have to be a whole lot nicer."

I took Bernice through the kitchen, where debris from Petal and Cullen's last meal told the story. Two wine glasses and one empty bottle of Merlot, and several empty cartons from a take-out Chinese restaurant.

Chinese food always had made Cullen horny. There were some things I wish I didn't know about my brother-in-law.

When I returned from the garage, Cullen and Petal were in the living room. Petal was wearing a real robe, one that actually covered something, and she'd lost the mules in favor of a set of Dearfoams. I was much relieved.

"So what's this about Ruby's murderer?" Petal asked the moment I walked in. "And what's that?" She pointed to the pink photo album, which I still clutched.

"I'll get to that in a minute." First I wanted to tell them the good news about Reverend Haglin. I related the whole story of how he'd come to my doorstep to apologize, and the matter of the mysterious disappearance of the jewel-headed walking stick, which had been discovered in Ruby's house and which was later purchased from my shop by Merrilee and identified as "very similar" to one her husband had owned and which had been "stolen."

Cullen was shaking his head. "I'm not making the connection."

"He said some of the stones were missing," I continued impatiently. "And that they weren't real stones, but colored glass. And that's when I figured it out. Colored glass. Remember that tiny sliver of colored glass Dr. Melrose found stuck in Ruby's hair?"

Now Cullen looked really confused. "What are you talking about? There was no mention of glass, colored or otherwise—"

"Yes, there was," Petal said, getting excited. "It wasn't in the preliminary autopsy report because Dr. Melrose didn't find it during his initial examination. That came later, the day Gypsy and I visited the morgue."

"How come no one told me about it?" Cullen wanted to know.

Petal shrugged. "I guess 'cause it's not your case. I'm sure Melrose told Norton. He said he was going to send the sliver to the lab for analysis."

Or maybe not, I thought. It might've slipped through the cracks.

Cullen scratched his head. "So you think the good Reverend, a man of the cloth, went over to a neighbor's house and whacked her over the head with his walking stick?"

"Yes!" Petal and I said together.

"With what motive?" he asked.

"What motive does he need?" I asked. "He's a religious nut! And he hated Ruby, thought she was an agent of the devil."

"So one night he just snapped, went across the street, and broke one of the Ten Commandments."

"Maybe he thought he was doing the world a favor," Petal countered. "The Bible says it's okay to kill witches. Or something like that."

"That's right!" I agreed. "Haglin was quoting that Bible verse when he crashed my yard sale."

"Look, ladies," Cullen said, "all theories aside, the police can't exactly storm the Haglins' house and arrest him just because Gypsy here noticed he was carrying a different cane."

"Whyever not?" Petal asked shrilly. "I was arrested without a shred of physical evidence, just because I had a silly motive. Haglin's got a motive and possible evidence."

"And don't forget," I added, "when Petal and I found the cane, it had crusty brown stuff all over it."

"I bet if we used Luminol on the cane," Petal said, "it would glow all over the place."

"If we had the cane," Cullen said. "Which we don't."

"Haglin said it had been sent out for repairs," I said. "I'll bet if you asked Merrilee where she sent it, we'd find out Haglin was telling a big, fat lie."

Cullen was silent, though I could tell the gears in his brain were turning as he mulled over the evidence I'd presented.

"Well?" Petal said. "Let's pull Norton away from his dinner and make him deal with this."

"I'll talk to him in the morning," Cullen said.

"What?" Petal sprang off the sofa, where she'd been seated next to Cullen. "Why can't we jump on this? Every minute we waste is another minute Haglin has to destroy evidence."

"Okay, let's think about this logically," Cullen said, hinting that Petal and I weren't logical, which irked me no end. "Say the cane is the murder weapon. Why would Haglin have left it behind at the murder scene?"

Hmm. I hadn't thought of that.

"He was upset," Petal said. "He was scared. Maybe he was interrupted. Who knows? Criminals don't think straight at the high-stress time of a crime. God knows I've defended enough of them who did utterly stupid things."

"Good point," I said, cheering her on. I felt a sudden surge of sisterly solidarity. Petal and I agreed, for once, and we had to unite against Cullen, playing devil's advocate.

"Okay, I'll give you that. He got so caught up in hiding the body that he left his cane behind. How did he get into Ruby's house? Remember, there was no sign of a forced entry."

"She let him in, of course," I immediately said. "He came to the door with some excuse, just like he did to me ..." I trailed off, thinking how easily Haglin had gotten me to open my door. He'd remained on the front porch, but he could have pushed his way inside once the door was open.

"Maybe," Cullen conceded. "Didn't you say the cane was wrapped in newspaper?"

"The bank hired someone to start packing up Ruby's things," I explained. "But they gave up after one day."

"Okay, then, I have one final question, and I don't think you'll shoot it down so easily. How did Haglin know where Ruby's land was?"

Ugh. I really hadn't thought of that.

"He could have known about the land," Petal argued. "Ruby could have told him about it as easily as she could have told me."

"And did he also get detailed directions from her before he hit her over the head?" Cullen asked. "If he was panicked enough to leave an identifying murder weapon behind, he wasn't thinking clearly enough to locate a clever hiding place for the body in advance of the murder."

Petal looked like she wanted to throw something at her husband. "I'm beginning to think you don't want to find the real murderer. Maybe you want me to go to jail, so you can just move Miss Sample Books into my house!"

"Petal," Cullen said, "don't be childish."

I winced. Sometimes Cullen had no sense, and he certainly didn't know how to diffuse Petal's temper.

"Childish!" Petal screeched.

Cullen stood and spoke in the booming voice he usually reserved for subduing criminals and yelling at incompetent pro football coaches. "Listen, you two."

Petal, perhaps sensing Cullen wasn't in a mood to toy with, sank back down onto the couch. But she didn't stop glaring at him.

"We've got a good suspect in Reggie Crane," Cullen continued. "First off, he's a family member. That automatically makes him a more probable suspect. He had loads of opportunity. He could walk into Ruby's house any time day or night, no questions asked. Means are no problem—anybody can hit a woman over the head with a heavy object. He had motive—he was heir to whatever money she had—"

"Which he couldn't inherit if no one knew she was dead," I pointed out.

"We have witnesses who heard the two of them argue—"

"Unreliable witnesses, if you ask me," I grumbled.

"And he's about the only possible suspect who would have had intimate knowledge of that parcel of land. If we go confusing the issue now with another suspect, not nearly as strong, it'll just take away from Reggie."

"But they haven't charged Reggie," Petal said.

"I think they will," Cullen said. "He simply can't explain away that truck full of blood. The deer-hunting story is ludicrous. I mean, gangbangers like guns, but they don't go hunting. That's honky red-neck stuff."

I cleared my throat. "Sorry to disappoint you, Cullen." I handed him the photo album, open to the relevant page.

His eyes got really big as soon as he spotted the photo. "Oh, shit."

"What?" Petal jumped up to peer over Cullen's arm. "No! No, no, no! We are not showing that picture to anyone, do you all understand me? We'll ... we'll just pretend Gypsy never found it."

Cullen sighed, and I knew he was torn. He was sworn to uphold the law, and he was an uncommonly ethical cop, if not always a hundred-percent-honest husband. He didn't want to increase Petal's chances of receiving a guilty verdict, but neither did he want to suppress evidence that might clear a possibly falsely accused suspect.

I decided to make the decision for him. "We have to show the picture to the police, Pet," I said. "I know you're innocent, but I don't believe Reggie killed Ruby, either. It's no more fair to make him pay for a crime he didn't commit than it is to make you."

"I don't believe you!" Petal screamed. "Have you gone crazy?"

"I just want to catch the real murderer!" My voice escalated right along with hers. Old habit. As kids, the loudest one usually won the argument.

Petal looked at Cullen. "Tell her we can't give the picture to Norton."

Cullen's silence was telling.

Petal, now enraged, tried to wrestle the photo album away from Cullen. But her physical strength was no match for his, and she quickly gave up. "Fine. If that's all either of you care about me."

She flounced out of the room and upstairs.

Cullen handed the album back to me. "You take it to Norton," he said, and I thought there might be just a hint of moisture in his eyes. "It'll look better, coming from you. And tell him about Haglin. It couldn't hurt for him to at least talk to the guy about his cane. I'll give you Norton's home phone if you want."

I decided first thing in the morning would be soon enough. Haglin didn't know I was on to him. I doubted he'd be grinding up any evidence tonight.

Petal stomped down the stairs wearing a pair of purple palazzo pants, a sheer lavender blouse, and a matching sports bra underneath. Even her sandals were purple. Just some old thing she'd tossed on to make an escape.

And escape was precisely what she had in mind. She was dragging a suitcase with her.

Cullen moved into action. "Aw, Petal, no. C'mon, don't leave. Let's talk about this." He trailed her through the kitchen.

Petal opened the door into the garage. Bernice streaked into the house, but Petal paid the dog no mind. She hit the button for the garage door opener, then opened the Jaguar's trunk and wrestled the suitcase inside, all while Cullen and I pleading with her to listen to reason. She acted as if we weren't there.

Moments later, she was behind the wheel. Before slamming the door, she yelled at Cullen, "I stole your gun!" Then she backed out of the garage with tires screeching.

I guess I couldn't blame her this time. She felt betrayed by her closest allies, the people who were supposed to be helping her, who'd pledged to keep her out of jail.

Cullen slumped against the garage wall. "She stole my gun? That's a scary thought. Why does she have to be so melodramatic? Why can't she be more sensible, like you? She's a lawyer, for Christ's sake. You'd think she'd use logic in her own life every so often."

"You didn't want the sensible sister," I reminded him, letting a teensy amount of bitterness creep into my voice. "You wanted the cute blond one with the long legs." With that blatantly unfair zinger, I left, too, dragging

Bernice away from the empty Chinese food carton she'd been licking. I guess none of us were behaving our best that night.

CHAPTER EIGHTEEN

At some point during the night, Bernice's growls woke me up. Instantly alert, possibly because the dog had bounded out of bed via my stomach, I sat up and listened.

Bernice growled, whined and pawed at the closed bedroom door.

"Shhh!" I hissed. She quieted long enough for me to hear someone clunking around downstairs. "Oh, Jeez, not again," I murmured, grabbing the phone off the night stand. I never went to bed now unless the phone was right next to me and fully charged.

Reggie was still in jail. So who could this be? His Pit Bull friend, coming to make good on his promise?

Without further ado, I dialed 9-1-1. While waiting for the operator to answer, I opened the bedroom door. "Sic 'em, Bernice, sic 'em!" Obediently she bounded out the door and down the stairs, teeth bared and hackles raised, and I sent up a fervent prayer that nothing bad happened to her. I was sort of starting to like her.

"Nine-one-one operator, what is your emergency?" a bored voice said on the other end of the phone.

"I have an intruder," I said.

"Are you at one-oh-two North—"

I didn't hear the rest. A loud clatter and a feminine scream claimed my attention. "Oh, for pity's sake," I said to the operator, "it's my stupid sister. Never mind. I'm terribly sorry for having taken your time." I hung up, then ran downstairs to assess the damage, turning on lights as I went.

I found Petal on her back in the living room with Bernice on top of her, huge paws on her shoulders, panting into her face. The dog wasn't growling anymore, but she looked decidedly triumphant.

"Gyp, get it off of me!" Petal screamed.

Somehow I managed not to laugh. Petal was not only allergic to dogs, she was a bit afraid of them.

"Bernice, down!" I said. She looked over her shoulder at me as I approached, but she didn't release her suspect. I had to drag her off by the collar.

"Good dog," I said, scratching her behind her ear.

"Good dog!" Petal sat up, testing for broken bones. "She almost killed me!"

"She thought you were a burglar, and so did I," I shot back. "You scared me half to death, breaking in here and fumbling around. I called 9-1-1 because of you!"

"I didn't break in. I used a key."

"Well, next time call and warn me." I was starting to get my breath back and calm down. My heart rate slowed to something that wouldn't cause cardiac arrest. "What are you doing here?"

Petal sneezed. "Could you put the dog outside?"

"Temporarily," I said. "But she sleeps inside. She's my bodyguard, now." And a darn good one, I thought, feeling inordinately proud. She'd subdued my intruder, but hadn't bitten anyone, which would have been unpleasant all the way around. I wasn't sure if I could keep a dog that bit my own sister. And, hell, Petal would probably have sued me over it.

Once Bernice was in the backyard with a handful of dog biscuits, I started the automatic movements of making tea. I knew, without asking, that Petal would want some.

"So, what are you doing here?" I asked again once the water was on and Petal stood at the sink, trying to wash dog prints off her blouse with a dishcloth.

"What do you think? I'm leaving Cullen."

Great. So we were back at square one. "But why come here? I thought you were mad at me, too."

"I am. I really can't believe you'd want to turn that picture over to the authorities. But Cullen's my husband, and he should be loyal to me no matter what." She paused to catch her breath. "Don't you like having me here?"

I refrained from answering that question directly. Sure, it'd been a little spooky staying in this house alone, with the bloodstain on the floor and Ruby's ghost around every corner, not to mention the threat of Pit Bulls outside. But it also had been kind of nice to be able to get into the bathroom once in a while and to eat all the pudding pops I wanted without hearing a lecture on how I was clogging my arteries.

"Cullen is in a tough spot," I said. "He's torn between being a good cop and a loyal husband. I don't think he'd turn that picture over if he didn't truly believe that you're going to beat the charges anyway."

"Hmph." Petal started opening cabinets, finding my stash of Snickers bars. She tore into them like a starving woman. Uh-oh. I suspected if she'd had a pack of cigarettes handy, she'd be chain smoking.

"He could lose his job if it were ever discovered he'd hidden evidence," I pointed out.

"Better his job than his wife," Petal said with her mouth full of chocolate and caramel.

We were saved from further discussion by the doorbell. What now?

"Don't answer it," Petal hissed. "It's probably Cullen."

The bell was followed by a loud rapping against the plywood. "Police. Open up, please."

Please? Since when did the cops say, "please"? I scurried to the door. "How do I know you're really a cop?" I yelled through the plywood.

"You called 9-1-1. Thought you wanted a cop. Ma'am."

I jerked open the door. "I told the operator it was a false alarm. It was just my sister. I thought she was a burglar."

"We have to check these things out." A bored-looking patrolman with an impressive gut stood on my front porch. "In case you were under duress. Mind if I look around?"

"Sure, come in," I said. He could check to his heart's content. Maybe he would find Ruby's lottery ticket.

I was just about to close the door when someone else called out in a whisper. "Gypsy?"

I peered into the darkness of my front porch. Didn't I have a porch light? Was it burned out? Had someone unscrewed the bulb?

Suddenly a form merged from the darkness. Ramone. The cop hadn't seen him; he was too busy checking behind the drapes and under the furniture in the parlor.

"Jesus, you scared me to pieces," I said, letting him in. "What are you doing, lurking about on my front porch?"

"The cops are here," he said by way of answer. "What's wrong?"

I wasn't letting him off the hook. "What are you doing here?"

"I was, um, watching your house."

"Why?" I couldn't believe he would actually stakeout my house. Surely he had better things to do with his time—like sleep.

"Well, because—"

"I know why he's here," Petal said from behind me. "Cullen sent him. He's a slimy little spy."

Petal's accusation made sense. Ramone's appearance was a little too coincidental to be written off to chance. "Is that true?" I demanded, dragging him inside and shutting the door before an army of moths invaded. "Are you Cullen's spy?"

"No! I was just—I'm smitten with you, Gypsy. Completely obsessed. I watch your house every chance I get."

"Bullshit." I recognized a last-ditch effort when I heard one. "You don't have a stalker's personality." And I would know.

He dropped his head. "All right, yeah. Cullen called and asked if I'd come over here and watch for his wife." Ramone glanced at Petal. "He was worried about you, Mrs. Ingalls."

"Oh, drop the Eddie Haskell routine." Petal swiveled on her purple sandals and drifted back to the kitchen.

"That vile, puling, two-faced hypocrite," I muttered.

"He's not so bad," Ramone said. "He worries about his wife's safety—yours, too."

"He told me to stay away from you. That you were just trying to stir up trouble, that you were dangerous. Then he calls you up himself. Tell me, does he pay you to do his little surveillances for him?"

"No!"

"Then why do you always jump through hoops for him?"

"He gives me tips. I scratch his back, he scratches mine. He told me something was going down tomorrow, that I needed to stay on Norton's back. That's why I wanted to talk to you. I bet you know what's happening."

He wanted to see me for no other reason? To say that out loud would have sounded petty and whiny, and Ramone and I didn't have any claims to each other. But he could have at least paid me a compliment, something to feed my girlish pride.

I looked down at myself. I was wearing boxer shorts and a ratty-looking red tank top with the hem half unraveled. My hair could've housed half-a-dozen small rodents. A compliment would've been insincere.

Pushing aside all those stupid romantic notions, I tried to figure out how to use Ramone's investigative skills for my own devices. And maybe get back at Cullen for his hypocrisy.

I grabbed Ramone by the sleeve. "Come with me. We're having tea. I'll share a few things with you if you'll help us catch a murderer."

His dark eyes lit up, if that were possible. He followed willingly to the kitchen.

"Gypsy, what's he still doing here?" Petal sniped.

"He's going to help us." I found him a clean mug, then offered him his choice of peppermint, raspberry, chamomile, or regular.

"You don't have a cold Corona handy, do you?

I selected peppermint for him.

The cop stuck his head in the kitchen. "All clear, Miss?-hey, what's he doing here?"

"It's okay. He's a friend."

"You sure?"

"Yes. Goodnight, Officer."

The cop shrugged. "I'll let myself out, but you better lock the door behind me." He gave Ramone one final surly once-over before leaving.

I waited until I heard the door close. "I think Reverend Haglin from across the street murdered Ruby," I declared.

Ramone looked at me like I was crazy. "Just 'cause he doesn't like fortune-tellers?"

So I related the entire story about the walking stick. The longer I talked, the more intrigued he became. But he came up with the same stumbling block Cullen had. "How did Haglin know about Ruby's land?"

"Maybe there was a tax bill for the property sitting on her kitchen table," I hypothesized. "Maybe, when he threatened her, she promised to move away to some land she owned, and he pressed her for details. Maybe he stashed her body somewhere else for a few days until he could find the optimum place for burial. That part could be worked out, I'm sure of it."

I set the steaming mug in front of Ramone. He blew on it and took a sip so as not to offend me. "Hmm. Not horrible. Okay, so what do the cops have to say about your theory?"

"Nothing, officially, because I haven't told them. I was planning on talking to Norton tomorrow." Petal gave me a warning look, which was unnecessary. I wasn't going to say anything about the photo album.

"Unofficially?" Ramone asked.

"Cullen thinks I'm full of it."

"Cullen would rather believe his own wife did it," Petal huffed.

A light bulb flashed above Ramone's head. "What if we could prove he did it? Or at least prove there's something suspicious about that cane. Like it's not being repaired after all."

"Like maybe he's got it hidden away some place where no one will ever find it," Petal said, catching the enthusiasm. "Except us."

"Who's 'us'?" I wanted to know.

"You and me, Gyp. Now that Haglin's made up with you, we could get into the house."

"Bring over a peace offering," Ramone suggested. "Then ask for a tour of the house. He's got one of the nicest properties in the Heights. You could say you're looking for renovation ideas for your own home."

"That's perfect!" Petal exclaimed.

"It's not perfect at all," I said. "Even if Haglin would let us anywhere near where he's got the cane stashed, it sounds like an illegal search to me."

"Our search will be strictly off the record," Petal said. "We'll just tell Norton if we see anything incriminating. Ought to be enough to at least prompt some curiosity on his part."

I slammed the flat of my hand on the table, causing Petal and Ramone to jump in unison. "You two are nuts. That cane is long gone by now. It's at the bottom of a lake."

"Maybe not," Ramone said. "He was openly using it, remember. Maybe he figures no one would suspect if he carried the cane around like it was nothing. Besides, there's other incriminating evidence to be found. Bloody clothes. Rubber gloves."

"This is an idiotic plan!" I said. "I'm having nothing to do with it."

Petal's face fell. "But Gypsy, it's the only plan we have!" She had me there. I sipped tea and reconsidered. "Okay, tell you what. If I can't convince Norton to question Haglin about that cane, then we'll get into the Haglins' house somehow and search for evidence."

Ramone rubbed his hands together. "All right. This is going to be great."

"And you better keep your itchy fingers off the computer keyboard until I tell you it's okay to write about it."

He held up his hands, the soul of innocence. "No ulterior motives here. Just trying to help, trying to get at the truth."

"Yeah, right," Petal said, voicing my thoughts exactly. She took her empty cup to the sink and yawned melodramatically, stretching her shirt tightly across her breasts, causing Ramone's eyes to bulge.

The hussy.

"I'm off to bed. I still have a bed, right? You didn't sell it or anything?"

"I didn't even wash the sheets."

She left, and I walked Ramone to the door, eager to reclaim what little of my night's sleep remained.

"Petal Ingalls is a lot different than I thought she was," he said with a crooked smile. "Not nearly as tough as she looks in the courtroom."

"She puts on a good show when she has to. But she's very sensitive."

"'Sensitive' might be pushing it," Ramone scoffed. "Hysterical, maybe. Anyway, she's very interesting."

Interesting? What did that mean? Now I was really sorry I wasn't wearing something sexy, like Petal's see-through purple shirt. The three of us, sitting at the kitchen table hatching ideas, reminded me of that weekend I'd first brought Cullen home to meet the family. Petal hadn't even been trying, and she'd lured Cullen away just by being her all-fired delectable self.

The thought that Ramone might find her cuter than me gnawed away at my insides. How could he not, when I looked like I belonged in Reverend Haglin's homeless shelter?

Perversely, I said, "She's available." At least for the moment, the fickle slut. What woman dressed so provocatively just to leave her husband? "She thinks you're a catch." I didn't explain that Petal's definition of "catch" meant a good-looking jerk with a job.

Ramone laughed. "Not in a million years would I go near your sister. She looks high maintenance to me. Without big sister to lean on, she'd have fallen apart long ago."

"That's me, good ol' dependable Gypsy. Good ol'—"

"Good ol' kissable Gypsy."

Before I could make a smart comeback, he'd swept me into his arms and kissed me, bending me back over one arm and doing a fair imitation of Clark Gable in that "Gone With the Wind" poster. I doubted anyone would mistake me for Vivien Leigh, but I indulged in the fantasy for a moment, anyway.

Oh, God, did he smell good. He even tasted good, like peppermint tea. His arms, all strong and muscular around me, made me feel fragile and petite and very feminine. Quite a feat, considering the boxer shorts.

"Don't suppose you'd care to show me your etchings?" he asked, breathing hard between kisses.

Very tempting. But then I thought about the sheets, which no doubt smelled faintly of dog, and the fact that I hadn't shaved my legs in a couple of days.

"Another time," I replied, behaving the perfect tease and sending him off with a pat on the butt.

Petal accosted me in the hallway outside my bedroom. "You're alone!"

"Of course! I keep telling you, you're the slut, not me."

"He's kinda cute, when he's not being a slime bucket reporter," Petal observed.

"Kinda cute" was an understatement. My hormones were in such a state of uproar, I took forever to fall asleep.

Norton was predictably moved by the photo of Reggie and his deer. We sat in the detective's little cubicle, scrunched over his desk, peering at the album. "Well, I'll be damned," he said over and over. "Never would have guessed. Never in a million years. The polygraph results were inconclusive," he added.

"Really?"

"He stayed cool as a cucumber when we asked if he murdered his aunt, but when the technician asked him if he knew anything about Ruby's murder, the needles went ballistic."

"So maybe it was one of his Pit Bull buddies!" I said excitedly.

"That's a possibility. Or," Norton continued, "Reggie might have practiced answering that one question—'Did you kill Ruby Casserly'—over and over until he could distance himself enough from the question not to show a change in heart rate and respiration."

"Can people do that?"

"Polygraphing is an inexact science," Norton said. "Some people can fool the test completely. Others are only partially successful."

He tapped the photo with one close-bitten fingernail. "This is troubling, though. This shows that he was telling the truth about some things, at least."

"I don't think he did it," I said.

Norton snorted. "Maybe he didn't wield the fatal blow, but he was there, all right, part and parcel to the crime."

I swallowed my fear and told Norton about the Pit Bull thug who'd accosted me in my car after Ruby's visitation. Instead of being sympathetic, the detective was livid.

"Why didn't you tell someone about this before?"

"Because I was scared, all right? He said it was my fault Reggie'd been arrested, and if Reggie went down, I was going down, too."

"So you've been doing everything possible to clear the dirt bag. You'd rather see a piece of filthy, amoral scum—who would kill his own dear aunty—get back out on the street than clear the charges against your own sister."

"I was hoping to do both," I said. "I don't believe either of them did it."

Norton sighed and shook his head. "So we're back to the mystery killer."

"Actually, I have an alternative suspect."

Norton threw up his hands. "Oh great, just great. Who? No, no, let me guess. An alien spacecraft landed in the front yard—"

"Reverend Wade Haglin, my neighbor across the street."

That revelation elicited a long belly laugh from Norton, complete with knee slaps. "The one who launched a hate campaign against you? Oh, there's not just the tiniest bit of vengefulness in your accusation, is there?"

I hadn't thought about how my claims would look in light of the fact that Haglin had sworn to destroy me. "I have evidence," I said calmly, though I was seething. All along I'd been trying to help this guy solve a murder, and he had no right to treat me like some crackpot. Even if I had oinked at him.

"Evidence? Oh, this I gotta hear."

So I told him about Haglin's apology and the cane, and Norton couldn't even contain his mirth until I was finished. He snickered the whole way through my story.

"So you want me to arrest a minister based on the fact that he's carrying a different cane?"

"But the other one was found at the scene of the crime!" I reminded him. "With blood on it!"

"It was found in a box in another room with rust on it," he corrected me. "And his wife said it was similar to one her husband had once carried—not the same cane at all. Case closed."

"But there was a sliver of glass—"

"I have no idea what you're talking about."

"Ask Dr. Melrose!"

He hustled me toward the exit.

"I've spent eighteen years in law enforcement, twelve of those working on homicides. That's why they pay me the big bucks to solve murders."

"I'll talk to the newspaper," I threatened. "I have connections."

"If you're talking about your lover boy, not even a muckraker like Ramone would touch a bunch of confused allegations like you're spouting."

I was going to kill Cullen, and then I was going to get my sewing kit and sew up his mouth for good measure. I'd never realized what a back-stabbing, sniveling little gossip he was.

"Good day, Ms. Larabee," Norton said, depositing me into the elevator. "And thank you for bringing the photograph to my attention."

I found myself out on the sidewalk, wondering if Norton would even use that photograph. Maybe I should have turned it over to Reggie's court-appointed lawyer instead. If Norton were bent on railroading Reggie, he could put the whole album through the nearest paper shredder.

By the time I got home, I'd worked up a powerful case of righteous indignation. How dare Norton treat me the way he did. Was he even worried that the Pit Bulls might try to kill me? Had he offered me any kind of protection or assurance that he would try to find the thug who threatened me? He hadn't even pulled out any report forms or made any notes about the assault!

Maybe because he wasn't going to say anything about it. Maybe he was intent on suppressing any evidence that didn't point directly to Reggie. Or Petal, who I think was secretly still his favorite suspect. The charges against Petal hadn't been dropped.

As I climbed out of the Jeep, Petal came barreling out the front door. "Hurry, Gypsy. Come inside."

Worried that something was wrong, I did hurry, but it was just Petal's impatience to talk to me.

"The Rev and his wife left their house about five minutes ago. This is our chance. Let's break in and search."

"Break in!" This was new to me. "I thought we were going to pay them a social call!"

"Oh, we won't be able to do any kind of thorough search if we have to sneak around. Let's just break in and be done with it. What did Norton say?"

"You don't want to know," I said glumly.

"Hurry, go change clothes."

"You really want to do this? We don't even know where the Haglins went. They might have just run to 7-11 for some milk. They could be back any minute!"

"I've thought of that. We'll bring Bernice as a look-out."

I realized the dog was not only in the house, but following us around, and Petal wasn't sneezing or freaking out. "What happened to your allergies?"

"I took an antihistamine. Found it in your medicine cabinet."

"Oh, no! Petal, you're not supposed to take those. Don't you remember? They make you crazy." No wonder she wanted to perpetrate breaking and entering. She was the victim of temporary insanity, though what judge would believe Actifed had driven her to it?

Still, I was just mad enough at Norton that I was a bit insane myself. I no longer cared solely about clearing Petal or Reggie. I wanted the truth. A defenseless woman had been brutally murdered, and I wanted the right person to pay for it. Unlike Norton, I wasn't just looking for the most convenient explanation.

I changed out of my khaki slacks into gym shorts, T-shirt and Keds, then scurried back downstairs. Petal, already wearing her fashionable burglar attire of pale peach leggings and darker peach Gap T-shirt, was champing at the bit. She had Bernice on a leash.

"How exactly do you propose we get in?" I asked as we charged across the street.

"We'll break a window in back."

"You don't actually believe Bernice will warn us if the Reverend returns, do you?"

"I've got it all worked out. If we get caught, we'll claim the dog got out and bolted across the street. We chased her around to the back of the Haglins' house and discovered Bernice had cornered a burglar. The burglar, frightened of the dog, fled. And innocent us, we're just trying to get our dog back."

As plans went, it was okay, I decided, just kooky enough to be the truth. And no one would believe we had any motive for breaking into my neighbors' house. No one except Cullen, Norton and Ramone.

I shoved that thought aside. We were fighting for truth, justice, and the American way here. Okay, we were turning ourselves into common criminals. But we'd been provoked.

CHAPTER NINETEEN

The side gate to the Haglins' back yard wasn't locked.

"Act casual," Petal said, looking anything but as she unlatched it. "Although who would be looking at us? In this weather, everybody's got their houses shut tight and the air conditioning on."

I didn't bother to remind Petal that in this neighborhood, lots of people didn't even have A/C. Like me. Lots of them didn't have jobs, either, which made it much more likely they'd have windows and screen doors open, or be sitting out on the front porch or the back deck. I was sure dozens of eyes had caught our blatant trespassing, and people all up and down the street were wondering about us, hands poised over their phones ready to dial 9-1-1.

The Haglins' back yard was a landscape architect's dream, and I paused a moment to marvel at it. Flowers I didn't know the names of, all different sorts, were in bloom despite the heat wave. The grass was green and free of weeds. A little fountain gurgled on the patio, lending a cooler feeling to the day.

"Do you think I could do this with my back yard?" I asked.

Petal grabbed my arm. "Quit gawking. We have work to do. Ah, this'll be a piece of cake." She studied the patio door with its many small panes of glass, then looked all around the patio. "We need something to bash with."

I broke out in a cold sweat. "Petal, what if there's an alarm?" Most of the nicer houses in the Heights had security systems.

"We run like hell. Anyway, I don't see any warning signs. People with alarms always use those warning window stickers."

"What if it's a silent alarm?"

"We stick to our story. Here, this will do." She reached for an empty clay flowerpot.

"Petal, wait. Fingerprints?"

"Oh, right. Almost forgot." She pulled a pair of plastic gloves, like the kind found in hair-dying kits, from the waistband of her leggings. "Although I don't think clay picks up prints very well. Just don't touch anything with your bare hands once we get inside. Use your shirttail, or a paper towel."

"And how do we explain the gloves to the cops?"

"If the cops show up, the gloves go down my panties."

Obviously she'd thought of everything. Without further ado, she pounded the pot against the glass. Both clay and glass broke with a terrifying amount of noise, probably audible at police headquarters downtown. But no alarm sounded.

Utterly calm, Petal reached through the broken pane, turned a dead bolt, and we were in.

Bernice immediately trotted around the perimeter of the downstairs, checking everything out. I left her to her own devices and started my own search.

"I'll take the upstairs," Petal said, which was just as well. I wasn't too keen on inspecting the Haglins' bedroom. Kinda gave me the willies.

The decor was surprisingly stylish. Obviously the Haglins weren't hurting for money, because their furnishings were top-notch, and the decor had an interior designer's stamp to it. I couldn't imagine Merrilee, with her shapeless dresses and convent hairstyle, coming up with the living room's amber, gold and maroon color scheme, or the sleek lavender mini-blinds in the kitchen.

Rather than haphazardly opening cabinets and peeking under couches, I tried to decide where I would hide something if I really didn't want it found. I checked the inside of the kitchen garbage can. Behind the refrigerator? No, too obvious. Inside the piano?

Really, if an army of cops came to search, none of those places would be safe. I'd seen what those cavemen were capable of. Yellow Jacket would have the piano in splinters.

Sewn into a piece of furniture, maybe?

I checked the sofas and plush club chairs for any recent tampering with seams, but found nothing promising. I stuck my head in the fireplace and looked up the chimney. Nothing. I checked behind pictures for wall safes, and I checked under rugs for trap doors. No luck.

Just as I was smoothing an Oriental rug down over its padding, I noticed something. A floor vent for the air conditioning, dark with age, sported fresh screwdriver scratches on the two screws that held it in place.

I ran to the kitchen. Where did people usually keep their screwdrivers? Where did I keep screwdrivers? In the kitchen junk drawer. I tried every drawer, forgetting my aversion to leaving fingerprints, but they were all neatly organized—silverware, color-coordinated tea towels, plastic wrap and foil aligned by the size of the box. Not even Petal, borderline compulsive, was this neat.

Still no screwdrivers. I'd have to improvise.

I found a dime in a china bowl in the living room. That would do. The screws turned easily, and moments later I had the cover off the vent.

The flow of cool air felt great as I put my face against the vent opening, but I couldn't see a thing. I reached my arm down and felt around on the bottom of the well. Nothing. I could feel only a short way into the round duct leading out of the vent well, because my arm was simply too short. Still nothing.

But I had a hunch I was on the right track.

Bernice had come to investigate. The A/C switched off, and the dog stuck her nose down the vent hole and sniffed. Which gave me an idea. Bernice was big, but not as big as me. Plus, she was thin and wiry, and completely fearless. Not to mention she was fixated on food.

I ran to the kitchen and rummaged around until I found an open bag of Fritos. I was pretty sure she would like those. I grabbed a handful, returned to the vent, gave Bernice a good sniff, then stuck my hand down the vent and pitched them into the duct. "Go get 'em, girl! Fetch!"

Bernice didn't waste a second. She plunged head first into the vent. I grabbed on to her back legs to make sure she didn't go too far.

Frenzied snuffling and crunching emanated from the vent as Bernice found her prize. She wiggled a little farther into the duct, or at least she got her head and front paws in there, and I heard more crunching. Then she started to whine.

About that time, Petal screamed.

"Did you find something?" I called out.

She scampered down the stairs. "They're back. The Haglins are back. I just saw their car drive up."

"Shit!" was my eloquent response. "Bernice, out! Come! Come on, girl!"

She came out part way, but then she whined and wiggled, seemingly stuck.

Petal screeched to a halt when she saw the spectacle of Bernice's hindquarters sticking out of the floor. "What are you doing?"

"Just a dumb idea," I confessed. "Help me get her out." We tugged and maneuvered, but she didn't budge. Could her head be stuck? I slid my hand down next to her wiry body and reached into the duct. Bernice had something in her mouth, and it was wedged tight inside the duct.

"Drop it," I said. "Uh, let go! Release!"

Suddenly she popped out of the vent like a champagne cork, aided by Petal's frantic pulling. I closed my hand around the object Bernice had been attempting to fetch and extracted it. It was the head to Reverend Haglin's walking stick.

Petal yelped in surprise. "You found it!"

We heard car doors slamming. Without thinking about the consequences, I replaced the vent cover. My hand shook as I turned the screws with my inadequate screwdriver.

"Hurry!" Petal urged, peering out a front window. "They're checking the mailbox now."

"Got it!" I jumped up and sprinted for the back door, clutching the head of the walking stick. Petal and Bernice were on my heels. We shut the door just as the Haglins came in the front.

Terrified they would see us if we exited the yard through the side gate, we headed for the back fence instead. I stuck the brass ornament inside my bra. The gate was locked, so we had no choice but to scale the fence. We hoisted poor Bernice over. She landed with a surprised bark. I would never have imagined I could scale a six-foot fence in four seconds flat, but abject fear is a powerful enabler. I landed in the weed-choked alley at virtually the same moment as Petal.

We ran down the alley, and we didn't stop running for three blocks. Then, sweating and puffing, we collapsed on the curb, hugging each other and laughing with no small amount of hysteria. Bernice flopped down in the grass beside us, thinking this was a great game.

"Oh, my God, Oh, my God," I mumbled over and over. I couldn't seem to get anything more articulate past my lips. What had we been thinking? I guess deep down, I hadn't truly believed Reverend Haglin was a murderer. But finding the carefully hidden murder weapon pretty much clinched it.

Said murder weapon was poking me in the boob. I reached down my shirt and pulled it out, then breathed a sigh of relief.

Petal gasped. "What are you doing with that?"

"What do you mean, what am I doing with that? This is what we just risked our lives to find. Right?"

"Find, yes, but you weren't supposed to take it!"

"If I hadn't taken it, who would believe we'd found it?"

"Who's going to believe where we found it?" she countered. "Norton could have gotten a search warrant if we told him where we saw the cane. But now ... my God, put it down! You're obliterating all Haglin's fingerprints!"

I dropped it like it was red hot. "Sorry, Petal. I wasn't really thinking. But, to be fair, Bernice's slobber probably did in Haglin's fingerprints before—"

"Do you realize what we've done? We've tampered with evidence!"

Given that we'd broken into someone's home and rifled through it, I couldn't see why tampering with evidence mattered so much, but apparently it did to Petal.

"Lighten up, Pet. At least we didn't get ourselves killed. If Haglin had caught me with my arm down his vent, he probably would have chopped us up into—"

"Stop." Petal was getting her breath back. "Okay, let's not worry about what might've happened. Let's just figure out what to do next."

"I, for one, could figure a lot better with a frozen margarita."

We took the evidence home and hid it in the umbrella stand, then walked the four blocks to El Mariachi, one of numerous Tex-Mex neighborhood dives that lined Jefferson Street. Today was their two-for-one margarita lunch special. Perfect.

The drinks were strong and tart. Petal and I shared a chicken enchilada platter while we plotted.

"Why don't we just take the thing to Cullen and confess?" I suggested.

"No way. I don't trust him. He wants to see me in jail so he and Miss Let's-Go-Over-These-Wallpaper-Samples can resume their torrid affair."

"That's ridiculous."

"We don't need Cullen," Petal insisted, daintily using a paper napkin to wipe guacamole off her lower lip. "We'll dig out one of the rhinestones from the cane head and give it to Dr. Melrose. He can send it to the lab without arousing suspicion. Once we have proof that the stones match—"

"I vote we break into the Haglins' house again and put the thing back where we found it," I said. Deep down, I was afraid we'd blown it. How could we prove, now, that the cane even belonged to Haglin? Sure, people had seen him walking around with a jeweled, brass-headed walking stick, but who could be sure this was the same one?

"No way," Petal said flatly. "Besides, I'll bet within two hours they'll have a lock on the front gate and a security company wiring the place."

I remembered how I'd felt after my break-in. Violated. Terrified. The Haglins probably wouldn't leave the house unguarded for at least a few days. "Maybe we could invite ourselves over and casually drop the cane head back down the vent."

"My way will work." She took another sip of her margarita, then a bite of rice. "Do you think I've gained weight?"

There was no dissuading Petal once she'd made up her mind. So after lunch we paid a visit to the M.E.'s office and tracked down Dr. Melrose. Petal had stuck the brass ornament in a Ziploc, though neither of us held out much hope that Haglin's prints were still usable. Just mine. As soon as we were in a private office with the doctor, she pulled the murder weapon from her purse and handed it to him.

"Can you take this to the lab and have them pull off the prints, then determine whether this could be the object that killed Ruby?"

Dr. Melrose's eyes got huge, and he rolled his chair back slightly, distancing himself from the object. "Where in God's name did you get that?"

"We can't tell you."

"Then I can't touch it. Without a proper chain of evidence??"

"This wouldn't be official," Petal hurried to assure him. "Are you kidding? I know the lab reports and such would be totally inadmissible. Do it just to satisfy our curiosity."

"I could lose my job," Melrose said.

Petal didn't say anything. She just batted her eyelashes at the poor man.

"Petal ..." he whined. At her continued silence, he finally nodded. "All right. But this is strictly unofficial. And if this proves to be connected, you better turn this thing over to Norton and spill your guts."

"I will," she said insincerely.

I was having second, third, and fourth thoughts about this whole thing. If only Norton had taken my suspicions seriously. If only I'd had the presence of mind to leave the walking stick in the vent. If only Petal and I hadn't been so stupid as to break into a murderer's house.

Petal's cell phone rang as we climbed back into her Jaguar. She answered it smartly, then handed it to me. "For you."

Who would call me on Petal's phone? Cullen? "Hello?"

"Gypsy. Where are you? What happened?" It was Ramone, and he sounded worried. Maybe even panicked. I had no idea how he'd gotten this number.

"We're downtown. Why?"

"Thank God. I thought maybe you'd been arrested. Cops are crawling all over the Haglins' house. I heard the call go out over the police scanner."

"Are you insinuating I would commit a crime?"

"Last night you were talking about making an illegal search. I was afraid Haglin had caught you. Oh, wait, they're talking again." I could hear the squawk of a police scanner radio in the background. "It appears your neighbors are the victims of a burglar. Don't suppose that has anything to do with you?"

Great. The one person in the world besides Cullen whom I wouldn't want to know about my crime had figured it out.

"The cops want to call out an evidence guy to take fingerprints," Ramone continued, giving me the play by play from his scanner, "but apparently the Haglins have refused."

Hmm. Guilty conscience, Wade? Afraid an evidence team will inadvertently turn up a murder weapon?

"I don't blame them," I said mildly. "That fingerprint powder is messy, and they have nice furniture." Immediately I clamped my hand over my mouth while Petal scowled at me. Okay, okay, so I'm not cut out for a life of crime. I'm too innately honest.

"Ah-hah!" Ramone pounced on my slip of the tongue. "How do you know what kind of furniture they have?"

"Just guessing?"

"Did you find anything? C'mon, Gypsy, spill it. I'm one of your fellow conspirators, remember?"

"You'll be the first to know after the police if there's anything reportable," I replied primly.

Ramone was understandably ticked. "Okay, that does it. Where are you?"

"Heading toward home."

"Good. Once I catch up with you, you aren't getting out of my sight."

Fine by me, I decided. He could hang around on my front porch any time he wanted. I would enjoy the scenery.

True to his word, Ramone became my shadow. When I was at home, he invited himself in, raided my refrigerator, and played with Bernice while I painted the dining room and did a couple of readings for customers who dropped by. Business had fallen off, but apparently even the stench of murder didn't scare some people off.

I also interviewed more neighbors about Ruby's activities, but nothing helpful came up. With Ramone's help, I read every piece of paper in her file cabinet and scrounged through box after box of junk, hoping to find a clue, but no dice.

When I got restless and decided to take Bernice to the park, he came with me. It almost felt like we were a couple. At night I sent him on his way, but I suspected he went home only to shower and change clothes. I noticed he kept a pillow in his car.

Petal took on a couple of court-appointment cases—low pay and not much fun—while she pretended she wasn't waiting for Cullen to call. She filed motions and pleadings. She interviewed everyone she could find who knew Ruby, including Judge Colter.

We saw little of the Haglins. It was mid-August, the true dog days of summer in Dallas, and I suspected they were staying inside with their lovely air conditioning. I wondered if Wade had thought to check the vent and see if his guilty secret was still there.

The glass people came and installed a new beveled window in my front door. I even called a flooring company to replace the bloodstained planks of my dining room floor. While that was going on, I ripped out the last of the old carpet in the foyer and parlor. Ramone helped me shuffle furniture around and sand floors.

Petal complained about the noise.

I felt like I was in limbo—or maybe in the calm before the storm.

"Why are you still here?" I asked Ramone on the third day of our pretended normal activities. Sure, I was being ungrateful after all the work he'd done. But he was getting on my nerves. He hadn't kissed me again, hadn't asked to see my etchings, and had resisted what little allure I could muster in the heat. "Don't you have work to do?"

"I'm on vacation," he said, draining the last can of Coke. He'd bought a couple of sacks of groceries on my last trip to the store, so I couldn't complain that he was sponging off me, but the fact that he was just hanging out was beginning to wear thin.

"Most people go somewhere on vacation."

"I like it here just fine."

"I'm going to start charging you rent."

He waggled his eyebrows. "You asking me to move in with you?"

"Hah! In your dreams." I wasn't willing to let the subject drop. "C'mon, Ramone, you don't really want to be here. It's boring."

"Something's about to happen," he said with utter confidence. "I feel it in my bones. I have a sixth sense about these things."

"Everybody's a psychic these days."

"You're not going to shut me out again."

"I've never tried to shut you out," I said. "It's not like I'm running to the TV station and giving them the scoop. But I do have a self-preservation instinct. I've been caught in the middle of this thing from the beginning, bouncing like a pinball between you and Cullen and Petal and Haglin and Norton. You can't blame me for not baring my soul every chance I get."

Though Ramone hadn't crossed any serious ethical lines with his reporting, seeing my name in the paper had made me feel icky. And violated. And scared, because Darryl was out there somewhere.

And that, I realized, was the crux of the problem for Ramone. I didn't trust him, and he knew it. That was why he hadn't tried lately to get in my pants. Funny, but I always thought guys didn't care about stuff like trust and honesty, that they'd take sex in whatever package it came, with whatever trappings. But apparently my lack of total honesty had caused him to pull into his shell a bit.

I could see where he was coming from, and I wanted to put things right between us. I wanted to get that warm fuzzy feeling that came from confiding and empathizing and putting our lots in together to battle the cold cruel world.

But the stakes were a lot higher now than they'd been early on. I had to worry about more than just simple embarrassment, or even Darryl. I'd crossed a line into criminal activity. I could face jail. Petal could face even worse.

"I didn't know you when I wrote that first article," he said, showing a little psychic ability of his own. "I admit it was kind of ... exploitative. And

I'll admit that when I first started hounding you, it was because I wanted something juicy to put my byline on. But things are different now."

I went to the fridge and got a pudding pop, holding the door open a tad longer than necessary. "How different?"

"I care about how this all comes out. I don't want your sister to go to jail. Or you."

"The trial would make great copy," I reminded him.

"So would Wade Haglin's," he countered.

"I thought journalists were supposed to be unbiased."

"We're also supposed to uncover the truth," he said. "I want to know who killed Ruby Casserly. And I'm not about to print anything that would mislead the public into believing the wrong person did it."

He seemed really sincere. But I knew how gullible I could be. If I confessed everything, even off the record, would that turn him into the romantic swain my girlish heart yearned for?

I snorted at the thought. Look after yourself, Gypsy, I cautioned myself. Don't fall for this line of crap. Santiago Ramone wanted to help Santiago Ramone. He wasn't hateful or vindictive, but if the truth as he saw it inadvertently hurt someone, that wouldn't stop him from printing it.

I should have kicked him out right then. But then the phone rang, and it was too late. Dr. Melrose was on the line. He didn't ask for Petal, probably because he found it easier to talk tough with me.

"Your hunch was on the money," he said, speaking softly, as if he didn't want anyone else to hear. "You've got thirty minutes to come get this thing and take it straight to the police. And I better not hear my name connected with it."

"We're coming right now."

"Coming where?" Ramone wanted to know.

I couldn't tell him. I just couldn't. With a look that pleaded with him to understand, I ran to the stairs and called up to Petal. "Get your butt down here," I said. "We have to go—now!"

Ramone steamed when I didn't let him come with us. He followed us in his own car, though. He saw where we went. He saw us come out of the M.E.'s office with a mysterious-looking brown paper sack. I know it must have been driving him crazy.

"You blew it with Ramone," Petal observed as we headed for The Castle. We'd decided we would confess our sins to Father Cullen and let him figure out what to do.

"I did," I admitted, maneuvering the words past the constriction in my lungs and the lump in my throat. "He's a reporter, and he can't be trusted."

He was ambitious. Any fleeting sentimentality he might feel toward me, any fledgling protectiveness, could so easily be overshadowed by his ambition.

"He's also right behind us."

I sighed. His photographer was nowhere to be seen, but I wondered if Ramone had a camera of his own. Was he using it to take pictures of us coming and going from the M.E.'s office with our mysterious package? What would happen when and if he found out it carried the murder weapon?

Now that I'd pissed him off, we were fair game. I was afraid he'd go for the jugular.

We pulled into the driveway at the Castle, and Ramone parked at the curb, not even bothering to be sneaky about it. I gave him a jaunty wave as we headed for the front porch. Cullen didn't answer, but his car was out front, so we let ourselves in, calling his name.

No answer.

"I know where he is," Petal said as we marched through the den to a set of French doors that led out to a patio/pool area. Sure enough, there Was Cullen, lean and tanned and looking very relaxed on a raft in the pool. He had a can of Coors in his cup holder and Pearl Jam playing on a boom box.

I went over to the boom box and shut it off. Cullen sat up abruptly and jerked off his sunglasses, then relaxed. "Oh, it's you." He didn't bother to move. Petal shot me an uneasy glance.

"Glad you're working so hard on the investigation," Petal said.

"I've officially been told to butt out or lose my job," he answered.

I, for one, was feeling the heat, and the swimming pool was just too inviting. I kicked off my sandals and waded down the steps of the pool until the water swirled around my knees. Petal, holding the paper bag, sat on the pool's edge and cooled her feet.

"Cullen, we have to talk," she said. "It's important."

"If you're looking for an apology," he said in a bored voice, "give it up. I'm done groveling, Pet." He put his sunglasses back on and ignored us.

"This has nothing to do with our dysfunctional marriage," she said. "Gypsy and I found the murder weapon."

Cullen sat up so quickly he unseated himself and landed with a splash in the water. I would have laughed if we hadn't been in such deep doo-doo. He came up sputtering. "What?"

Apparently Petal decided to blurt out the worst and get it over with. "Gypsy and I broke into the Haglins' house while they weren't home."

"What?" Cullen said again, treading water.

"We found Haglin's walking stick hidden in a vent," I said, continuing the story. "We sent it to the police lab for analysis."

"What?"

"Cullen, do you need your ears checked or something?" Petal snapped. "We found the murder weapon. The lab found a little bit of dried blood in the crevices around the rhinestones. And the piece of colored glass found in Ruby's hair matched those rhinestones exactly."

"Wade Haglin's your man," I said.

"Do you have any idea what you idiots have done?" Cullen said, nostrils flaring and the tips of his ears turning bright red. "Breaking & Entering is just the tip of the iceberg. You've tampered with evidence. You've compromised a police investigation. You've used government resources for personal—"

"I'll deal with that," Petal interrupted. "If that asshole Norton would do his job, we wouldn't have had to take matters into our own hands."

"Yeah," I said, full of righteous indignation as I remembered how the sniveling little jerk had patted me on the head and sent me off with a few patronizing words. "Norton refused to even question Haglin."

Cullen turned pale under his tan. "Goddamn," he muttered. "How in the hell are we ever going to make this right? No one will ever believe you found that cane in Haglin's vent! If anything, this'll make Petal look even more guilty!"

"No," I said, searching for the thread of reason I'd found earlier. "Dozens of people can link that cane to Haglin. He was carrying it when he picketed my house. I'll bet it's on videotape."

"But his wife purchased the cane from you! After the murder! Jesus Christ, do you limp-brained females ever think before you do something stupid?"

I'd anticipated Cullen being angry, but I couldn't believe he was resorting to chauvinistic slurs.

"He wouldn't have hidden it in the vent if he weren't guilty," Petal said sensibly. "Listen to what we're saying, Cullen. Yeah, we made a mess of this. But we know Haglin's the murderer. Now we just have to figure out how to prove it."

Cullen hauled himself out of the pool and, without even drying off, headed into the house. With a collective shrug, Petal and I followed. Cullen was acting like a hot head, but when he cooled down, I was sure he would figure out the best way to present our evidence to Norton without landing both our butts in jail.

CHAPTER TWENTY

With Cullen dry, dressed, and slightly calmer, we called Norton and asked him to meet us at the station. The scene that followed wasn't a pretty one. Petal and I groveled like a couple of schoolgirls caught smoking in the bathroom. We did everything but offer him our bodies if only Norton wouldn't arrest us for the B&E.

"It was really my doing," I said magnanimously, since I didn't have a career as a lawyer to protect. Last I heard, you could still be a psychic if you'd been convicted of a crime—once you got out of jail, that is. "We really did chase my dog across the street," I improvised. "Then, once we were that close to the house, and no one was home, the temptation was so great—"

"Spare me," Norton said. He hadn't been as angry as Cullen, particularly when we mentioned the lab test linking the cane to the corpse. In fact, I think he was pretty pleased that we'd found the murder weapon for him, though not too happy about us mishandling the evidence.

Personally, I thought he owed me an apology for laughing at my theory that Haglin was responsible for Ruby's death. But even after I gave him the spiel about his ridicule driving me to commit a crime, no apology was forthcoming. Big surprise. If I knew Norton at all—and I was beginning to—he would pretend his own little gray cells had come up with the answer.

"So what now?" Cullen asked.

"I don't have any choice but to arrest these ladies," Norton said, pursing his lips—to avoid smiling, I bet. "They came to me and confessed to a crime. It's my duty."

Petal and I both opened our mouths to sputter outrage when Ramone appeared from behind a cubicle divider. He made it look as if he'd just arrived on the scene, but I suspect he'd been eavesdropping. In fact, I hoped he'd heard everything. He was my ace in the hole.

"You're going to arrest them, huh?" Ramone asked, scribbling in his notebook. "That'll make a nice story—how a couple of bumbling, two-bit female burglars—"

"Hey!" Petal and I objected together.

"—solved your big murder case for you."

"Now wait just a freaking minute," Norton said. "You can't print that, you sneaky little shit."

"He can if I tell him all about it," I said brightly. "About how I came to you with my suspicions and you brushed me off—"

"Okay, okay," Norton said, backing down in a hurry. "I won't arrest you. For now." He stared darkly at me and Petal. "You two keep your mouths closed. I don't want any leaks to the press that might tip off ... well, you know." He glanced uneasily at Ramone.

"Tip off your new suspect?" Ramone repeated. "You mean, Reverend Haglin?"

Norton gave me a long-suffering look. "How much does this jerk know?"

"He follows me around," I admitted with a shrug. Norton took his gun and shoulder holster out of his desk drawer, checked the gun's magazine, then shrugged into the apparatus as he bellowed at someone over the cubicle partition. "Baker! Got a lead on the Casserly murder. I need you to come with me to question a witness."

We all heard a grunt of assent from the invisible Baker.

Norton put on his jacket. I didn't envy him, having to wear a coat and tie in this weather. He fixed each of us with a steely-eyed gaze, even Cullen. "I want all of you all to stay out of my way or face obstruction-of-justice charges." Then he softened—or it could have been my imagination. "Maybe I should have taken a harder look at Haglin to begin with. I will now. But unless he admits to ownership of this object," he said, taking the paper sack with the cane head from Cullen, "I don't see any way to make a murder charge stick. Talk about a fucked-up chain of evidence."

He left. The rest of us sat or stood there, feeling the brunt of his disgust with us. Deserved, I supposed.

"We can prove he owned it," I said. "I bet people in his church and at the homeless shelter saw him using it before the murder."

"Using what?" Ramone asked. "Oh, hell, don't tell me you actually found that walking stick."

Cullen gave me a look. "You blabbermouth!"

"Hey!" Petal said, springing to my defense. "It was half Ramone's idea that we go look for it! And if you don't want us talking to reporters, quit sending them to spy on me. Especially don't send cute ones," she added, her voice softening until she almost purred. "What if he isn't telling the truth about my activities?"

Everyone's expression changed. Ramone looked horrified, Cullen looked pissed, and I had to struggle to keep from laughing. Leave it to my sister to manipulate any situation into her favor.

I cleared my throat and tried to distract everyone before we had a fistfight in the middle of the detectives' bullpen. "Let's get out of here before Norton changes his mind and arrests all of us."

There was nothing left for us to do but wait until Norton let us know how his meeting with Haglin went. I wasn't about to go back to my house. I didn't want to be anywhere near the Haglins when Norton arrived with his bombshell.

I had another reason for avoiding my home. Norton had let it slip that Reggie had been released from jail, no charges filed for the time being. Petal's charges still were pending, which pissed her off. She was convinced the D.A.'s office would have already cleared anyone but her, given the lack of witnesses or physical evidence tying her to the crime.

"I think Cullen had the right idea," Petal said as we all filed onto the elevator. "Nothing to do in this heat but swim."

"You're coming home?" Cullen asked.

She wrinkled her nose at him. "I'm still pissed."

"You'll have to stay pissed, then," Cullen retorted. "I didn't do anything wrong this time, and I'm not spending the rest of my life kissing your ass."

Ramone's eyes lit up at the possibility of a marital tiff. Although this wasn't something he could possibly write a story about, he was interested anyway.

I realized, then, what drove Ramone. More than deadlines, more than Pulitzer Prizes, more than front page bylines, he was just a plain ol' drama fan. He'd chosen a career that allowed his nosy curiosity about everybody else's lives to enjoy a socially acceptable outlet.

"You watch soap operas?" I asked him.

"Real life is a lot more interesting."

"I didn't used to think so." That was because I used to veg out in front of the TV and think, No matter how lousy my life is, at least it isn't as bad as the lives of the people who live in Pine Valley. That axiom didn't apply anymore.

The afternoon turned into a pool party, and I took the liberty of inviting Ramone. He tried to demure, said he wanted to stake out the Haglins' house in case an arrest was made. But the man was dead on his feet, and I couldn't imagine he wanted to sit in a parked car with his binoculars when it was a hundred-and-two degrees outside.

"We'll be the first to know what happens," I told him.

"Yeah, but you won't tell me anything," he countered, sticking out his full lower lip in a sexy pout.

"If you're hanging out with us, you won't be able to miss it when we find out." And anyway, I really wanted to see Ramone wet.

If he hadn't been so tired and frustrated, I don't think he would have given in. But the promise of frozen margaritas and me in a bikini finally did it. Cullen wasn't terribly pleased at Ramone's inclusion, but I whispered to him that Petal's flirtation with the reporter was meaningless, and that Ramone was actually my possible squeeze.

I'd learned to make frozen margaritas during college—probably one of the reasons I never graduated—and they were the best, even if I do say so myself. I took charge of the blender. Petal made some Rotel cheese dip in the crock pot. I put on an old two-piece swimsuit of Petal's, Ramone dug a pair of cut-off shorts from his trunk. We put Jimmy Buffet and Prince CDs on the boom box, and for a few hours, we partied like a bunch of idiot college kids at the beach during Spring Break.

We were all in perfect denial.

But even during the hilarity, the possibility of arrest wasn't far from my mind. I didn't know how far the threat of negative publicity would push Norton. But, just in case, I, for one, wasn't going to waste what were potentially my last few hours of freedom.

Petal, greased up with Hawaiian Tropic and mellow with Tequila, lay on the raft Cullen had occupied earlier. Cullen had his arms and chin propped on the edge, and they were talking.

A good sign. Even during their brief, tenuous reconciliation, I wasn't sure they'd done anything but drill for oil. Figuring a little privacy might be good for them, I motioned for Ramone to follow me inside.

"It's been a couple of hours," I said, pouring us each another margarita from the blender. I was feeling more than a little buzz myself. "Shall we call Norton and pester him for details?"

Ramone, looking like a bronzed Mayan god in his cut-offs and nothing else, refused the drink. "If I drink another one of those things, I'll pass out cold. You think Norton will tell you anything?"

"He might." He'd been amazingly forthcoming, on occasion. I suppose it wasn't strictly kosher, but I didn't delude myself into thinking his generous gestures were out of pure kindness. Each time he dropped information to me, or Cullen for that matter, he was trying to get something back—a reaction, a slip of the tongue, something. He was known as a diligent and wily investigator. There had to be a reason for that reputation.

Sitting in the kitchen, with Ramone listening closely, I called the station, but Norton wasn't in. No problem. Cullen's Rolodex was right there. It had Norton's home number, his cell phone, his beeper. I tried the cell phone first, but it was turned off. So I tried the beeper, punched in Cullen and Petal's number, and hung up.

"Why are you including me?" Ramone asked as he swirled a tortilla chip into the crock pot, coating it with cheesy-tomato sauce.

I shrugged. "'Cause I like you?"

"I'm a reporter. I'm the enemy."

"Sometimes," I agreed. "But overall you've been pretty decent. Other reporters want a sexy sound bite, something to boost ratings or readers."

"So do I."

"Yeah, but there's more to it with you. You want ..."

"The truth."

"Yeah," I agreed cautiously.

"Sounds like a pretty high-flying ideal. You believe it?"

"I don't know what I believe," I said. "But I don't think you'd print anything deliberately hurtful or scandalous."

"Hurtful, no. Scandalous, maybe, if there was a good enough reason. Like, it's pretty hard to resist a story about two white-bread ladies breaking into a reverend's house and finding a murder weapon."

"If you do, Norton will have to arrest us."

"So, you cooperate as witnesses in the murder trial. The charges get dropped."

"The D.A.'s office hates Petal. They're salivating at the chance to put her out of commission, and they won't drop charges if they don't have to. If she's convicted of anything serious, she can't practice law anymore."

"Is that why you tried to take the rap?"

"Yeah. If I'd thought of it, I'd have pretended she wasn't even there."

He studied me for a moment. "You're a pretty nice sister. And you look awful damn good in that swimsuit."

In truth, I was spilling out of the swimsuit. I had a couple of pounds on Petal.

Tension sizzled between us, charging the very air around us. I fancied I could smell the ozone. Slowly, he walked around the island until he was a few inches away. Then he reached up, grabbed a lock of my untamable hair, and reeled me in with it.

The first kiss was a half-drunken one, but at least half the intoxication came from the pure deliciousness of being in his arms again. Especially with neither of us wearing much in the way of clothes. His hard-on, impossible to hide behind his wet shorts, jutted pleasantly against my belly.

His hands, tangled at first in my hair, moved lower to explore my back. Every place he touched quivered. Then he found the bow that held my bikini top up around my neck. Without any hesitation, he pulled it.

"Ramone ..." I cautioned. We were, after all, in my sister's kitchen.

"They're busy," he said. "They won't bother us."

"But—" He silenced my objection with his mouth. Another bow came loose, and my top sailed through the air, narrowly missing the Crock Pot and the cheese dip. I was standing there topless under the unflattering fluorescent lights.

The bikini bottoms were held in place with similar bows at the sides, and I knew what was coming next. Maybe I'd subconsciously chosen this particular swimsuit from Petal's drawerful because of this very feature.

Ramone leaned down and yanked first at one bow, then the other, with his teeth. I thought I was going to vaporize.

I don't know how or when he got rid of his shorts. Suddenly all I could think about was that we were naked in Petal's kitchen and I didn't care. All I cared about was having Ramone inside me. I'd never known a thirst so powerful.

I'd also never had sex standing up, but Ramone seemed perfectly comfortable with the idea—as comfortable as a man can be with an erection the size of a telephone pole. He backed me up against the refrigerator, placed one hand on each of my cheeks, and lifted me up, poising me above him.

Then he paused. "You're ready for me?"

I was pretty inarticulate at that point, but I managed a jerky nod.

"Say it."

"Yes!" I ground out. If he didn't put me out of my misery within two seconds I was going to grab a meat cleaver and make like Lorena Bobbitt.

Fortunately for him, he accommodated me. And I accommodated him, all of him.

With a very subtle movement on his part—no crude pumping for this guy—he started up an excruciating friction that just about had me crawling out of my skin. And speaking of my skin, it registered every sensation, not just the main event. I felt his warm breath on my neck, the cold fridge against my back, the breeze from the A/C vent gently stirring my hair.

I wondered how long I could stay poised at that incredible point of total awareness, a Zen-like living in the moment that made me forget everything, everything.

Then the phone rang, jangling my finely attuned nerves and spoiling my concentration. The phone was right there on the counter. I could reach it.

"Touch it and die," Ramone said as his movements became less poetic and more frenzied.

"It might be Norton!"

"He'll call back—"

True enough. I let the thing ring long enough for Ramone to finish, but I was no longer in an altered state. Now I was just a girl getting boinked in her sister's kitchen by an incredibly gorgeous Latin lover. That was okay, but near-nirvana had been better. I wondered if I could ever recapture that feeling long enough for it to reach its logical conclusion.

When Ramone finally slumped against me in a good imitation of sudden death, I slowly reached for the phone. The answering machine in the den had already picked up, but I hoped to catch the caller still on the line.

"Hello? Hello?"

"Ms. Larabee, it's Norton. Cullen paged me, I think."

"Cullen's tied up at the moment," I said, not bothering to correct Norton's misconception about who had called him. And I really didn't want to bother Cullen, since he was busy trying to patch up his marriage. "You can tell me."

"There's not much to tell." It sounded as if Norton relished the news.

"What? You couldn't find Haglin?"

"I found him. He recognized the cane, all right, and claimed it as his."

"See? See there?" I said excitedly. "He claims the murder weapon. Isn't that enough?"

"Gypsy, his wife bought the walking stick from you!"

"But ... but ... it was his before it was mine," I said weakly. "I found it among Ruby's things, with blood ..."

"It's not the same cane as the one Haglin carried before," Norton said. "The missus says it's very similar to one he used to carry, but not the same."

"She's mistaken! Trying to protect her husband. And anyway, if he's not guilty of anything, why was the cane head hidden in the vent?"

Ramone came alert at this. I'd momentarily forgotten about him, though how I could forget a man still buried inside me is a mystery. Now he leaned his ear up to the phone and shared the conversation.

What the hell.

"Was it hidden in the vent?" Norton asked. "Really? Or was this some elaborate hoax to throw suspicion off your sister?"

"Of course it was in the vent!" I huffed. "How else would I have gotten hold of it?"

"Exactly what I was wondering. The Haglins wondered, too. Merrilee remembers that she left the cane on a table in the entry hall, intending to take it for repair."

"You didn't tell them I broke into their house, did you?"

He hesitated while I died a thousand deaths. "I might've let it slip."

"Lieutenant Norton, how could you?" I wailed. "That man is a cold-blooded murderer, and now you've got him mad at me again!"

"Couldn't be helped," he said easily. "They want to press charges."

"Terrific," I grumbled. "Prison, here I come."

I hung up on him.

Ramone, bless his heart, hugged me. That was exactly what I needed at that moment. "Not the news you wanted to hear, I guess."

Not by a long shot.

Sobered considerably, Ramone and I tidied ourselves, then returned to the pool to give Cullen and Petal the bad news. They hadn't moved, other than to drift a bit.

Petal took it stoically. I guess she was getting used to bad news.

"Do you think they'll really arrest us for burglary?" I asked Cullen.

He gave a not-too-reassuring shrug.

"Don't worry, Gyp, I'll get us off," Petal said.

"Like you've done such a sterling job getting yourself out of a murder charge?"

"You won't be able to mount a defense from jail, Petal," Cullen reminded her. "If you're arrested for burglary, they'll revoke your bond."

Petal paled beneath her burgeoning sunburn.

Now I felt really bad. If only I'd left that cane head where I found it. "I'm sorry, Pet."

"Don't be. I was the one so anxious to break in."

We'd forgotten about Ramone, sitting quietly in a deck chair listening to our conversation. He knew the whole story, now, and in our anxiety we hadn't sworn him to secrecy or made him pledge everything was off the record.

Now he started making restless noises about needing to get home and feed his cat.

"Yeah," I said. "Cat must be getting pretty hungry by now. What time is your deadline, anyway?"

He looked at me with those soulful eyes. "That's not fair."

Well, I was scared and pissed and not in a very good mood. He'd just banged me, I was facing arrest and imprisonment, and he was going to leave? Who could blame me for snapping at him?

"Let him write whatever story he wants," Petal said glumly. "How much harm could it do? We're about as screwed as we can get."

Cullen, looking battle-weary, didn't disagree.

I shrugged. "Fine," I said. "Let it all be on the record. Every last friggin' word."

Ramone flashed his mega-watt smile. "Thanks, Gypsy. It'll be fine, I promise."

He left without even a kiss good-bye, the rat. I wondered if I'd ever see him again, or how he would react if nine months from now I presented him with a dark-haired, brown-eyed bambino.

"Guess I'd better get home and put my affairs in order," I said, only half joking. If I went to jail, who would take care of Bernice? What if Reggie's gang was still mad at me? Could they get to me behind bars? Jeez, I'd be like a fish in a barrel.

"Take the Jag," Petal said. "I'll be along a little later to pick up my stuff. You can stay with us if you want, you know."

I guessed that meant my sister and brother-in-law had reconciled again. "Maybe," I said, though for some reason I felt compelled to spend time at home, with my dog and the quirky old house I was starting to think of as home. How long had it been since I watered the rose bush?

All these thoughts, and more like them, chased their tails in my head on the drive home. The sun was setting, but it was still in the nineties. I cranked up the A/C in Petal's jag, figuring I'd better chill off while I had the chance. I wondered how much it would cost to install air conditioning in my house.

My house for the foreseeable future, anyway.

Maybe I could buy it, I mused. The bank might sell it to me for a song. Maybe, if they were desperate enough, they would qualify me for a loan. When I'd first discovered the bloodstain, I'd thought, no way could I sleep there again. But I could, and I had, and it was fine. Ruby's ghost was almost a comforting presence. I wished I'd known her when she was alive.

Bernice was ecstatic to see me. I fed her and petted her, then turned on the sprinkler in the front yard. That accomplished, I wondered what to do next. What did one do to get one's "affairs in order"?

It was getting dark when I remembered the sprinkler. Not paying the least bit of attention, I opened the front door and barreled outside, running into a stout body. I backed up and looked into the blazing eyes of a red-faced, irate Reverend Wade Haglin.

CHAPTER TWENTY-ONE

Instinctively I backed away as my heart galloped like a racehorse on amphetamines. Without hesitating, Haglin advanced, pushing his way into my house.

"How could you!" he bellowed.

Where was Bernice, I frantically wondered? Crap, she was in the back yard! How was my personal protection dog going to help me locked out in the back yard? Why hadn't I been more careful? Surely Haglin would have been plainly visible through my newly installed, very expensive beveled glass.

"I had made peace with you!" he continued. "I had agreed to live and let live. I had apologized to you! I'd even prayed for you!"

"Isn't that what ministers are supposed to do?" I asked a bit hysterically, still backing away. "Pray for sinners?" The man had clearly reached the end of his sanity rope. He just kept coming forward, and I feared that if I stood my ground he would plow over me like a bulldozer.

His head looked like a big, red balloon, and as he railed at me, little drops of spittle landed on his chin.

I was more afraid now than I'd ever been in my life, more afraid than when Reggie's gang friend had accosted me in my car, even. Because I was looking into the eyes of a murderer, one who'd crossed over from sanity to insanity.

"You broke into my house!" he cried. "You violated the sanctity of our privacy, you looked through our things!"

He'd killed someone, and he thought my crime of peeking into his pantry so terrible? Okay, he was over the bend. Would he respond to reason? No. Threats? Probably not. Religious fervor? Hmm, possibly.

"I'm really sorry!" I said. "It was the wrong thing to do, and I humbly apologize."

He just kept coming, as if he hadn't heard me. I'd backed all the way through the foyer now and was moving through the doorway into the parlor. This room was still in disarray, and I occasionally had to glance behind me to keep from tripping over a pile of books or a box.

"I trusted you, Gypsy," he said. "I'd come to believe you were sincere, that you really meant no harm. And how do you repay me?"

"What if I start going to church?" I babbled. "You could save me. I know you could. Wouldn't that earn you some brownie points with God?"

"You broke into my house, and you tried to frame me for murder!"

"Right, you're right," I agreed, nodding. "Rotten, rotten, rotten. I'm a sinner! I know it!"

Just then I heard a key in the front door. Petal! Thank God. Only, would she blunder in here and simply succeed in getting herself killed along with me?

"Petal!" I screamed. "Call 9-1—" I didn't get the rest out. I'd backed into a seven-foot column of precariously stacked boxes, and the box on top toppled off and hit me in the head. Damn, it must have been full of bricks, because I dropped to the floor like a rag doll, striking my poor abused head on the corner of a coffee table.

I was thoroughly stunned, though not unconscious. Unconsciousness would have been a blessing, actually, since I was fully aware of an excruciating pain enveloping my head and running down my neck all the way to my lower back. I figured I'd compressed all umpteen of my vertebrae.

Haglin's expression changed abruptly. "Gypsy? Gypsy, are you all right?"

The big phony, I thought, though when I opened my mouth, nothing came out. He did what every grade school child knows not to do when someone's taken a fall—he grabbed my shoulders and shook.

"Say something!"

I closed my eyes against the crushing pain, praying—yes, praying—for a coma. Anything to stop the knives stabbing into my back.

As if from a long distance, I heard Petal scream. "Get off of her! Get away from her! Let her go!"

"She's hurt!" Haglin said. "The box—I didn't mean—"

"Freeze! Police!" Cullen's voice.

Haglin's hands left my shoulders. There was a loud thud, an oomph from Haglin, along with protestations of innocence. Hurried, urgent conversation between Petal and Cullen.

"Police brutality!" Haglin cried.

Cullen grunted something I couldn't understand. Then, mercifully, I did black out.

When the fog lifted, a couple of EMTs were leaning over me with an oxygen mask. I panicked at first, not knowing quite what was going on. Not remembering exactly what had happened. Had Haglin tried to kill me? Yes, I recalled the image of his florid face leaning over me, his hands around my neck, throttling ... No, that didn't seem quite right. But Petal and Cullen had rescued me. I remembered that someone had pulled Haglin off me.

"Can you hear me?" the woman EMT asked. "Gypsy?"

"Unhhhh!" I said. "Hurts."

"Don't move," she said. "We're taking you to the hospital."

Oh, terrific. I had no insurance. Only after I'd addressed that worry did I wonder how badly I was hurt. Was I paralyzed? No, I hurt too much to be paralyzed. I could move my fingers, I noted with some relief. And my toes.

From the corner of my eye I saw a couple of uniformed police officers standing around talking to Cullen—and Norton! Was that Norton? I couldn't really tell, because my vision went in and out of focus. I saw no sign of Haglin, and I hoped they'd carted the son-of-a-bitch off to jail.

The EMTs stuck needles in my arm and attached an IV Now, ordinarily I go berserk at the sight of a needle, but my back hurt so much that the needle hardly registered.

I was lifted onto a board and my head wedged into what felt like some sort of clamp. One of the EMTs shined a flashlight in first one eye, then the other. "You doing okay?" she asked.

Of course not! Couldn't she see I wasn't okay?

I thought I heard Petal crying, and that scared me. I must be in bad shape, I decided. I must be dying.

But I wasn't. I became increasingly alert as they put me in an ambulance. I made them get rid of the oxygen mask, which I didn't need—I hadn't injured my lungs that I knew of. Petal was allowed to ride with me. From her seat, she couldn't reach my hand, so she held my bare foot and snuffled.

"I'm okay, Pet," I said.

"You'll be fine," she agreed. "Just fine." She sounded like someone reassuring a relative after a fatal diagnosis.

The female EMT asked me some questions—my name, address, the date. If she asked me to produce an insurance card, I was going to hit her. Then I realized she was trying to find out if my brains were scrambled. As far as I know, I answered the questions correctly.

The driver drove like a bat out of hell to get me to Methodist Medical Center, the closest hospital. I was rolled into the emergency room, where a doctor gave me a cursory glance, spoke briefly in hushed tones with the EMTs, ordered some x-rays, and left. I was completely abandoned in a treatment room with only Petal to reassure me. Yeah, I was pretty scared. I kept moving my toes, just to make sure they still worked.

"Are you in a lot of pain?" Petal asked solicitously.

"You could say that." Though it didn't seem quite as bad now. Maybe the morphine they'd given me was kicking in. Or maybe I was getting used to the pain.

Cullen found us. Petal slipped out to find a bathroom, leaving me alone with him. He looked really worried when he peered into my face. And guilty, too.

"I guess maybe we shouldn't have let you go home alone."

"No, it was my fault. Did you arrest Haglin?"

"Yeah. For assault."

"But not for murder?"

"That'll come. The D.A.'s office is moving slowly. They don't want to make another embarrassing mistake."

"They should have thought of that before they rushed to charge Petal," I huffed.

"They're going to take a beating from the press, that's for sure."

The press. That made me think of Ramone, off writing his story, completely oblivious to the final chapter. I wanted to call him and let him know. Then I remembered how impersonally he'd treated me after he finally got in my pants, how quickly he'd tossed me aside in favor of his deadline and his hungry cat.

Hell, let him dig up his own scoop. I didn't owe him anything. Now that he had what he wanted, I'd probably never hear from him again.

Cullen lightly stroked my hair. "I'm sorry this all had to land on you. The investigation into Ruby's death was screwed up from the start."

I didn't care anymore. I was just glad the mystery had been solved. The murder charge against Petal would be dropped. She still had some ethics complaints to deal with, and we still faced the threat of arrest for B&E, but I was convinced the worst was over.

"Tell Reggie," I said. "Call his mother and make sure he knows he's completely off the hook. And tell him to tell all his buddies."

"I will. Gypsy ..." He struggled with his next question. "About the walking stick."

"Yes?"

"How did you know where to look?"

I started to tell him about searching for a trap door and spotting the fresh screwdriver scratches on the vent cover. Then I had a better idea.

"I saw it in my crystal ball," I answered matter-of-factly.

"I was afraid of that."

The young pup of a doctor in charge of my case had a grave expression on his face when he entered the treatment room. He put the x-rays onto a light box where I couldn't see them, and proceeded to discuss me with Petal and Cullen as if I wasn't there. He threw out a lot of medical jargon, but I caught the gist of it. I'd broken my neck.

"It's essential that she remain completely immobilized for the next several days," he said. "I'll want to put her in traction."

I objected vociferously to this idea. Couldn't I just lie still in my bed at home?

Then the doctor got stern. He said I was lucky I wasn't paralyzed, that on false move could have put me in a wheelchair for the rest of my life. It still could.

I became very meek after that. Traction, body casts, hospital food— whatever they wanted to do to me, I'd go along with it. A hospital stay would be restful, I reasoned. I could watch soap operas and trash talk shows all day. I'd make Petal bring me some books on tape. No murder mysteries, though.

Petal went back to my house to get a few things for me and freshen up herself. When she returned, after I'd been wired up to a torture machine in my private room, she'd undergone an amazing transformation, having reverted to her usual glossy, composed self. Not a hair out of place, make-up, coordinated accessories—even her nails were polished.

"You know, I think we should sue the police department," she said. "False arrest and imprisonment, dereliction of duty, endangerment, reckless disregard for ... I don't know what. I'll come up with something."

I groaned. "Petal, no lawsuits, okay? I just want to put this behind us. I want to get well and go back to ..." It occurred to me I really had nothing to go back to.

"Your fortune-telling?" she asked. "Do you think you'll still do that?"

"I'm not sure." The moneymaking potential couldn't be overlooked. Then, there was the fact that it drove Cullen crazy. That had a certain appeal.

"Do you think you're really psychic?" Petal almost whispered the question.

"I'm not sure about that either."

"You found the cane head. It was hidden pretty well, and you found it in less than ten minutes."

"There were clues."

"But would a non-psychic person have picked up on those clues?"

"Before, you didn't believe I was psychic."

She thought a moment. "I'm changing my thinking about a lot of things lately." She stood up. "Is it okay if I leave now? I left all the Jag's windows open so your damn dog won't suffocate. She's probably eaten the upholstery by now."

"She would never do that," I objected. Then I added, "Thanks for taking care of her."

"I couldn't just leave her," Petal said. "I'll send you a bill for the dog food and antihistamine."

"Deal."

She left me alone to wallow in my drug-induced lethargy. I wanted to sleep, but the traction was hideously uncomfortable. So I channel surfed until the flickering images induced eye fatigue. Even when I did manage to drift off, nurses came in every ten minutes, it seemed, to check on me.

A hospital stay would be restful. What had I been thinking?

Along about two o'clock, the pain started getting to me. Though I felt like a real weenie, I buzzed the nurse and asked for more drugs. She accommodated me without blinking, dumping something into my IV and leaving without comment. The effects were almost instantaneous, a warm, comforting lethargy creeping through my veins as the pain ebbed, like the tide going out.

I'd almost dropped off again when I heard a noise—the whisper of a door opening and closing, the squeak of crepe soles on linoleum. Someone was fumbling with my IV, and it wasn't my nurse.

"Wha—?" I managed.

"Your pain med," said a low voice.

"No, I just had it!" Now, I might've been groggy, but even in that state I knew that a double dose of morphine couldn't be good for me. How could a hospital make mistakes like that?

When no argument came from the nurse, I realized something wasn't quite kosher. She hadn't even turned on the light.

I jerked my arm away—as much as I could jerk, given I was strung up like a Thanksgiving turkey. The light flipped on. And there stood Merrilee Haglin, wearing a nurse's uniform and an evil smile.

"Surprise."

Yeah, no kidding. "What are you doing here?" I said, hearing the words, hearing how stupid they were. Merrilee Haglin could have only one reason for visiting me in the dead of night.

"Ministering to the sick, dear."

"You're not a nurse."

"I am so! Well, I used to be, before I met the Reverend. He didn't like it that his wife worked. So I quit. Wade, and Wade's church, are my full-time job now."

I was suddenly fully alert, my surge of adrenaline overcoming the morphine. "Get out of here." I tried to shout. But the cervical collar had my neck, throat and mouth locked into place so thoroughly that I couldn't get up any volume.

"Not 'til I'm through with you," Merrilee said. She seemed to be enjoying my predicament. She took a step away from the bed, thoroughly examining the elaborate weights and pulleys that kept me stretched out and immobilized. "Did Wade do this?" She sounded almost proud.

"Read the police report." The police had questioned me about the assault. In truth, my memory wasn't too sharp. I recalled Haglin advancing on me, purple-faced, livid, out of control. But the actual assault was pretty hazy. Still, Petal had found me on the floor with a broken neck and the Reverend bent over me, so one would assume ...

Merrilee held up a syringe containing a clear liquid. "You know what this is?"

I guessed it wasn't sugar water. "Why don't you tell me?"

"It's an anti-coagulant. A large enough dose will cause a hemorrhage in your brain. The doctors will be surprised, but not shocked, given your head injury. They'll assume there was some damage that didn't show up on the x-ray."

Brain hemorrhage. That sounded serious. Like, lethal.

I broke out in a sweat. I wasn't surprised that Merrilee, unhinged from learning of her husband's arrest, wanted to hurt me. But kill me? That mousy-looking woman was a murderer?

"Wait a minute," I said as my hand inched toward the nurse call button. "Have I got this right? You're going to murder ... me?"

"It's amazingly easy to kill. Human bodies are fragile in so many ways. If I'd had more time to think about it, I'd have gotten rid of Ruby in a less ... messy way. But I didn't think about it. The opportunity presented itself ..." She shrugged.

"You killed Ruby?" I squeaked, though the conclusion was inescapable.

She flashed a smile that chilled me to the bone, the smile of a zealot. "It was my present to Wade. I was fulfilling my destiny as Wade's helpmate, carrying out his wish to be rid of Ruby Casserly's scourge on our community, though perhaps not in the exact way he would approve of. And I was fulfilling God's will, of course."

"Wade wasn't even in on it, then?"

"Heavens, no. Deep down he is a gentle man, well suited to spread God's word, minister to the poor, counsel those in despair. I don't believe for a minute he hurt you on purpose, either. He was out to give you a good tongue-lashing, yes, but he would not have raised a hand to you."

"Then how do you explain my broken neck?"

"Wade says you ran into a pile of boxes and one fell on you."

Hmm. Her explanation, I was afraid to admit, had the ring of truth about it. I thought maybe a box had fallen on me.

"But God needs soldiers as well as ministers," she went on. "I'm a soldier, a warrior for God." She sounded really proud.

I'd just about reached the call button when Merrilee spotted the small movement of my fingers. She leapt across the bed and grabbed my hand. "Don't you dare! You'll ruin everything."

The abrupt addition of a hundred plus pounds on to my trussed-up body caused a searing pain down my back, and all I could think of was, any false move ... wheelchair the rest of your life.

"Okay, okay, I won't call the nurse. Just get off. Slowly, please." On the off chance I survived the next few minutes, I wanted to do it in a non-paralyzed state.

"Put your hand in your lap," she instructed, threatening me with the syringe. "And don't move it again."

"Yes, ma'am."

When I'd meekly followed orders, she slid off the bed and composed herself.

"How did you do it?" I asked, thinking that if I kept her talking, someone might intervene. In fact, I closed my eyes and sent out a mental cry for help, a psychic S.O.S. to anyone who might pick it up. If I had any special abilities at all, this was the time for them to work.

"I was coming home late from the homeless shelter," Merrilee said, more than happy to accommodate me with a full description of her revolting act. After all, when else would she have the chance to brag on her exploits? I guess she figured I wouldn't be around to repeat the story and get her in trouble. "As I pulled into the driveway I heard a terrible ruckus going on across the street. Ruby stood in the open doorway, and that nephew ..." She shivered delicately. "... was standing out in the driveway, yelling and screaming, high as a kite on coke or pot or something worse."

As she talked, Merrilee kept her eye on my hands. But she couldn't see my feet, which were encased in these boot things and attached to ropes and pulleys. At the end of each pulley was a five-pound weight. If I bent one knee I could bring its attached weight level with the other foot. But I couldn't kick it, not unless I got the weight swinging.

"Wade had left that brass-headed cane in my car a few days earlier—he's always leaving them some place. I took it with me, for personal protection, initially, and headed for Ruby's, intending to break up the fight—and I was willing to bash a few heads if I had to."

I pretended rapt attention while I subtly bent and straightened my left knee. Pretty soon the traction weight was swinging gently back and forth, like a pendulum. I shuddered to think what I was doing to my spine, which was supposed to be immobilized, but since I'd just received morphine, nothing hurt, so I kept at it.

"Just as I got to Ruby's yard, however," Merrilee continued, spinning her yarn in a way that would have been entertaining had it not been so horrifying, "the boy jumped in his truck and screeched away, and Ruby just stood there in her doorway, crying or something. Well, I'd had enough. I marched up to her and told her all the things I'd been keeping to myself, about how tired I was of the noise and the cars, not to mention the devil right there in our neighborhood. I'm here to tell you, she didn't like it. Didn't care for my scolding at all."

And who could blame her? I thought, having so recently been treated to a similar verbal attack from Merrilee's husband.

"All the sudden, she got an evil light in her eye," Merrilee said. "She raised her hands over her head like a witch or something, and said she was going to put a curse on me! Well, I couldn't let her do that, could I? What good would I be to Wade if I were cursed? I held up the walking stick and told her to stop it, but she went right ahead and started chanting in some foreign language that decent people don't speak. So I hit her."

I cringed at the matter-of-fact way Merrilee recounted her foul deed.

"I guess I didn't really mean to kill her, but I did none the less. She fell to the floor and bled all over the rug. It was really quite a mess." She thought for a moment. "I suppose, if I'd gotten caught, I could have pleaded self-defense."

Against a curse? Please. "But how did you know about Ruby's land?" I asked. "How did you know where to bury her?" The traction weight swung higher and higher. A little more, a little more ...

"Oh, I had nothing to do with that. I was planning to put her in my deep freeze and dispose of her later. But that blood stain! I had to do something about that. You know, blood sets if you don't take care of the spill right away."

She'd played Heloise while Ruby's dead body lay there on the floor? God, Merrilee was a cold bitch.

"Unfortunately, Ruby had nothing in the way of cleaning products. But she had an old scrap of carpeting rolled up in a corner, just about the right size. It only took me about an hour to move the furniture, tack down the carpet, then move the furniture back. It looked better than when I started, actually, though I don't care for shag carpeting."

"You'll be pleased to know I got rid of it."

"I was just about to do something with the body when I heard tires screeching in the driveway. The nephew was back. I didn't think he would understand, so I got out of there, only I left Wade's walking stick behind."

"So Reggie did bury the body!" I concluded.

"Uh-huh. Most ordinary people would have called the police when they found their aunt deceased. But that kid must have had some guilty conscience. I watched from the window while he put her in his truck and drove away with her."

I could just imagine what poor Reggie thought. A noisy argument overheard by the whole neighborhood, then Aunty gets snuffed. He knew, and rightly so, that he would be the number- one suspect. He hid the body out of pure, unadulterated fear.

"So why didn't you go back to get the walking stick?" I asked Merrilee.

"I tried. But the door was locked."

"And you didn't break a window or something?"

"Well, my dear, that would be a crime, breaking into a house that wasn't mine."

Merrilee's code of ethics was a little skewed, but I didn't mention that to her. The traction weight was spinning in just the right arc, now.

"Well, that's enough chit-chat," Merrilee said, raising the syringe menacingly.

CHAPTER TWENTY-TWO

"**Why** are you doing this?" I asked. "Just because I fool around with a crystal ball?"

"That's a good enough reason in itself," Merrilee said. "You're consorting with the devil, whether you think so or not. As human beings, we aren't meant to know certain things. Only Satan tempts us with that knowledge. But that's not the true reason I decided to dispatch you."

Dispatch. What a lovely, harmless-sounding word.

"Without your testimony, they probably can't convict Wade. And I would do anything, anything, in support of my husband. That is my God-given role in life, and I take it very seriously."

I take my life pretty seriously, too. Merrilee reached for my IV. The traction weight reached the apex of its backward swing. I hit it with my right foot as hard as I could, and it swung right into Merrilee's head.

Merrilee went down, but she wasn't out. I couldn't see her, but I could hear her moaning.

She would recover in a minute or two, and I'd really be in trouble. Where was the nurse call button? I jammed my thumb into it, though normally it took my nurse several minutes to respond. Too long, much too long.

I tried, really tried, to scream. And yes, yes, yes, the door opened. Someone had heard me.

"Look out!" I croaked as Merrilee, crouching like a cornered cat, sprang at the newcomer, who issued a decidedly male oomph as he went down.

I recognized that oomph. Ramone?

"What the hell!"

I could hear them scuffling on the floor, but I couldn't see anything, since I couldn't move my head. "The syringe!" I yelled. "Watch out for her needle!"

Something light clattered across the floor. Maybe it was the syringe.

"Stop struggling," Ramone groused, not sounding too worried. "I outweigh you by a hundred pounds. Ouch!"

Then the door opened and all hell broke loose. Nurses screamed. Doctors stood around debating whether they should join the scuffle and risk damage to their Rolex watches. Finally it took three nurses and one three-hundred-pound orderly to subdue little Merrilee.

As soon as he was sure Merrilee was no longer a threat, Ramone came to me. "Gypsy? Jesus, you look awful!"

"So? I'm breathing. I'm not bleeding out my ears. That woman tried to give me a cerebral hemorrhage! How did you know I was here?"

"Cullen."

Figures, the blabbermouth. But for once I couldn't complain about my brother-in-law gossiping. He'd saved my life.

"I dropped everything and came as soon as I heard."

"And to get an exclusive," I added.

"Screw the stupid story! Can't I just be worried about you without your assigning ulterior motives?"

I wanted to believe he was sincere. But I also didn't want to be a gullible dope. "Haglin didn't kill Ruby," I said. "Merrilee did it trying to save herself from an evil curse. Then Reggie found the body, panicked, and took it out and buried it."

Ramone actually smiled. "Ah. That makes sense."

That was all the conversation we were allowed before he got kicked out of my room. Doctors and nurses were all over me, making sure I hadn't done any permanent damage to myself with my unique self-defense tactics. Cops arrived and declared my room a crime scene, even going so far as to put up yellow tape and try to keep medical personal out.

"Let them in, for God's sake," I complained. "I need my morphine."

But they wouldn't give me any more morphine. Some cruel doctor decided I'd gotten addicted to the stuff in record time, so they changed over to wimpy codeine.

I answered questions, and for a change, the cops listened to every word I spoke as if it were gospel. Not a single snicker, not even when I described how I whomped Merrilee in the head with my traction weight.

Cullen and Petal showed up. Norton showed up, full of apologies and regrets and self-recriminations. I lapped it up with a spoon, and I even got Norton to promise that the B&E file would disappear.

Cullen flirted with a nurse. Petal got mad and declared she was moving back into my house to house-sit 'til I came home.

I was kind of hoping I'd get the chance to talk to Ramone again—and thank him for picking up my psychic S.O.S. and saving my life. But in the middle of all the hubbub, I fell asleep.

I came home from the hospital a week later wearing a neck brace that made me look like a total nerd. I was going to have to wear it for two solid months, during which I couldn't do much of anything except lie in bed. I could only hope the bank didn't kick me out once they discovered they'd hired an invalid to fix up their house.

Petal volunteered to stay with me and nurse me back to health. I wasn't particularly thrilled. I much preferred the idea of my mother, who could at least cook. But since Mother hadn't come home yet from Tibet, I was stuck.

"Won't you be going back to work soon?" I asked hopefully as Petal helped me up the porch stairs. One of the law firms she'd applied to had offered her a job.

"Not for a while. The Ethics Committee came to a decision. They suspended my license for a year."

"Oh, Petal."

She brightened. "It's okay. I was tired of lawyering anyway. I can hang out here and help you fix up the house, maybe help you market your fortune-teller services. It'll be fun."

I decided now wasn't the time to mention we'd be running my business from under a bridge. Petal was fully enmeshed in her plans, and if they took her mind off her career and marriage woes, then we'd manage somehow.

We went inside. Bernice trotted up to me, stopped about five feet short, and growled.

Petal laughed. "It's the neck brace. She doesn't recognize you."

"Bernice, it's me!" I patted my thigh. "Remember? The one who saved you from the gas chamber?"

She approached cautiously, sniffed, then allowed me to pet her. Not the joyful reception I'd anticipated.

In my absence, Petal had tidied up the parlor, unpacked some more boxes, and cleared off Ruby's comfy old sofa as a sick bed. Since walking from the car to the house had exhausted me, I gratefully sank into the sofa.

"Yeah, this is nice," I said. "Thanks. Do we have anything to eat?"

Petal frowned. "No. Guess I'll have to go grocery shopping."

I could see playing nursemaid-cum-housekeeper would not sit well with her for long. She wasn't the domestic service type—unless she was hiring someone to do it. But she made a list, gathered up her keys and purse, handed me the TV remote, then braved the triple-digit heat.

I would have loved a trip to Fiesta. At least it was air-conditioned.

I'd just found Gilligan's Island and was happily trying to sing all the words to the theme song when I heard the front door open. "Did you forget something?" I called out.

No answer.

"Petal?" The hair on my arms stood at attention, and Bernice growled softly.

"Guess again." Darryl stuck his head through the doorway, smiling that Charles Manson smile. "Your sister should remember to lock the door."

My heart fluttered in momentary apprehension. I waited for the outright fear to grab me by the throat, but it didn't. After all I'd been through the last few days, Darryl's appearance hardly registered on my terror scale.

I was more annoyed than scared. "Oh, hell."

"You don't seem happy to see me."

The phone was in the kitchen, and in my present condition I stood zero chance of beating Darryl to it. Still, I wasn't really afraid, not even when he pulled a Bic lighter from his filthy jeans pocket and started idly flipping it on and off.

"Oh, get over it," I said tiredly. "Just leave, and I won't call the cops. How's that for a deal?"

He stared at me, puzzled. "Aren't you afraid?" He looked almost disappointed that I wouldn't produce any histrionics.

I looked him in the eye. "I'm not afraid of you. I pity you. You're pathetic."

His face hardened. "You'll think pathetic when I burn your whole house down around you!" He grabbed a piece of newspaper and applied the Bic to it.

I sighed tiredly, hoisted my bruised, complaining body off the couch, and grabbed the newspaper out of his grasp. I gingerly smacked the flames out with my hand. "This isn't working very well, is it?"

About that time, a face appeared in my open living room window. "Gypsy? Is everything okay? I saw some strange dude just walk into your house."

It was Reggie. What was he doing here?

"Actually, no, everything's not okay. I have a giant piece of scum that needs removing." I nodded toward Darryl, who'd frozen at the sound of Reggie's voice.

"I was just leaving, man." He held both hands out in a gesture of surrender and started backing out of the room.

Reggie, never one to heed barriers, kicked in my window screen and climbed through. "I don't think so." He bunched up his fists and advanced on Darryl, who ran into the coffee table trying to escape.

Darryl made another lunge for the door, and Bernice sprang into action. She sank her teeth in his butt before he could clear the room, then knocked him down and sat on him.

"Help!" Darryl screamed. "It's gonna kill me!"

"Oh, don't be such a baby," I said.

Reggie just smiled. "Me and some of the brothers been keeping an eye on your house, makin' sure everything's cool. But I guess you don't need our help after all."

Well, what do you know. I'd made friends with the Pit Bulls. I smiled at him, and he smiled back. What a difference that expression made to his looks. He was quite a handsome kid.

"If you'll bring me the phone from the kitchen," I said sweetly, "I'll take care of this mess." I nudged Darryl with my toe.

Poor Petal. She came home from the store to be greeted by flashing lights in front of the Purple Palace and Pit Bulls loitering in my front yard. When she saw I was all right, she actually hugged me—not an air kiss, but a real, bone-crushing hug that almost undid a week of traction.

When the two of us were finally alone again, Petal put away the melting groceries, fixed me a sandwich, and brought me a huge wad of mail.

"What the hell's all this?" I leafed through the envelopes, not recognizing any of the return addresses.

"Your fifteen minutes of fame," Petal said. "Enjoy it while it lasts."

True to my word, I'd given Ramone an exclusive. But the story of Merrilee's attack on me and Ramone's nick-of-time arrival had received quite a bit of media coverage without my help. Everything came out, but what the press had seemed particularly fascinated by was how I'd found the walking stick in the Haglins' vent. The psychic angle came alive again.

The story had been picked up by the wire services and printed in newspapers all over the country—all over the world.

The letters, too, were from everywhere—New York City; Tampa, Florida; Hickman Mills, Missouri; even Manila. I ripped the Hickman Mills one open.

"Dear Ms. Larabee," I read aloud. "I read about how good you are at finding missing people and things. My brother's been missing for fifteen years. Do you think you could find him? I would pay you handsomely."

"Wow," Petal said.

I opened another one. "'Dear Gypsy Moon Larabee:' Hey, how'd they know about my middle name?"

Petal shrugged. "Beats me."

"'Recently I lost my wedding ring in an apple orchard,'" I continued. "'I've drawn you a map of the orchard. Can you tell me where to look? I've enclosed money to cover return postage.'"

Sure enough, there was a five-dollar bill folded up in a meticulously drawn map.

Petal started opening the envelopes, too. There were requests from people who'd lost their children, their dogs, their cars, their girlfriends. Some of the envelopes contained checks. Others merely promised exorbitant payment if I agreed to help them. There was even one envelope from the FBI asking if

I'd work on some cold missing persons files—on the Q.T., of course. The FBI didn't want it to get out that it consulted psychics.

"I guess this'll give me something to do while I'm waiting for my neck bones to grow back together," I said. I didn't know how successful I'd be, but I could at least give it a try. The income would come in handy.

Petal smiled wistfully. "Must be nice to be able to see into the future," she said. "I wish I knew what my future held."

"It'll all come back together, Pet," I said. "A year's not such a long time."

"Oh, I'm not so worried about that," she said. "It's Cullen. I'm afraid we're at an impasse."

I couldn't offer an optimistic rejoinder. Unless they agreed to counseling, which they hadn't so far, they were doomed to repeat the same patterns over and over.

"Hey, do you think you could read my future?"

I started to laugh, but then I saw she was serious. "You ... you really want me to?"

"Sure. You helped all those other people. Why not your own sister?"

For starters, because I couldn't possibly be objective. But Petal looked so hopeful, I couldn't turn her down. "Okay."

"Great." She jumped up and fetched the crystal ball from its spot on the shelf and brought it to me. I couldn't lean over the table, so I leaned back and settled the brass stand in my lap. It wasn't the best angle for intense study, but since the glass ball was just a prop anyway ...

Bernice, suddenly alert, sniffed at the crystal.

"What do you see?" Petal asked impatiently.

"Besides a dog nose? I see you and Cullen visiting a marriage therapist."

"Will you be serious?"

"I am serious. His name is ... no, her name is Dr. Landers." I'd asked for a referral while I was in the hospital, just so I'd have someone to send Petal and Cullen to.

"Come on. What do you really see?"

"I see ... I see ... Hmm." I really did see something in the crystal.

"What? What is it? Am I going to divorce Cullen and marry a rock star or what?"

"I see ... 38."

"The bra size of Cullen's next bimbo."

"No, really." There were numbers clearly visible in the glass. I removed the ball from its stand and examined the felt liner. It was peeling back on one side, and underneath it was a piece of paper. I pulled it out. Petal's eyes bugged out.

It was a lottery ticket.

www.ingramcontent.com/pod-product-compliance
Lightning Source LLC
Chambersburg PA
CBHW070117260626

47160CB00004B/1508